something like winter

Jay Bell Books
www.jaybellbooks.com

Did you buy this book? If so, thank you for putting food on our table! Making money as an independent artist isn't easy, so your support is greatly appreciated. Come give me a hug!

Did you pirate this book? If so, there are a couple of ways you can still help out. If you like the story, please take the time to leave a nice review somewhere, such as an online retail store (my preference), or on any blog or forum. Word of mouth is important for every book, so if you can recommend this book to friends with more cash to spare, that would be awesome too!

ISBN-13: 978-1479261727

Cover art by Andreas Bell: www.andreasbell.com

-=Books by Jay Bell=-

The *Something Like...* series

#1 Something Like Summer
#2 Something Like Autumn
#3 Something Like Winter
#4 Something Like Spring
#5 Something Like Lightning
#6 Something Like Thunder
#7 Something Like Stories - Volume One
#8 Something Like Hail
#9 Something Like Rain
#10 Something Like Stories - Volume Two
#11 Something Like Forever

The *Loka Legends* series

#1 The Cat in the Cradle
#2 From Darkness to Darkness

Other Novels

Kamikaze Boys
Hell's Pawn

Other Short Stories

Language Lessons
Like & Subscribe

This book is dedicated to all the wonderful readers who opened their hearts to Ben, Tim, and Jace. Thank you for making them a part of your lives, and thank you for demanding more.

Something Like Winter

by Jay Bell

Part One:
Kansas, 1996

Chapter One

This is my coming-out story. No, that's too simple. This is the story of the man I fell in love with, the hero who reached out to me all those years ago and turned my life around. I first met Scott, my husband, at the company Christmas party. Oddly enough, that party was my first day at work. The ad agency had lost their top man to a corporate head hunter and rushed me in mid-December to take his place. I was scheduled to start the following week, but my new boss insisted I attend the festivities. That's where I met Scott.

Forget love at first sight. My first impression was that I hated the guy. Scott kept giving me the eye. I thought he was sizing me up, comparing me to the executive I had replaced. After a few drinks, I felt ornery and decided to stare back. And that's when I knew. Maybe I didn't call it gay, homosexual, or anything else, but I knew I wanted to be with him, and from the fire in his eyes, I could tell he wanted the same thing. I'm not proud to admit it, but the first time I ever had sex with another man was that night in the—

"Ready to go?"

Tim Wyman shoved the magazine back on the rack just as his mother came around the corner. He could already feel his face burning as she looked the one place he wouldn't—back at the rack. Luckily he was in the men's interest section, which aside from a few gay magazines was mostly about working out, health, and fashion. Almost all the magazine covers had shirtless men on them, so it's not like the gay ones stood out.

Unless he had put the magazine back in the wrong place, or left fingerprints on the slick cover. Shit!

"Find anything good?" Tim asked her, successfully drawing her attention away.

Ella Wyman held up two paperbacks, one thin, the other thick. Both had Spanish titles on their covers. "Enough to make the trip down a little more bearable. You?"

"No. I'll probably just listen to music."

"Okay. Well, I'm going to the register. Are you coming?"

"Yeah."

As soon as her back was turned, Tim glanced once more toward the magazines. The gay one was where it was supposed to be, thank god. He glared at the cover accusingly. The guy on the front was doing the classic "thinker" pose, his body just as ripped as the famous statue. The thing was, the model looked so *normal.* That's exactly what had piqued Tim's curiosity. Despite being a gay magazine, the cover model wasn't feminine, dressed in leather, decked out in drag, or anything else outrageous. He was just a guy with an enviable physique.

Tim followed his mom, browsing through a display of sketch books as they waited in line. He chose a small one with a plain black cover and slid it on the counter without having to ask. His mother knew he liked to paint and assumed this passion extended to drawing as well. In truth, Tim would probably use the book to write, which he did almost exclusively in Spanish. He could speak it too, but often felt self-conscious when doing so.

Once outside the store, Tim scanned the parking lot, a habit he would be glad to leave behind. He did this when entering and leaving every location, seeking out people his age who might attend the same high school—people who might have heard. With school out for the summer, his chances of running into someone were high. That's why the past month had been spent mostly at home, but now hiding was pointless because today was the last day.

"Can I drive, Mom?"

"Of course."

She fished a keychain out of her purse, Tim taking it and pushing the button to unlock the doors. A few minutes later they were cruising down the street toward I-35, the very interstate that would soon get him the hell out of Kansas.

"How long of a drive is it to Texas?" he asked.

"Oh, twelve, thirteen hours. Maybe longer depending on how often we stop to eat. It's going to be grueling on your father."

"I can drive part of it," Tim offered, but he knew his father would never accept. Thomas Wyman wouldn't let his own wife be anything but a passenger. Maybe his father found it too emasculating. Not Tim. He just enjoyed driving and hadn't had much chance lately while playing hermit.

Soon his problems would be left far behind, a thought that had him in high spirits—until they pulled into the driveway. The garage door was slowly opening, revealing walls of packed boxes on one side, when Tim noticed her sitting on the steps.

"Oh, it's your little girlfriend!" his mother said.

Tim hit the gas too hard, the car lurching. His mother made a quick plea to saints in her native Spanish while he got the car under control, parking in the garage without further incident. His hands were already clammy with sweat when he took them off the steering wheel.

"I can carry the bags in," his mother said. "Go talk to Carly."

"Carla," he said distractedly. The difference was one letter, but *Carly* sounded much too cute for her now.

Carla was still waiting on the porch step when he came around the corner, which was so like her. He should have just gone inside, let her wait there for eternity instead of coming to her like an obedient puppy. Except then she might ring the doorbell and talk to his parents, and lord only knew what she might say to them.

Carla raised her eyebrows and smiled demurely, cute as a baby doll.

Tim glared back. "What do you want?"

"Nothing," Carla said, ignoring his gruffness. "I just came to say goodbye." She stood and offered a delicate hand.

Tim just stared at it. "Why?"

"Why? Because we were together for ten months. Because you were my first, and I'll never forget that. And because we love each other."

"Carla, you told everyone that I raped you!"

She shrugged, her fine features betraying no hint of remorse. "All's fair in love and war."

Right. And Carla won the war long ago. Almost a year, to be exact. Tim had met her last summer, swimming with friends at the community pool. Normally Tim stuck to the pool in his backyard, but one of the girls from school had recognized him walking by and called him over. Tim, along with his former best friend Brody, had been happy for the chance to flirt. A dozen or more girls were there celebrating a birthday. Their eager faces had been a blur until Tim saw Carla, lithe in a black bikini that matched her hair.

She knew exactly what to say to Tim, how to stroke his ego just right to make him want to give her more. And he had, emotionally and physically, and it had never been anything but consensual.

"You still never told me why," Carla said. "You owe me that much."

"That's why you came? You want to know why I dumped you? Fine. Because you're so fucking mean."

Carla shook her head. "I wasn't back then. I was always good to you."

Hardly. The truth was, she had often demeaned him in front of her friends, like he was a trophy she kept for bragging rights. At first that wasn't too big of a deal. Most of their time together was spent alone, and in *those* moments she had been kind. Socially, she would parade him in front of her friends like a prized pet, which made him feel oddly proud, until her comments became more critical than praising.

And of course there were other reasons Tim had left her. Like her brother, who shared the same dark eyes that were locked on him now, waiting for an answer.

"You know what?" Tim huffed. "It doesn't matter why. You showed your true colors when we broke up. You ruined my life!"

Carla rolled her eyes. "Stop being so dramatic. It's not like I went to the police."

"You might as well have. I lost all my friends. The whole freaking school turned against me! Even Brody won't talk to me anymore."

"Probably because he's too busy trying to get into my pants."

"Yeah, keep twisting the knife. Just because it's true doesn't mean you have to say it."

"Fine." Carla took a step closer and put a hand on his arm. "I'm sorry, okay? I was mad. But this is our last day together. Do we really have to fight?"

Her eyes moved across his face, flicking down to his neck, shoulders, and chest. This was something Tim was used to, not just from Carla, but strangers as well. He owed a lot to his parents for the genes they had given him. From his mother, he had inherited the Hispanic skin tone—light enough to be mistaken for a tan—and his silky black hair. The silver eyes from his father drew the most compliments. The muscular build also came from him. Tim knew because next to her bed, his mother kept a photo of Thomas in his college rowing days, pale as ever and hair starting to gray even then, but his arms rippled with effort. No doubt those muscles had won over his mother, just as Tim's physique had impressed Carla.

Right now Tim would trade his looks for flab and acne. He

couldn't count the number of times Carla had spoken about the children they would have, swapping their traits around to design the perfect child. Her dark eyes, his olive skin. His nose, her smile. For one chilling moment, he wondered if that's why she was here now. One last shot at tiny versions of Carla and Tim. The hand on his arm was warm, almost hot, so he pulled away.

"I won't look back," he said. "As soon as I'm in Texas, I'll forget you. By this time tomorrow, you won't even be a memory."

"I don't believe you."

"No? Why would I remember? You never meant a thing to me."

Carla's face finally registered anger, making it anything but pretty. He stepped past her, wanting to get away before whatever venomous words she was cooking up spewed out. He tried the front door. The stupid thing was locked, so he jabbed at the doorbell.

"I guess I'll just go over to Brody's," Carla said.

She didn't get a rise out of him. Tim couldn't care less who she fucked now. His mom peeked out the side window, and he mouthed for her to open the door. Hurry the hell up!

"Goodbye then," Carla said. "I'll be sure to tell my brother that he was right about you."

Tim stiffened. His mom opened the door and greeted Carla, who replied back in pleasant tones that belied her serpent's tongue. Tim was terrified that she would say more, would drop a bomb that would follow him to Texas, but he made it inside and shut the door before the worst could happen.

"Are you okay, *Gordito?*"

"Fine," Tim said. His mother smiled sympathetically, misinterpreting his distress. He wanted to get away from her before she said something kind about the witch outside. "I'm going to make sure everything in my room is packed."

Once he was upstairs, Tim went to his father's office and peeked through the curtains overlooking the driveway. Carla had gone. Exhaling in relief, Tim tried to force her from his thoughts, but those dark eyes came back to haunt him once more. Then he realized that the penetrating gaze in his mind didn't belong to Carla, but to her brother instead.

* * * * *

"You can kiss me if you want."

Tim paced his near-empty room, frustrated by the lack of distraction. An inflatable mattress his mother had bought for this occasion, a blanket, and a pillow were all that remained. The only signs left of his world were scuff marks on the blank walls and patches of pressed carpet where furniture had once stood. He had nothing left to escape into. No books, music, or TV—not even his studio. His home had been hollowed out completely, empty now of all but memories.

Except the ghost of the room Tim found himself in didn't belong to this house. Memory brought him to Corey's room, a place on the brink of transformation, just like its occupant. Childhood toys competed with posters of bikini-clad girls on the wall. CDs of Disney soundtracks were shuffled up with grunge bands. Stuffed animals and designer clothing shared piles on the floor. Not the coolest place to hang out, but Tim was happy to escape the party. And Carla.

"Go upstairs and check on my brat of a brother," she had snapped at him when he offered to get her a drink.

Tim happily complied, because that night he felt he could hardly breathe. Her brother's room had been the perfect sanctuary. Fourteen years old, Corey and his world still mostly revolved around video games and cartoons, but he was changing. Most recently his glasses had been replaced by contacts, revealing eyes that matched his sister's, so dark that the pupils were nearly lost.

With his parents out of town and none of his friends allowed over, Corey had been glad for the company. He even shut off his games and focused on Tim, watching him with transparent admiration as Tim nursed a beer. An hour passed easily. They bragged, laughed, and talked, Tim wondering if this was what having a brother was like. Then Corey spoke those crazy words that haunted him still.

"You can kiss me if you want."

Tim's grin had abandoned ship. Maybe the bass thumping from downstairs had affected his hearing.

"Why would I?" Tim replied.

Corey's face had fallen, which was enough to make Tim backpedal.

"I'm almost seventeen," he continued lamely, "and you're—I'm dating your sister!"

"I won't tell her." Hope lit Corey's face, as if there was room for negotiation. "I never tell anyone."

Corey made it sound like a game, a secret that guys kept. Like telling your best friend about the girl you wanted to hook up with, or those shitty moments when you cry or something vulnerable like that. But kissing each other? That wasn't a secret that guys kept. Was it?

Those dark eyes, so like his sister's, watched and waited for Tim to give the word. What if he had said yes? Would Tim have leaned forward, or would Corey have come to him? He would never know, because Tim had stood and walked to the door. When he turned around, the hurt had returned to Corey's face, and Tim couldn't leave him like that.

"Anyone would be lucky to kiss you, Corey. It's just... Your sister would never forgive me."

When Tim arrived back downstairs, he nearly wished he had done it, just to spite her.

"Where the hell have you been?" Carla said with a withering glare.

"I was just upstairs, trying to figure out if I want to molest your brother or not."

Of course Tim hadn't really said that. Memory could be toyed with, twisted to suit his needs. As he flopped down on the inflatable mattress, Tim tinkered with another memory. What if it had been Corey sitting on the doorstep today? No parents at home, no ugly relationship with Corey's sister, just them alone, the crazy offer repeated one final time.

"You can kiss me if you want."

Chapter Two

The small sketchbook pages felt impossible to fill as the Oklahoma scenery whizzed by. Not that scenery was an apt description, since there wasn't anything to see. Tim had grown up in Kansas, accustomed to horizons filled with farmland, but also housing developments and strip malls. Oklahoma seemed deserted by comparison, so Tim tried creating more interesting worlds on paper, but sketching wasn't his forte.

When creating art, he found the pen frustrating, its scratching ugly compared to the silken motion of a paintbrush. Ink was stationary, permanent, and damning once on paper. A thick glob of paint could be sculpted, scraped, and moved. He missed the colors the most, the wet hues. Markers, chalks, and various inks—Tim had tried them all, but none were vibrant enough or spoke to his soul like paint did.

The SUV pulled to the right, slowing as his father guided it down an exit ramp. Tim tossed aside the sketchbook. He had managed a couple of drawings, but they would remain chicken scratches until the movers showed up with his art supplies.

"Where are we?"

Neither parent responded from the front seat, so Tim looked out the window until he spotted stores and car dealerships that incorporated the location's name: Oklahoma City. They had returned to civilization.

"That looks like a nice restaurant," his mother said at a stop light.

His father's eyes met Tim's in the rearview mirror. What was he thinking? That they usually dined out alone? That it would be awkward having Tim along for what was normally a romantic occasion?

"Thomas," Tim's mother prompted.

"We're making good time, Ella. After the tank is full, we'll get some fast food on the way out of town."

"Well, stop there anyway so I can use the restroom. At least it will be clean."

Tim turned his attention back to the outside world. When the car parked and his mother got out, he found himself more comfortable people-watching than facing the silence in the car.

What would they talk about, anyway? Besides sports, of course, but Tim wasn't in the mood for that.

The radio clicked on, voices babbling back and forth rather than singing. Thomas liked talk radio, Tim's mother tiring of it easily, so now was his father's only opportunity. The voices were prattling on about some Defense of Marriage Act, a title that sounded ridiculous, like too many weddings had been gunned down by mobsters and needed military protection. Tim paid more attention when the debate became heated.

"This isn't a bipartisan issue," one voice on the radio argued. *"President Clinton himself said, when interviewed by gay magazine,* The Advocate, *'I remain opposed to same-sex marriage. I believe marriage is an institution for the union of a man and a woman. This has been my long-standing position, and it is not being reviewed or reconsidered.' So you see—"*

Thomas turned down the radio. "Maybe there's hope for the Democrats yet," he said as his wife reached the car.

Tim didn't respond.

Next they cut across the street to the nearest gas station. Only when Thomas finished pumping gas and went to pay, did Tim's mother turn around in the seat to face him. She was always like that. Her husband was the focus of her world. Tim admired her devotion, in a way, but it always came at his expense. The irritation must have shown on his face, because she responded to it.

"There will be other girls," Ella said. "I know leaving your girlfriend behind can be hard, but you are young and handsome."

Could she be more clueless? Tim was sure he told her that he and Carla had broken up. As soon as Carla had started spreading the rumors, all Tim had done was mope around the house. How could his parents have missed that? Hadn't they sensed his relief when they announced the move to Texas?

The timing couldn't have been better, not that the two events were related. His father wanted to sort out the southern division of his company, the regional manager having been dismissed under allegations of embezzlement. Ella worked as a translator for a company that had locations all over the country, so the move wasn't inconvenient for her. If his parents had wondered what Tim thought about being uprooted halfway through high school, they hadn't bothered to ask.

"You know I hate it when you look sad, *Gordito*."

Tim sighed, his anger draining away. His mom *did* hate seeing him unhappy. When she wasn't preoccupied with her husband, like when Thomas was out of town for business, she lavished attention on Tim. Her elegant lashes would bat in his direction, like they did now, and she would smile until he couldn't help joining her. Then she would baby him like he was still a kid and treat him like the most important person in the world, Tim forgiving her for all the lonely days when he felt ignored.

He forced himself to smile. "I'm all right."

"Moving can be hard," Ella said. "When I decided to come back here with your father—oh, my heart nearly broke! You always see Mexicans on television eager to get into the USA. Not me. It was the most difficult decision I ever made."

Tim could sympathize. His parents visited Mexico City every couple of years, and for those trips only, they actually brought Tim along. That had everything to do with his grandmother, a leathery old woman who had spent a lifetime in the sun. She insisted on seeing her grandson. The one visit he hadn't been brought along, his grandma had chewed out "The American," as she called his father in sarcastic and heavily accented English. She was just as feisty and vital as the city she lived in, and Tim adored them both.

"Too bad we can't move there," he said. "Couldn't Dad commute to work from Mexico City?"

Ella's eyes lit up with the idea, and she laughed. Then the driver's side door opened, and her head turned back to her husband. His parents haggled over the choice of fast-food restaurants, Tim forgotten until it came time to order. He wanted his burger without pickles or onions, and when they got to the window, they were told to pull forward to wait while their order was prepared. His father's eyes met his again in the rearview mirror, seeming to blame him for the inconvenience, until Ella filled the silence.

"We have to pray before we keep travelling."

"We did before we left." Tim complained.

"And it got us this far safely."

Ella closed her eyes and bowed her head, her husband doing the same as she launched into her favorite Spanish prayer. Tim watched her. She wasn't pushy about religion. Her devotion was so strong that she assumed everyone shared her belief. No one needed to be converted to Catholicism because in her mind, everyone already belonged to God, one way or another.

Even when Tim refused to go to church anymore, she simply said she would pray for them both—that God was always with him no matter where Tim did or didn't go. To his mom, even the interior of an SUV could become a church, the beige leather seats transformed into pews, the dashboard an altar.

What the hell. Just for her, Tim closed his eyes and bowed his head.

The rhythm of the tires changed, Tim jarring awake in response. He smacked his mouth and pulled his head away from the puddle of drool. Not the best treatment for leather seats, but oh well. The car stopped, the turn signal clicking. With any luck, they had finally arrived. His mother kept murmuring how beautiful it all was. Tim remained reclined until his head cleared and his hard-on subsided. Then he sat up and took in his new home town.

The Woodlands. The name sounded like a country club, not a city. What sort of place started with "The"? Inspiration for the name was obvious: trees, trees, and more trees. Aside from the occasional shopping center sign, they could have been in the middle of a forest.

"Doesn't look like much is here," Tim said loud enough to be heard in the front seat.

"There's plenty," his father responded. "It's all behind the trees. I couldn't find a thing the first time I visited. The offices are just through there."

The street split off to the right, and for a moment they could glimpse a parking lot and a generic office building before the camouflage of trees returned. As they drove farther into town, they saw some areas that were more exposed. Man-made lakes, for instance, nestled up against parks and housing developments.

One thing was for sure—and Tim hoped this was the last time the damned saying would spring to mind—he wasn't in Kansas anymore. Everything here was flat, the horizon hidden. The sensation was almost claustrophobic, but he soon took to the idea. He had wanted to flee his former life. What better place to hide than a city that couldn't be seen?

The neighborhood they pulled into fit the anonymous theme, its houses soullessly new. Some didn't appear lived-in yet, a handful still under construction.

"*¡Muy hermosa!*" his mother said in approval as they pulled into a driveway. The three-car garage meant room for both cars—once Ella's was transported down—and his father's boat. To the left, entryway windows stretched up to the second story, a huge iron lamp hanging over the front porch. For one *Twilight Zone* moment, the house looked so similar to their previous home in Kansas that Tim thought they had returned there. He knew this one didn't have a pool, which sucked, but he hoped his room and the studio space in the basement were decent.

He helped his dad get the luggage out of the back and followed him to the garage entrance. Tim expected the inside of the house to be hollow like the one they had left behind. Instead he found a half-furnished home. A dining room table without chairs was already decorated with fabric placemats and a floral centerpiece, even though no one could sit there.

The other rooms were in a similar state. The living room had curtains and a couch, but nothing else. Toward the back of the house, down a hallway and past the guest bathroom was another room with a leather sofa that smelled new. A big-screen TV dominated one wall. To the side, a built-in mini bar was just begging for someone to mix a cocktail.

"Please tell me this is my room," Tim said as his mother entered.

"Uh-uh. This is your father's den, as he calls it." She snorted. "Like he's a bear."

"So where's my den?"

"Upstairs, first on the left." Ella considered the walls and tsked impatiently. "The decorators didn't hang a single thing!"

He left his mother to fuss over some frames leaning in one corner. Returning to the front of the house, Tim grabbed his suitcase and sprinted up the stairs. Everything had that brand-new feel only found in model homes. Nothing had been used yet, like all of this was part of some weird museum exhibit, forever preserving what life was like in nineteen ninety-six.

Tim checked the other rooms first. The largest was obviously the master bedroom, another had a stylish writing desk in it, and one was completely empty. Finally, Tim went to his room, feeling more excited about the move as he opened the door. Inside was a bed, already fully made, and an entertainment center/dresser combo where his TV should fit. One long window provided a view of the backyard, and best of all, he had direct access to his own bathroom. No more darting through the hall in a towel every morning.

Tim sat on the bed. For the first time in his life, he had a blank slate. He could reinvent himself, become something more. His life was the canvas now, empty and begging for lines and color, direction and depth. This room, a simple space and four walls, would be the center of his new world, beyond it a city and people unknown to him. No more familiar streets burdened with names of old friends and tired memories. Just fresh potential for him to breathe in and revitalize himself with. Tim was on the verge of something exciting and new. Life would be better, more than it had been before. *He* would be better.

Tim sprang off the bed and swung his suitcase onto the mattress. He dialed in the combination, the locks clicked open, and the suitcase opened to a whiff of air from another state. Hello, Kansas. Goodbye, Kansas. Opening a dresser drawer, he started shoveling in his clothes, taking extra care when he got to the T-shirt with the porn magazines wrapped inside. Not wanting the movers to discover them, Tim had packed them himself, but now he felt seedy unloading smut from his suitcase, like a desperate travelling salesman. Something about a long drive always made him horny, probably the constant vibration of the road. In fact, he wouldn't mind a quick—

The door to his room opened. In one smooth motion, Tim tossed the contraband-stuffed shirt into the drawer and shut it. His mom strolled in none the wiser and gave a cursory inspection.

"I told them the cranberry comforter, not brown. Why in the world would the decorators choose brown? Cranberry would have looked so nice next to your dark hair." Ella's gaze swiveled between Tim and the comforter, trying to decide if they matched or not. Depending on how expensive the comforter was, Tim wasn't sure if it would go or he would.

"Hey, where's the basement door?" he asked. "I want to check out my studio space."

His mother shook her head distractedly. "There aren't any basements down here."

"What? Why wouldn't they have basements?"

Ella looked puzzled. "Because there aren't as many tornados, I guess. No tornados, no need to hide in the basement like rats."

"Well, where am I going to paint?" Tim huffed.

"We'll find you a space, *Gordito,* don't worry."

"What about the empty room up here?"

"Don't be silly. That's the guest room. Your old bed is going in there."

Tim stared at her. When did they ever have guests? His parents didn't have friends, aside from his father's business associates and their spouses. None of them would stay over for some sort of grown-up slumber party. He tried picturing his father having a pillow fight with some other old guy in a business suit and couldn't.

"If they think that's cranberry, they're color blind," his mother said, her attention back on the bed.

Tim spotted his jogging clothes in the suitcase and grabbed them. If he wasn't going to find release sexually, this was the next best thing. He went downstairs to the guest bathroom, which was completely bare and should be safe from his mother's inspections, and stripped off his clothes. After flexing his muscles in the mirror to satisfy his inner narcissist, he pulled on the navy shorts and gray Kansas University tank top. He made a note to toss the shirt in the trash later, rather than the laundry hamper. Then he sat on the toilet and slipped on his blue running shoes. Half a minute later, Tim was outside pounding pavement.

This. Oh god, this! There was nothing that made him feel so centered, so calm, as running did. Not at first, of course, but as he warmed up and his breath found the right rhythm, all his worries melted away. He'd heard people talk about endorphins, and maybe that was part of it, but there had to be more. Jogging was like meditation on the go. How monks could meditate while sitting on their butts, Tim had no clue. He needed to move, his body completely occupied, skin covered with sweat, hair sticking to his forehead. Only then could silence fill his soul.

He slowed to a trot, almost unwillingly, and stopped. Between two houses was a paved trail a bit wider than the average sidewalk. In the summer dusk, he couldn't see much except the path leading into the shadow of trees ahead. Fences lined either side, meaning it couldn't belong to the neighboring homes. Still panting, Tim ran toward the darkness to see what he would find.

What Tim discovered over the next month is that the trees of The Woodlands hid more than just buildings. Winding throughout the city like a miniature network of roads were bike paths—as the natives called them—that snaked through neighborhoods, connecting everything from shopping centers to public parks.

Tim explored them with caution. The only downside to the bike paths going everywhere was that if he wasn't careful, he could end up anywhere. Those nearest his home led to a small park—not much more than a playground and a small lake. Tim always began by jogging around this body of water, returning the same way. Each time he would run a little farther, explore the paths a bit more before retracing his steps. If he tired of a route, he would choose a different fork and begin again.

With his things unpacked, his room set up, and summer drawing to a close, Tim found himself glad that school was starting soon, if only for the chance to socialize. Exploring his new surroundings was becoming dull, and with both his parents working, Tim longed for something more.

Of course, he still couldn't paint. A week before his birthday, Tim decided he'd had enough. He set up an easel in the guest room and grabbed a canvas he had made a rough sketch on. No one had been in this room since his mother finished decorating it. His hands shook with excitement as he squeezed paint on to the palette, but grew steady again when he dipped in his brush. Sometimes he worked cautiously, every stroke bringing his vision into reality. That had been his intention today, but as soon as the brush touched canvas, his joy was too great.

Like fevered sex after a long period of abstinence, Tim gave into instinct, letting passion dictate his every move. He started with greens, browns, and whites, thinking of the trees he'd been running past and the way light filtered through their leaves. Then he went for purple, just for the sheer hell of it, dragging it through this world of branches over and over again and creating segments, each separated by dark borders like stained glass. A forest of stained glass… stained wood. He liked that.

"Tim."

He spun around. Usually his mom was the first one home, but not today. His father eyed the surroundings, the mess Tim had made, everything but the painting itself. "Your mother is going to be furious."

And that was that. Thomas left the room, not needing to say more. Tim looked around, noticing paint splatters on the carpet. He should have put down newspaper first.

"It's not like anyone ever comes in here!" Tim shouted after him, but there was no reply.

He considered the painting once more. For a first try, it wasn't bad. He'd have to go over the purple with midnight blue to pull in the theme of sky, but it had potential… if he ever found a place to finish it.

As if to prove him wrong about the guest room, Tim's aunt and her husband came to visit the following week. As aunts went, Emily was all right. She was usually good for a laugh, unlike her stoic brother, but as the 24th of August rolled around, Tim began to worry. Like a rare eclipse, his mother's obsessive focus on her husband ceased briefly on one special occasion, but his aunt's visit threatened to ruin that.

As it turned out, he had nothing to fear.

On Tim's birthday, balloons and streamers invaded the house, turning the perfect décor garish. There was cake and ice cream and only one present—but holy shit—it was a big one! The wrapped gift was no larger than a ring box, and inside was a key. Tim knew what that meant. He was out the front door in seconds, his family close behind.

"Oh, wow!"

The car was sleek and black, its curves designed for minimum wind resistance. The three diamonds on the hood screamed Mitsubishi, and that company made only one sports car this boner-inducing: The 3000GT!

Tim jumped and punched the air. "I can't fucking believe it!" His mom's eyes went from bright to flat in the fraction of a second. "Oh, sorry, mom. It's just so fu- freaking *awesome!* Thank you!"

"Happy birthday!" Aunt Emily chirped. "We pitched in on the rubber floor mats. They're a godsend on a muddy day, believe me. Oh, and the air freshener. Ha ha!"

"Just be careful," his father warned, but his cheeks were flushed, perhaps from the memory of his own first car.

"Thank you so much!" Tim opened the driver's side door and jumped in. He couldn't get the key turned quick enough. The engine roared to life with a ferocity that would make a lion piss its furry britches. Tim checked out the dashboard and was about to adjust the seat when he remembered his family standing outside. Finding the right button, the passenger's side window lowered.

"Wanna go for a ride?" he shouted.

He watched them debate over who would go, surprised when his father got into the car with him. He hadn't let Tim drive him anywhere since a few basic lessons last year.

"I have an errand to run," Thomas said.

Tim grinned. "Hold on tight!"

He put the car in gear and hit the gas, the car's engine more powerful than he was expecting. He nearly ran over some guy who was gawping at him instead of walking his dog. Tim couldn't blame him. The car was pure sex. He turned the steering wheel before committing involuntary manslaughter, then zoomed down the street and around the corner, laughing with mad power. When he looked over, his father was holding on to the door handle for dear life, complexion even paler than usual.

"Let's take it easy, son!"

"Sorry."

Tim brought the speed down before turning on to the main road. This was too cool! Maybe his parents were a little preoccupied most of the time, but they sure knew the right way to compensate.

"Thanks," he said again. "I honestly wasn't expecting this."

"I hope not," his father said, but added, "A man should have his independence. Turn here. I need to go to my office."

Tim was dying to gun it, but he didn't want his dad to regret giving him such a souped-up car. He stayed on his best behavior all the way to the generic office building where his dad's company was located. The parking lot was empty on the weekend, so he pulled right up to the door. Tim wanted to wait in the car while his father went inside, unwilling to be separated from his gift. Hell, he might even sleep in the backseat tonight! But his father wanted him to come along, so Tim grudgingly killed the engine.

Once inside, they walked past the reception area and a row of cubicles to a hallway where the real offices were. When they reached a door as nondescript as the others, Thomas dug a key from his pocket and handed it to Tim.

"As I said. Independence."

Tim's stomach sank. His father was giving him a job. He could see through the window in the door that the room beyond was empty, but he took the key and used it anyway.

"This is more a necessity than a present," Thomas said.

Tim opened the door and stepped inside, unsure what to say. His father filled the silence for him.

"This was your mother's idea. I had the carpet taken out so you wouldn't get paint on it. We can always lay it again when you move out, but try not to get paint on the walls."

A studio? Tim felt so relieved that he laughed. He wasn't against getting a job, but he didn't want to work for his father. "Cool! So I can move all my stuff in?"

"Anytime you want."

Tim turned in a circle, viewing the space in a new light. "Can I cover up the window in the door? I don't want people looking at what I'm doing."

"That would be fine."

Tim stopped short of asking if he had the only key. He could always go through his father's keychain sometime and snag any duplicates. Tim was never fond of showing his paintings to other people, and he was planning one that would raise uncomfortable questions if anyone saw it.

"Ready?" Thomas asked.

"Yeah. Thanks. This is really good."

They talked cars on the way home, conversation coming effortlessly. Once back home, the adults poured drinks and discussed subjects that bored Tim to tears, but this made it easy to slip away.

Loading up his car with painting supplies, and feeling more free than ever, Tim headed toward his new studio. He could hardly wait. There was so much he needed to get out of his head, ideas that hounded him until they were released on canvas. Or in some cases, images that he needed to exorcise for his own well-being.

In the backseat was a canvas with a rough sketch. The dark

eyes were apparent, but the shape of the face around them was drawn in light lines hard to see. If someone were to look close enough, they would discover the features were male, even though they shared traits with his ex-girlfriend. Except in the drawing Corey was older, enough so that when he made a pass at Tim, it wouldn't have felt like his kid brother was hitting on him. Old enough that Tim might have given Corey a different answer.

Chapter Three

Tim shifted in the hard plastic seat and resisted moaning in miserable boredom. Had he really wished for the school year to begin? At the front of class, a thin woman with wiry gray hair read passages from a book. The idea was to entice them, since they were about to read it themselves, but so far nothing much of interest seemed to happen in Holden Caulfield's life.

The words blurred together, Tim's mind turning to sex as it always did when he was bored. When his brain checked out and left his body in charge, it only ever wanted a few basic things. This class was almost over, and getting hard now would be inconvenient when the bell rang, so Tim tried to find something else to occupy his attention.

He covertly eyed the other students. The guys didn't look so different from those back in Kansas, except for a handful who dressed like cowboys. The hats weren't there, at least not in class, but the picnic-patterned shirts and massive belt buckles were. Girls in Texas favored more makeup and often wore their hair up. Literally. Hairspray must be in constant short supply here because a lot of the hairdos—especially the bangs—were sculpted to defy gravity.

Tim felt someone watching him and caught them in the act. A girl, and a pretty one at that. She had a little of the heavy makeup and sprayed hair, but it worked for her. Ramrod thin with pale blonde hair, she wore an open expression that made her appear timid, like a woodland creature. Their eyes still locked, Tim gave a tentative smile. She smiled back, adorable as a doe.

Beyond her was a bear, a hulking package of muscle squeezed into his desk chair. The guy looked like he belonged in college, maybe as a linebacker on the football team. He seemed annoyed at the exchange Tim and Little Miss Doe had shared. The guy had blond hair and green eyes too—not the same shade as the girl's, but he could be her brother. Or boyfriend, since they didn't share any family resemblance. Tim returned his attention to the teacher, keeping his eyes averted even when the bell rang and he left the class.

Time for lunch. Tim strolled around the cafeteria, checking out the vending machines full of sugar-free drinks. He got a lemonade, and though he was hungry, he didn't line up for food, not wanting to be the pathetic new guy sitting alone at a table. Making new friends was more daunting than he'd expected. In Kansas he'd been around the same people all his life and knew who everyone was, even if he never interacted with them. And he had been popular. Here, he was a nobody.

But that anonymity was what he wanted. Tomorrow he would swallow his pride and sit alone, but today he went outside and walked around the school, enjoying the weather. When the bell rang, he went back in for his other classes. In U.S. History, the teacher didn't seem interested in starting the year quite yet and let them "get settled," as he put it. This meant everyone could talk. Tim had a conversation with a girl who was nice enough, but her cheeks kept flushing like they were on a first date or something. They didn't have much in common.

When the school day finally ended, he was eager to get to his car and head home. The new house was close enough that he could make the trip a long walk or a short jog, but today Tim had driven. He wanted to make a good first impression, and this didn't go unnoticed.

"Nice car."

Tim turned, his hand on the Mitsubishi's door handle. The guy eyeing his car like it was a naked woman was stocky, bordering on chubby. But his clothes were all designer-label, and his hair might have been highlighted, since it was darker underneath than on top. One thing was for sure: No common barber had ever touched those locks.

"Thanks. Just got it for my birthday."

"Sixteen?" the guy asked.

"Seventeen."

"Ah. Well, that's what I got for my sixteenth."

The guy pointed to a cherry-red Porsche. Several people were gathered around it, most of them watching Tim and the guy talking. Little Miss Doe was there, as was her huge companion and a number of other beautiful people. High school royalty. Farther away was their court, the people not quite in their inner circle but desperate to be.

"You new here?"

"Yeah. Just moved down this summer." He held out his hand, giving the other guy a firm grip. "Tim Wyman."

"Darryl Briscott. Hey, we're having a party to help wipe today from our minds. You want to come?"

Tim nodded. "When and where?"

Darryl's smile was smug. "My place, right now."

Before they went anywhere, Darryl walked Tim over to the group for a round of introductions. His woodland creature was Krista Norman, the tower of muscles Bryce Hunter. Definitely not brother and sister then. The other names and faces Tim would have to catch on the sly because he had already forgotten most of them.

He followed Darryl's Porsche to a neighborhood that made his own look destitute. A lot of his friends in Kansas were rich, so his mind wasn't blown, but for the first time in his life he wondered if he was going to make the cut. This invitation was obviously the beginning of an interview. Tim had the looks and he had the car, but there were still plenty of ways to fall out of grace, as he had learned back home.

Three other cars were in their convoy, and once parked, Darryl's driveway looked like a sports car showroom. The inside of the house was spacious. Rich homes either had a ton of rooms or scaled-up versions of the normal amount. Darryl's home was of the latter variety. Every room was like a cathedral, the ceilings so high they could have easily supported an additional floor halfway up.

"This way, my man," Darryl said.

He led Tim through the house to a room that nearly made his jaw drop. He supposed it wasn't so different from his father's den, but taken to a whole new level. Instead of a big-screen television, the room had a movie screen and a projector built into opposite walls. Beneath the projector was a long L-shaped couch that could seat at least ten.

Instead of a mere wet bar, the far wall looked like it had been stolen from a British pub and teleported to Texas. Set against a giant mirror were shelves and shelves of liquor bottles, all lit tastefully from below.

In front of this was an ebony bar with brass accents and half a dozen empty stools. Tim happily plopped down on one. Darryl played bartender, switching on some music as everyone got settled. Then he turned to Tim and asked a question that sent his mouth watering.

"What'll it be?"

"A beer."

"A beer man, very good." Except Darryl didn't open a fridge and pull out a bottle. Instead he grabbed a mug, held it tilted under a nozzle, and pulled a handle. Tim died and went to heaven. They actually had beer on tap! In their home! He needed to have a serious talk with his dad. Of course his father wouldn't be cool about it, even as a joke.

Darryl set the glass on the bar, but it was only two-thirds full. "Beer isn't very strong, especially for the first day of school. Ever had a depth-charge?"

Tim shook his head. Darryl grinned and grabbed a bottle of whiskey. He filled a shot glass full before dropping it straight into the beer mug. The beer fizzed and foamed, but didn't overflow. Pushing the mug toward him, Darryl started taking other orders. He certainly knew his stuff. He whipped up everything from cocktails to daiquiris, always knowing a way of making the requested drink stronger. No wonder he was popular!

"What do you think?" he asked, nodding toward Tim's beer.

The foam had died down enough for Tim to take a sip. It tasted like someone had pissed in his beer, but he nodded appreciatively and lied. "Fucking delicious!"

Darryl was having the same and clinked mugs with Tim before nodding to the room. "Looks like you have a fan."

Tim turned around. A dozen other people were there, but he only remembered the names of two. Doe-eyed Krista Norman was staring at him, but laughed and looked at her friend like she hadn't been. And that friend of hers was something else! Krista was pretty, but the brunette next to her was beautiful. Dangerous too, judging from the power Tim felt behind her gaze. Unlike Krista, the brunette offered no bashful flirtation. Instead she sized him up in seconds and looked away again. Tim, feeling a little uncomfortable, did the same. He spun back around in the stool, catching a hulking giant glaring at him as he did so.

"A fan, huh?" Tim said. "You mean Bryce?"

Darryl guffawed. "Don't worry about him. Not only is he big as an ox, but he plays like one too."

"Football?"

"That, and women." Darryl gestured to the room with his mug. "He thinks all these cows belong to him."

Charming.

"The problem is," Darryl continued, "everyone here has dated everyone else. Some of us have a harder time letting go, is all."

"So you talking to me is making Bryce jealous?"

Darryl laughed again. "He's nothing to worry about. He's with Stacy Shelly now, and believe me, she's the kind of girl who keeps you in line."

"The brunette?" Tim asked as if disinterested.

"Yeah. That's Krista's best friend. Speaking of which—" He nodded over Tim's shoulder. "What do you think?"

"Krista? I think she's hot."

"So do I, but no one ever gets anywhere with her. She's a prude."

"Or maybe none of you guys have the right moves." Banter. It was so damn easy.

A cocky smile spread over Darryl's face. "All right. Let's see what you've got."

They went to join the others on the couch, Darryl telling people to move over, making room for Tim to sit next to Krista. When Tim put his mug on the long coffee table, he noticed it was more than half-empty. That explained the warm feeling inside.

"Hey," Tim said, focusing on Krista. She turned bright red, like he had asked to see her panties.

"Hi," she managed.

Stacy leaned forward on the couch to get a better view of him. "So, Mr. Tim Wyman, where exactly are you from?"

Tim managed to meet her gaze, but only just. "Kansas." He could see her tallying the points in her head. Had he been from somewhere cool, say California, he would have earned more.

"Trying out for any of the teams?" she asked next.

"Yeah. Not sure which, though."

"How about football?" Bryce said.

Right. Like Tim was looking forward to getting crushed beneath him during practice. Tim had given football a shot in freshmen year and hated it. People in Kansas were fanatics about high school football, especially the teachers. While it was an easy way to get good grades—since failing meant the team lost a player—Tim hated the intense pressure. Basketball was out too, since being six feet tall didn't amount to much on the court. That left cross country in the fall, which they probably wouldn't care about, but in the spring…

"I'm thinking about baseball," he said.

"Wait, there's a baseball team?" Darryl said sarcastically.

Stacy played off this, sounding bored. "I can't say I've ever heard of one."

"Trust me," Tim said, looking her in the eye. "When I'm on the team, it's all you'll ever hear about."

Most people chuckled at his joke, but Stacy's eyes lit up with scored points. Darryl hopped up to get more drinks, and the rest of the party was much more relaxed. Tim was in. For now. They would never stop watching and judging him, but that was high school. The wine flowed like wine, and so did the depth-charged beers. Considering he had skipped lunch, every beer felt like two, maybe four including the whiskey. Soon enough, Tim had his arm around Krista, and she was either flushing or giggling in response to everything he said.

At some point Darryl's parents were mentioned, which was the alarm that sent everyone scurrying for their cars. Tim knew he shouldn't drive, but he couldn't crash at Darryl's place. The streets were a distorted blur, and he managed to get lost a few times, but an army of exhausted guardian angels guided him home safely. The last of them helped him up the stairs and to his bathroom. Tim barely managed to get the toilet seat up before he puked his guts out.

All in all, a fairly normal first day of school.

"Timmy!"

Krista Norman darted down the hall and put a hand on his arm. Funny how first impressions could be so wrong. Last week Krista had seemed so shy. Now she never stopped talking. Not that Tim minded much, since it meant less effort on his part. Usually he would daydream about other things while she rattled on.

And Bryce, who had seemed so big and scary before… Well, he was still both those things, but he had warmed up to Tim, probably because he'd kept his distance from Stacy. And maybe Bryce didn't worry about Tim getting anywhere with Krista, since more people than Darryl had since told him she was a prude. That was fine by him. Horny as Tim might be, he still felt shell-shocked from the rape rumors in Kansas.

"Hey, faggot!" Bryce rumbled.

Tim looked up and followed his gaze. The intended target

was obvious, since he was the only guy standing still as everyone else hurried to class. Brown eyes stared at him from below perfectly styled blond hair, and for one moment, Tim thought of Corey.

"He really is, you know," Krista said in a stage whisper.

The guy's face turned red, but he seemed more angry than embarrassed. He glared at Bryce, even though he was skinny enough to be crushed by one of those ham fists. Then he waved sarcastically at Krista, imitating her snobby body language. The guy had guts! Finally he looked at Tim, as if he was still unsure about him. Tim returned the wave, which didn't seem to please him, since he spun around and stalked off down the hall.

"Who was that?"

"Brian Bentley," Krista said, rolling her eyes.

"No, it's Benjamin," Bryce corrected, "as in bend over!"

The joke didn't make sense, but for Bryce it was probably his wittiest moment.

"Walk me to class?" Krista said.

"Yeah," Tim answered distractedly.

He said goodbye to Bryce and let Krista guide him down the hall. Krista started talking about a shopping trip or something involving shoes, Tim nodding along until they reached her class. Then he interrupted her.

"How does anyone know?" he asked.

"What?"

"That Benjamin guy. How does anyone know he's gay?"

Krista looked repulsed. "Because he told everyone."

"Seriously?" Tim considered this in surprise. "That takes balls."

"More like he's crazy. Who cares anyway? He's just some loser."

"Well, if nobody cares, then why pick on him?" Tim had never understood the way popular kids picked on those who weren't. He got along with everyone, really. But here, just like back in Kansas, being on top seemed to require making everyone below you miserable.

Krista rolled her eyes. "Do you want me to get you his number or something?"

"Why would I want it?" Tim said forcefully enough that she blanched.

"I was just kidding. Geez."

Tim glared at her. "Why would you even joke about that? Huh?"

Krista grasped for words and for once couldn't find any.

"I'll see you during lunch."

Tim sulked his way down the hall. He had only asked a simple question. Krista didn't need to jump to conclusions like that. Just because he didn't hate someone for what they were, didn't make him the same thing. He felt irritated at himself for even broaching the stupid subject. But once he was in class and had calmed down, part of him couldn't help smile that there was someone crazy enough to stand up to Bryce Hunter.

Tim waited in line for lunch, the smell of greasy cafeteria food making his stomach growl. Bryce's stomach roared back, echoing the sentiment. They did this every day, grabbing two trays each and bringing them back to Krista and Stacy like waiters on a date. Tim only started doing it because he enjoyed the quiet that came from leaving Krista at the table.

"I've got this one."

They turned in unison, puzzled at Stacy's presence.

"What?" Bryce asked.

"Today I'm bringing you your food. Go sit down."

Bryce shrugged and did as he was told, leaving Tim and Stacy alone for the first time. Tim knew this had never happened before because he made sure it didn't. As hot as she was, Stacy scared the hell out of him. Maybe because she was as mean as Carla could be, except Stacy usually didn't bother playing nice.

Not that she couldn't, when she wanted. A male teacher had once come up to her in the hall and asked why she had missed class. Stacy went all giggling dingbat, her every movement adorable and flirtatious. The teacher had forgiven her pretty quickly and headed down the hall, probably so no one would notice the growing tent in his pants.

"Double date tonight," Stacy said with a calculating smile. "Or at least, it was supposed to be."

"The four of us?" Tim asked.

Stacy nodded. "Don't you think it's time you make it official? I know Krista is an idiot, but believe me, there are benefits to dating someone so stupid."

Tim didn't reply.

"You're a very careful person," Stacy said. "Why is that?"

Tim shrugged and gave an easy smile. "I've got nothing to hide."

"I didn't say you did. Look, Krista thinks you're mad at her. Something about Ben Bentley, the gay guy."

Tim played dumb. "Oh, is that his name?"

There was a long pause before Stacy answered. "Yes. Yes, it is." Forget Bryce. She was way scarier. What a monster couple they made! The beauty and the beast, but it was Stacy's intelligence that made her dangerous.

"Yeah, well, that guy smarted off to Krista," Tim huffed, "and I wanted to know who he was. It pissed me off, that's all."

Stacy searched his eyes, but seemed satisfied. "You like her, and she likes you, right?"

"Obviously."

"Then ask her. Dinner and a movie, tonight. Unless you want people to start asking why you're still single."

Stacy walked away. A minute later, her boyfriend was sent back over to wait in line with him.

"I don't understand women," Bryce huffed.

Tim did. He understood them all too well.

Chapter Four

Krista, as it turned out, made a decent girlfriend. Sure, she talked a lot, but when Tim did have something to say, she listened with rapt attention. She laughed at all his jokes and was so slender that she made Tim feel as big as Bryce. He liked that. He also appreciated that she had none of Carla's meanness. Occasionally she could be a bitch, but only when she was following someone else's lead, usually Stacy's.

Mostly she was just as happy and dumb as the doe he first pictured her as. Like today, when he hadn't been in the mood for company. Instead of driving to school, he had walked. He forgot to tell her until the end of the day. When he mentioned he was jogging home, she didn't mind having to find a ride. Carla would have chewed his head off, but Krista simply went with the flow.

Tim was starting to realize she was safe. As he ran along the bike path on the way home, the fabric of his shorts feeling good against his package as it bounced around, Tim considered taking things further with her. He couldn't be celibate his whole life, just because of what happened in Kansas. Krista didn't seem the type to spread lies. With his parents out of town for the next two weeks, now was the perfect opportunity to get—

Boom!

Weight slammed into Tim from behind, knocking him off the path. Unfortunately, this particular path ran along a drainage ditch, a deep ravine which left him nowhere to go but down. Tim tumbled, rolling over and over, thankful that the ditch was grass and dirt and not hard concrete—until he skipped into the air at the end and landed on one leg with a crunch.

Pain! It seared up from his leg and into the rest of his body, his brain burning as he swore out loud. He managed to roll off the leg, easing his suffering, and raised the limb into the air. Blood covered one shin. As bad as that hurt, the source of the worst pain throbbed from further down.

Tim carefully lowered his leg, putting pressure on it. A fresh wave of hurt washed over him. This wasn't good.

"Oh, god! I'm sorry. I'm sorry!" Someone slid down into the drainage ditch with him. Whoever it was, they were to blame!

"What the hell happened?" Tim spat.

"I don't—I'm just a klutz."

The guy acted like he was going to pick Tim up and carry him to safety, which was ridiculous because he was so scrawny that Krista could probably take him in a fight. In fact, he looked familiar. They went to the same school, if Tim wasn't mistaken.

"Is your leg broken?"

"Leg's fine," Tim looked back at it. "It's my ankle that's jacked."

The guy dropped to his knees to examine it, like he could fix it with a little tape and glue. Tim stared. Now he recognized him! Benjamin Bentley, shameless homosexual and brave glarer at Bryce. He had inline skates on his feet, which presumably had propelled him into Tim.

"We have to get you to a doctor," Ben said. "Can you walk?"

Tim tried putting weight on his leg. Even though the worst of the pain had receded, walking on it now would bring it all back again. "You're going to have to help me."

"Wait." Ben flopped on to his rump and started undoing his skates.

Tim watched him work. There wasn't really anything feminine about him. Aside from being a little small he looked just like any other guy. Except apparently he couldn't skate without leaving behind a wake of destruction. With the skates finally off, Ben dug in his backpack and pulled out a pair of shoes. Jesus, how long was this going to take?

"Right." Finally dressed for the occasion, Ben stood. "How do we do this?"

Tim looked up the hill he had fallen down. "You pull me up there, I guess."

"Pull you how?"

Ugh! Tim would die down here before he got this guy to do anything. "Just grab me under the arms and pull. I'll help as much as I can."

Ben scuttled behind him, and Tim lifted his arms. After another uncertain pause, Ben's arms hooked beneath his and pulled. Tim moved half an inch. Maybe. Now he was sure Krista could win that brawl. Ben pulled again, and this time Tim kicked with his good foot. Now they were getting somewhere! After some grunting and no doubt a ton of grass stains on his backside, they made it to the top.

They both panted from the effort before Tim asked for help standing up. Ben handled this much better. Soon Tim had an arm draped over Ben's shoulder for support. His ankle was still too sensitive for any pressure. Tim could kind of hop along with assistance, but it was slow going.

"Okay." Tim sighed. "I guess we make it to the nearest house and have them drive me home."

"Your house is really close if we cut through the trees there."

Tim tensed. What the hell was that supposed to mean? If Ben had only known his name, Tim wouldn't have been surprised. That was one of the perks of being popular. But how could Ben know where he lived?

"Let's go, then," Tim said. The sooner he got home, the sooner he could forget this had happened.

Ben held tightly to him as they made their way through the trees, and for a moment Tim imagined himself being led to some pit dug in the woods where no one would see him again. Instead they reached a privacy fence. Left and right, that's all there was—one long row of fences.

"Fuck," Tim swore. "How much further would it be if this fence wasn't here?"

Ben looked away, ashamed at having been called out. "Half a block."

Tim hopped toward the fence and grabbed its top. If they couldn't get around it, they would go through it. "Support me," he said. Tim yanked on the plank, muscles flexing with effort. Ben grabbed him just as the board came loose. Cheaply built, the fence only had two nails holding it in place. The plank fell to one side, so he worked another free, and then a third. Now they had plenty of room to squeeze through. If the owners saw them and came running, at least they could give Tim a ride the rest of the way home.

As it turned out, the place was empty, not having been lived in yet. They were close to his neighborhood, all right. In fact, when they made it to the street, Tim saw they were just a few houses away.

"Which one is yours?" Ben asked.

"You tell me," Tim snapped. A little late to play coy, stalker boy. He glared at Ben, who was staring at the ground, cheeks red. The rest of his skin had a nice tan, the edges of his blond hair bleached platinum from the sun. Tim's hair never changed color like that. A sheen of sweat covered Ben's upper lip, either from the heat or the exertion of supporting him. Was it the pain that rendered everything in such stark detail? Maybe they should head to the studio instead. Tim watched in fascination as Ben's mouth formed a sentence.

"Is anyone home?"

"No."

"Then shouldn't we drive straight to the hospital?"

Which would involve his parents being called, and them being angry with him, like last time. Tim turned his attention back to the goal. "I just need to take the weight off my leg."

The front door was unlocked, the cold air inside already feeling good on his ankle. Thank god for air conditioning! Tim had left the curtains closed last night to keep the house cool. By this time of year, Kansas was usually dropping hints about fall, but summer seemed to reign eternal in Texas.

He flipped a light switch and headed for the couch in his mother's living room. That's how he thought of it, since it was just as flowery and dainty as his father's den was masculine. After lowering himself to the couch, wincing with every inch, he told Ben to fetch a washcloth and first aid kit from the bathroom. Once he got his leg cleaned up, it should be a lot easier to see the damage.

"Are you sure we shouldn't go to the hospital?" Ben held out a washcloth and a little first aid kit. "Or call a doctor at least?"

"No need. Same thing happened to me freshman year." And that was the other reason Tim wasn't interested in football. "I still have a brace upstairs. A couple of days with that on, and I'll be fine."

Ben was staring at him with saucer-sized eyes overflowing with guilt. "It's just—"

Tim cut him off. "Thanks for helping me get home." Ben took the hint. Well, first he apologized about ten more times, but then he finally headed for the door. Tim was about to sigh in relief when Ben turned around.

"Are you sure you're going to be all right? When do your parents get back?"

"In about two weeks. They're in Switzerland." Tim worked on wrapping a cloth bandage around his shin. He made sure not to look up again until he heard the front door close. Then he leaned back on the couch and sighed.

What a weirdo.

Tim sat there, breathing deeply and forcing himself to remain calm. The pain receded a little, but seemed to have reached its minimum level, which unfortunately still hurt like hell. Last time the doctor gave him pills that not only killed the pain but made him feel drunk. Some of those would be good about now.

Tim sat upright. The movers had packed absolutely everything. Maybe that included old prescriptions. Unless things had changed, his mother kept those in a kitchen cabinet. Tim considered several ways he could get there. Finally he sat on the floor and used his three good limbs to move himself backward. That way his leg could drag along the floor without getting hurt. In theory. His ankle still bumped against things and made him suffer for it, but Tim got to the kitchen, pulled himself up on one of the counters, and opened cabinet after cabinet.

His reward was a vintage bottle of pills from 1993. After grabbing a Coke from the fridge, he doubled the recommended dose, chugged them down with half the soda, and started back to the couch. It was that or lay on the kitchen floor. When he made it to the living room, he noticed the clock. He had spent half an hour doing what would normally take a minute. Those pills better work miracles, or he was royally screwed.

In a way, they sort of did. Soon Tim was feeling pretty damn good. His body thrummed with pleasure, even though the pain was still there below the surface. Trying to stand brought the pain back with a vengeance and had him shrieking until he sat down again. Then the opiate haze resumed, soothing him, but he clearly needed help. Tim lay on the couch, wondering what to do and zoning out occasionally until the doorbell rang.

Help had come! He heard the front door open before someone said, "Hello?"

Crap. It sounded like Ben. Then again, help was help. "Hey," he shouted. "Come in!"

Sure enough, Ben came in the room, still looking guilt-ridden. "Good that you're here," Tim said, hoping to bolster his spirits. He needed action, not more apologies "The ankle might be worse than I thought."

"Yeah." Ben held up a thick tome with a diagram of human

anatomy on the cover. "I think you have a third-degree sprain. Either that or it's broken. You really need to get to a hospital."

Tim didn't need a book to tell him that. He kept a straight face and said as solemnly as possible, "Probably should."

"Er, I know this is a really stupid question, but are you all right?"

"Yeah. After you left I dragged my ass into the kitchen and remembered some pills from last time. They've got me feeling…" Floaty? Cosmic? Rainbow flowery? "Oh man," he said instead.

"I'll call an ambulance."

"No, fuck that. I'm not dying or anything. We'll take my car. You can drive, right?"

"Um… Yes?"

"Well, get me up and we'll be on our way."

Setting aside the book and approaching the couch, Ben wrapped an arm around his back. He was still warm from being outside, and his touch felt good on Tim's cold skin. Lying on the couch for so long in his jogging clothes probably hadn't been the best idea, but soon they were standing outside in the heat.

"Actually," Tim said when he saw his beloved car, "just get me seated and I'll drive."

"With one foot?"

"Yes," Tim said slowly. "That's usually how it's done."

Ben shook his head. "You're too doped up."

"And you can't rollerblade without killing someone," he countered.

"You're not dead yet," Ben said defiantly.

Tim laughed. This guy really was crazy. "All right, fine. You can drive. But be careful." He wasn't laughing for long. As soon as he was in the passenger seat, Tim braced himself for disaster. He even flinched when Ben jammed the key into the ignition, as if he could make the car explode just by doing this. Instead, the engine growled like it always did.

Tim relaxed into the seat, but his repose didn't last for long. Ben drove like he was in a dream, Tim suffering the experience like a nightmare. Ben made casual conversation, twisting the wheel at the last second to avoid bikers, pedestrians, or oncoming traffic. Maybe an ambulance would be taking him to the hospital after all, but only after Ben wrecked his car. Now it was all too clear how he had managed to crash into Tim while rollerblading.

By some miracle, they reached the hospital without creating extra victims to bring with them. Ben pulled up to the emergency entrance, where he jumped out of the car and snagged a wheelchair. That was a welcome convenience. Once inside, Tim expected a team of concerned doctors and nurses to rush him down hallways on a gurney, like they do in the movies. Instead they sat in a waiting room with other despondent souls and struggled with paperwork.

When a nurse finally called his name, Ben wheeled Tim into another room… where they waited some more. But first she and Ben helped Tim onto the examination table. He was getting sick of being so helpless. The nurse took his vital signs and promised the doctor wouldn't be long.

Tim sighed and glared at his ankle. "Can't you do that thing where you twist it real fast, I scream, and then I'm miraculously better?"

"That's only for dislocated bones," Ben said, "but I can give it a try anyway."

"Nah. Better not. So what did that big medical book of yours say? Think I'll need a cast?"

"Honestly, they'll probably just amputate."

"What?"

Ben exhaled. "I'm afraid there's no other option, but just think how cool your new peg leg will be. I hear the pirate look is all the rage in Europe right now. A frilly shirt and an eye patch, and you'll be the most popular guy in school."

Tim considered the idea. "Do I get a parrot?"

"Of course."

"Then you've got a deal."

Ben's expression grew somber. "Seriously, though. You're going to be okay."

"Thanks, Doogie Howser," Tim retorted. "I'm not really scared for my life, you know."

"Sorry. I just feel so guilty."

"Don't start that again!" Tim shifted, the paper beneath his butt crinkling. Ben had really loosened up on the drive over, and kept flashing smiles that caught Tim's eye. Those teeth were perfect, lined up like little soldiers that saluted him every time he tried to be funny. Something about that smile made Tim want to be wittier than he'd ever been before, and oddly, that pressure made finding the right words so much harder.

They were quiet for a moment. Then Ben nodded at the exam table. "Why do they always put paper down? It's so weird."

"No kidding. I figure it's for sanitary reasons, but how many naked people show up at the ER?"

Ben laughed. "Huh?"

"You know. Most people sit here in their clothes, so I don't see how they could get the table messy."

"Unless a lot of people wet themselves." Ben suggested thoughtfully. "Or worse."

"Yuck!"

"Who knows how many years of fecal matter have soaked through the paper to stain the exam table?" Ben's grin was wicked. "I dare you to pull the paper back and lick the spot where you're sitting."

"Dude! Shut up!" Tim laughed, even though he was repulsed. "You're crazy, Benjamin!"

"It's Ben."

"Yeah," Tim said, wiping tears from his eyes, "but Benjamin is better."

"Better?"

Tim shrugged. "It's a nice name."

Ben didn't respond, an awkward silence trying to ruin their fun. Tim didn't want their banter to end. Talking to Ben felt good, maybe because if Tim screwed up, it wouldn't count against him like it would with his friends. He wasn't sure how to jumpstart their conversation again, but thankfully a distraction walked in the door and introduced himself as Dr. Baker. The doctor barely needed to look at the ankle to see what was wrong. Ben's diagnosis seemed to be right. Most likely they were looking at a class three sprain. Tim would need X-rays and probably a cast so it would heal right. He could live with all of that. The words Tim really dreaded came next.

"I'll need to inform your parents about this, of course."

"They're in Switzerland." Right now it was probably late there. Tim could imagine them being awakened in the middle of the night and told they needed to come back home.

"Any other family in the area?" the doctor asked.

"Nope."

Ben piped up. "My family can take care of him until they're back."

Tim raised his head. Was he serious? If Tim could avoid ruining his parents' trip, he would get a lot less grief.

Dr. Baker was less enthused by the idea. With no family to look out for him, Tim would have to stay in the hospital overnight. It was getting pretty late anyway, so that wasn't a big deal.

"I have to get home," Ben said. "Can I pick him up tomorrow?"

"I suppose," Dr. Baker replied. "Could you please bring the phone number of his parents' hotel with you? Or better yet, phone it in tonight?"

"Absolutely."

What was Ben playing at? He didn't have access to their number—unless he used the keys still in his pocket. "Wait, you're taking my car?"

"It's not like you can use it," Ben said cheerfully. "See you tomorrow, tiger."

"You know," Tim said to the doctor after Ben had left, "I'm starting to think he did this to me on purpose."

"Must be a nice car to go through all this trouble," Dr. Baker said, helping Tim back into the wheelchair.

"It is," Tim murmured, "but it might not be in the best shape when I get it back."

Chapter Five

Tim's night in the hospital passed in a welcome haze of painkillers. He got his X-rays, then his cast, and flirted with every nurse who came in the room—reveling in the giggles of the younger girls, and the barely-suppressed smiles of the older ladies. As much fun as he was having, he dreaded the next morning. Ben would bring the phone number of his parents' hotel, and from there, history would repeat itself.

Tim was thirteen when his parents cancelled a trip to Japan because he had come down with the flu. At first he was glad they decided to stay home, still young enough that it bugged him when they took trips alone. Instead of fawning over him at his bedside and catering to his every need, his parents treated him as an inconvenience, remaining bitter until they were able to reschedule their trip.

He understood now that the vacations his parents took together were a way of recapturing the childless life they had once planned. As far as Tim was concerned, he was a mistake. His parents never talked of having another child. They still loved him, when they found the time, but he had learned long ago not to ask for too much or get in the way.

As the morning progressed, he tried to imagine what their reaction to his accident would be. Even worse, what if Ben called them to explain? This was the first question out of his mouth when Ben showed up at the hospital.

"Did you call my parents?"

"No," Ben started to say, but when Dr. Baker came in the room, he changed his answer. "Yes. They don't think they can change their flight, but they've arranged for a nurse to take care of you and everything."

That didn't sound so bad, if it was true. The doctor asked Ben for their number, which he had rather conveniently forgotten to bring along. Dr. Baker seemed to share this suspicion, but he checked his watch and gave Ben a quick earful about everything Tim would need. After being presented with crutches and making a quick trip to the hospital pharmacy for pills, Tim let Ben wheel him outside to the car. He insisted they do a loop around the Mitsubishi before they got in so he could check for damages.

Amazingly, he didn't find a scratch.

Once behind the wheel, Ben was pensive. With Tim starting to feel his most recent dose of pain medication, they didn't talk much on the way home. When they arrived, Tim made use of the crutches, swinging up the driveway so fast that Ben had to rush to keep up.

"I feel like Tarzan," Tim said.

"Or his chimp," Ben retorted. "Wait up. I'll get the door for you."

"Thanks." Tim watched him fumble with the keys. Ben shot him a nervous look, as if concerned about messing up such a simple task. Not that Ben didn't steal little glances at him at other times. Tim was used to girls finding him attractive, but now he wondered what other guys thought. Gay guys, obviously. Corey had expressed interest, but that whole situation had been weird. Of course, so had Ben's knowledge of where Tim lived.

As soon as Tim was inside and seated on the peach-colored couch, Ben stood in front him nervously. "There's something I need to tell you."

For a moment, Tim thought Ben was about to confess his feelings. The idea made him both uncomfortable and excited.

"It seemed kind of pointless to worry your parents for nothing," Ben said instead. "Or mine. It's just a sprained ankle, right? A nurse seemed overboard too. I mean, we can call one now if you really want. Or I can just take care of you."

Tim stared at him. "So, no nurse?"

"No nurse."

"And you never called my parents? They have no idea I was in the hospital overnight?"

Now Ben looked guilty. "They have no idea."

Tim relaxed. He would have thanked him, if this whole mess wasn't Ben's fault in the first place. Ben was more than willing to make up for it. He promised to swing by every day to cook and clean. So Tim *would* have a nurse. One who would destroy his reputation at school if anyone found out, but for now he was so relieved his parents weren't involved that he didn't care.

But if they were going to do this, they were going to do it right. Tim stood with a little wobbling and crutched his way to his father's den in the back of the house. Maybe the room couldn't compete with the set-up Darryl's father had, but it was still nice. Everything was dark wood, brown leather, and most of all, comfortable.

"I figure this is a good place to make camp," Tim said, settling down on the couch. He nodded at the wet bar. "There's even a fridge to keep drinks in."

"So what all do we need?" Ben glanced around. "Blankets and pillows obviously… Um…"

"In one of the hall closets," Tim said. "I want my pillow from upstairs. And some real clothes. Throw something in the oven too, will ya?"

"Right."

Tim turned on the TV, allowing himself a chuckle once Ben left the room. He would cut Ben loose after today. Tim figured he was trying to make amends or searching for an excuse to be around. Either way, Tim could take care of himself. But for now, he only wanted to kick back and relax. He flipped through the channels, settling on music videos.

Soon the smell of pizza filled the house. When Ben came into the room with two plates loaded with slices, Tim was nearly drooling in anticipation. They watched videos together, poking fun at all the bad ones and flipping between VH1 and MTV to avoid commercials. When they had finished eating, Ben took the plates to the kitchen, then hurried back and plopped on the couch. Tim was about to change back to MTV when Ben made him stop.

"Wait! I love this song!"

Tim had heard it plenty of times already. The radio stations were going crazy playing The Fugees' *Killing Me Softly,* but the song had never caught his ear before. Nor had the silky male voice that came in halfway through.

Tim looked to his left, jaw dropping. Ben was singing, but not how other people crooned along with real music. Ben's voice was studio sweet, sounding so perfect that Tim wanted to snap at Lauryn Hill to be quiet so he could hear better.

Instead Tim covertly turned down the TV's volume, which wasn't hard since Ben's eyes were locked on his. Gone was any sign of passive interest or furtive glances. Ben's full attention was on Tim now as he sang. And it was beautiful. Scratch that, *Ben* was beautiful. Forget Darryl's money, Stacy's cunning, or Bryce's muscles. Ben had the voice, and that should have made him the most popular guy in school because it was so damn hot! Girls should be heartbroken over him, and guys should be doing everything to be more like him.

Then the song ended and Ben looked away, his cheeks a little red. Tim stared dumbfounded for a couple more seconds before he clapped and cheered, happy to make an ass of himself.

"You can sing!"

"Yeah," Ben said with a nervous chuckle. "I do all right."

"Why don't you do that all the time? I mean, if I had a voice like yours, I would sing everything instead of talking like normal people do."

Ben laughed. "That might get oooold after a whiiiile!" he sang opera style.

Okay, so maybe that sounded dumb, but Tim wanted to hear Ben belt out a real song again. "Do this one!" he said, turning the volume up a little.

"It's the Beastie Boys," Ben said. "They aren't singing, they're rapping. Or whining. Wait until a song like the last one comes on. Hey, have you ever heard the original *Killing Me Softly*?"

Tim shook his head.

"Roberta Flack! She's a goddess. I'll play that version for you sometime. Then you won't think I have a good voice. I get goose bumps every time I hear it."

Tim had goose bumps still, so he tried to chill out and stop acting like a groupie. They watched another couple of videos together until one came on that Ben liked. Then he started singing again, this time with his eyes closed, and Tim felt those same feelings come rushing back. It hadn't just been the song or the moment. That voice was freaking magical! Tim really couldn't understand why Ben wasn't more popular. Maybe it was the gay thing, but surely people would forgive Ben for anything if they could hear him sing.

Once the song was over, Tim did his best not to gush. "Are you in choir or anything like that?"

Ben nodded.

"So people at school have heard you sing."

"Yeah, but usually just the people who go to recitals. I also sang in the talent show freshman year."

And the school didn't worship him? Ben sang another song for him—at least it felt that way—and once he was finished, Tim shut off the TV. Then he asked the question that kept popping up in his mind. "So what's it like being gay?"

"Like anything else, I guess. What's it like to be whatever you are?"

"Straight," Tim said firmly before getting back on track. "Don't you catch a lot of flack for it? I mean, everyone at school knows, right?"

"Yup."

"I'm surprised you don't get your ass kicked every day."

"I get a lot of crap." Ben shrugged like it didn't matter. "But I got crap before I came out for totally different reasons. It's no different now. Not really."

"True, true." Tim nodded sagely. "If it's not one thing, it's another."

Ben rolled his eyes. "Like you would know! It must be hard being a jock with rich parents and a brand-new sports car. People must tease you mercilessly."

Tim grinned in response. "When you put it like that, I do have it good, but I still get crap from people. Miss a catch or don't make it to base and your team turns on you, especially if you lose the game."

Ben looked unconvinced. Tim would have to give him more. Being popular wasn't all it was cracked up to be, and if Ben only knew what had gone down in Kansas—

Tim could tell him. Doing so would mean summoning up the past. Speaking those words here, even just once, could mean they were repeated again and again until they ruined Tim. But surely Ben understood what it was like to be an outcast.

"How about this?" The smile dropped from Tim's face. "At my last school my ex-girlfriend went around telling everyone that I raped her, just because I dumped her. I had every girl in the school coming up to me and saying the craziest shit. A few even tried to knee me. It was insane."

Ben seemed more curious than judgmental. "What happened?"

"What do you mean? Nothing happened. It was her word against mine, but she didn't take it to the police or anything because she knew the truth. It blew over after a while, but people never treated me the same afterwards. You don't know how glad I am to have a fresh start."

Ben sighed. "The idea sounds appealing."

"Would you still come out? If you moved to the other side of the country where no one knew, would you come out again?"

"Yeah," Ben answered immediately. "Are you kidding me? What would I do otherwise? Pretend I'm into girls and start sleeping with them?"

Tim felt uncomfortable, like he was being accused of doing just that. Maybe because being with Krista involved so much pretending.

"I'd definitely come out again," Ben continued. "It's the only chance I have at meeting another gay guy. It pays to advertise. That's the theory at least."

"No luck in the romance department?"

"Not really. Not love at least."

The cuckoo clock his parents had brought back from Germany sprang to life, the little bird tweeting the hour.

"Jesus, I should get home." Ben started pulling on his shoes. "Are you going to be all right? There's drinks and stuff in the fridge and leftover pizza on the counter. Should I bring it in?"

Tim fought down a grin. "Naw, I can manage."

"I thought I'd come by in the morning to make breakfast and check on you, and then again in the afternoon?"

"Yeah?" Tim meant to tell Ben that he could manage on his own, but instead he said, "You'd do that for me?"

"That and a hell of a lot more." Ben laughed, like he was joking, but they both knew he wasn't. "Uh, so see you tomorrow then."

He practically ran for the door, probably embarrassed by his confession, but Tim didn't mind. It was quite the compliment. If Tim was a girl… Well, that was just a weird thought. But if things were different, he would be thrilled that someone like Ben was interested in him. At least, more thrilled than he already was.

Ben was the first thing Tim saw every morning, since the painkillers made him sleep deeply. Usually Tim was roused, back aching from sleeping on the leather couch in the den, and Ben would look at him in that funny way—like this was all too good to be true. Then Ben would hurry off and make breakfast. Tim was served pancakes the first day, fried eggs the next. Today was only frozen waffles, so he must have really been in a rush.

"It's nine thirty," Tim said when Ben set the plate on the coffee table. "Aren't you missing school?"

"Well, yeah." Ben checked his watch. "It's okay though. Allison, my best friend, has the inside scoop. They only take attendance in second period; otherwise they'd get false positives from the people who are late in the morning. Before or after that, I'm in the clear. Sort of. Teachers will start asking questions eventually, which is why I'm going to most of my classes."

Tim gave him the smile, the one usually reserved for girls who did something he liked. That always caused them to melt, and to his amusement, it worked on Ben as well. Seeing a guy react like that was somehow more satisfying. Tim had already won the affection of more girls than he had time for, but getting another guy to look so flustered felt like a new achievement.

"At least tomorrow is Saturday. Have any big plans?"

"Well, maybe," Ben said.

"I see." Tim put on a pouty face. "You're leaving me here to fend for myself."

"I *was* going to cook you a real meal. No frozen pizzas or quick breakfasts. But come to think of it, I might be too busy. I can't waste all my time on straight boys." Ben winked. "I'm sure you understand."

"I'll make it worth your while," Tim said. Of course he had no intention of doing so, but he loved flirting.

"Like what?" Ben pressed.

"I'll let you smell my socks." A pillow smacked into Tim's face, and when he moved it away, Ben was on his way to the door. Tim called after him. "*And* I'll let you keep using my car, you thief!"

So it went. The days were lonely until Ben was out of school. Then Ben would spend all his free time with him, Tim grateful for every second because the days could get long and boring. Besides, Ben took good care of him. The cooking and cleaning was enough, but he also did laundry, even though Tim hadn't asked him to. Ben ran baths for him too, Tim having to bathe with the cast propped up on the tub's edge. Once, during their first weekend together, he even let Ben keep him company in the bathroom while he bathed. The shower curtain had been pulled, of course, but not completely, since the way Ben snuck looks at his body definitely wasn't bad for Tim's ego.

In a way, they were like an old married couple not interested in sex anymore. At least Tim wasn't. Not even thoughts of scoring with Krista could rouse his appetite. Maybe the pills were to blame for that. The constant drowsiness was starting to annoy him, so after being on them nearly two weeks, Tim decided to quit. He was out of the pills anyway, and not having them refilled would give Ben less to complain about, since Tim had fallen asleep early the last couple of nights.

When the phone rang Thursday afternoon, Tim grinned as he reached for it. Most likely it was Ben, worrying about what they were going to have for dinner. "What's up, sweet cheeks?"

"Hey man, where you been?"

The voice was unmistakable, possessing the smooth confidence of the rich and popular.

"Hey! Darryl! Didn't Krista tell you?"

"Krista? Don't you mean sweet cheeks?"

Tim choked but managed to make it sound like a laugh. "Yeah. I thought she'd be calling. Anyway, she didn't fill you in?"

"She did. Your ankle is jacked up, huh?"

"Yeah."

Krista had called last week, but Tim had only told half the truth, saying his parents weren't letting him go out. He wasn't sure why he lied. Maybe because he was enjoying the easy evenings with Ben. Now the idea of hanging out with the guys, sneaking a few beers after school at Darryl's place, sounded nice. As did the attention Krista normally lavished on him.

"We thought you'd be back by now," Darryl pressed. "Bryce broke his arm last year and only got a few days off."

Tim probably wouldn't have gotten that much if his parents had been in town. "I'm milking it, man. I should be back on Monday."

"Krista says she hasn't seen you. Want me to send her over for a get-well hand job?"

Tim snorted. "I mentioned my parents are Catholic, right?"

"Ah," Darryl responded as if this explained everything.

"Besides, she's a prude."

Darryl laughed. "Surely she's not *that* much of a prude! Maybe you've been playing it too safe."

"Yeah, maybe." Tim's cock twitched at the idea. Yup, those pills had definitely kept his libido down.

"All right, get well soon, I guess. *Ciao!*"

"Peace."

Tim hung up and sat in silence. Something about the call made him nervous. Hearing from Darryl was like a wake-up call. His parents were due back on Sunday. After that, it was back to reality. Playing house with Ben had been fun, but Tim couldn't see this world and the one he had known coming together.

Unless he could bring Ben with him somehow, get his friends to appreciate him. But how? He couldn't imagine Bryce being moved by Ben's singing, and exposing Ben to Stacy Shelly and Darryl Briscott wouldn't be doing him any favors. Tim didn't mind them, but by comparison, Ben was too nice and innocent.

Except for the gay thing, which was pretty wild, but that was another problem. Ben didn't keep a low profile, and if Tim's parents found out, they would flip. No, there was only the weekend left, and then it was as good as over. All he could do was try to enjoy what time remained.

Despite his best efforts, Tim felt moody when Ben showed up. The fridge was getting empty, so Ben had brought fast food with him, but Tim only picked at it. Afterwards they hung out on the couch, Tim increasingly sick of being there. Without the pills, it wasn't just sex that he missed. Painting, running, driving—anything sounded better than more television. He switched off the TV and tossed aside the remote with a sigh.

"You okay?" Ben asked.

"Not really." Tim pushed himself up. "Let's go for a walk or something."

"The way you swing around on those crutches, I'd never keep up with you." Ben chewed his lip, searching for inspiration. "How about the back patio? You guys have a nice yard. We can hang out there."

"Yeah, okay."

Tim wasn't sold on the idea until they were outside. A nice stretch of lawn—made secluded by strategically placed trees instead of a fence—awaited them. The bugs were humming a mellow tune, nearly drowning out the neighborhood air conditioners that clicked on and off in the distance. Ben helped Tim get settled into one of the wooden lawn chairs, adjusting the pillows for him. Then Ben lit the Tiki torches, and in the dwindling daylight, Tim found himself relaxing.

"Grab me a beer from inside, and this will be paradise."

Ben hesitated. "Won't your parents notice?"

"I don't care. Get one for yourself too."

Ben came back with only one can of beer, which he handed to Tim.

"Thanks." He cracked it open and took a sip. Yeah, not bad at all.

They sat together in silence—just what Tim needed. That's something else Ben was good at. He could read Tim's moods like nobody else. Krista was a nonstop chatter box, but Ben was content to just hang out with him. Not that it was fair to keep comparing them, but it was hard not to. If things were just a little different, if Tim was gay or if Ben was a girl, he would be walking down the halls with Ben hanging off his arm. The thought made him laugh.

"What?" Ben asked.

"Nothing. Just thinking about school."

"You miss it?"

"Are you kidding?" Tim took another swig and set the beer down on the patio. "I wouldn't go again if I had a choice."

Ben scrunched up his face. "Weird."

"Why's that?"

"Well, I just figured that you'd like it more. I mean, you're popular."

Tim drew out his reply to make it all the more sarcastic. "Which is so… very… fun."

"Isn't it?" Ben challenged. "I have one real friend, and hanging out with Allison is the only thing that makes school tolerable. Without her, I'd go crazy."

"So what's your point?"

"Well, you have way more friends, so it would be like having more Allisons. That sounds like a good time to me."

Tim laughed, but inside he wondered if he was missing something. Multiply the Darryls and Bryces, or even the Carlas and Brodys from back home, and it sounded like one giant headache. His friends kept him entertained and made him feel important, but they could also be tiring. They were just as demanding in their needs as he was, and probably felt the same way about him.

"Let me tell you a secret," Tim said. "Popular people are

insecure as hell. All they worry about is staying on top and being loved by everybody. To do that, they obsess about what everyone thinks of them. Most are downright desperate for any vote of approval they can get."

"Present company excluded."

Tim was sure Ben meant it as a compliment and not a jab, but he shook his head. "I'm just as bad, and I can't even tell you why. Popular kids are just a powerful union of needy, insecure losers. Remember that next time someone stupid like Bryce mouths off to you. You're better than them, Benjamin. You don't have to be anything but yourself."

Ben looked embarrassed, but he flashed Tim a goofy smile. And it made Tim sad, because he had been telling the truth. Come Monday, his life would center around keeping up appearances, because he needed people to love him. Maybe he didn't get enough from his parents, or maybe he was just pathetic, but Tim lived for admiration. He'd been milking Ben for it the past two weeks, which probably wasn't fair.

Tim rubbed his neck and sighed. He needed to go running. "Once this cast is off, I'll never sit down again."

"Do you want a massage?"

Tim was about to give a snarky response, thinking it was their usual fruitless flirtation, but Ben looked serious.

"Put the seatback down and flip over," Ben said. "Trust me, I give great massages."

Why not? Tim leaned the chair flat and rolled over, the foot of his cast banging against the patio, but he was doing so much better that it barely hurt. Ben sat on the side of the chair and started kneading the muscles at the base of Tim's neck.

"So you've done this a lot?" Tim asked, wanting to keep their conversation going.

"Nope. First time."

Tim lifted his head. "But you said—"

"Yeah, well, I say a lot of things." Ben laughed and started kneading harder, forcing Tim to put his head back down.

Maybe Ben lacked experience, but the massage sure felt good! He worked the area between Tim's shoulder blades next, then squeezed Tim's deltoids a few times, slowly kneading his way toward the lower back. Tim shifted in the seat, his shorts tight.

Fuck.

He was hard or very nearly there. Another guy was touching him, and his stupid dick had responded. Part of him was tempted to roll over. He knew it would make Ben happy but—holy shit!—what did this say about him?

"All right," Tim said. "That's enough."

Ben kept massaging.

"Fucking stop!"

Ben's hands lifted away. "Sorry. Did I hurt you?"

"No." Tim kept his head turned away from Ben, his line of vision nearly level with the beer can dripping condensation on the patio stones. Beyond, the flame of a Tiki torch danced, sending strange shadows across the grass. Tim scowled. Maybe things had gone too far. He pushed himself up on his elbows. "I'm tired," he said, without looking at Ben. "You should go."

"Oh. Okay." Ben stood up, but he didn't go anywhere. What did he expect? To be walked to the door? When Tim didn't move, still didn't look at him, Ben took the hint. The sound of his footsteps went to the house. Tim heard the sliding glass door open, but didn't hear it close. He could picture Ben standing there, looking back at him and wondering what he had done wrong. He must have been right, because Ben spoke.

"So, do you still want me to come by tomorrow?"

No! Of course not. That's why I'm sending you away! But Tim couldn't bring his lips to shape these words. "Yeah. See you tomorrow."

When Tim heard the car drive away a few minutes later, he got up and struggled with his crutches. Once inside he would jack off. He hadn't done that since he was injured, which was crazy. Pent up hormones could make just about anything sound like a good idea.

Tomorrow would be different. Tim would start taking care of the house himself, become self-sufficient again. Ben was a good guy, but he wasn't his freaking girlfriend. Tim wouldn't punish Ben for what was his own fault, but after this weekend, playtime was over.

Chapter Six

Ben showed up the next day with an armful of groceries. Tim followed him out to the driveway, determined to help carry in the rest, though Ben wouldn't let him. Back in the kitchen, he helped put everything away. Ben didn't stay long after that, having promised to eat dinner with his family. A couple of hours later, Ben called, anger in his voice.

"My stupid sister figured out I was skipping and ratted me out."

"Oh." Tim's response wasn't the best, but he had mixed emotions. The night wouldn't be as much fun without Ben, but maybe it wouldn't be as confusing either.

"It's not just today," Ben explained. "I won't be able to come over all weekend."

"What can you do, man? That's life."

They didn't stay on the phone long after that. Tim microwaved some frozen burritos, then sat at the dining room table and ate without really tasting them. His head was buzzing from too many thoughts that, despite his best effort, kept circling back to Ben.

After dinner Tim grabbed his sketchbook and went to the back patio, lighting the torches and trying to recreate the mood from yesterday. Somehow it just wasn't the same, but he sat there and drew a little. Next he wrote, trying to get his thoughts down and becoming increasingly aggravated. Then he saw the butterfly fluttering through the air with lazy ease, as if life had always been simple and without consequence. Thinking of Ben again, Tim switched to poetry, and the words finally flowed, his feelings easier to express in the abstract, especially when wrapped up in Spanish. Tim found the language beautiful, the words exotic enough to be almost mystical, their power undiminished by constant exposure.

His mind and soul satisfied, Tim slowly crutched upstairs and flipped through his old porn magazines. He relieved more tension that way, although he felt frustrated with the familiarity of the images, how all the women with fake breasts and men with pumped-up gym bodies looked the same. At least being upstairs meant he could sleep in his own bed again, which was ten times more comfortable than the couch.

Tim's dreams that night weren't restful. He found himself in Corey's room again, except bizarrely, Ben was sitting there talking to him. But he wasn't really speaking. He was singing, every word a melody. When the dream reached its climax, Ben sang the same words over and over again until they became a song with one lyrical line: *You can kiss me, if you want. You can kiss me, kiss me, kiss me, if you waaaant.* Finally Tim gave into temptation and leaned forward, jolting awake the moment their lips touched.

Enough was enough. Tim called Krista later that day.

Ben had once said the cast would be good for getting sympathy. As it turned out, he was right. Tim was back on the leather couch, but now the slender form next to him kept giggling and saying "Timmy!" in chastising tones. He loved kissing Krista's neck to make her squeal. More than that, he loved how easily he got hard in response to this, the doubts about his sexuality now distant.

"Let me sign it!" Krista said.

"And then?" Tim asked.

"Um..."

Ugh, did he have to write a script for her? "Will you give me a reward?" Tim prompted.

"Oh!" Krista stared. "What do you mean?"

Seriously? "I'm sure you'll think of something you can do for me."

"Oh. Oooh!"

There we go. Now she was finally getting it. Krista took one of the markers from the coffee table to write on his cast. His irritation with her had made his hard-on go down, but he would get there again. He kept jiggling his foot, making Krista laugh more, when he heard a noise in the hallway. Tim glanced over and saw Ben, eyes wide before he backed away from the door. Good thing, because Krista had heard him too.

Tim struggled to his feet. "Be right back."

"Is someone here?" Krista asked, looking worried.

"It's just my neighbor. He promised to bring something by. Wait here."

Tim grabbed his crutches and hurried to the hallway. Not only was Ben there, but he had a dog with him. Tim brushed by them, motioning with his head that Ben should follow. He didn't stop until he reached the front door, which should be hint enough.

"What are you doing here?" he hissed. "I thought you were grounded?"

"I snuck out," Ben said.

"Jesus, man! You almost gave me a heart attack."

"Sorry. I wanted to surprise you."

"That you did." The dog made a grumbling noise to get his attention. Tim had wanted a dog for ages, but to his parents, that was like asking them to make another kid. "Who's this?" he asked, reaching down to pet him.

"Wilford, my faithful companion. I thought taking him out for a walk would be a good excuse to sneak over here."

But Tim barely heard him. Instead he was thinking of his birthday, when he had nearly driven over some guy and his dog. It couldn't be… could it? "You know, he looks oddly familiar."

"He looks like Wilford Brimley," Ben explained. "The old guy in the oatmeal commercials?"

"Oh yeah!" Tim laughed. "He totally does."

"That's why we named him that. He just needs a pair of glasses, and the look is complete."

They laughed together, and it felt easy. Too easy. Krista could walk into the entryway at any moment.

"Look, you can't stay," Tim whispered. "I'm trying to get laid. I'm playing up the injury thing like crazy, and she's eating it up."

"Yeah, sorry." Ben looked embarrassed, like he'd done something stupid. "I, uh, yeah. Good luck, man."

God this sucked, but it was going to happen on Monday anyway. Tim gave him a friendly punch to the arm, the sort that was really just pressing your fist against someone's deltoid. "You too. I hope you sneak back in without getting caught."

"Shouldn't be hard. My parents are out running errands."

"Oh."

Ben shuffled awkwardly. "Well, see ya."

"Yeah. Wait!"

Ben turned around, Tim regretting his carelessness because Ben looked so damn hopeful. "I need my car keys back."

"Oh, yeah. Of course."

Ben fumbled the keychain out of his pocket, not making eye

contact with Tim. Then he left the house, cutting across the yard and practically dragging Wilford along in his haste.

Sorry, Benjamin.

When Tim got back to the living room, Krista was still sitting on the couch, upright and alert. "Just my neighbor," he reminded her. "I missed a delivery the other day."

"Oh."

Tim sat back down on the couch, took the marker from her hand, and kissed her with a vengeance. After a moment of surprise, she responded. To his relief, so did the rest of him, but it wasn't easy because Ben's hurt expression kept flashing through his mind. If the world were a different place, Tim would make Ben happy, give him what he wanted. And Tim had to admit, that's what he wanted too. Maybe he didn't understand it or even like it, but Tim wanted him. He grabbed Krista's hand and moved it down to his cock.

She pulled away instantly, face beet red. "Sorry," she said.

"What?" he asked, completely puzzled.

"I just don't..." She looked scared! "I don't want to do that."

"Okay," Tim said quickly. "That's all right."

The look of fear didn't fade.

"Seriously," he said. "I don't mind."

And he didn't. As much as he wanted to get laid, it wasn't with her.

Krista flashed a nervous smile. "Really?"

"Really. We're good. Come here."

Tim pulled her close, and she leaned into him, resting her head on his chest. He grasped around for a subject, anything that didn't have to do with Ben, being gay, or sex. "So have you missed me being at school?" he tried.

"Yes! Stacy told Bryce he had to bring me my lunch while you were gone, but he can't carry three trays at once, so he had to go back and wait in line for his food. I thought it was mean and told her to stop, but Stacy thought it was funny. Finally—"

The "finally" was just the beginning of what Krista did best. She prattled on, and Tim relaxed. He let her talk for the next hour, kissing her a few more times, but only to show her that things were okay. Then he lied and said the pills were making him tired. He walked her to the door and kissed her goodbye, but she didn't go just yet.

"Timmy?"

"Yeah?"

"Do you think I'm a prude?"

And there was the hint of fear again. Of course she had heard what everyone said. Rumors always made it around to the person they were about. She was terrified of what other people thought of her. Just like he was.

"You're not a prude," Tim said. "You're perfect."

She stared at him. Then Krista kissed him one more time and practically skipped to her car. He'd probably regret that. Lord knows it would only make her like him more. But maybe, just for today, it would be enough to make her feel good about herself.

Tim's breath caught as the phone rang. Was he really going to do this? His body responded. Yeah, he was. Assuming Ben didn't say no. The story Tim had concocted was so stu—

"What?" snarled a voice in his ear.

"Benjamin?"

"Tim?"

Okay. Contact established. "Man, I'm glad I didn't get one of your parents. Are they still gone?"

"Don't worry about it." Ben's tone sounded warmer. "What's up? Are you calling to brag or something? Tell me you aren't screwing her right now!"

"No, almost." Tim did his best to sound frustrated, which wasn't a stretch. "Came close, but she got freaked out by the European standard."

"O-kay."

Tim winced inwardly. Had he really said that? Brody used to give him hell after noticing in the shower room that Tim was uncut. For a while he called Tim "the Frenchman" because he claimed that only the French were uncircumcised. Tim did a little research and found that most of Europe didn't circumcise. Of course Brody only gave him more hell for this, eventually referring to it as the European standard.

"Uh, anyway," Tim said, changing tactics, "we got into an argument and she's gone."

"Sorry?" Ben said, sounding anything but.

"So you want to come over?" The phone line was silent. This

wasn't going well. "Maybe you and I can pick up where she left off."

"I'll be right there!" The line clicked and went dead.

Tim grinned. That was more like it! Ben was on his way over and... Man! Was he really going to go through with this? If he was, he was going to do it right. Tim hurried to the bathroom as fast as his crutches would allow, brushing his teeth, spraying on cologne, and trying to fix his hair before he gave up. He considered waiting by the door until he realized how pathetic that would seem, so he returned to the couch in the den.

You can kiss me, if you want, said the ghost in Tim's mind, but this time he had an answer. *Hell yeah I'm going to kiss you!*

Tim heard the front door open. His loose fitting jogging shorts—easy to get on over his cast—doing nothing to hide his anticipation. But maybe that was okay. This is what they both wanted, right?

He looked up to find Ben standing in the doorway. He appeared uncertain too, but when their eyes locked, Tim guided his gaze downward. When he looked back up again, Ben's expression was just as lustful as his own.

"C'mere," Tim invited.

Ben came to him, sat next to him on the couch. One of them would have to make the first move. Ben took the initiative, reaching his hand toward Tim's crotch, but Tim caught his wrist and stopped him.

"What's the rush?" He used his grip on Ben's wrist to pull him closer. Hungry, Tim put his other hand on the back of Ben's neck and drew him in. He saw the expression of surprise on Ben's face just before their lips met, the kiss clumsy. Then they tried again. Tim put all of himself into that kiss, capturing Ben's lips with his own over and over again, holding Ben's head in both his hands now as he let his tongue slip inside.

This was good. Not so different from kissing a girl, but somehow better, somehow right. Tim never wanted to stop, but then Ben's hand found his chest, feeling his muscles and reminding Tim of what his body needed. He stopped their kiss long enough to strip off his shirt, grinning cockily as Ben looked him over with admiration. Then he put Ben's hands on those muscles, tingling where Ben's palm moved across his skin. Tim stole a few more kisses, but Ben's hand was moving lower and lower.

Tim squirmed, and Ben went for it, grabbing his cock through the shorts.

"Wow!" he said.

That sounded good! Tim had no idea how he stacked up to other guys. Everyone snuck sly peeks in the showers, doing a little covert comparison, but no one walked around hard. None of them could really tell what anyone else was packing, but Ben seemed impressed and intent on *un*packing. The elastic band of Tim's shorts was pulled down, causing him to tense and sit up.

Ben was staring at Tim's dick. Then he pulled the foreskin down experimentally before moving it back up again.

"The European standard?" Ben inquired.

Oh, man. What if it *was* an issue? "It's normal over there," Tim explained.

"It's gorgeous."

To prove it, Ben took it into his mouth, and Tim collapsed into pleasure. This wasn't his first blowjob, not by far, but Benny-boy knew his stuff! Tim usually prided himself on lasting a long time, being able to run the marathon until his partner was satisfied, but in Ben's hands and mouth, he was helpless. His hips started bucking of their own accord, and he couldn't stop moaning. Then he came like a frothing horse across the finish line. Ben kept him in his mouth. No girl had ever swallowed, and oh man, did it feel good. Too good!

"No more, no more, stop!" Tim pleaded. He had to pull Ben off before he would let up. Then Tim tried to catch his breath. "Fuck, that was good," he panted. Ben looked proud, but something a little unsure flickered on his face.

Oh. Right. What about him?

Tim had spent all his time fantasizing about kissing Ben, maybe getting blown by him. But he hadn't taken it further. He needed time to figure this out. "Man. I have to take a piss."

"That's cool."

Neither of them made eye contact as Tim pulled up his shorts, fumbled with the crutches, and left the room. Tim stared at himself in the bathroom mirror, his hair twice as messy now, his silver eyes glazed over like he was on drugs. The sex had been freaking incredible, but it had also been selfish. Poor Ben was sitting out there, probably with an erection so hard it threatened to tear through his shorts.

And the idea was kind of exciting.

Tim grinned at his reflection. Why the hell not? He was in this deep already. Tim flushed the toilet, just for appearances, and headed back to the den. Ben licked his lips nervously and stood when he entered.

"I guess I should get back," he said

"What?" Tim laughed. Poor guy thought he had served his purpose and was no longer needed "You're crazy." Tim reached him and shoved Ben back on to the couch. He tossed his crutches aside, falling on him in a clumsy wrestling move. Ben cried out in amused shock. This was familiar territory. Tim was the guy, Ben was the girl, and it was his role to be the dominant one, to take what he wanted. He got Ben on his back, kissing him, tasting his lips and indirectly tasting himself. Jesus, this was crazy, but Tim was already getting hard again. He reached down to Ben's package and found it in the same state.

"Your turn," he huffed into Ben's ear.

Tim slid off to the side, his knees on the carpet. He pulled up Ben's shirt, admiring the narrow waist and the lines of ribs sticking out. So like a girl, but still a guy. Speaking of which. Tim ripped open the jean shorts, the buttons popping loose one by one, before yanking them—and Ben's underwear—down.

For the first time, he saw another guy hard. Strange how different the same body part could be when it belonged to someone else. Ben was cut, of course, the head always exposed and much more purple than his own. But for a scrawny little guy, he sure was packing. Tim was bigger, which made him feel more like a man, but Ben had nothing to be ashamed of.

"Nice," Tim said, taking hold of it and starting to pump. Ben's skin felt tighter, probably because he was circumcised. That made the technique Tim used on himself impossible, but Ben responded as if Tim was doing fine, moaning and writhing beneath his touch. The experience was hotter than Tim had imagined. He pulled Ben's shirt higher with his free hand, teasing his nipples with his tongue. Then Tim did what he loved best, and started kissing Ben again. He was still kissing him when Ben exploded in his hand.

Tim grinned as Ben groaned and jerked, taking his revenge until Ben too begged him to stop. "I'll grab a towel," he said. Tim's stomach rumbled. "And then you're going to cook for me."

Sliding back into their old routine was easy. The more time Tim spent around Ben, the more he appreciated that. Nothing was complicated with him. There was no dramatic discussion about what any of this meant. They had sex, simple as that. Then they hung out like they always did, watching TV or putting on music and just talking about whatever.

Ben slept over that night, making himself a bed on the floor and giving Tim the couch. Somehow the idea of going upstairs to his room seemed too intimate. Would they sleep cuddled up together? Despite everything they had done, the idea sounded weird. Until the next morning, when Tim very much wanted Ben on that couch with him.

They started off the day by reenacting the events of the previous evening before it came time to face the facts. Tim's parents were coming home, which meant dismantling this fantasy world, gathering up the pieces, and putting them away. They were both a little subdued as they cleaned the house, not wanting their fun to come to an end. But it had. Tim had to say goodbye.

"You should probably get going," he blurted out. Ben was wiping down the kitchen counters, even though they clearly didn't need it. "Just in case my parents catch an early flight or something."

Still Ben worked, his brow furrowing as if the task required his full concentration.

"Look," Tim began, but while the words were easy to find, saying them wasn't. "What happened between us, well…"

Ben's hand stopped wiping. He looked Tim straight in the eye, giving his full attention. Maybe they could still do this, if they could find somewhere to be alone. But there was something even more crucial than that.

"It's probably best we keep it a secret," Tim said. "I just don't want people to get the wrong idea."

"Wrong idea?" Ben repeated.

"There's nothing *wrong* with it," Tim backpedaled. "I just don't want people thinking I'm gay when I'm not."

Ben looked at Tim curiously, like he was speaking a foreign language. But then he said, very carefully, "Okay. Not a big deal."

All right! That wasn't so hard. He thought Ben would be upset. In a strange way, Tim was kind of disappointed he wasn't.

"So are you going to call me?" Ben added.

"Yeah, totally!" Tim felt he said this with a little too much enthusiasm, so he added, "We're buds."

"Cool," Ben replied. "I'm off, then. Good luck with your parents when they get here."

"Good luck with yours! I hope you won't be in too much trouble." Tim reached out and tousled Ben's hair, thinking about drawing him in for a kiss, but that wouldn't be fair. Not if this was the end, and he couldn't be sure that it wasn't.

Tim matched Ben's smile as he left, but as soon as the door shut behind him, he didn't feel so happy. He slowly made his way through the house, doing one final inspection for any damning evidence. Already the place seemed a lot colder, like Ben had taken the heart of the home with him.

Chapter Seven

"Oh, you're home! Didn't you hear us honk? Go help your father with the luggage."

"I can try," Tim said with a grunt, grabbing his crutches and pulling himself up from the kitchen table.

"*¡Gordito!*" His mother set her bag down, staring at his cast with concern. Even his father, hauling in the first suitcase from the garage, appeared worried. "What happened?"

Tim had thought about dramatizing events, running with a story about thugs who had jumped him, or maybe how he kicked down the door of a burning building to save orphans or some crap like that. Obviously he didn't want to tell them that a gay guy on skates knocked him over and later seduced him.

"Some crazy biker ran me off the path when I was out jogging," Tim said. "Fell right into a drainage ditch. Don't worry, it's just a sprain."

"My poor baby!" His mother took his face in her hands and kissed his cheeks. "Sit! We'll get the rest of the luggage."

Tim smiled and sat, enjoying the attention, but his parents began to fuss over where the laptop bag was, if they had packed the charger in a separate suitcase, and if his mother should do a load of laundry. He was pretty damn sure he sat there for half an hour waiting for more from them. Maybe something like: *Why didn't you call us? Did it hurt? Is there anything you need?*

Finally his father brought out a ridiculously huge bar of Swiss chocolate and set it in front of him. "Did the hospital get your insurance information?" he asked.

Tim nodded. "We got it figured out eventually."

"Good. I broke my arm when I was a kid." His father chuckled at the memory. "Casts are terrible, aren't they?"

"Yeah," Tim said, taken aback by this divulgence. "How did you break it?"

"Oh, my kid brother and I were—" Tim's mother walked by with a laundry basket, distracting him. "Ella, if you're washing shirts for tomorrow, I need the blue one. I have a meeting with a new client. No, not that one. The light blue shirt. I'll show you."

His father left but didn't return. Tim let another ten minutes of solitude pass before he gave up and went upstairs to his room.

His mom knocked on his door an hour later, asking if he had eaten. She never failed in this area. Tim never went hungry, but they seemed to have already forgotten his injury. He supposed they were jet lagged or tired from their trip, so he tried not to blame them. When the house went silent, his parents retiring for the night without saying another word to him, he wished Ben was still there making him feel special.

Monday arrived like a Kansas tornado, tearing up and sweeping away the two oddest weeks of Tim's life and returning the world to normal. Getting back to school helped. Tim was the center of his friends' attention, and even though he had been gone for nearly as long as they had known him, they still acted like his absence was a big deal. After school, Darryl threw another of his impromptu parties, this time in Tim's honor. And without the depth-chargers, thank god.

Krista was crazier about him than ever, clinging to him like her life depended on it. But in a way, that felt nice. The only time it got weird was when she kissed him, because for a second he felt like he was cheating on Ben… but then he reminded himself that Krista was his girlfriend. If anything, he should feel guilty about what he had done behind her back. But he didn't.

Tuesday wasn't quite as good. The excitement about his return had died down, and he had cross country practice after school, so no partying. Tim could only sit on the sidelines and watch, but being part of the team was more than just competing. He watched the other guys, asking himself if he found them attractive, trying to see them in a new light. But it wasn't the same. He knew which ones were handsome and who had the nicest body, but he didn't feel that connection like he had with Ben—or that desperate need to kiss any of them. If he was gay, wouldn't he want them too? Tim began to wonder if he had been the victim of hormones and two weeks of cabin fever.

On Wednesday, while strolling to class with Bryce at his side, Tim noticed Ben walking down the other side of the hallway, head forward but eyes watching him. And it was funny, because a whole team of athletic runners didn't do much for him, but seeing Ben for one brief second called up all those feelings of home, of being cared for. Tim brought a quick finger and thumb to his face, signaling that Ben should call him. Ben gave a hint of a smile and a nod before they broke eye contact.

Tim felt strangely elated by this small interaction, his good mood lasting until he got home in the afternoon. His mother was there, which wasn't surprising since she did much of her translation work from the house. But his father was home early too, and that was rarely a good omen.

"Your school called," his mom said, after asking him to sit down at the kitchen table.

"What did they want?"

Ella's face was strained, bringing out the lines and making her appear older. "They said the reason for your absence wasn't reported."

"Oh. I had a friend of mine pick up homework for me, but not from all my classes. One of the teachers made a big deal about it on Monday, but I explained everything."

"Including that we were out of town and couldn't call?" his father chimed in. "You've made us look incompetent."

"Sorry!" Tim said, getting his back up. "I'll go into school tomorrow and tell them I kept you in the dark. God forbid anyone think ill of you."

"Don't get smart!" Thomas growled. "A counselor wants to meet with us, which I sure as hell don't have time for!"

"We know the school called while we were gone," his mother said in gentler tones. "All you had to do was pick up the phone and explain the situation. And really, a sprain isn't a good enough reason to miss two weeks."

Now his father chimed in again. "The counselor asked if we felt you should be punished for skipping, since you were capable of attending."

Tim gritted his teeth. "I had a lot to deal with, okay? I didn't want to ruin your stupid trip, and it's a class three sprain, by the way, which is pretty damn close to being broken."

His father's face turned red. "Don't use language like that in front of your mother!"

Tim looked to his mom, whose eyebrows were raised. Tim couldn't believe it! Out of everything he had said, all they heard was a cuss word? "I'll take care of it. I'll talk to the school counselor tomorrow and get it all cleared up. I promise."

But this wasn't enough. His father was still angry, and worse, his mother appeared hurt.

Tim's shoulders slumped. "I'm sorry."

That satisfied them enough that they let him escape to his room. Once he got there, his phone rang. His parents had splurged for a private line—for their convenience more than his—and if he had been smart, he would have given the school that number instead.

Tim picked up the receiver. "Yeah?"

"Hey."

Benjamin, like a lifeline from another world, one that Tim was eager to escape into. "Hey. You have to come get me. I'm totally sick of it here."

"I don't have a car," Ben reminded him.

"I think you've driven mine more than I have. Get over here."

And Ben came, lightning fast. Tim met him in the driveway, and before long, he had relaxed again. He wasn't sure if Ben would be able to recreate the magic, to make Tim feel good outside the bubble they had existed in for two weeks, but once again, Ben knew just what to do. Commandeering his vehicle and taking him hostage, Ben brought him to the city of Galveston, where the beaches overlooked the Gulf of Mexico. Tim had never seen the ocean before, and even though he technically still hadn't, the waves and sand sure looked like the real thing.

Together they sat on the beach, talking until the sun went down. Ben was easy to be around, like he always was. There was nothing weird. Tim didn't have to hold his hand or constantly fend off his advances. When a group of college girls spotted them and offered to share their beer, Ben grew a little quiet, but that could have been because the girls were so loud. Of course they flirted with Tim, which he couldn't help but enjoy. One of them even followed him down the beach when he went to relieve himself. She kissed him, the fumes on her breath much stronger than his, and he kissed her back, curious if his body would react. A kiss was a kiss, it would seem, because Tim began to get turned on and started to feel her body. But it seemed empty. Like masturbation, it felt good, but it didn't mean a damn thing. Then the girl tried groping him, which only reminded Tim how much he had to pee. He untangled himself from her so he could go.

He swayed a little as he relieved himself, trying to force Krista and Ben out of his mind. Sometimes he felt like he didn't have room for himself anymore. He glanced over his shoulder to see another ghost. The girl waiting for him, the evening shadows obscuring her features, could have been Carla, back from the past to ruin the one good thing that had just begun. And Tim realized that good thing wasn't Krista.

"I have to get my friend home," Tim said.

"Why? Does he need to be tucked into bed by a certain time?"

"Something like that," Tim replied.

The girls wanted them to come back to their hotel, but Tim managed to bluff their way out. The relief at breaking free of them, of being alone with Ben in the car, weighed heavily on him. If Bryce or Darryl had been in the same situation, they would be in that hotel right now, living a story worthy of *Penthouse Letters*. Instead, Tim was happier cruising along with his new gay buddy. What did that imply?

Tim put on a CD to avoid conversation so he could sort through these thoughts. Ben sang along to a few of the songs, making up lyrics once he caught the rhythm of the chorus. Every time Tim looked over at him, he seemed happy. Unpopular, scrawny, and about as uncool as you could get, but happy. Tim wanted to be like that too, to not give a shit about what anyone else thought, to not need so much from every stranger he met. To the untrained eye, Ben had nothing, at least by the bizarre rules that governed high school. But really, Ben was one of the few who wasn't pretending, one of the few who was free.

The school counselor was an older woman with short gray hair. Tim supposed she looked wise, like a frumpy old owl. He just hoped she wasn't so shrewd that she saw through him. He smiled, which helped like it always did. People put an amazing amount of stock in beauty. A handsome face could open doors, inspire confidence, and most of all, deceive. Tim's mother had once said—the palm of her hand on his cheek—that he was beautiful because he had been touched by God. Sometimes Tim wondered if the other guy down below hadn't touched him instead.

"Mr. Wyman," the counselor said, "I was hoping to meet with your parents soon."

Tim glanced at the nameplate on her desk. "That's why I'm here, Mrs. Hewitt." Tim leaned on his crutches like a beggar from a Charles Dickens novel. God this was humiliating, even if he was playing a role.

"Sit down," Mrs. Hewitt said.

Tim thanked her and sat. "I wanted to tell you the truth. My parents were out of town when I got hurt, and even though I could have called their hotel, I didn't."

Mrs. Hewitt nodded. "That's exactly what your parents told me, but I also feel that leaving someone your age alone for two weeks isn't appropriate."

"Oh. Well, I talked them into that. Argued, is more like it. I kept saying it was time they treat me more like an adult, but I guess I let them down."

Mrs. Hewitt considered this. He was halfway there.

"We just moved here from Kansas. Usually I stay with my aunt when my parents aren't home. Everything is kind of new for us, and I guess I took advantage of that."

Now Mrs. Hewitt looked at him more sternly, no doubt seeing a rich spoiled brat who tricked his parents. Maybe that's all he was.

"Well, Mr. Wyman, what do you feel a suitable outcome to this would be?"

Ugh. She wanted to know who was going to get the blame so she could cross his name off her list. "I didn't show up for two weeks, so two weeks of detention, I guess?"

"Your parents have at least raised you to admit your mistakes." Mrs. Hewitt made some notes. Tim watched her and wondered if she really did have a list of names. "I trust you'll convey the details of this conversation to your parents?"

"Yeah," Tim said.

Mrs. Hewitt raised an eyebrow. "Excuse me?"

"Yes, ma'am."

"Good. You'll report to room 2W26 today after sixth period for your detention."

"Yes, ma'am."

Tim slunk out of the room. He may have pulled the wool over an adult's eyes, but he felt anything but victorious.

Tim opened the front door before Ben could ring the bell, hobbling out to the front porch. The afternoon was cooling off, the fresh air welcome after being cooped up inside. Days like today made Tim feel like he could break into a sprint, running past the neighborhoods, into the wild, and away from the world he knew.

Maybe he'd throw Ben over his shoulder and bring him along. Of course with his ankle, he wouldn't be running anywhere just yet.

"Take me for a walk," he said instead.

"I left Wilford's leash at home," Ben replied, "but I can run back and get it."

"Ha ha. Seriously. I need some exercise."

Ben looked him over. "You sure?"

"Yeah, doctor's orders." The cast had come off last night, a removable plastic brace taking its place. His ankle was a little stiff and the pain came and went, but mostly he was okay walking on it.

"Okay," Ben said. "Where do you want to go?"

Tim gazed at him. They hadn't had sex since those first tumbles on the couch. Since then, Ben hadn't made a move. Tim had been glad for that, but now he wouldn't mind a relapse. If you had to go to confession, you might as well enjoy the sin.

"Somewhere private," Tim suggested.

"Ah!" Ben fought down a smile. "Well, we could walk to my place."

"Are your parents there?"

"Yeah."

Tim shook his head. "No way."

"Okay—" Ben turned this way and that, as if to get his bearings. "Follow me."

Tim followed him down the street and to one of the bike paths, enjoying the physical exertion. He hoped he could start jogging again soon. He needed the release, although Ben might have a different sort for him, depending on where they were headed.

"Think you can handle going off road?" Ben asked.

The bike path ran ahead, the backs of houses to the left and trees on the right. It wouldn't be easy, but Tim thought he could manage. He nodded, and Ben led him into the woods. They walked a fair distance, following a small winding dirt path before abandoning it. Not much farther ahead was a tree with low branches, each thick and long, some burdened with a wooden construct of some sort.

"My tree house," Ben declared.

"How many rooms does it have?" Tim asked.

"One," Ben said proudly.

"More like a tree shack then."

Ben laughed, then scurried up a couple of wooden boards hammered into the trunk to form a ladder.

"Unless you're going to carry me up there," Tim said, "I don't think I'll be able to join you."

But he tried anyway, using his good foot to get on the second rung and pulling himself up so he could at least see over the edge. Forget tree shack! A hobo would turn up his nose at this place. It didn't even have a proper floor, just a bunch of criss-crossed boards. What passed for a roof strained where rain water had collected. Of Ben's many talents, carpentry wasn't included.

"Very nice," he lied. Then he lowered himself back down, his ankle twinging, so he took pressure off it by sitting and stretching out on a bed of fallen leaves.

"I've gotten a lot of good thinking done here," Ben said, his legs dangling over the edge.

"Oh yeah?"

"Yeah. This is where I figured out I was gay." Ben watched him from above, waiting for him to ask more.

Tim bit. "How did you know?"

"I fell in love. Well, sort of. I thought it was love at the time. Really it was probably just a crush, but there were feelings nonetheless."

"Who was the lucky guy?"

"Kevin, a friend of mine. When he moved away I was heartbroken. I was just twelve at the time. I guess there had always been guys I liked, but with him, I took it to a whole new level. I tried to catch a bus to Utah just to see him, and when that failed, I wrote him a love letter."

"So did you two ever hook up?"

"I was twelve!" Ben brushed some leaves down on Tim's head.

"So? I lost my virginity when I was thirteen."

"Why am I not surprised?" Ben was quiet a moment. "You're ruining my story."

"Sorry."

"So anyway, shortly afterwards, a girl in school asked me out. Not like on a date, but to be her boyfriend or whatever. That was the missing puzzle piece. The idea of being with a girl that way, of being romantic, had never occurred to me. I mean, it was fine for other people, just not for me. But when I thought of Kevin, it felt right."

Tim shook his head. "That's not me, Benjamin. I like girls. They turn me on."

"But you like guys too," Ben pointed out.

"Maybe."

Ben lowered himself over the edge and hopped down. He got on the ground with Tim, crawling over him like an animal, bringing their faces close together. He was so damn ballsy! They hadn't done a thing since last weekend, and Ben acted certain Tim would still be willing. Of course he was right. Ben kissed him, and Tim kissed back, reaching to stroke his hair when Ben moved away.

"*Maybe?*" Ben said with a smirk. Then he sat back, pulling his legs up in front of him.

Tim sat up too. "You sure know how to make a point!"

Ben grinned. "What I'm trying to say is that it's not just physical. I've messed around with a lot of straight guys before."

"What? How does that work?"

"Well, it was mostly in junior high when guys are a little more experimental. Or desperate. So there were a handful I would do stuff for."

Tim wasn't sure if he should be turned on or jealous. "What sort of stuff?"

"You know firsthand," Ben said pointedly. "Anyway, I thought there were a lot of other guys like me. I'd already sat in this very tree and put a name to it. I even said it out loud. 'I'm gay.' You have to come out to yourself first, so I did. I thought these other guys hadn't done that yet, so I started talking to them about it."

"And?"

"And it got around the school. I lost all my friends except for Allison, and most of those guys I thought were like me now have girlfriends."

Tim watched Ben's face closely, trying to imagine how that must have felt. In Kansas, the school had turned against Tim because of a lie. But for Ben, they turned their backs because of who he was.

"Sorry, man." The words were far from sufficient, but they were all Tim could manage.

"It's okay. I keep getting sidetracked, really. My point is that just because these guys messed around with me, doesn't make them gay. We all do crazy things when we're horny. So you sleeping with girls doesn't mean you're straight."

Tim stared at him. Then he laughed. "You think I'm just a very experimental gay guy? I've had sex with women enough times that it's gone *way* past the experimental stage. Is there an expert phase? Because that's where I'm at."

Ben tried a new tactic. "Did you love any of them?"

That shut Tim up. The longest relationship he ever had was with Carla, and half the time they were together he didn't even like her. But part of him cared enough to stick with her. Sort of like he was doing with Krista. He would never be her friend, but as a girlfriend it somehow worked.

"I've never been in love with a guy either," Tim said.

Ben shrugged. "So the jury is still out. At least until you fall in love."

Tim shook his head ruefully. "Whatever makes you happy." He glanced up at the tree. "Speaking of love, who is A.C.?"

Ben looked embarrassed and followed his gaze. Carved into the tree were two sets of initials. The B.B. could only belong to Ben Bentley.

"Allison Cross."

"So Benjamin *has* had a girlfriend before?" Tim said with a cackle. "How experimental of you!"

"Shut up!" Ben laughed. "We were young and dumb. Allison and I thought it would make a good best friends oath. You know, like how people cut their thumbs and press them together or whatever. We carved our initials on this tree."

"And then carved a heart around them," Tim pointed out.

"Young and dumb," Ben repeated. "Don't tell me you're jealous."

"Of her or the countless straight guys you've toyed with?"

Ben's face grew serious. "It's not like that."

"I was just teasing."

"I know, but you're different."

Tim wasn't sure what that meant. Was he different because Ben thought he was gay, or was he different because Ben had feelings for him? Either way, the intensity of that look had Tim interested in anything but more conversation. "Kiss me."

Ben came to him and did as he was told. Tim started gently but then nibbled and gnawed on his lips. He felt like he could eat Ben up, like some sort of cannibal vampire. Kissing Ben drove Tim wild, maybe because he didn't have to be as cautious as he was with girls. He would have gladly spent the rest of the day lying together in the leaves, but a twig snapped and they both jumped. They froze, only their eyes moving as they tried to detect more noise. When it didn't come, they both chuckled. Then Ben attempted to unbutton Tim's shorts.

"Not here!" Tim said, sitting up and knocking his hand away. "Jesus, we're out in the open!"

Ben's brow furrowed. "We're not exactly in public. No one ever comes out here."

"But they could," Tim said. "There are houses just over there."

"Fine." Ben rolled his eyes before a different idea occurred to him. Tim knew from his expression that he was in trouble. "Come home with me. I'll smuggle you upstairs to my room, and you can stay the night."

"Like your parents wouldn't notice?"

"My parents won't care," Ben said. "Those are your choices. Whip it out here and now, or come home with me."

"Or I can go home and jack off," Tim said.

Ben's smile was way too confident. "You can't say no to me."

Instead of arguing, Tim proved him right.

True to his word, Ben smuggled him inside the house and up the stairs undetected. Ben lived only a few blocks over, in a neighborhood old enough to have character. The houses were a little smaller than those in the new subdivision where Tim lived, but still decidedly middle class. Once they reached the safety of his room, Ben slipped out again to order a pizza for dinner.

Ben's room wasn't quite what Tim had expected. That is, it contained nothing conspicuously gay. No posters of guys on the wall or rainbow bedspreads. Tim couldn't even say it was tastefully decorated, since it was all a little eclectic. The wrinkled-up bed had probably been made in haste. A coat rack in the corner held a jacket or two and a couple of hats, and two identical CD shelves were maxed out. A small writing desk against one wall held a laptop, and of course the requisite stereo and TV finished the decor. All in all it was a typical guy's room, except maybe for the scented candles on the windowsill.

Tim felt restless, sitting on the edge of the bed briefly before rising again to check out a collage of photos on the wall. Most were of Ben and a pretty black girl—the fabled Allison, most likely. In one Ben had his hair dyed black and Allison was pretending to smoke a pen like it was a cigarette. In another they were younger and dressed for Halloween. Allison was wearing a man's suit, a false mustache, and slicked-back hair. Ben was dressed up like a woman, wearing make-up, a horrible wig, and a tank top stuffed with two oranges for boobs. Tim leaned in, trying to decide if Ben as a girl did anything for him when the bedroom door opened.

Ben walked in wearing a hopeless expression, his mother close behind. She couldn't be anyone else, the family resemblance all too clear. Take Ben, make him shorter and style that blond hair into a bob, and *voilá!*

"Sorry!" she said. "I don't mean to intrude. I'm June, Ben's mom."

"Tim," he said, accepting her extended hand.

"Aren't you handsome! We're just about to order pizza, and I wanted to know what you like."

"Which I told her I would run up and ask," Ben muttered.

"Oh. Uh." Tim tried to remember what he usually got, a task made harder by the way June's eyes twinkled—like her son had brought home a girl for the first time. "Canadian bacon and pineapple," he managed at last.

"Yuck," Ben said. "Just cheese and diced tomatoes on my side."

"Okay. Well, you two have fun tonight. I won't barge in again, I promise."

"It was nice meeting you," Tim said.

Ben's mom checked him out once more, looking a little less certain. No doubt about it, she was trying to figure out if they were an item or not.

"Sorry about that," Ben said once the door was shut and locked.

"It's cool." Tim sat on the bed again. "She seems nice."

"Yeah. Well, the good news is that you're all clear to spend the night."

"Isn't that a little weird?" Tim asked. "I mean, that would be like asking my parents if a girl could spend the night. They would flip, even if she was just a friend."

"I guess. I had guy friends spend the night when I was a kid, so there's precedent." Ben moved through his room, self-consciously straightening different things. "Anyway, do you need to call your parents or something?"

Tim shook his head. "They won't notice."

"Oh."

For a moment, everything felt awkward. Mothers could be a tremendous mood killer, and they weren't going to get it on while waiting for pizza to arrive.

"Oh, I know!" Ben said. "I've been dying to play this for you."

He moved to his CD racks, running his finger along one of them until he found what he was looking for. "Roberta Flack," he said, but it didn't ring a bell until the stereo started playing *Killing Me Softly.* But this version was much more chill, without all the bored rappers in the background making random noises. Ben gave him an "is this cool or what?" look, to which Tim nodded in response, but he wasn't completely satisfied.

"Sing," he said.

Ben gawped at him, as if the idea was unthinkable. "It's Roberta Flack!"

Tim crossed his arms over his chest and scowled until Ben gave in. Roberta sounded good with a guy backing her up. Ben's voice chased away the awkwardness, casting a spell on his room and conjuring their private fantasy world back into existence. And Tim was happy.

The rest of the night was easy. They made small talk, Tim asking about different things he saw in the room, like the stories behind the various photos of Ben and Allison. When the doorbell rang, Ben rushed out to get their pizza, making another trip for a two-liter bottle of Coke and some glasses. They watched *Toy Story* while they ate, a movie Tim missed when it was still in theaters. Ben's dad managed the local cable company, so they had every possible channel and even got their pay-per-view movies for free.

The side of Ben's bed was shoved up against the wall directly across from the TV, doubling as a long couch. Tim stretched out his legs, and as the movie wore on, he moved one so it touched Ben's. Then Ben scooted over, their arms brushing and making

Tim's skin tingle. Tired of being coy, he took Ben's hand in his own, and it didn't feel strange like he thought it might.

Ben must have seen the film before, because he sang along with *You've Got a Friend in Me* whenever it played in the story, shooting a few coy smiles in Tim's direction. When the movie was over, Ben shut off the TV with the remote, neither of them moving from the bed. The room was dark, lit only by a street light outside.

"It was never like this," Ben said. "Those other guys, they never held my hand."

Tim wished he hadn't said that. If a bunch of other horny straight guys didn't cuddle up with Ben, then it made him look, well—

"They didn't even kiss me," Ben said. "Everything was one-sided."

They didn't kiss him? Now Tim felt more conflicted than ever. If given an ultimatum between kissing Ben and getting blown by him, Tim thought he could go without the oral sex. Those other guys had no idea what they were missing.

Ben squeezed his hand. "I just want you to know that this isn't a game I've played dozens of times before."

"Okay." That's all Tim could think to say. He didn't want to delve into what any of this meant. Doing so made it too hard for him to enjoy.

"Ready for bed?" Ben asked.

Tim smirked. "Something like that."

They took turns using the restroom, with Ben going first. Tim went second. Outside Ben's room, the house was dark and quiet, the only light a sliver in the bathroom that Ben had left on for him. Tim thought he could hear snoring downstairs, either Ben's father or the family dog. Finding his way back without the bathroom light on was even harder. Ben's bedroom was next to his sister's. Wouldn't she be in for a surprise if Tim accidentally slipped into bed with her!

Fortunately, he made it back to the right room. The lights were still off in Ben's bedroom, but the candles in the window had been lit. Ben was already beneath the sheets, shirtless at the very least, lying on his side but facing the door. Tim stripped off his shirt, Ben's brown eyes watching his every move, absorbing the details of his body. Tim stood at the side of the bed, close enough for the candles to illuminate him, but far enough away that he couldn't be touched. He unbuttoned and unzipped his shorts next, the boxers underneath already tenting. When he lowered the shorts and boxers down and off, he waited, basking in Ben's attention.

Then he crawled into bed and pulled back the sheets. Ben was already naked, lifting his hands to touch, but Tim moved Ben's arms away. Instead, he did the touching, kissing every part of Ben's body he could find. As Ben lay on his back, arching and moaning, Tim showed him just how different he could be from those other guys.

Chapter Eight

It was over.

The past month had been the best of Tim's life. He'd been to crazy parties—not just sneaking some quick drinks at Darryl's before his parents got home, but all-night affairs that probably cost more in damages than they did in alcohol. Tim reached a happy impasse with Krista. Their relationship wasn't going any further, and both were content with that. And then there were the nights spent with Ben. *They* were the highlight, the times Tim looked forward to most, but now they were over.

Tim attacked the canvas. He wasn't usually into abstract expressionism, but today he needed to see the reds of rage blurring together with oranges of anxiety. He needed to purge his system of the anger and despair he felt before he crumpled beneath their weight.

He had never wanted things to become complicated. Not with Ben. That meant juggling more separate lives than he usually did, but Tim was skilled at this. Like now, since painting was something private he didn't share with anyone, even Ben. Such things were necessary. Keeping his parents pleased by not attracting unwanted attention. Maintaining his image at school. Both of these were crucial to making his time with Ben possible. No one was asking questions, drawing unwanted conclusions, or getting in their way. Ben might create the world they shared, but Tim protected it. And now he was being punished for having done so.

A shopping trip to the mall with Krista. That's when it all started to unravel. As usual, Krista held on to his arm as they moved from store to store. Tim had spotted Ben and his mother first. Thank goodness Krista was distracted by a window display of jewelry when they passed by. Tim nodded at Ben, which was all he could do, but then everything had exploded. Not there at the mall, but the next time they were alone.

Tim could understand how Ben felt. If he had seen some guy hanging off Ben's arm, it would have hurt, but Ben had known about Krista from the start. He understood she was necessary to maintain the right image—or so Tim had thought. The last time they had seen each other…

"Who do you like more, Krista or me?"

"You," Tim had told him. And it was true. Ben knew it was. "I like you more. When you're not pissed at me, at least."

"Who do you sleep with? It's not Krista, is it?"

"No. I sleep with you."

"So why do you need her when you have me?"

And Tim knew that the usual reasons weren't enough for Ben anymore, that like everything good, things had gotten complicated. Tim attacked the canvas again, but the red he had mixed was a little too pink. He tried adding some yellow near it to make the hue appear deeper, but this only seemed to highlight it.

Tim stepped back and sighed. The painting appeared more amorous than angry. In the center, created by chance, was a shape like one lonely heart, surrounded by a mess of emotions. Feeling sorry for it, he gave the heart a partner, tracing the edge of another right behind it, so close that they almost appeared as one.

He had fucked up. Ben had done everything right, and Tim had ruined it. Of course being with Krista hurt Ben's feelings. Right from the beginning, Ben had made sure Tim knew he was special, more than just a fling. And Tim had responded by keeping Krista around. And kissing that girl on the beach. What the hell had he been thinking?

Sometimes he wondered if something was wrong with him. Tim felt like a flower starved of sunlight, and every time that fiery orb rose in the sky, he jumped at the opportunity to soak up its warmth. He basked in attention like it gave him life. And now he had caused night to fall on the brightest days he had ever known.

His time with Ben had been precious. No, his *relationship* with Ben. That's what it was—could be still—if he somehow salvaged it. If Tim was going to keep Ben, he would have to start taking risks. Starting with Krista Norman.

The flagpole dinged, the halyard and hooks blowing repeatedly against the metal cylinder. The noise seemed to haunt every school Tim had attended. The sound was desolate, one he usually noticed only when the parking lot emptied and everyone had gone home. Like now. School was out and cross country practice was over. Krista had come to watch him, as she sometimes did, and Tim had decided not to delay anymore. Surely this was better than calling her, like he had originally planned.

But watching Krista's face, he wasn't so sure.

"Why?" she asked.

"I just can't be with anyone right now," Tim said.

"Is it because I—"

"No. It's not because of that, I promise."

"Then why?"

Tim had struggled to find the right excuse, anything but the truth. The most effective reasons were also the most hurtful; another girl or that he simply didn't like her. But he couldn't bring himself to say any of those things, because as ditzy as Krista was, she was all right.

"There's stuff going on at home," Tim said. "It's complicated, and I don't like to talk about it. I'm sorry."

Krista covered her nose and mouth with her hand, as if she could hold back the tears this way. Tim felt terrible.

"You're the only girl for me," he said, hoping to make her feel better. "You won't see me with anyone else. Maybe once everything blows over—"

A false promise, but he hated letting anyone down. For once Krista didn't have anything to say, so he walked her to her car, which she had parked next to his. When he hugged her, he pretended not to notice her tears. Then he turned, got into his car, and drove away.

Tim stood in front of Ben's front door, steeling himself. The driveway was overflowing with cars. The street too. Tim had to park half a block down. Five balloons were bundled together and tied to the mailbox. If this wasn't indication enough, colorful paper letters on the door explained the rest, quivering in the October wind.

Happy Birthday!

Ben's birthday bash was in full swing. They had talked about Tim attending before their falling out, and of course he had remained silent, not wanting to be around Ben's family more than he had to. Not that they didn't seem wonderful, but Tim felt what he and Ben had together was private.

That was about to change. He rang the doorbell and stood

there ten seconds before he felt like ditching the present on the porch and jogging to his car. Before he could, the door opened. Ben's face was lit up, like he'd been on a smiling marathon all day, but his expression shifted to surprise.

"Hey!" Ben said, sounding more upbeat than negative. "Uh, come on in!"

Tim could hear numerous voices elsewhere in the house. He wasn't ready for this. "That's okay. I just wanted to bring this by."

Ben looked down at the present. Tim felt what the paper concealed must be obvious, considering the long thin shape.

"Oh, hi!" Mrs. Bentley appeared behind Ben, beaming at Tim like she always did. "I was wondering when you would show up! Come on in and grab some cake."

"No really, I—"

Mrs. Bentley waved a hand dismissively. "Come on, don't let Wilford get out the door, or we'll never see him again."

Tim slinked inside, nearly jumping when the door shut behind him. He needed to chill, and quick.

"Time to meet the family," Ben said with a nervous chuckle. "The extended version."

"Great." Tim smiled at him, trying to put an apology into it. As always, Ben seemed to understand. They stood there, eyeing each other like years had passed instead of a week. He could almost imagine them going up to Ben's room, but Tim was led to the heart of the party—where about ten thousand relatives waited for them.

Well, not that many, but they certainly made Tim's family seem small. He shook a lot of hands, missed almost all the names, and suffered a few old lady hugs. Then someone tall, dark, and gorgeous hopped in front of Tim's path like a ninja.

"Allison," she said by way of introduction, smiling broadly at him.

There was no mistaking that look. She knew everything, absolutely everything, he and Ben had been up to. Tim took her hand and gave her his best smile, which only made her grin grow wider.

"Up close, I can see why Ben puts up with you," she said playfully.

"Don't worry," Tim said. "Once the looks go, I'll be ancient history and he'll be all yours again."

"I'd rather you stick around," Allison replied. "I've had my hands full with the boy for far too long. The break has been nice."

"I'm standing right here," Ben said testily.

Tim and Allison laughed. Maybe everything was going to be okay.

"Wait, everyone!" Mrs. Bentley declared. "We have one more present before we light candles."

"No, you can open it later," Tim said, his panic rising again as everyone focused on him. "Really!"

Ben snatched the present from his hands, and Tim's world receded to the shreds of wrapping paper that were flung into the air, revealing his art. Then he could only focus on Ben's face. Tim was proud of the painting. It wasn't his usual style, but he felt the blizzard of colors showed passion, the overlapping hearts in the center evoking the right emotion without being too hokey.

Ben seemed lost for words, so his mother spoke for him.

"Isn't that gorgeous? Did you paint it yourself?"

Tim's instinct was to lie, but Ben was smiling. Maybe he understood what Tim was trying to say. He was opening his mouth to take credit when Karen, Ben's sister, spoke first.

"It looks like someone barfed up paint on a canvas."

"We should have cut your tongue out at birth," Mr. Bentley scolded.

Tim's stomach sank. This is why he didn't tell anyone about his paintings. All of them, even the ones that didn't turn out well, were close to his heart. Having one out in the open was like having a dagger pressed against his bare chest. Anyone could nudge him and drive the blade in, which Ben's sister had done.

"It's just something I found somewhere," Tim said lamely. "You don't have to keep it if you don't want."

Ben's eyes, more watery than normal, turned toward him. "I love it!"

Mrs. Bentley looked between them, seeing it all with a mother's insight, and heroically called attention away from them.

"Okay, everyone! Time for cake!" That did the trick. The relatives hustled away, eager to get a slice. Ben went to claim the first piece, setting aside the painting for now. Tim was tempted to steal it back and smuggle it home. Instead he retreated to the back of the crowd.

"Sorry about Karen," Allison said, joining him. "She's one of the most miserable people on the planet. I don't see how she and Ben can possibly be related, but Ben got all the charm."

"The looks too," Tim said, glaring in Karen's direction as she joined the others in singing *Happy Birthday.*

"Anyway, he likes the painting," Allison said. "A lot."

If anyone would know, she would, so Tim felt a little better. "Thanks."

"No problem. Just a second," Allison stepped forward and started singing, just as the birthday song was winding down. She sang an extra verse on her own, her voice like honey. Tim could see why they were best friends. He hoped being able to sing wasn't a prerequisite of their clique. If so, Tim was screwed.

Ben continued to be held prisoner by his family, each relative eager to have a word with him, so Tim stood back and watched. Part of him was envious that so much love was showered on Ben, but there was no one in the world more deserving. Tim could see Ben had a similar effect on everyone around him. That inner light, the fearless pride inside him—who wouldn't want to be near that?

Allison dove into the fray and returned with two slices of cake. Tim accepted one of the paper plates gratefully.

"Ben said you weren't coming," she remarked.

"To be honest, I wasn't sure I was still invited."

Allison smiled slyly. "Either way, I think you're out of the dog house now. Showing up like that was smooth. I'm going to be hearing about it for weeks."

"Oh? Does he talk about me a lot?"

Her expression turned coy. "Occasionally." Allison toyed with her cake, mashing the frosting around in a way that made Tim think of paint. "Just try not to break his heart. You being here today speaks volumes. I'm not going to give you a tired speech about how if you hurt him, I'll make you regret it. I think you've already figured out that losing Ben is much worse than anything I could do to you."

"Yeah," Tim said, his voice sounding hoarse.

"Good. Don't look so down, because he's heading this way with his happy face on."

"Hi," Ben said to him, like they had only just met. "I was thinking we'd hit a haunted house or two. Maybe Ronnie could come along."

"Ronnie?" Tim asked.

"My boyfriend," Allison explained before addressing Ben. "Sure. I'll give him a call."

She walked away to do just that, Tim's nerves acting up again. "Does Ronnie go to our school?" he asked.

"Yup." Ben's smile faltered a little. "Is that okay?"

"Yeah. Totally."

Tim wanted to be more open with Ben, but school wasn't part of that plan. He trusted Allison, since she was Ben's best friend, but he didn't know anything about this Ronnie guy. Tim needed time alone with Ben to explain where he was coming from, to tell him how important their secret was, but not so soon after getting back in Ben's good graces. Like it or not, he'd have to risk an evening out.

Tim didn't have much to worry about. Ronnie turned out to be pretty cool. He was into sports, which gave them common ground. Tim spent a lot of the drive down to Houston talking to him, feeling unsure what to say to Ben in front of others. The line for the haunted house was long and full of people their age, but Ronnie was still chatting him up. Even if Bryce or Darryl happened to see him now, it wouldn't be obvious he was hanging out with Ben.

The haunted house itself wasn't as cool as the ones back in Kansas, but it had all the basic requirements. Some rooms had cheap animatronic monsters; others had costumed actors who did their best to scare them. The chainsaw-wielding guy at the end could already be heard, but first they had a pitch-dark maze to navigate. Tim grabbed Ben, pulling him down a corridor and whispering the words he had been dying to tell him.

"I broke up with her."

"With Krista?" Ben's voice was so hopeful that Tim chuckled.

"Yeah. You were right. It's you I like and it's you I want."

He pressed himself against Ben, found his lips in the dark, and kissed him. Soundtracks of creaking boards and howling monsters serenaded them, the smell of smoke machines in the air. Tim couldn't think of a stranger place to get so turned on, but he could have taken Ben right then and there. Unfortunately, a group of girls bumped into them and shrieked. Why was the universe always throwing women at him?

Tim shouted, causing another round of shrieks that sent them away. Then he took Ben's hand and led him out of the maze.

*****

The candles were lit one by one, the Zippo lighter singeing Tim's fingers as the last wick sputtered to life. He turned around. His room looked good in candlelight, especially with Ben in his bed. This was another birthday gift. Tim had given Ben a house key and asked him to sneak in. Having come close to losing him, Tim now needed more than just the weekend nights they shared in Ben's room.

Of course that meant one more calculated risk. Tim waited farther down the hall, watching Ben creep into his room like a thief. Tim's parents were out of town for the weekend, but they wouldn't have heard a thing. Even if they did, they so rarely paid attention.

And now Ben was in his bed, curled up on his side and grinning. "So I hear you're officially single," he said. "Does this mean you're back on the prowl?"

"I never stop prowling." Tim flicked the Zippo shut, growling like a tiger.

"I see. At the ripe old age of seventeen, don't you think it's time you settled down with someone special?"

"Meaning?" Tim inquired.

"I want to be your boyfriend."

"Jesus, Benjamin! You don't let up do you?" It took all of Tim's effort not to smile. Why not make it official? But he didn't plan on making it easy. "It's not enough that you make me dump my girlfriend?"

"If she was good enough for you to date, then I am twice as qualified." Ben smirked and then sang, "Anything a girl can do, I can do better."

"Off hand, I can think of a few things that you can't!"

"Well, anyway. What do you think?" Ben's expression became vulnerable. "Seriously."

"I think I want a test drive before I buy the car." Tim pounced on him, and after some wrestling around, shrieking and laughing, their touches became intimate. They didn't get much sleep that night.

The next morning, Tim had the talk with Ben, hoping he had given enough to get something back. He had just returned from the bathroom when he noticed Ben was awake. After a little banter, Tim decided now was as good a time as any.

"My parents can't know about this. No one at school either."

Ben didn't hold back. "So just like things were before?"

"Not like before. No Krista, no other girls, and definitely no other guys. Just me and you. I want it to stay that way."

Ben didn't look convinced, but Tim hoped some part of him understood. He was protecting what they had. The doors to Tim's heart were open now. He would be Ben's boyfriend, be loyal, do everything he could to make him happy—but Tim would never let others get near what they had.

Chapter Nine

"Trouble at home, Tim?"

Stacy Shelly sat down at the lunch table across from him. When Tim had broken up with Krista on Friday, he hadn't imagined what the following week would be like. Parties would be easy, since they could mingle on opposite sides of the room, but school was tricky. He and Krista shared a class together and had long ago swapped seat assignments to sit next to each other. And then there was lunch. Tim didn't know how he was supposed to handle that, so he sat alone at a different table. Until Stacy found him.

"What's wrong?" she continued. "Daddy sleeps around? Mommy drinks too much?"

Tim glared at her. "I broke up with your best friend, and now I'm on your shit list? Is that how it's going to be?"

Stacy pursed her lips. "Well, I did have to listen to her cry all weekend. You owe me for that. No, what really bothers me is the transparently fake reason."

Tim kept quiet.

"'Trouble at home.'" Stacy laughed. "Has anyone broken up over a bad home life? Ever? Come on! Krista may be stupid, but give me some credit."

"You don't know what you're talking about," Tim said. "You don't know a thing about me."

"Is that a challenge?"

"No."

Stacy Shelly eyed him like a viper. "Well, whoever she is, you better keep her a secret."

Tim didn't ask her to expound on that threat. "Are you done?"

"Almost. She wants you to come sit with us."

Tim stared. "Krista?"

"Yes, Tim. She's in love with you. That means she's already forgiven you or thinks she can win you back. Or maybe she's just dumb. Regardless, you don't need to sit here like a scrub."

But Tim did just that for the rest of lunch period. The next day he tried a tentative smile in class that Krista returned, which made him comfortable enough to sit with her at lunch. She didn't try anything, didn't put her hand on his arm like she always used to or press him for answers. Stacy still scrutinized his every move, but with Krista, Tim felt things were going to be okay.

"Are you sure you want to go through with this?" Tim asked, stopping before the office door to his studio and turning around.

"What?" Ben asked, his eyes big with concern.

"Me painting you nude."

Ben pushed him playfully. Tim laughed, unlocking the door. This wasn't the first time Ben had been here. That had been Christmas, a holiday Tim usually despised, but Ben had made it just as magical as those cheesy television specials. Even more so. Then Tim had brought Ben to his studio, opening one more door to his soul. In the months that followed, they would often hide away here on the weekends when the office was empty. Or on a Friday night, like this one, after everyone had left. All his father's employees were either out wining and dining dates or at home comforting themselves with tubs of ice cream, for today was the most dreaded holiday of them all.

Tim always found the pressure behind Valentine's Day irritating. Everyone had to hook up with someone before the holiday or feel left out. Or jump through hoops for who they already had. Krista found someone new just the day before, conveniently enough. The guy was handsome, plucked from the semi-popular crowd where Darryl usually got his eager-to-please girls. Krista invited her new beau to sit at their lunch table, which was awkward because she kept watching Tim for a reaction.

So school had been miserable, but the evening held potential. Tim walked around the studio, clicking on the lamps Ben had helped him shop for to replace the cold fluorescent light. The lamps cast shadows and created warmth, setting the right mood for him to paint. And tonight they would help set the scene. Tim didn't want flowers or chocolates for Valentine's Day. He wanted to paint.

"The clothing stays on," Ben said, sitting on a stool.

"For the painting at least," Tim murmured, taking his place behind the easel.

Truth be told, it wouldn't matter either way. Ben's face was his solitary focus. Tim had tried from memory a couple of times already, but his mental images were too fluid and shifting. Besides, he'd never had a live model before. Tim didn't paint in front of anyone, didn't even take art classes. Everything he knew was learned through trial and error or gleaned from the books he kept in his studio.

"So what do I do?" Ben asked, shifting uncomfortably.

"Just relax." Tim squeezed paints on to the palette, eager to begin.

"Can I still talk to you?"

"Sure, but that doesn't mean I'll listen."

"Ha, ha," Ben deadpanned, but then he smiled when he saw Tim make the first couple of strokes. "You're going to let me see, right?"

"Maybe." Tim worked in silence a few minutes. Then his subject spoke again.

"Ronnie is taking Allison to Café Annie."

"Never heard of it."

"It's supposed to be one of the best restaurants in Houston. It's really expensive."

"Hm. Well, I'm lucky I have such a cheap date." Ben was quiet, so Tim stopped painting and looked at him. "I thought you wanted to do this?"

"I do!" Ben said. "I really like the idea."

Tim resumed painting, knowing the topic wasn't over. The silence grew thick over the next ten minutes, but he kept his focus on the canvas until Ben spoke again.

"It would be nice to go out with you sometime."

"We do," Tim countered, but he knew what Ben meant. Usually they would go for long drives or nighttime walks. Tim never wanted to hit the mall with him, go out to eat, or even catch a movie, since there was always the possibility of them being seen. The most they had ever done was go to AstroWorld, Houston's theme park, in the cover of night. That had earned him some major points, but lately Ben had been pushing hard for—

"What about dinner with your parents?"

Exactly. Tim chose his answer carefully. "I don't get why you want to meet them. I know what you said," he added quickly. "If they ever catch you sneaking in, they'll at least recognize you—"

"And they're a part of your life," Ben said.

"Right." Tim didn't hide his sarcasm. "That aside, why can't you just pop in and say 'hi' to them before we go somewhere? Why does there have to be an awkward dinner?"

"Because I want them to get to know me," Ben said.

Tim considered this. "You're going to tell them?"

"That I'm gay? Of course! Before I came out to my parents, they had no idea what gay people were like, aside from what they had seen in comedies and gay pride parades."

"The fools," Tim said, hiding his smile. Not long ago he hadn't been so different.

"One of the biggest shocks for them was how someone normal, like their son, could be gay. I think they kept waiting for me to sprout a feather boa and strut around the house in leather chaps."

"You mean you don't?"

"Seriously. I think it would be good for your parents to meet someone like me."

Tim shook his head while he worked. Every time he looked up from the canvas, he saw his boyfriend looking expectant. "Your parents are cool, Ben. The gay issue aside, they're way more laid back about everything. And more supportive."

Ben squirmed a little. "I know I'm lucky."

"Good, but not everyone's parents are like yours. I know you think I should come out and that all the pieces will fall into place like they did for you, but that's not how it'll work for me. Not everyone who comes out gets a happy ending."

"You won't know until you try."

Tim snorted. "I can make an educated guess."

Ben didn't give up. He *never* gave up. "I don't see the harm in me being the test subject. Let them meet me—for dinner, not just a few seconds—and we'll see what they think. Anyway, you promised."

"Did I?"

"Yes!"

"It must have been a moment of weakness."

Ben scowled in response.

"Fine. Dinner with my parents. Don't say I didn't warn you."

The next fifteen minutes were spent in blissful silence, but Ben's mind was always working. "You mentioned coming out to your parents."

Tim laughed, knowing exactly what Ben was getting at. "Don't read into it."

This was another of Ben's crusades. Titles made Tim

uncomfortable, and Ben was always pushing for him to choose something. Maybe he was bisexual, maybe he wasn't. What Ben had said about sexuality being emotional had stuck with him, and yeah, what they had together involved feelings. But maybe he was also capable of loving the right kind of girl.

Regardless, Tim knew if he started getting all emotional, Ben would treat it as evidence. It's not like there was any rush. They had all the time in the world together.

"Hey."

Tim looked up from his canvas. "Yeah?"

Ben licked his lips, his chest rising and falling a few times. "I love you."

The breath caught in Tim's throat. His mouth opened, ready to reply, then snapped shut again.

That bastard! Tim had never doubted that Ben loved him, but the timing was no coincidence. Maybe Ben wouldn't play that card now, but it wouldn't be long before he used it to define Tim's sexuality. Still, hearing him finally say it felt amazing.

"Come here," Tim said softly.

"Won't that ruin the—"

"Just come here."

Ben got off the stool and walked toward him, standing next to the canvas. His eyes searched Tim's, waiting to discover what his response would be. Tim dipped the paintbrush into the yellow paint without breaking eye contact.

"Hold still," he said. "Please." Then he brought the paintbrush up to the center of Ben's forehead and pulled down, making one fat stroke of yellow between his eyes, over his nose, and down to his chin.

"What was that for?" Ben spluttered.

"To make you prettier," Tim said before laughing.

"You're such an asshole!" Ben swung at him, Tim dodging easily and laughing some more. Ben chased him around the canvas a few times, swearing in frustration. On one of his rounds, he noticed what Tim had painted and stopped.

Despite all the distractions, Tim was proud of what he had managed. The painting was just Ben's nose and lips. So far he had put most of the detail into the lips, working out his obsession with kissing Ben. The painting needed more work, but it had serious potential.

"Those are my lips!" Ben exclaimed. "I mean, they look exactly like mine!"

"Don't sound so surprised."

"I don't mean it like that." Ben stared a little longer. "I like it, but why?"

He looked at Tim, who let his eyes dart down to the real thing. His own lips moved a little in response.

"Oh, I see," Ben said knowingly. "You like what these lips can do."

"Yeah." Tim gave a sly grin. "I guess so."

"You *know* so." Ben grabbed a tube of blue paint, squeezed a glob on his fingers, and smeared it over his lips. Then he moved menacingly toward Tim. "Well? Come kiss me, baby!"

"No thanks." Tim backed up until he felt the wall behind him, staring horrified at the blue fish puckers coming toward him.

"If you love me, you'll kiss me," Ben said.

Well, it beat having to say it. Tim closed his eyes and braced himself for the sloppiest kiss of his life.

"Are you sure your parents aren't home?" Ben whispered as Tim unlocked the front door.

"Positive. They're never home on Valentine's Day. Usually they shack up in a bed and breakfast somewhere." Tim did a double take. "Wait, I thought you wanted to meet them?"

"Not like this!" Ben gestured to his face where the yellow and blue paint had smeared together, making it look like green slime had leaked from his nose before drying.

"You've never looked better," Tim said. "Ouch," he added when Ben slugged him.

Tim must have looked just as bad. He could feel paint crusted on his mouth where Ben had kissed him. Hopefully it was non-toxic. He imagined the newspaper story, complete with a color photo of their bodies lying next to each other, their mouths stained with the same green hue. *Paint Fetish Kills Gay Couple!*

Tim grabbed a beer for himself and a Coke for Ben, but the war paint had weirded him out. "Come on, Benjamin. It's time for your bath."

As romantic as a candlelit bath sounded, the tub was barely big enough for them both, and Tim would have a hard time doing half the things he wanted to. So he turned on the shower and let the water get hot while he undressed his boyfriend. Ben was wearing a tangerine dress shirt Tim had never seen before, probably bought for this occasion. He slowly undid each of the buttons, adoring how Ben had trouble meeting his gaze at times like these. Crazy, considering everything they had done together. As wildly brave as Ben could be, he still had a bashful side, and it came out every time Tim touched him.

Tim wasn't so ceremonial with his own clothes. As soon as Ben was nude, he tore off his clothing so they could get in the shower. Ben was under the water first, holding his head up to the stream, green water swirling around his feet. Then he switched places with Tim. When they were both warm and wet, Tim grabbed the shampoo and squirted some into his hands.

"Come here."

"Oh, no!" Ben replied. "I'm not falling for that again."

"I'm just going to wash you." For some reason, Tim found the idea erotic. After a couple more suspicious looks, Ben came close. Tim met him halfway, letting their bodies press together as he worked shampoo into Ben's hair. They both laughed at the process, but it turned Tim on like crazy. He went for the liquid body soap next, letting his sudsy hands rub all over Ben's body, running them into every nook and cranny.

"Now I'll wash you," Ben said. He hadn't rinsed off yet. Instead he grabbed Tim and pulled him into a hug, the soap acting as lube, Ben's thin body squirming against his muscles.

"Way better than a loofah sponge," Tim said, leaning back to squirt more soap between them.

Ben's hand found their cocks, squeezing them together before he started pumping. Tim went for those lips he was so crazy about, but after a few kisses Ben turned around, having something else in mind. That was another first that had happened during Christmas, and they didn't do it often, but Tim would never turn down the offer.

He grabbed the real lube, a small bottle he kept hidden behind the cluster of shampoos and conditioners. Ben was already going wild, grinding his butt against Tim's crotch. Only when Tim moved away to apply the lube were they both more cautious.

Tim let his fingers explore first, whispering into Ben's ear occasionally. "You okay? Does that feel good?" All he got was nods and moans in response, so Tim added more lube to his dick before he pushed inside a little bit.

This killed him every time, just as much as Ben's songs did. There was something so undeniably emotional about the act, so bonding, that it was a miracle he hadn't already let loose those three magic words. Tim could say them without lying, if he really wanted to. If they woke up tomorrow to find the rest of the world obliterated, Tim imagined it's all he would say.

"Harder," Ben hissed.

That was new! Tim wrapped his arms around Ben's torso, hugging him tight as he pumped faster. He chewed on Ben's earlobe, then rested his head against Ben's neck like they were spooning, but of course they were doing much more. Tim was ready—had been for the last five minutes—but he held back, monitoring how tense his boyfriend's body was. When Ben's breathing quickened, Tim held back no more, his timing perfect. They came in unison, but Tim didn't let go of Ben until their fingers and toes were wrinkled like prunes.

"Next weekend," Tim said while they were toweling off.

Ben was getting the water out of his ears like he couldn't hear, but said, "Really?"

"Yeah. I'll ask my mom to make *chile rellenos*. She always makes too many. You show up spontaneously, and I'll ask if you can stay. Sound good?"

"Yeah." Ben smiled. "You won't be sorry."

Looking into those sweet cocoa-brown eyes, Tim couldn't help believing him.

The smell of battered peppers frying in canola oil filled the house, making Tim's stomach grumble. Or maybe it was churning because of nerves. He paced the front room, wondering what was taking Ben so long. Dinner was going to be served any second, and if he didn't get here—

The doorbell rang, Tim sprinting to answer it. Ben looked good. Almost too good. They were supposed to be catching a movie, or so the story went, with Ben showing up a little early. But the dress shirt he wore, while smoking hot, seemed too dressy for two guys catching a flick together. Two straight guys, anyway.

"Get inside!" Tim hissed.

"And hello to you too," Ben said.

"Just stay here. I'll be right back."

Tim dashed to the kitchen. His mom was singing in Spanish while poking at the peppers in the frying pan, occasionally turning or moving them to a dish lined with paper towels.

"Hey, Mom," Tim said, coming up beside her. "Smells good!"

Ella smiled and kept singing. She always got like this when preparing Mexican food, the sights and smells whisking her back home again. Maybe that's why she always made too many.

"You know that friend I'm going to the movies with? Well, he showed up early and hasn't eaten."

His mother stopped singing.

"I keep telling him what real Mexican food tastes like and how it's different from the Tex-Mex around here, so I thought maybe he could stay."

"Why don't you ever bring your girlfriend by for dinner?"

Tim's stomach sank. "Because she eats like a bird. So what do you think?"

His mother was quiet a moment.

"Please?"

Ella dropped a couple more peppers into the oil. "Set another place at the table."

"Thanks!"

Tim kissed her on the cheek and ran back to the entryway, feeling twice as nervous now. Ben didn't seem too comfortable, either. He was staring at the stairs he had snuck up so many times at night, but when he saw Tim, he put on an easy smile.

"How'd it go?"

"We're good. I hope you're hungry."

"Starving!"

Tim took a deep breath. "Look, I was thinking. Just let them get to know you this time. Don't play the gay card. Not tonight."

"Tim—"

"Some other time, okay?"

Ben's expression was grim, but he nodded. The knot in Tim's stomach loosened slightly. Then he remembered he had to set an extra place at the table. He was doing so when his father came in the dining room, followed by his mother a second later, carrying the peppers.

"Mom, Dad, this is my friend Ben."

His father's brow furrowed.

"He's staying for dinner," Ella explained. "*Gordito,* get the rice from the kitchen. Your friend can bring the salad."

"See?" Ben said when they were in the kitchen. "I'm part of the family already."

Tim didn't laugh. Was it too late to bail? Couldn't they slip out the back door and disappear? The atmosphere at the table felt tense when they returned and were seated. Ben had met his match this time, Tim was certain. At least Ben was prepared. Tim had coached him as best he could, starting with the way his family said grace. Without any prompting, Ben bowed his head before reaching for any food, intoning the words seamlessly along with the rest of his family.

"And thank you to the Wymans for being kind enough to share this food with me," Ben added at the end.

Tim glanced at his parents. His mother appeared pleased or amused, but his father watched with stoic puzzlement. Tim helped his mother serve. Ben made a big deal over how good the food tasted, launching into a big speech about how interested he was in Mexican culture, and how he had done a paper for school about Mexico City, where—surprise!—Tim's mother just happened to be from. To Tim it all sounded phony, but his mother laughed at all the right moments and seemed genuinely flattered by his interest.

Tim was sure they were doomed when Ben started talking sports with his father, but that went even better. Ben got Thomas raving about the Kansas City Chiefs—a smart move since it meant Ben spent most of his time listening and nodding. Tim stopped waiting for the world to end and focused on stuffing his face. Really, this was nice. Usually when Tim ate with his parents they spent most of their time talking to each other. Now, with Ben playing moderator, they were treated like the couples his parents occasionally entertained.

"It is so nice to finally meet one of Tim's friends," his mother said. "He's been so protective of his social life since Kansas."

"Not protective," Tim said. "I just like going out instead of staying home. I'm too old for sleepovers, you know."

Ben's mouth twitched with amusement, but he hid the smile, thank god. They weren't playing a game here!

His mother turned to Ben. "Do you know his other friends? His girlfriend?" Mrs. Wyman asked.

Tim nearly choked on his food. He hadn't thought to brief Ben about this. Romance was his mother's passion. She loved her husband more than anything, more than him, so the one aspect of Tim's world she always inquired about was his love life. If he didn't have a girlfriend, she obsessed over it, so it was easier to lie and say he had one. "Of course he knows Krista!"

Ben didn't miss a beat, even if his voice was strained. "She's really pretty. Popular too."

Tim's mother was pleased. "And what about you? A fair-haired boy like you must also have a pretty girl."

"Well, actually—"

Ben had that look on his face, so Tim kicked his leg under the table. Their eyes met for a fraction of a second. *Krista?* that look said. *For that, I'm telling them.* And to drive the point home, Ben kicked him back.

"I have a boyfriend."

The words were out. Permanently. Ben had spoken them and there would be no taking them back. His mother appeared puzzled, maybe wondering if her near-perfect English had failed her. His father cleared his throat repeatedly like he had swallowed a bug.

"He's really great," Ben pressed on. "Goes to the same school as we do."

Tim was sure Ben was going to out him to his parents, right then and there. But then Ben started talking about Mexican cuisine, as if the bomb he had dropped was nothing more than idle chitchat. And Ben kept talking, tossing out subjects that his parents grasped on to because they were much more comfortable. By the end of the meal, it was like none of it had happened.

"If I knew one of *Gordito's* friends was coming by," his mother said, "I would have made *tres leches.*"

"Three milks?" Ben tried.

Tim chuckled. "It's a type of cake."

His mother smiled. "And it's your favorite, isn't it?"

"Yeah," Tim said. All right, enough weird family time. "We have to get going or we'll miss the film."

Ben insisted on staying to help clear the table, Tim practically shoving him out of the house afterwards. Not because he was upset, but because he couldn't wait to be alone. He kissed Ben the second they were in his car.

"That was awesome!" he said.

"Yeah." Ben gave a humble nod. "I think I did okay."

"You were incredible! You got more conversation out of my parents than I have in the last ten years."

Ben smiled. "They didn't seem so bad."

No, they didn't. Maybe the silence over the years had been Tim's fault. He could learn a lot from Ben. Tim started the car and revved the engine.

"Where are we going?" Ben asked.

"To the movies."

"On a Saturday night where everyone can see us?"

Tim grinned at him and nodded. Why the hell not? Ben had been right this whole time. There wasn't anything to be scared of. Once they were cruising down the street, he reached over and took his hand.

"There's just one thing I don't understand," Ben said.

"What?"

"Why did your mom keep calling you *Gordito?*"

Tim groaned. "It's just a pet name, like how your mom calls you 'honey' in English."

"Oh." Ben mulled this over. "Well, doesn't *gordo* mean fat?"

"Mm-hm."

"So your mom is basically calling you 'fatty?'"

"I was a big baby!" Tim said defensively.

"A fat baby?" Ben asked before laughing.

Tim smiled. "Hey, all this muscle had to come from somewhere!"

"Well, in that case I'm glad." Then Ben added, so quietly that Tim almost didn't hear him, *"Mi Gordito."*

When Tim returned home that night, his parents were still awake. That wasn't so strange, considering the hour, but normally they would be in their bedroom by now, watching TV or whatever else they got up to. He was glad that he and Ben had decided to play it safe tonight, because his parents had been waiting for him.

"Sit down."

His mother was already seated on the living room couch, his father standing over her with arms crossed as he waited for Tim to do what he was told.

"What's going on?" Tim asked.

Ella patted the couch. "We just want to talk to you."

Tim took a seat at the opposite end, turned slightly so he could see her.

"We're concerned about the kind of people you associate with."

Tim's insides became a void that he tumbled into. He knew it had been too good to be true.

"He's just a friend," Tim said, wishing his voice had more power, but it never seemed to. Not when his parents were unhappy with him.

"He's a homosexual," his father said.

"Yeah. He didn't exactly hide that fact."

Thomas huffed. "Is that accepted at your school?"

Tim tried to meet his eyes and failed. "Not really. He has a hard time. But you saw him. He's a nice guy."

"He was very polite," his mother chimed in, "but you know it's a sin."

"Not to mention how this reflects on our family."

How it reflects on *them.* That's what his father truly meant to say. But Tim had to try. For Ben's sake, he had to say something.

"Didn't you like him? Everyone got along so well during dinner."

"We're not barbarians," his father snapped. "We don't treat our guests poorly."

"We did like him, *Gordito,* but unless you think he can change his ways, he's going to Hell. There's no way around that. It breaks my heart to think of a sweet boy like him there, but you can't argue with God."

Tim looked at his mother, at the tears in her eyes. She possessed as much sympathy as his father did anger, but was so wrapped up in her religion that Tim knew he could never change what she believed. He wished he could see her, just once, without his father and without her faith, because he was certain she'd be amazing.

He thought about telling them the truth, of daring them to judge him as they did Ben. Those tears in his mother's eyes—for a person she barely knew—would be magnified a hundredfold. Whether it was true or not, his mother would believe with complete conviction that her son was going to Hell, and it would break her heart.

"What do you expect me to do?" Tim rasped. "He's my friend."

"No, he isn't," his father announced, as if it were up to him to decide. As it turned out, he could. "I'll pull you out of school if those are the sorts of friends you have. You can go to a military academy instead. Then you'll regret abusing the freedom we give you. Is that what you want?"

"No," Tim said.

"Maybe we shouldn't have left Kansas," his mother said.

Yeah, like there weren't gay people there too. But what his father said next made his blood run cold.

"We can move back if we need to."

They would do anything to split him and Ben up, and they only knew half the truth.

"You should be going to the movies with your girlfriend on a Saturday night," his mother said.

Tim met her gaze, wondering if she saw the jolt of fear he felt. Did she know? She must be suspicious. She certainly wasn't stupid. Maybe she liked Ben, but while they were laughing through a cheesy Jim Carrey movie, holding hands even though the film wasn't the slightest bit romantic, she had been at home putting the puzzle pieces together. The tears in his mother's eyes took on new meaning. They were tentative, an expression of the pain caused by her suspicions.

"Krista wasn't feeling well," Tim said, his tongue feeling numb. "Girl problems. I only went out with Ben because I felt sorry for him."

"Of course!" His mother sounded so hopeful, ready to accept any other conclusion than the one she feared.

But when Tim glanced at his father, he saw none of that. Instead his father's silver eyes watched him intently, daring him to hurt his wife again. Tim knew he couldn't say or do anything to reassure him. Thomas would be monitoring him closely from now on. Tim supposed he should feel happy. He had always wanted his parents to take an interest in his life. Now they had.

Chapter Ten

Tim pounded on Ben's front door the next morning, having barely slept at all, alternating between anger and despair so often that he didn't know who he blamed anymore. The only certainty was that his worst fear had come true. What he and Ben had together was ruined.

Ben answered the door wearing the same stupid smile they shared last night, like they had won an election or something. Tim hated the reminder of how naïve they had been, so he said something guaranteed to wipe the smile from Ben's face.

"They don't want me to see you anymore."

"What?"

"My parents. They don't want me to be your friend."

Ben's hurt expression almost extinguished the fire inside, but Tim had tried to warn him. No, he couldn't stop feeling pissed, because all of this was Ben's fault!

"What happened? I thought they liked me?"

"They did, Benjamin, but Jesus Christ, they're Catholic! They aren't going to ignore their religion just because you can bullshit about sports or geography."

Ben glanced behind him, checking to see if his family had heard before stepping outside and closing the door. "Maybe they just need some time to—"

"To what? Call the Pope and ask him to change the rules for you?" Tim kicked at the concrete walkway, trying to keep his anger from turning into tears. "I told you this would happen. I told you they would get in the way. How could I have been so stupid?"

"Nothing is in our way!" Ben sounded more desperate than confident. "So they aren't going to invite me to dinner again. Big deal! We just go about things like we did before."

"Do we? We just keep screwing around until the day they find us together? Jesus!"

"I think we can definitely leave him out of this."

Tim glared at him. "This isn't funny! My parents are going to be looking at me differently now. Questioning why their son is hanging around with someone like you!" Tim did his best impression of his father. "Gee, honey, how come our son brought a gay guy to dinner and not his girlfriend? Hm. I fucking wonder!"

"Stop it."

"That's exactly what we should do!"

He hated the words, but he wouldn't take them back. They were inevitable. Ben had pushed and pushed and pushed, and now everything was broken. Tim didn't know how to fix it. No one could. He turned and walked away, desperate to put space between him and the hurt shock on Ben's face.

"Don't ever come back!" Ben shouted after him.

Tim swore to himself that he never would.

The door to Tim's bedroom clicked open. He glanced at the clock without shifting in bed. Just after midnight. Their usual time. Sometimes when Ben arrived, Tim was already asleep, not waking until he felt Ben's body next to his. On nights like tonight, Tim hadn't slept a wink. He was exhausted, tossing and turning and regretting the scene at Ben's house.

He rolled over in bed and watched Ben as he undressed, moving the sheets back when he came near. Ben lay facing him, reaching out to touch his face, but Tim grabbed his wrist and used it to pin him, the anger and desperation rising up and manifesting as hard kisses. Ben fought back, wrestling him and grabbing him without permission, like two mad men trying to violate each other. Then, at the same time, they slowed, their bodies pressing together, the kisses soft again.

"Why does everything have to be so stupid?" Tim whispered to him.

Ben sighed. "I don't know."

Then they made love, comforting each other with gentle motions. In the morning, they didn't talk about sexuality, parents, or coming out. Tim breathed a sigh of relief. Finally Ben had seen the truth, understood how the world would get between them if they weren't careful. They had come dangerously close to losing each other, but now, with this new understanding, they would be safe.

The stereo speakers thumped with bass, family photos shaking on the wall. Everyone at the party was shouting to be heard. Disgruntled neighbors summoning the police was inevitable. Maybe that's why people guzzled their drinks down so desperately.

Bryce's parents were crazy to give their son the run of the house, even if it was his birthday. Good thing the Hunters were staying at a hotel for the night. They'd probably keel over from heart attacks if they could see their home now. Already the house was trashed, the birthday boy not even conscious to enjoy the chaos. Bryce's massive form was passed out in a recliner that barely held him, his limbs hanging off the front and sides. He looked like a giant in a child's chair.

Tim turned the music down slowly so people wouldn't notice. No sense in the police coming before he drank his fill. Once everyone was talking instead of shouting, he grabbed another beer from the ice-stuffed cooler and flopped down on the couch. Krista was across the room, flirting with some guy who Tim had never seen. The previous boyfriend had barely lasted a week, so she was fair game again. Krista had followed Tim around the party until this new guy showed up, giving him much-needed space.

To Tim's dismay, that space was now filled by Stacy Shelly. She slid on to the couch beside him, raising a glass of wine in toast. No one else at the party was drinking wine, which meant she either brought her own or had raided the Hunters' cabinets.

Tim clinked his beer bottle against her glass and asked, "What are we drinking to?"

"Ben Bentley," Stacy said.

Tim shrugged and took a drink, not showing a hint of the adrenaline that shot into his system. "Who's he?"

"AstroWorld," Stacy said next.

Tim shook his head. "I know it's difficult, but try forming complete sentences."

This earned him a scowl. "Molly Desai works at AstroWorld. Although I can't stand her, apparently she has the hots for you. I had the ill fortune of being teamed with her in English class, where she bemoaned all the beautiful gay men she couldn't have. Really, I think the issue is her acne, not the sexuality of her infatuations. Regardless, Molly named you among the elite homosexual untouchables."

Tim laughed and didn't even have to fake it. "Some girl I've never heard of can't have me, and that makes me gay?" But Tim knew there was more to it than that. Stacy had already told him everything he needed to know, but still he played stupid.

"Molly claims she saw you and Ben Bentley at AstroWorld together, and as you know, Ben is the biggest fruit in town."

Tim took another swig of his beer. That had been what… four months ago? They had been so careful the last couple of weeks, ever since dinner with his parents. Now some stupid past indiscretion had crawled from its grave to haunt them.

"First of all, I've never been to AstroWorld. Second, I think Krista can attest to just how gay I am."

Stacy laughed. "So she felt your boner once. Yes, she told me about that, but for all I know, you could have been thinking about Ben at the time."

Tim leaned forward, close enough that he could taste the fumes on her breath. Stacy didn't lean back to get away from him. Instead she moved closer, just the fraction of an inch. And he knew he had her. "This isn't about some gay guy or how far Krista and I went, is it? This about you, wondering if I can fuck as good as you've been imagining. Do you want to find out, Stacy? Do you want me to take you in that bathroom right now, put you on the sink, spread your legs, and fuck you?"

That vicious fire was back in Stacy's eyes, but she wasn't angry. She was ready.

"Fine," Tim said, leaning back. "Let's do it. But you run along ahead of me. No matter what you've heard, I can be discreet."

"So can I," Stacy said. Then she stood. "Master bedroom, upstairs, last door on the right. Bathrooms are for trash." Stacy stood and walked into the party, saying hello to a few people so she was seen. Then she doubled back and headed up the stairs. Tim waited until she was out of sight, then got to his feet and went to where Bryce was slumbering. Tim slugged him in the arm twice, as hard as he could, to wake him up.

"Huh?"

"Hey, birthday boy. Your girlfriend wants you to fuck her. She's waiting in your parents' bedroom."

"Oh, okay."

Bryce stood, swiped the half-empty beer bottle from Tim's hand, and went upstairs. Tim grabbed a fresh one from the cooler on his way out the door. Stacy would be furious with him, but Tim now had dirt he could use against her. If she wanted him to keep quiet about her near-indiscretion, then she better not utter a word about him and Ben.

"Thank you."

These were the last words Tim expected to hear breathed over the phone. Stacy sounded hung-over as hell, but she didn't sound angry.

"For what?"

"You know what," she replied. "I was really, really, drunk."

But not so drunk that she didn't know what she was doing. Tim had seen her out-drink Bryce before, her mind remaining razor sharp, but he played along. "Yeah, I figured. I had a few too many myself."

"Does Bryce know?"

"No," Tim said. "I just sent him upstairs. I didn't think you would mind."

"Of course not."

There was an awkward moment of silence. Tim was wondering if he should blackmail her into keeping quiet, or if deep down she was decent enough that he wouldn't have to ask. He decided to give her the benefit of the doubt.

"Well, I'm going to pop some aspirin and sleep this off," he said.

"Good idea."

Another pause.

"Hey, Tim?"

"Yeah?"

"Would you have? I mean, if Bryce wasn't in the picture."

No, because of Ben, and because Tim doubted he would survive the experience. She still scared the hell out of him, but at least he had convinced her the gay rumor wasn't true. "Yeah," he lied. "Of course I would." His ego grumbled in hunger. "Would you? If you were single and sober, I mean."

"Don't flatter yourself."

Tim chuckled and Stacy laughed before they said goodbye and hung up the phone. Close one! Tim had played it sloppy and loose, but gotten lucky. Stacy thought he wanted her, which should take the heat off Ben. But Tim would have to be smart. The first crack in his mask had shown, and if he wasn't careful, it could crumble into pieces.

*****

Tim was running, and for once it didn't feel good. Fucking hormones! They caused temporary brain damage, he was sure of it. That, and the evening had been one giant adrenaline rush. Summer was fast approaching. Baseball was in regional playoffs, and today's game had been one of his best. When he had met Ben in the park afterwards... well, he had been horny as hell. Not that he planned on doing him right then and there, but they were both victims of their stupid urges.

Ben had been blowing him when the police flashlights shined in Tim's eyes. Now they were screwed, but in another way entirely. In that split second Tim could see his world falling apart. The police at his house, the looks on his parents' faces, time in juvenile hall followed by the military academy. Hell, he'd sign up to be shipped away considering what would happen when word got around school.

Those nightmares only came true if they were caught. Tim could run. He did almost every day, so he doubted the cop huffing behind him would ever catch up, but he still worried he had been recognized. As for Ben, Tim had abandoned him, saying they should split up. He sure as hell hoped his boyfriend could run too, because Ben was on his own now.

Tim made it to his neighborhood with no sign of pursuit. Still he ran, slowing to a jog to appear casual until he reached his house. The driveway was full of cars, none of them familiar. He swore. His parents had that stupid dinner party tonight, plying their favorite business contacts with food and drink. Tim wiped the sweat from his brow and tried to slow his breathing—not an easy task since his insides were sizzling with panic.

Calming down as much as he could, Tim went inside. Thankfully, the festivities were still confined to the dining room. The front room was decorated but empty, ready for the mingling that would follow the meal, allowing him to go upstairs to his room undetected. Once there he paced restlessly. Maybe he had gotten away, but Ben could be sitting in the back of a police car right now, the cops grilling him. Ben wouldn't rat Tim out—ever—but who knew what the Bentleys might say when the police arrived at their door.

-clink!-

Tim spun around, facing the window.

-clink! clink!-

Shutting off the light, he returned to the window. Ben was down there in the backyard, face upturned to him. He hadn't been caught, but his presence here didn't ease Tim's anxiety. He snuck out the front door and hurried around to the back. If anyone at the party glanced out a window they would see Ben waiting there, so Tim grabbed his arm and took him around to the shadows at the side of the house.

"Did they catch you?"

"No. Well, yeah." Ben stuttered. "I don't know. They're at my parents' house."

"Shit!" Tim stepped away from the wall, checking his driveway for red and blue flashing lights.

"Don't worry, they only—"

"Don't worry? The fucking cops caught us screwing!"

Ben sighed, like Tim was being unreasonable. "They don't know about you! They only know about me because I ran into Daniel Wigmore."

"Who?"

"A guy who goes to our school."

Tim's stomach sank. He had barely dodged a bullet with Stacy and AstroWorld. She hadn't mentioned Ben since, but now some guy had seen them going at it. "Someone was watching us?"

"No!"

"How do you know?"

"He was too far away." Ben shook his head, irritated. "I don't know!"

"No, you don't know." Tim wanted to shout, but he didn't dare risk being overheard, so instead his voice came as a barely controlled growl. "You don't know what your parents are saying to the police right now. Who do they think you're out with tonight?"

Ben crossed his arms over his chest, meeting Tim's scowl with one of his own. "Look, I'll tell them I was blowing Daniel. Problem solved."

"They saw me," Tim stressed, his throat raw. "We're fucked!"

"No, we aren't." Ben reached out, like they were about to get sentimental at a time like this, but Tim stepped back.

"Yes, we are. Everything's fucked up." And it would keep

being that way. Eventually Tim's parents would catch Ben sneaking in, or enough people at school would come forward with stories and sightings. He could only fight off the rumors for so long. And like Kansas, all the admiration paid to him now would turn to hate. He liked Ben, maybe more than that, but their relationship would explode into the open eventually. Worst of all, his mom would never stop crying if she found out. His parents would turn their backs on him completely. And for what? It's not like they could get married or have a life together. Ben made everything sound possible, when really, the opposite was true.

What they had together wasn't love. It was an addiction. Even looking at Ben now, Tim's body was screaming to be near him, to hold him, even if it would destroy them both. "Jesus, what did I let you do to me?"

"Do to you?" Ben was incredulous, moving dangerously close to him. "I didn't 'do' anything. This isn't a choice. It's who we are!"

But Tim did have a choice. He had been with girls before and could be again. But not while Ben was around. "Get away from me." Tim shoved him and tried to walk away, but Ben caught his arm and swung him back around.

"This isn't something you can control!" Ben's grip was tight, his words desperate. "You can't just push me away and expect to stop feeling—"

No! Tim didn't want to hear it! "I can't do this anymore!" He pulled his arm away, but Ben wouldn't leave him alone, coming nearer. He knew. If Ben touched him enough, he knew Tim was too weak to resist. He pushed Ben away again, half-blind from the tears in his eyes. "It's over! Go home."

Ben shook his head, refusing to accept what Tim had said. When he tried to come close again, Tim shoved him hard enough that Ben hit the ground, eyes wide as he tumbled backwards. Ben clutched at the grass, staring up at him in complete disbelief, probably because he would never in a million years do the same to him. Tim hated himself more than ever. The hurt and shock on Ben's face was killing him, so he turned away and went back inside.

Of course the stupid party had adjourned to the living room, every head turning his direction when he entered.

"This is our son, Timothy," his mother announced.

He stopped on his way up the stairs and stared at them—all those happy couples, dressed in their nicest outfits and beaming at him over their drinks. Boy-girl, boy-girl, boy-girl. They existed in pairs, and no one would ever question their right to do so. Tim despised them for being normal, for being happy.

"Everything okay?" his father asked, an edge of warning in his tone.

"It was a rough game."

"He plays baseball," his mother explained.

There was chorus of murmured understanding. Of course! What else would a guy be upset about?

Tim turned and tromped up the stairs to his room, locking the door. He left the light off so he could see out the window. There, just off to the side, stood a shadowy form with its head bowed, shoulders shaking. Ben kept standing there, waiting for Tim to come back, waiting for him to undo the horrible things that he had done. But he wouldn't. Tim watched him, one step back from the window so he couldn't be seen, and joined Ben in his tears. Eventually, the lonely silhouette shook its weary head and disappeared into the night.

Chapter Eleven

There were no happy gay couples on TV. No gay president with his handsome and charming "first gentlemen" at his side. Ellen DeGeneres had come out earlier in the year, and the media had exploded, making Tim squirm as much as Ben had grinned. Ben saw it as progress, while Tim felt it was evidence that the world wouldn't accept them, that being gay was A Very Big Deal. He supposed he could name some musicians who had come out once their bank accounts were fat enough to make them untouchable, but Tim didn't know if any of them had healthy long-term relationships.

Ben probably knew. If Tim called him right now, he would probably rattle off a list of inspiring role models. Then again, he never had before, and Ben had never held back in his attempt to convince Tim that being gay was okay. The irony was that Ben *had* finally convinced Tim of one thing, but the price of that truth was saying goodbye.

Tim was gay. He had to be, because his insides ached without end. He had never felt this way about anyone. Krista was more a necessity, Carla a strange sort of infatuation, but neither they nor the girls that came before them had carved their names into his heart like Ben had. Or become so intertwined with his soul that he questioned who he was without them. He loved Ben, but that didn't change a thing.

He couldn't relive Kansas again, couldn't bear the brunt of all that hate. And his parents—he barely had them as it was. They would finally have an excuse to get rid of him, to toss him in a military academy or boarding school and leave him there to rot. Then they would be free to live their lives as they had intended while Tim was left with nothing.

He couldn't stand the idea. Maybe he could handle losing his father, but not his mother or his grandmother with her big open arms. She was just as Catholic and would cry even harder over Tim dooming himself to Hell.

Coward.

That was the word that stood out most the next time Tim heard Ben sing. He knew Ben would be at the high school talent show, performing a song with Allison. They had been practicing for months. Tim didn't want to go, but his friends had egged him on, not wanting to miss making fun of all the losers. But even they had taken a break from flinging insults when Ben and Allison broke into song.

Ben had found Tim, searching the audience until their eyes met. Then Ben sang like never before. His voice had always brought Tim to new emotional heights, but now it smacked him down, cutting him just as much as it had once healed him.

The verses of the song couldn't have been more appropriate, crafted just for him, and *coward* was the word that stung the most. Because it was true. *Frozen* stood out too, but more as sage advice. Over the coming weeks, Tim tried to kill his emotions, to clamp down on his love for Ben. Eventually he began to get the hang of it. He tore up the letter Ben left in his locker that said there wouldn't be any trouble from the police. And when Tim went to his studio, shredding the painting of Ben's face with a box knife, he didn't feel a thing. Almost.

There were parties and there were friends, and when Tim's parents bothered to turn their attention to him, it wasn't with sorrow or hate. That's more than Tim could say for himself when he looked in the mirror. But he pressed on, because that's all anyone could do. Just keep moving on.

When the doorbell rang one evening, Tim remained in bed. For a while he had been on edge, expecting Ben to do something crazy, but he no longer had that fear. Not after the song Ben had sung. A pang of doubt came when his mother called him from downstairs, but her voice sounded much too happy for the visitor to be Ben. He soon saw why.

Waiting at the bottom of the stairs was a beautiful girl, exchanging pleasant words with his mother, to which Ella responded with smiles and happy little laughs.

"Stacy!" Tim said, not hiding his surprise. "Come on up."

His mother made a face, like he was being naughty and she approved. The idea hadn't even occurred to him.

"Not bad," Stacy said when she was in his room, walking around and inspecting the details.

They had gotten along well over the past month. Ever since her drunken pass at him—or vice versa—she had treated him with a little more respect. And she never mentioned Ben. Done looking around, she sat on the edge of the bed. Tim seriously hoped she wasn't here to take him up on that offer.

"What's up?" he asked.

"Darryl is planning to ask Krista to the prom."

Tim shrugged. "She doesn't belong to me. I'm not going to get jealous or anything."

Stacy fixed him with a patient expression. "Darryl," she repeated. "Think about it."

True, it was odd for Darryl. He usually chose from the circle of girls who wished they were popular, girls inevitably dazzled by his status and then dumped as soon as they put out.

"Oh."

"Exactly," Stacy said. "I guess he's looking for a new conquest, something more of a challenge, because we all know what happens on prom night."

"Should I have a talk with him?" But Tim already knew what she was asking.

"Do you think talking to him would make a difference?" Stacy made a show of checking her nails. "Krista still raves about you. A lot. I know men live for the thrill of the chase, so I probably shouldn't tell you this, but she regrets that you weren't her first. I mean, you still could be. She hasn't made any mistakes, but I know firsthand how pushy Darryl can be."

"Oh yeah?"

"Yes."

And even though Krista had never meant that much to him, Tim hated the idea of Darryl plying her with depth-chargers or some other kind of alcohol before putting his toadish hands all over her. So yes, Tim would take Krista to the prom, take her in any way she saw fit. He would smile at her, whisper sweet words into her ear, and make her feel like a princess—but he wouldn't feel a thing. He knew now that he couldn't.

Despite his resolve, Tim still felt a spark the next time he ran into Ben. They hadn't seen each other since the talent show two months ago. Just the sight of him was enough to conjure up conflicting emotions. Ben was wearing a pale green polo shirt with an ice cream cone stitched on the left side of his chest. That he had a summer job now made Tim feel empty, like they were already strangers.

Ben seemed distracted, looking at the houses beyond the bike path. He hadn't yet noticed Tim or the two people he was with. Bryce was on his left. Tim could tell from his low chuckle that he had noticed Ben. On his right was Bryce's cousin Trey, visiting for the summer and also the one to blame for them walking. They were on their way back from buying weed, and Trey was jittery, not wanting them to drive in case they were pulled over.

"Well, well. If it isn't the village faggot!" Bryce rumbled.

Ben was startled, noticing them at last. First he looked up at Bryce. Then he saw Tim. When their eyes met, Tim tried to send him a telepathic message. *Just keep walking. Don't stop and don't respond.*

And maybe Ben would have if Bryce hadn't blocked his way. "What are you doing out here? Looking for some cock to suck?"

Tim clenched his jaw, but it fell open when he heard Ben's response.

"You'll have to pull your skanky girlfriend off the football team if you want that. I'm definitely not interested."

Tim nearly laughed, but then Bryce grabbed Ben by the shirt and yanked him forward. This wasn't good. Not good at all.

"What did you say?" Bryce shouted, spittle splattering Ben's face.

"Leave him alone," Tim said, moving forward to break it up.

"He called my girlfriend a slut!" Bryce snarled.

"Technically," Ben replied, "I said she was skanky. She's also a brain-dead snob, but I guess that's your common bond, isn't it?"

Bryce dropped Ben, causing him to stumble, and hauled back his fist. Tim barely got there in time, pushing himself between them.

Bryce eyed him like a bull seeing red. "What the fuck?"

"Forget him," Tim said. "Let's just go."

Bryce considered him a second longer, then with surprising speed, shoved Tim aside with his left arm and brought a right hook around. But Tim wasn't the target. He heard a sound like a fleshy thunderclap before Ben hit the ground.

That piece of shit! Tim leapt like a tiger, his insides a volcano. He got two punches to Bryce's face while he was still airborne, and had only landed on his feet for a second before a meaty fist crunched into his nose. Seeing stars, Tim punched blindly, connecting with what felt like Bryce's thick neck. Then his right eye closed instinctively before being struck twice. It was like getting hit by a car! Tim put everything into his next swing, knowing he didn't have too many left, and—bull's-eye!—hit Bryce on the side of the head, his class ring connecting with his temple.

Bryce groaned, swayed on his feet, then hit the ground. Tim wasn't leaving anything to chance. He leapt on top of Bryce and kept on swinging.

"Get off my cousin!" he heard Trey yell from behind, but no one tried to pull him off. He turned to see Ben plowing into Trey. Unlike Bryce, Trey was just a normal-sized guy, but Ben was smaller than most. Tim winced as Trey elbowed Ben in the face, knocking him down. He was on his feet when Ben counterattacked, punching Trey in the nuts. Ben was still kicking, punching, and screaming when Tim grabbed his wrist.

"Run!"

For once Ben listened. They took off down the path, this time staying together. A couple of twists and turns and they were in familiar territory. Tim followed Ben's lead, and before long they were standing in the Bentleys' driveway, clutching at their stomachs and trying to catch their breath. Tim raised his head at the same time Ben did, their eyes meeting. Then they laughed.

"Thanks," Ben panted.

Tim shook his head ruefully. "You and your big mouth."

Ben chuckled, his puppy-dog eyes wet with joy before they softened. "Do you want to come inside?"

Yeah. More than anything in the world. But the bloody nose and the soon-to-be bruises were nothing like the pain Tim had felt that night in his backyard. And Ben, so much better than he was, so fearless with his love, must have suffered even more. Tim would only hurt him again, hurt them both. The judgmental world around them hadn't changed. Nothing had.

"Goodbye, Benjamin."

Despite the heat of summer, when Tim turned away, he was certain he could feel the chill of winter inside his chest.

The phone kept ringing. Tim rolled over and put a pillow over his head to drown out the noise, wincing at the pressure on his bruises. His nose was the worst, swollen up like an apple in the center of his face. The answering machine kicked in, and a previous version of himself—sounding cocky and self-assured because the world still belonged to him—asked the caller to leave a message.

"Look," Stacy said after the beep, "you can either pick up the phone, or I'm coming over there."

Tim sighed, tossed the pillow away, and grabbed the phone. "What?"

Stacy recovered quickly. "You know you've committed social suicide, right?"

Tim sighed. "I'm hanging up."

"Wait!"

Despite his better judgment, Tim kept the phone pressed to his ear. "Just tell me what you want."

"I want to know the truth. You and Ben—"

"We were friends." Tim had already given thought to this. He wouldn't be able to salvage his reputation at school. It was Kansas all over again, but he had to do everything he could to keep attention away from Ben. "His dad knows my dad, so when I first moved here, we hung out a couple of times."

"And then?"

"And then school started, and I had my social status to think of."

"Which you should have done yesterday before you jumped Bryce."

"Maybe," Tim said. "Look, I didn't want to see Ben get beat up. He's an okay guy, even if he is gay. There's nothing more to it. If anything, I probably stopped Bryce from killing him and getting arrested."

The line was quiet. Then Stacy said, "What are you going to do? When summer is over I mean."

"Go to a different school. Maybe a private one. I don't know. I won't be back."

"That's probably for the best." Stacy almost sounded sad. "I'd fix this for you if I could, but even Darryl is screaming for your head."

"I figured." Tim sighed. "And Krista?"

"Well, it's hardly going to work, is it? She either has to lose all her friends and change schools to be with you, or she moves on."

Tim closed his eyes. "Which do you think she'll do?"

"Whatever I tell her to," Stacy said matter-of-factly.

"I'm not going to be around, so—" He let the sentence hang.

"I'll plant the seed in her vacant little head," Stacy said, "but I'm not breaking up with her for you."

Oh well. Worth a shot. Tim had done it once before. He could do it again.

"Well," Stacy said, "I guess this is goodbye."

"Wait! I need a favor. I mean, I figure you owe me."

Stacy scoffed. "I don't owe anything to anyone."

But Tim had to try anyway. "Just make sure they don't come down on Ben."

"Do you really think I can control what my boyfriend does?"

"Yes!" Tim gave an exasperated laugh. "You have us all wrapped around your little finger. So will you?"

"Why should I?" Stacy pressed.

Tim swallowed. He would have to gamble, once last time. "You know why."

This time the line was quiet for so long that Tim wondered if she had hung up on him. "I guess Molly Desai was right about the cute ones."

"Don't tell Krista." He didn't know why it mattered. Maybe because he didn't want her to think that everything between them had been an act.

"The last thing I need is her crying about that too." Stacy paused. "I suppose beating up a gay guy is like hitting a girl. At least I'll convince the boys of that and make them feel like wimps if the thought crosses their minds. They won't touch Ben unless they want to be emasculated in the eyes of the school."

"Sounds good." It was the best anyone could do. Hopefully Ben would make it through his senior year without any more trouble. "Thanks."

"Consider it a parting gift. For Ben, more than you, I suppose. Salvaging your social status is beyond even me."

"I can take care of myself."

"Not if Bryce gets a second chance," Stacy said. "So what are you going to do with yourself, Mr. Wyman?"

"Keep on running." Tim sighed into the receiver. "It's what I do best."

Part Two:
Austin, 1999

Chapter Twelve

Tim traced his finger along Travis Kingston's back, playing connect-the-dots with the freckles scattered across his shoulders. The sheets were pulled down to his waist, the morning sun already hot. Travis stirred and yawned, running a hand through his mop of dark brown hair. Tim could imagine him rolling over, greeting the day and stealing a kiss, regardless of morning breath. Instead Travis jolted awake, like he always did, flipping over and sitting upright.

He looked down at Tim, who almost mouthed the words along with him. "We shouldn't have done that."

"But you were drunk," Tim finished for him, flopping on his back with a sigh.

"I was!"

"So was I. So was the whole damn fraternity, but you don't see them in bed with us, do you?"

"Don't be disgusting." As Travis got out of bed, Tim checked him out and wished, just once, that they could have a normal morning. That as closeted as they were, they could recognize the door was locked, their fraternity brothers were sleeping off their drink, and this private moment was perfect for a little fun.

Instead, Travis knocked over empty beer bottles on his way out of bed, scurrying with a panicked expression to stop them from rolling too far along the floor. As if the noise would give away what he and Tim had done—what they always did, but only when drunk.

That wasn't quite true. Sometimes Tim was sober, like the first time Travis had stumbled into their room and climbed into Tim's bed by complete accident.

Right.

"I'm hitting the shower," Travis said, one hand on the doorknob, the other full of clean clothes. He stared at Tim like he was missing the obvious.

"So?" Tim prompted.

"So you're in my bed!"

No one would come in their room at this hour, and even if they did, Tim doubted they would remember which bed belonged to whom. But he knew Travis would stand there like an idiot until he did something, so Tim got out of bed and leisurely scratched himself, giving Travis a good look at his morning wood. Face flushed and jaw clenching, Travis turned his head, refusing to look at him.

Tim had meant to be funny, but now he was pissed. "Stupid hick," he huffed, stomping over to his bed and ripping back the sheets so he could get in. He even smashed a pillow over his head until he heard the bedroom door shut. Then he tossed the pillow aside and groaned.

The thing was, he liked Travis. They had first met as University of Texas freshmen and pledges to the fraternity, the noble Alpha Theta Sigma, the very same fraternity his father had belonged to. What he couldn't picture was his father going through initiation. Most of the hazing was harmless and dumb, like having to answer trivia questions correctly or do pushups. Or race to eat an entire large pizza alone, chugging a beer between each slice. Sometimes they faced sleep deprivation or had to exercise until they dropped. But the worst had been when they were teamed up, handed shaving cream and razors, and told to shave each other completely from the neck down.

Tim had been teamed with Travis, the experience anything but erotic. For him, at least. Travis nicked him so many times, Tim worried he would lose his junk completely, so self-control hadn't been an issue. Travis wasn't so lucky. Maybe Tim was a little too careful with the razor, because when he got to his pubes, Travis started getting hard. Fraternity brothers were walking around like drill sergeants, screaming at each team to be the first, but Tim also couldn't help wondering if they were weeding out the gay guys.

So Tim had started talking about his grandma and her foot fungus that spread up her whole leg, smelling terrible as it ate her flesh. All fiction, of course, but Tim's descriptions were repulsive enough that Travis got himself under control. They weren't the first team done, but they weren't the last. They made the fraternity. Tim didn't interact with Travis much after that until his second year when they were assigned as roommates.

Tim never thought they would end up sleeping together, or that he would like Travis as anything more than a frat brother. Not that Tim's interest hadn't been piqued. Travis spoke with a country drawl, the sort of accent everyone assumed Texans had. In the Houston area, everyone sounded normal, aside from saying "y'all" instead of "you guys." Austin wasn't so different, but in some places, like Dallas, the accents could get just as exaggerated as those on TV. That's how Travis sounded, and that, combined with his freckles, gave him country-boy charm.

Travis often spoke of his family back home in Kentucky, especially his little sisters. He seemed like the kind of guy who would be a good dad, a family man. Or a good boyfriend, if he could accept himself. Only when drunk did the real Travis emerge. He even told Tim once, slurring heavily, that he loved him.

But he didn't. Tim knew what it was like to be loved, and this wasn't it.

Travis didn't return to the room after showering. He would avoid Tim for the day, maybe longer. Then he would get over it, acting like nothing happened until the next time he decided to get drunk. Being in the closet was one thing; being in denial was a completely different game. Fate had found someone even more messed up than Tim to give him a taste of his own medicine. If only Benjamin could see him now.

Tim rolled over and sighed. Thinking about Ben would only make a bad morning miserable, so he closed his eyes and tried to get some shut-eye. He had just managed to doze off when the longhorn jolted him awake.

The longhorn was a compressed air horn, like the kind used at sporting events, that was taped to a megaphone. The result was excruciatingly loud. And annoying. When a fraternity meeting was called, some poor sap would be sent walking down the hallways, blaring the longhorn to get everyone's attention. They had five minutes to reach the main common room unless they wanted to get demerits, and those meant cleaning up puke after a party or other horrible jobs they couldn't even get maids in to do. Being part of a fraternity was about as much fun as being in the military, especially the way Quentin ran the house.

And of course it was Quentin who had called this meeting. He stood at the speaker's podium they normally dragged out for rituals, waiting for all the brothers to file in the room. Quentin was the consummate frat boy: white as the suburbs—despite the fake tan—and decked out in a polo shirt tight against his muscles. When he smiled, his teeth were just as bright as the gold chain around his neck. The All-American Boy look was shared by most of Tim's other fraternity brothers, enough that they could have been clones. Lately, when Tim looked in the mirror, he felt disturbed rather than proud.

That's one reason he liked Travis. That Huck Finn vibe really stood out. Travis was already in the common room, the only person other than Quentin who was showered and alert. Everyone else was still recovering from the excess of drinking and drugs the night before.

"Fund raising," Quentin said, his booming voice answered by a number of groans, Tim's among them. "Stop your bitching! The roof isn't up to code, one of the air conditioners stopped working, and the floor is completely fucked. If you pussies want to keep living here, you'll get out there and bring in some money. No fraternity house, no fraternity."

Tim kept looking over at Travis, hoping to catch his eye. He was sure, from the way he moved his head slightly, that Travis saw him. Naturally, Travis then turned away, which Tim supposed was all the answer he needed.

"We've got a number of schemes this year," Quentin continued. "Some of you will be hitting the streets, selling scratch tickets. People can't win money, but some of them have invitations to our best parties and events, so don't forget to remind them how much booze and pussy we get here. Charm the hell out of girls to make sales, but for fuck's sake, don't give away any tickets. I know how many there are, and it'll come out of your wallet if any go missing."

Tim let Quentin drone on. He knew the drill. Quentin always made up excuses as to why they needed money. It was always the roof, curiously enough, but no one here seemed to remember him saying that the year before or didn't call him on it. The truth was, most of the money went to the parties, but whatever. One week of work for all the benefits they received wasn't bad.

And Tim knew he wouldn't get one of the crappy jobs like selling tickets or working the car wash. Quentin came from a long line of Alpha Theta Sigma brothers and took it seriously. Most guys here just wanted status, but Quentin upheld a tradition started by his great-grandfather. That Tim's father was also a brother earned him major points.

"Each of you will be paired with your roommate. Only one of you report for your assignment. Figure out who's talking to me. Don't both come up here or it'll piss me off."

Tim looked over at Travis, who grudgingly made eye contact. Tim pointed at himself, and Travis nodded. Now Travis would have to interact with him today if they were going to be hitting the alumni for money. That was by far the easiest fund-raising job. All they had to do was talk to some old geezers and listen to their fondest memories or whatever before a fat check was cut.

Tim waited behind a few other guys, and sure enough, when he talked to Quentin, this was the assignment he was given.

"Get out there today," Quentin said. "A lot of these guys still work, so the weekend is your best chance. You should be able to get them all by the end of tomorrow." He handed Tim a list, glancing at it first and smirking. "Eric Conroy is on there. Start with him. He's loaded and always happy to dish out cash."

"No problem."

Tim scanned the list of names and addresses, glad that all were in Austin. Last year he had to drive an hour out of town for a lousy hundred dollar check. He looked up when he reached Travis and grinned.

"Good news. We're spending the weekend together!"

The interior of the 3000GT felt like it was stuffed full of cotton balls, only the muffled sounds of traffic outside invading the silence. Every movement felt deliberate and awkward. Tim had tried everything to make Travis unwind. Music didn't help, since Travis wouldn't speak over it. Any conversation he attempted was met with grunts or silence.

Travis wasn't in a slump. At the last house they visited, he'd been as animated and charming as ever. The alumnus there was from Kentucky as well, giving them plenty to talk about, along with a five hundred dollar check. But as soon as they were back in the car, Travis clammed up again.

"What do you think the trade-in value on this car would be?" Tim asked. "I mean, I wonder if selling it would get more cash."

He wasn't really planning on getting rid of his car. He had taken the best possible care of it. Not that he wouldn't mind trading up, but he doubted his parents would fork over the cash to get something new. Travis was a car enthusiast, jabbering nonstop the first time he rode in Tim's car, talking about tweaks he could do on the engine or cars he had driven back home.

"What do you think?"

"You always get more selling," Travis said, looking out the passenger window. "If you do it right."

Okay. That was a start. "It just sounds more convenient going to a dealership and driving away with something. What sort of car do you think I should get?"

No answer. Tim waited, hoping Travis was mulling it over, but nothing. They were only minutes from the house Quentin suggested they visit first. They'd hit a few others on the way, since Tim didn't want to waste time driving back and forth through the city. Plus, Tim didn't want to ruin a good prospect with Travis acting moody. Now the idea of him returning to his usual chipper self at the next house was irritating.

"Look, I don't get why you can't be yourself around me, of all people." When there wasn't a response, Tim pulled over to the side of the road. They were in the West Lake Hills area, where homes had multi-million dollar price tags. The house ahead was a sprawling one-story ranch with so much land there were no neighbors in sight. "Travis! Would you fucking look at me?"

Travis did, his eyes angry and accusatory. "Why won't you leave me alone?"

"Because if I do, the same shit will keep happening. You'll ignore me for a while before you loosen up again. Then we'll be friends until the next time you decide to get trashed, and you know damn well what happens next."

"It won't. Not again."

"Why not?" Tim said. "We both have the same secret! I won't betray you to anyone. Ever. You don't have to be drunk to hook up with me. You don't need an excuse."

"I don't want to be with you!" Travis snarled, ripping at the door handle. "I want a family!"

And then he was out of the car, tromping down the road. Tim let him go, figuring he needed to blow off steam. Travis was almost over the next hill when he stopped and leaned against a brick pillar of the cast iron fence. Still Tim waited, giving him time. Then he put the car in park, got out, and went to Travis, hearing the sniffs and seeing the tears before grabbing and hugging him. To Tim's relief, Travis hugged him back.

"Until you find the right girl," Tim whispered. "The one who can give you that family. Just be with me until then."

Travis tried to say something, his voice coming out a squeak, but he nodded against his shoulder. Tim hurt inside as much as he felt happy. This was progress, right? Once Travis had pulled himself together, they got back in the car and kept driving. This time Tim stayed quiet, not wanting to push his luck.

"A Plymouth Road Runner," Travis said eventually. "That's what you should get."

Tim fought down a smile. "Do they even make those anymore?"

"Nope. They're classic. Especially if you can get one from '68 or '69 before they updated the body. If we shop around, get a fixer-upper, you might end up with left-over cash."

Tim doubted that. He was a latest-and-greatest kind of guy when it came to cars. But hell, if it brought Travis around, maybe he would sell his car for an old junker. Travis sang the praises of a Road Runner for a while, Tim's focus split between where they were going and Travis's need for a normal life. Once Tim had yearned for the same thing, but he knew now that it was impossible. He could pretend, and would probably have to his entire life, but nothing would ever be normal for him again.

Tim turned his attention to their surroundings before he became even more disoriented. Most of the houses were set back in the trees, with only the driveways and spindly mailboxes indicating where the residences were. Tim slowed next to each, reading the number before driving farther along as the curving roads rose with the hills.

"Are we lost?" Travis asked.

"Quentin smirked when he mentioned this guy," Tim said. "Probably because he knew his house would be so damn hard to find. Left or right?" he asked at a fork in the road.

"Right."

Travis's guess was lucky because they found the correct address just two properties down. Tim pulled into the driveway and parked in front of a separate garage that looked outdated rather than ritzy. The rest of the house was pure money, if not from sheer size then from the complexity of the design. The owner must have gotten the architect high before showing him a bunch of Picasso's cubist paintings. Wood, iron, stone, wire—it seemed any material possible was integrated to create the right lines and definitions. Viewed from afar, Tim had no doubt the house was a work of art. Up close, it appeared confused at best, the white cube buildings arranged together awkwardly. Then again, the design was gutsy and wholly original.

"Whoever lives here must be crazy," Travis said.

"Eccentric," Tim corrected. "The rich are eccentric."

"What's this guy called?"

Tim checked the list again. "Eric Conroy. Let's go say hello."

They took their time walking to the front door, scoping out the whole thing. When Tim rang the doorbell, he expected to hear a bizarre noise, maybe a baaing sheep, but the chime sounded as normal as could be. Nor was there anything unusual about the man who opened the door. He was older, his hair charcoal gray and his build small. His clothing didn't seem expensive, the navy blue shirt and gray slacks appearing comfortable and worn. He arched a brow and waited for them to address him.

"Eric Conroy?"

"Yes. Let me guess. Alpha Theta Sigma."

Tim grinned. "How did you know?"

"Oh, something about your appearance." Eric winked and motioned them in.

Most large houses have a huge entryway built to impress or a staircase curving up to the second floor. This house had neither. Beyond the front door was a comfortable sitting room, almost like a hotel lobby. Practical, since Eric was able to offer them a seat without leading them through his home. Four couches embroidered with gold thread faced each other. A mini-bar in one corner stood near an unlit fireplace. Tim could see a guest bathroom through one door and a glimpse of the rest of the house beyond another. He and Travis took a seat next to each other, Eric sitting across from them.

"Something to drink?" he offered.

"I'm fine. Travis?"

"No. Thank you, sir."

"How polite," Eric said. "Travis, is it? And you are?"

"Tim." He half-stood to offer his hand, which Eric rose to take without a firm grip or a hearty shake—like holding hands for the briefest of moments. Then the process was repeated with Travis, who pumped Eric's arm up and down like a proper country boy.

"It's always good to meet a brother," Travis said with an appealing grin.

Tim wished fleetingly that he could get Travis to smile at

him like that before turning his full attention to Eric. "This is a beautiful home," he said. "Are you the original owner?"

"Yes," Eric said. "I had it built some years ago, before you were even born, I'd wager."

"Did you design it yourself?"

"I had input into it. Why?"

"I'm just wondering if you're a fan of cubism." If this worked, Tim just knew a fat check was waiting for them. "Picasso, maybe?"

Eric nodded in appreciation. "I'm more a fan of his friend Georges Braque."

Close enough. "*Man with a Guitar?*"

"*Violin and Candlestick.*" Eric laughed. "I'm going to have to see some identification. You can't be from the fraternity."

"If it makes you feel better," Travis chipped in, "I have no idea what you two are on about."

"Your friend is wowing me with his knowledge of art," Eric explained.

"Just don't quiz me," Tim said, "or you'll find out how limited that knowledge is."

"Well, you have countless years to brush up on the old masters." Eric leaned back, seeming more relaxed. "To what do I owe this pleasure? Air conditioner broken again? Or is it the roof?"

"Both," Tim laughed. "I take it we hit you up every year."

"Always in pairs," Eric nodded. "Last year it was Corey and Stephen, the year before Quentin and Jerry, if I'm not mistaken."

"Quentin is still around," Tim said. "The others must have graduated."

"Or been kicked out," Eric said, his smile fading.

Tim wasn't sure what to make of that. "Let's hope not. When were you a brother?"

"Oh, don't make me reveal my age. And to be honest, I'm no longer a member of Alpha Theta Sigma—not even an alumnus. I'm afraid you've been sent here as a joke."

Tim shook his head. "But you were a member once."

"Once." Eric swiftly changed the subject. "That accent, Travis, are you from Tennessee?"

"Kentucky," Travis said. "I'm from Bowling Green."

"Ah, not far from the state line, then. I had a cousin from

Clarksville with a similar accent that I could listen to all day."

Eric and Travis bantered on for a while, giving Tim time to figure out the situation. Eric might have parted with the fraternity on unhappy terms, but Tim still didn't understand why being sent here was a joke. A waste of time maybe, but Eric seemed like a personable guy with good taste. Unless Tim was missing something. He looked Eric over for clues. No wedding ring, the gentle handshake, the tidy appearance. On their own, these things didn't really have meaning. There was no surefire way of knowing. But maybe…

"If there's something I can do for you," Tim said when conversation died down, "just let me know. I mean, if you were kicked out of the fraternity, that doesn't mean you can't be let back in. Time heals all wounds."

Eric appeared amused. "Time can also create wounds. Some issues are even hotter now than when I was young."

"Such as?" Tim prompted.

Eric's tone grew serious. "Who one chooses to love."

Bingo. Tim played innocent. "You mean going after another brother's girl?"

"Or after another brother." Eric's smile was bitter. "So now you know why your brothers sent you up here. I was caught in a compromising situation, which I'm sure you'll hear all about when you return. The story has become legendary and no doubt exaggerated. Every year two of you are sent here, and every year that pair leaves empty-handed."

"Things change," Tim said.

Eric shook his head. "Not that much, they don't. Not in that fraternity."

"I'm gay."

"*Really?*" Eric's disbelief was more than apparent.

Tim let a slow, cocky grin spread over his face. "Yeah. Want me to prove it?" He looked over at Travis, one of the stupidest things he had ever done. Travis was already tense, but when Tim looked at him, he shot up off the couch and headed for the front door.

Tim swore, standing to follow. Eric stood too. Lord only knew what he thought. Probably that Tim was playing him and was willing to do something gay for the money, but that his friend wasn't. "Sorry," he said as the front door slammed. "He's got issues."

Tim turned to give chase, car keys in hand, and was at the front door when Eric called out.

"Wait!"

"I really have to get after him," Tim said.

"He won't get far. Just a moment."

Tim turned, but Eric had already left the room. He thought about leaving. Staying was pointless, and Travis was getting farther away by the second. "Come on, old man," Tim muttered under his breath, jumping when Eric appeared one second later, holding out a check.

"What's this?" Tim asked.

"What you came here for." Eric waved the check until Tim took it. "I hope things have changed as much as you say they have. Now get after your friend and be patient. We've all been there, haven't we?"

"Yeah, we have. Thanks."

As appreciative as Tim was, Travis was his only concern right now. He bolted out the door, but needn't have worried. Travis was sitting in the passenger seat, glaring at the empty space ahead.

"You okay?" Tim said as he climbed in.

"Let's just get out of here."

"Yeah, okay." Tim didn't start the car. "Nothing happened. He doesn't know about you. Just me."

"That's not it," Travis said. "Why do you think the brothers sent us up here?"

"Like Eric said, every year—"

"But you and me specifically. They know."

"That's it?" Tim felt like laughing. "When Quentin gave me the list, he only noticed Eric's name at the last minute. Believe me, it was pure chance that we got sent here."

"You sure?"

"Yes! You've seriously got to chill!" Tim looked down at the check. "Besides, we're going to have the last laugh."

"How so?"

Tim handed Travis the check and watched his green eyes grow wide at the sight of a one followed by four zeros.

Chapter Thirteen

When they returned to the fraternity house that night, a party was in full swing. He and Travis had collected eight checks total, and while none were nearly as generous as Eric's, they had managed to scrape together a fair amount of cash. Plus a free meal, since the last alumnus they visited insisted on taking them out to dinner.

Girls crowded the house, the guys being obnoxiously loud to impress them. Tim walked from room to room, hoping to tell Quentin the good news. He lost Travis somewhere along the way, but wasn't worried. The day had been nice, Eric's fat check cheering Travis up and returning everything to normal.

Tim failed to find Quentin, who was probably boning some sorority girl. Not in the mood for the noise after such a long day, Tim grabbed a beer and headed to his room. To his surprise, Travis was already in bed.

"Yeah, I'm tired too," Tim said, finding an old envelope for the checks and stashing them in a drawer. When he turned around, Travis patted the bed. An invitation—even if he appeared scared shitless.

"Oh!" Tim grinned and headed straight for him.

"Is the door locked?"

He made sure it was, stripping off his clothes on the way back. Then he slid between the sheets and wrapped his arms around one hundred and ninety pounds of pure Kentucky muscle.

When they awoke the next morning, neither had the smell of stale alcohol on their breath, nor did Travis jolt upright and give a tired speech of regret. Instead he rolled over to see if Tim was awake, his grin goofy when their eyes met.

"Good morning," Tim murmured.

"Morning!"

"How do you feel?"

For a moment the grin faltered. They weren't out of the woods quite yet. "It's a lot better when I can actually remember what we did."

"I'll take that as a compliment. Ready for round two?"

But the longhorn cut these plans short.

"Another fund-raising day," Tim said with a sigh. "Hey,

maybe Quentin will give us the day off once he sees what we came back with."

They felt self-assured enough that they took showers—separately to Tim's dismay—before heading downstairs to the common room. Quentin was already dishing out new assignments or criticizing poor performance. When he noticed Tim standing there he waved him over.

"How did you do?"

"See for yourself." Tim handed him the envelope. Quentin shifted through the checks one by one, grunting after reading each number. Then he got to Eric's check, which Tim had intentionally put last in the pile.

"Holy shit!"

Tim grinned. "I know, right? Pretty sweet!"

"And it's from the faggot! What'd you do, suck his dick?"

Tim's face fell. "Dude. That's not cool."

Quentin shrugged, still beaming at the check. "I'm joking. I know you didn't go down on the old geezer."

Tim felt heat rising. "Eric's a brother. You shouldn't talk about him like that."

Quentin reluctantly pulled his eyes away from all those zeros. "He's not a brother. Do you know what he did?"

"I don't care," Tim said.

"Well, I'm going to tell you," Quentin said loud enough for everyone to hear. "Eric Conroy *was* a brother once, until he was caught sucking off the pledges. He was taking advantage of his status to blow most of them before he got caught."

"Bullshit!"

Quentin's brow came together. "Are you calling me a liar, Wyman?"

"I'm saying the story doesn't add up. Eric was sucking off a bunch of straight guys against their will? How does that work? If some guy put your dick in his mouth, would you get hard?"

"A mouth is a mouth," one of the brothers shouted with a cackle.

"Just put a wig on the faggot," another said. "Or a paper bag with a hole in it."

Tim ignored them, still holding Quentin's glare. "Well, would you get hard?"

"Hell no!" Quentin snarled.

"There you go. The story is bullshit, so stop bad-mouthing him."

Face red, Quentin stared long and hard at Tim before he spoke. "You're lucky I'm your Big. Now get back out there and finish the list."

"Fine."

"Hey," Quentin called after him.

Tim turned around. "Yeah?"

"Good job getting the queer's money."

Tim shook his head and left, the chorus of laughter drowned out by the drumming in his ears. What an asshole! What sucked most is that Quentin could be so cool. He had sponsored Tim during the rush, acting as his Big. This meant he helped Tim, his Little, get through and avoid the early pitfalls new brothers are tricked into. Quentin did it mostly because Tim was a legacy, but he could be a warm and protective guy. Except, apparently, when it came to this. Tim wanted to believe that Quentin was only harping on Eric because he had been kicked out, but the homophobic slurs were impossible to ignore.

Quentin had met Eric once and seen how nice he was, which made Tim even angrier. He couldn't tolerate ignorance like that. Not since Ben. What if Quentin had been talking about Ben just now? Or Travis, who had overheard everything and was no doubt freaking out.

Tim hurried back to their room, which was empty, then checked out the rest of the house. Only when Tim walked out into the yard did he spot Travis sitting morosely on the curb.

"People talk shit," Tim said, standing behind him. "It comes with the territory."

Travis didn't respond.

Tim's patience exhausted, he left to get the car. Then he took Travis to breakfast but didn't try to make conversation. The tables around them were full of parents and kids. Travis fixated on these families like his future was calling to him.

The day went downhill from there. Every house they visited had family photos on the wall. Wives brought in drinks while the husbands chatted with them about the good ol' days. The background sounds of children playing only drove the point home.

The timing couldn't have been worse. Just when Travis was

coming around, all this stupid fund-raising had come along and wrecked it. Eric, Quentin, all of it made Tim's mood grow dark as the day wore on. When they were finally through visiting the alumni, that anger found a target.

Quentin.

He could have accepted Eric's donation with grace. Here was a guy who, despite being kicked out of the fraternity and treated as a joke, still gave an enormous amount of money to them. And Quentin had stood in front of everyone and talked trash about him like an ungrateful dick. Tim wasn't going to let him get away with it.

Once they were back at the fraternity house, Travis slunk off somewhere while Tim put in an appearance to show the other brothers that everything was cool. He was even friendly to Quentin, giving him the day's checks and asking how the others had done. Then Tim made himself a sandwich and ate it in the common room, keeping watch until Quentin took the envelopes upstairs.

That's all he needed to know. Quentin had the only bedroom on the first floor—a sprawling space on one corner of the building. He wasn't keeping the checks there. That left the second floor office. Tim sat around, watching a movie and waiting until most of the brothers went out for drinks or on dates. Then he went upstairs.

The office door was locked, but the doorknobs were the cheap kind that could be picked by inserting a paperclip into the hole. The brothers trusted each other; such flimsy precautions were only to keep visitors out. Tim picked the lock and slipped inside the office, locking the door after him. There weren't many places to look. Aside from a computer and desk, the office was furnished with filing cabinets stuffed with paperwork. Tim searched those first, finding the section with the current year written on it. Soon he had a fistful of checks, but he only sifted through them until he found Eric's. Then he folded it and put it in his back pocket.

He thought about taking the check to the bathroom and burning it, but he felt Eric was owed more than just his money back. Hopping in his car, Tim headed for the outskirts of Austin.

Tim found himself not in the luxurious front room with its burgundy and gold-threaded couches, but deeper in Eric's home in what was introduced as the living room. One wall was dominated by bookshelves of different widths, between them equally tall and narrow windows that also varied in breadth. A couch and a number of armchairs filled the rest of the space, with thick carpets cast seemingly at random across the hardwood floors.

"Do you recognize it?" Eric asked, nodding to the shelves. "This room is also inspired by one of my favorite paintings."

Tim was at a total loss in regard to both the right answer and the situation. He had imagined speaking to Eric at his front door, but the older man had greeted him with enthusiasm, practically dragging him inside when they shook hands.

"I don't know," Tim said, grasping for anything. He considered the windows, how lights in the yard lit them from behind like stained glass. "It sort of reminds me of a forest, how trees form dark lines and the empty gaps between them glow."

"Exactly!" Eric gently turned him by the shoulder so Tim faced the opposite wall. There hung a painting of a woman riding through the woods, except something was amiss, because it wasn't clear if the woman was in front of the trees or behind them or entirely there at all. "René Magritte's *Le Blanc-Seing*. The bookshelves are trees, the windows— Well, you've already figured it out. Here, sit down."

Tim was directed to a couch, its fabric the same color as the horse in the painting. Eric took a seat in one of the comfortable chairs across from him, cheeks warm and red as if he had enjoyed a glass or two of wine.

"You have an artistic eye," Eric said. "Do you draw? Or paint?"

"Uh, listen," Tim said. "I really need to get something off my chest." He stood enough to get the folded check from his jeans pocket and stretched out his arm, handing it to Eric.

"What's this?"

"Your check. You were right about the fraternity. They *are* a bunch of homophobic assholes." Tim sighed. "Well, not all of them, but they don't deserve your money."

"I take it you heard the gruesome legend of Eric Conroy?"

Tim nodded.

"Well, go on. No doubt it has changed since the last time I heard it."

The idea of repeating the story made Tim uncomfortable, so he tried to present it in the most polite language. "They said that you were taking advantage of pledges, uh, sexually. But it didn't make sense, because the pledges weren't the ones pleasing you. Um."

"I was sucking their dicks?" Eric said candidly.

"Yeah."

"Thrilling." Eric rolled his eyes. "Next time I hear the story I'll probably be sodomizing the entire fraternity against their will."

Tim shook his head. "It's stupid because it's not like there aren't gay brothers in the fraternity. One night I got up the guts to visit Oilcan Harry's, the gay bar in the warehouse district."

"I'm familiar with it."

"Oh. Well, I walked in and almost had a heart attack because one of my fraternity brothers was sitting right there at the bar."

Eric snorted. "What did you do?"

"Uh." Tim scratched the back of his head. "Ended up getting it on in his car. He didn't even recognize me until afterwards."

Eric laughed so hard he started coughing. "And I take it he's not the only one? Your friend Travis, for instance."

"Exactly. The guy at the bar has since graduated, but there's at least one other besides us, and that's a story I'm definitely not telling."

"At least not sober," Eric said. "If you weren't driving I'd offer you a drink."

"Thanks anyway," Tim said.

Unfolding the check, Eric studied it. "I take it you're still in the closet?"

"That's the other thing," Tim said. "I acted like Alpha Theta Sigma was all progressive just because I'm gay, but none of them really know. That was misleading of me."

Eric shrugged. "I've never needed any help in leaping to conclusions." He looked up from the check to consider Tim. "For someone in the closet, you seem very comfortable with your sexuality."

"I've had a lot of practice." Tim saluted. "Proud closet case since I was seventeen!"

Eric gestured for him to continue.

Tim shook his head. "It's a long story."

"Then you have time for that beer after all."

And when Eric came back with an ice cold bottle, plus a glass of wine for himself, Tim told him everything. Talking about Ben again, even saying his name aloud, opened up so many old wounds. Those old emotions, both good and bad, had never left him completely. Even though he tried to kill them—turn his heart to ice—all he had really done was enter a fragile denial. These days he didn't suffocate his feelings. Like the dull throb of a toothache never tended to, Tim had slowly learned to live with the pain.

"You know what the worst part is? I still remember that feeling when we first moved to Texas. All the potential I saw, how my life was going to be bigger and better. When I was with Ben, it was. Everything else was Kansas, act two. Darryl was just another Brody, Stacy another Carla. The only new thing was Ben. Once he was gone, the same boring pattern repeated itself. Even now. Quentin might as well be Darryl or whoever."

"Except now you have Travis."

Tim didn't respond to this. There was no comparison to Ben. Instead he took a swig of beer and said, "What's it say about a person when they know they have a problem but never do anything to fix it?"

Eric smiled. "That they're human."

Tim shifted in his seat and stretched, stiff from sitting for so long. "Man, I've just been rambling on and on about myself. Sorry."

"There's nothing to apologize for. I enjoyed it."

"It's been one-sided though. Tell me about your life."

"Well, I'm usually in bed by now," Eric said.

"Oh! Sorry."

"But if you let me take you to dinner tomorrow, I'll talk your ear off."

Tim paused. "Are you asking me on a date?"

"You think you're man enough to handle me?" Eric winked. "No, no strings attached. Just a nice meal and an old man droning on about all his regrets."

Somehow Tim doubted it would be anywhere near that boring. "Then it's a non-date!" he said as he stood.

Eric walked him to the front door, fussing over Tim being able to drive, but he'd only had the one beer. Life at a fraternity meant he had a high tolerance. He was below the legal limit anyway.

"You can have this back," Eric said, holding out the check.

Tim shook his head. "They don't deserve it."

"You're one of them, and I think you do. Besides, won't someone notice it missing?"

"I don't care."

"But I do," Eric said, shoving it in his hand. "Please. I can't stand the thought of you living without air conditioning or a roof over your head."

They laughed together, and Tim gave in. He would accept the donation, but he wasn't going to let his brothers bad-mouth Eric again. Maybe he could even find a way to stop them telling that horrible story. Of course he would need to know the truth first.

"I'm holding you to that non-date," Tim said.

"You name the hour, I'll choose the place."

"Okay." Tim nudged him playfully. "Don't stand me up!"

"The pretty ones are always the most insecure," Eric teased.

They said goodbye, and despite how crappy the day had started, Tim grinned most of the drive home.

Tim was dozing off when something thudded against the door to his room. From the snort and the hissing laughter that followed, the smart money was on Travis. His country boy crush had made himself scarce the last couple of days. Tim hadn't seen him at all Monday or Tuesday, even though there were little signs in their room that Travis had come in late and gotten up early, just to avoid him.

But now Travis had abandoned these tactics, stumbling into the room, shutting the door behind him with a bang, and tromping over to Tim's bed. Keeping his back to the room, Tim was determined to ignore the racket, but a heavy weight fell halfway on top of him.

"Are you sleeping?" Travis said, throwing an arm around him. His breath smelled like rubbing alcohol.

"No." Tim replied, straining to breathe. Travis was heavy!

"I'm sorry." Travis kissed his neck, his lips sloppy and wet. "I just got a little scared. I want to be with you."

The way he ground his crotch against Tim's back left little question as to what he wanted. They were entering familiar territory, but Tim wasn't eager to return there.

"Let me up. I have to take a piss."

"And then you're coming back?" Travis slurred.

"Yeah." The weight rolled off him. Tim got out of bed, surprised by how wasted Travis looked. His hair was a mess, mud smeared one cheek, and a couple leaves were stuck to his shirt, like he had just crawled out of the gutter. Tim started unbuttoning Travis's shirt, the fabric damp in places with something strong, like whisky.

"You get naked too," Travis said.

Tim was wearing only a pair of flannel boxers, so he wouldn't have far to go, but he focused on undressing Travis instead. Then, dodging a few kisses, Tim managed to get him over to his own bed. Travis wouldn't lie down completely, instead reaching out and trying to pull Tim down with him.

"I have to pee," Tim reminded him. "I'll be right back."

"Hurry." Travis fell backward carelessly.

"I will." Tim left the room and slid to the floor with his back against the closed door. Travis was drunk enough that he should pass out quickly. All Tim had to do was wait.

They couldn't do this anymore. Nothing would change if Tim allowed Travis to use alcohol as an excuse to do what he wanted, to be who he really was. Besides, it wasn't gratifying to be with someone who would only sleep with him when wasted. Even though Tim's body wanted to give in, he was cutting Travis off. They could be together sober or not at all.

When he was sure enough time had passed, Tim quietly reentered the room to a chorus of nasal snores. Travis still lay above the sheets, so Tim took the blankets from his own bed and covered him. Then he lay down next to his country boy and held him—just for a little while.

Chapter Fourteen

When Tim pulled up to Eric's house on Tuesday, another car waited in the driveway. Parking next to the old Honda Civic, he wondered if someone would be joining them for dinner. He was halfway up the front walk when a middle-aged woman with brown curly hair and a plump frame left the house. She appeared distracted as she dug in her purse for keys, a manila folder stuffed with papers pinned beneath one arm.

"Hi," Tim said, mostly so she wouldn't run into him.

"Oh! Hello!" She looked him over once, her face flushing slightly before she continued on her way.

Tim looked back while waiting for Eric to answer the door, nodding at her as she pulled out of the driveway.

"I thought she would never leave!" Eric said. "Come in, come in. I'm running late because she never stops chatting."

"Friend or family?" Tim asked.

"Neither."

Eric led Tim to a grand kitchen. Pots and pans hung everywhere like decorations, all gleaming as if they were polished every morning. Tim noted a pair of ovens, an electric grill, and a refrigerator so tall and wide that a small family could live inside.

Leaning against the island in the room's center, Tim whistled in appreciation. "You like to entertain?"

"Ask me that again next week. I'll be right back. I have to run upstairs and get changed. Help yourself to a drink, if you'd like."

Tim checked the refrigerator, mostly just to waste time. Every shelf was crammed with food. How many people lived here? Eric was about Ben's size, so it was hard to imagine him packing away all these munchies. Closing the refrigerator, he strolled around the room, running his hands along the marble countertop. When Eric came back downstairs, he wore a maroon dress shirt and gray slacks the same color as his hair. A fresh puff of cologne followed in his wake. Tim was wearing the same T-shirt and jeans he had thrown on in the morning.

"Are we going somewhere fancy?" he asked self-consciously.

"Yes," Eric said, "but don't worry. The restaurant is so expensive that it's actually comfortable." He laughed at his own joke before adding, "Would you mind driving?"

"No problem."

They made small talk on the way to the restaurant, Eric just as curious about Tim as he had been the night before. Between asking about his car, what classes he was taking, and anything else that came to mind, Eric gave directions, leading them to a corner of downtown Austin that looked run-down. They pulled in behind a building where a small parking lot held expensive cars. Tim never would have guessed a restaurant was here. Aside from stenciling on a tinted glass door, it had no outside sign.

"What is this?" Tim asked.

"A place where a master works his magic."

The door swung open for them as they neared the entrance. A stiffly dressed maître d' invited them inside, his tidy little mustache wiggling. "Mr. Conroy, Mr. Wyman, please, right this way." The only thing missing was the French accent.

The inside of the restaurant wasn't at all what Tim expected. Eric was right about the comfort. Instead of starched white tablecloths and confusing cutlery, rustic tables were surrounded by plush chairs. Only six tables were visible in the low lighting, each separated by plants or dressing screens to provide privacy.

"How did he know my name?" Tim asked as soon as the maître d' seated them and glided away.

"He asked when I made the reservation."

"How did you know?"

"Your last name? I found it on the fraternity's website."

Tim stared at him.

"Are you surprised an old man can use a computer," Eric asked, "or are you disturbed that I stalked you?"

"A little of both," Tim said before laughing.

"Champagne?" The maître d' had reappeared, popping open a bottle with flair, the cork blasting away into the shadowy restaurant. People were lucky not to lose an eye here! Tim would have to remember to duck if anyone else was offered champagne. Golden bubbles filled their glasses before the maître d' bustled away. Apparently he would be their waiter as well. Hell, he could even be the chef, as small as this place was.

"Here's to new friendships," Eric said, raising a glass.

Tim toasted him, feeling a little overwhelmed. He wondered if that was the intention. As nice as Eric seemed, gay was gay, and Tim hadn't met a gay guy yet who didn't find him attractive.

"So, uh, where are the menus?"

"There aren't any." Eric took another swig, gave a satisfied smack, and set down his glass. "Whatever Jeffery cooks is what we get. You aren't a vegetarian, are you?"

"No."

"That's the one exception he'll make. Trust me, we're in good hands." Eric, elbows on the table, rested his chin on his hands. "So, how are you and Travis doing?"

"Oh no you don't!" Tim said. "This dinner was supposed to make up for me blabbering about my problems. It's my turn to ask you questions."

"Oh, I'm boring."

"I doubt that!"

"Very well." Eric smiled. "I can't promise you honest answers, but give it your best shot."

"Do you live alone?"

"Yes."

"But your house is huge!"

"It didn't feel that way five years ago."

"So there was someone else?"

Eric coughed, taking another sip of champagne to soothe his throat. "Excuse me. Yes, there was someone else. Gabriel, the love of my life. I built that home for the both of us. He left all the details to me, happy with how I threw myself into it. I had just decided to retire, and I think he worried I would become a different person, but I attacked the project with just as much gusto as I did our work."

"You guys worked together?"

"Mm-hm. Our relationship was very much career-based. We were both stockbrokers. Gabriel had the connections and clients, and I had the foresight to invest in little-known technology companies that have now become household names."

"Microsoft?" Tim guessed.

"Among others. We got rich and made our clients even richer. I was happy to become independently wealthy, but Gabriel—" Eric shrugged. "We lived in that house together for six years, and it was one of the happiest times of my life. That's all that matters."

The first course appeared—an appetizer that looked more like modern art than food. Delicately arranged cubes were decorated with sprigs and savory syrups. Tim couldn't tell exactly what they'd been served, but as soon as the first bite was in his mouth, the food was so delicious he decided he didn't care if he was eating poodle.

"So what happened?" Tim asked.

"You'll have to be more specific than that," Eric teased. "My life is twice as long as yours." He peered at Tim. "Oh god, maybe even three times!"

Tim grinned. "With you and Gabriel. Did he run off with the pool boy?"

"The pool boy, yes."

"Dude! Sorry! I was trying to be funny."

"So was I." Eric winked. "It wasn't the pool boy, but it was a much younger man. Gabriel didn't take to retirement. He kept working as a broker, only from home, which isn't the same as being in the thick of it on Wall Street. Myself, I didn't see the point. Once you're rich, what's the sense in getting richer? But what I failed to understand was Gabriel's need for a challenge. Eventually he met someone who became that challenge."

"That sucks."

Eric shrugged but then nodded. "At least the young man was stunningly handsome. Somehow that made it almost forgivable. Why, he could have given you a run for your money."

"Impossible!" Tim said mockingly. This made Eric laugh, which was good, but he felt bad for the guy. "Sounds really shitty. How long were you together?"

"Seventeen years. It was a good run. And yes, for the first few years apart, it was shitty, but I've made my peace. Knowing what I know now, I wouldn't have it any other way." Eric gave a brave smile and tackled his food.

Tim joined him, considering the similarities of their stories. More than once, Tim had given himself the same pep talks—saying it was for the best that he had split up with Ben, because Tim couldn't give him what he needed. Ben had surely found his Prince Charming out there, someone who could be as bold and open and as wonderful as Ben was. Someone better.

Just the thought made his stomach tight. "You don't mean that, do you?"

"What?"

"That you're happy with how things turned out."

"I do," Eric said firmly. Then his cheeks grew red. "Most of the time. Maybe I'm kidding myself. I mean, I still carry his photo around with me."

"Really? Let me see!"

Eric shook his head ruefully and pulled out his wallet. In the plastic envelop that people usually stuffed with pictures of their kids was a black and white photo folded at the bottom. Eric handed it to Tim, and he discovered it was from one of those novelty photo booths. Unfolding the strip of photos, he saw the same two faces repeating. Eric's hair was darker, his face tighter. Next to him was a handsome black man with a pencil-thin mustache. Their expressions changed slightly from each photo, all of them happy, except in one where Eric appeared slightly surprised. Tim wondered if that's the way he looked when finding out about Gabriel's new lover.

"You guys made a cute couple," he said, handing back the photos.

"Thank you." Eric carefully folded the strip and returned it to his wallet. "Even though the relationship ended on a sour note, I don't regret a thing. Do you?"

"You mean Ben? Absolutely not. Best thing that ever happened to me."

Their empty appetizer plates were replaced by an entrée. Tim was happy to see this wasn't so dainty. A drumstick sat on one side of the plate, poultry of some sort but too big to be chicken. Something like mashed potatoes—which Eric soon identified as a parsnip and truffle purée—accompanied by a side salad with so many ingredients that Tim didn't think any of them were repeated twice.

"So," Eric said between bites, "do you carry a photo of Ben in your wallet?"

Tim snorted. "Are you kidding? I was way too careful to have something like that. I don't have a single photo of him anywhere." He frowned at his plate. "I kind of regret that. His face gets a little fuzzier in my mind every year that goes by. Sometimes I worry I'll forget it completely."

"You won't," Eric said. "You may not remember every detail, but most of it stays with you. Have you ever tried looking him up?"

"No." Tim shook his head. "What if I found him? Nothing has changed, at least not for me, so I wouldn't have anything to offer."

"Nothing's stopping you from coming out," Eric said carefully. "You aren't living with your parents anymore."

Oh, yes. Eric had quite a few things in common with Ben. Tim sunk his teeth into the drumstick. Goose, he guessed as his mouth came alive with heavenly seasonings. How could he ever return to eating normal food again? "It's not my parents I worry about. At least not as much as I used to."

"The fraternity?"

"Yeah."

Eric cocked his head. "Which you joined because—"

"Because my dad offered me five hundred bucks if I got in."

Eric smiled. "I'll give you a thousand if you leave."

Tim laughed. "I don't want your money. How is the topic back on me again? Tell me about you. When did you come out?"

"Ages ago. And just yesterday to you. Coming out is something you never stop doing. You start by telling your friends and family. Then you tell new acquaintances or coworkers who invite you out for a drink. Even the telemarketers who call and ask if my wife is home. You don't have to tell everyone you meet, of course, but coming out is something that accompanies your entire life." Eric carefully cut the meat off the bone with his fork and knife. "I've known I was gay since I was fifteen. I told my best friend that same year, and have been coming out ever since. When did you first know?"

"That I was gay?" Tim's laugh was hollow. "The very moment I broke up with Ben."

Eric raised an eyebrow. "You didn't know all those times you slept together?"

"Well, I wondered, but Ben was always going on about how straight guys experiment and stay straight, but what really makes a person gay is who they love." Tim took a swig of champagne. "When we broke up, it hurt bad enough that I knew it had to be love."

Silence followed this statement, and Tim knew the question Eric wasn't asking. Once he realized it was love, why didn't he go back? Tim was glad for the silence because he wasn't proud of the answer.

"I think Ben has it half-right," Eric said eventually. "Who we love is definitely a strong indicator of our preference, but by no means a definitive answer. Have you heard of the Kinsey scale?"

Tim shook his head.

"Basically you choose a number from zero to six. Zero means you're straight. Six means you're gay. All the numbers in between are the varying degrees. A number one might be a straight guy who experimented as a horny teenager or got a little too drunk one night. Likewise, a five would be someone who mostly identifies as gay, but might have given girls a try while figuring that out. A three, right down the middle, is what we call bisexual."

Tim mulled that over, wishing he could have more champagne, but his head was already a little light and he still had to drive them home. "I would be a four, I guess. Honestly, there are probably more girls who catch my eye than guys, but I never connect with them emotionally."

"Fair enough." Eric moved his plate aside, the food half-eaten. "I suppose I would be a five. I had a girlfriend once, and I enjoyed sex with her. But once I discovered guys, I never looked back."

"Then why don't we call ourselves bisexual?" Tim asked, eyeing Eric's leftovers. When Eric gestured he should help himself, Tim nearly tackled the food.

"I suppose it's easier to simply say you're gay, especially if you plan on mostly being with guys. Otherwise there's a lot of explaining to do, or the misconception that bisexuals need to be with both genders to be satisfied. Personally I don't believe anyone is completely gay or straight. There's always an exception to the rule, be it the right person or the right situation. In the future, I doubt we'll use any of these terms at all."

"Nhr-mrr?" Tim asked with a mouth full of goose.

"Never. You'll simply ask out the person you're interested in, and they'll say yes or no. Preferring guys won't be any more controversial than favoring blonde hair or dark skin. We already use the right term when we say sexual preference, but for now people treat it like an identity." Eric sipped at his water. "Of course, that's only if gay people still exist by then."

"Huh?"

Eric chuckled, as if embarrassed. "It's all this genetic research. What if they find a gene that controls sexual orientation? If parents are allowed to genetically design their children—which seems inevitable—then of course they'll want children who can give them grandchildren."

"How is that inevitable? Won't people say it's—I don't know—immoral?"

"Ah, but what a slippery slope! Imagine a pre-birth health scan that checks for diseases and corrects potential defects. If infertility is among them, couldn't a preference for the same sex be grouped in with that? Then—boop!—the doctor flips a switch and the kid comes out straight as an arrow."

Tim blinked. "You're freaking me out."

Eric laughed. "If it makes you feel better, I think we'll be okay as long as technology doesn't develop faster than human rights."

"And you made all your money from technology," Tim said with exaggerated disapproval. "You're to blame for the future being heterosexual."

"My money is also about to buy a dessert that will blow your mind. How does that sound?"

Mother-fucking glorious!

Tim managed to contain this reaction and civilly nod his approval. The sugar-laced dessert and a coffee made Tim sober enough to drive Eric home. Dropping him off seemed too cold, especially since dinner had been so expensive. Eric did his best to hide the bill, but Tim saw the triple digits. So he walked Eric to his door, which made it feel like a date.

"Thank you for a wonderful evening," Tim said.

Eric turned and smiled. "Believe me, the pleasure was all mine. There's nothing more valuable in life than companionship."

Hokey but true, and something Tim had learned the hard way. "I was scared," he blurted out. "That's why I never went back to Ben. I was too afraid of what everyone would think. And that he wouldn't want me anymore."

Eric considered him, house keys in hand. "The more we love, the more we fear. Rejection, or what others might think, these are just the beginning. In a perfectly happy relationship, we fear losing the other person to disease or chance."

"Or letting the other person down. Or them realizing that you aren't good enough." Tim laughed. "Fear and I are old friends. I could stand here all night listing off its different guises. Ben only made it through my barriers because of those first few weeks we spent together. I wasn't in school and my parents were away, so I felt safe. If only I could do the same for Travis."

"Why don't you take him on a trip?"

Tim paused, surprised by the simplicity of the idea. "Maybe I should on the next break. I don't have any money, though."

"I can—"

"No!" Tim said, not wanting Eric to think he liked him for that. No doubt countless people had hit him up for cash over the years. Tim was determined not to be one of them, although that's exactly what he'd done the first time they met. "I appreciate the offer, but I'll get a job or something. Really."

Eric's response was cut off by a coughing fit. He waved at Tim when asked if he was okay, like he should simply leave. "Just an old smoker's cough," Eric insisted. "I need to get inside and have a drink."

"Okay. Thanks again for dinner!"

Tim walked back to his car, thinking about Eric's idea. A trip somewhere with Travis could be just the thing. A place for the two of them, far away from it all, where Tim could show Travis the potential they had together.

Chapter Fifteen

Wind picked up, sending orange and yellow leaves—still moist from the recent change in weather—swooping to the ground. With just a few weeks until December, winter should be asserting its hold, but that never seemed to happen in Texas. Most of Tim's classmates were already bundled up and shivering, but the weather seemed mild compared to Kansas winters. Tim sat on the porch steps leading to the frat house, wearing an old pair of jeans and a long-sleeved shirt, while pushing buttons on his cell phone.

He could never get a strong signal inside the house, but he didn't mind going outside since it afforded him more privacy. Tim checked the time before making the call. Monday mornings were always the best for calling home. His father would be at the office, but his mother always needed time to ease back into her work week. "People say Friday night is part of the weekend," she would say. "Why can't Monday morning be as well?"

Tim greeted a frat brother heading out for an early morning jog and considered skipping class to do the same after the call. He pushed the send button and counted the number of rings before the phone was picked up. This time it was four.

"Hello?"

"Hey, Mom."

"*¡Gordito!* How are you doing?"

"Fine. Heading out to class soon."

"I was just about to get to work," his mother said with a yawn, but he knew she would make excuses until after lunch. "What have you been doing lately? Have you met a girl?"

Her favorite question. "Yeah, too many. I don't know how I'm supposed to choose."

His mother laughed. "With your heart, *Gordito.* You'll settle down when the right one comes along."

That one had already come and gone, as far as Tim was concerned, but Travis had potential. He was no Ben, but then who was? He changed the topic, like he always did. Besides, he had a reason for calling. "Thanksgiving is this weekend."

"Yes. Did I tell you that your Aunt Emily is coming down?

She's had a terrible time with the divorce, but met someone new she's bringing along."

"Really?" A family Thanksgiving was rarer than rare, even when they still lived in Kansas. Usually his parents would go to a friend's house for cocktails or something adult-ish, but with Aunt Emily there, maybe this year would be different. "I wouldn't mind seeing Emily again," he hinted.

"Oh, well, she's only down for the weekend, and I'm making your father drive us down the coast to Matamoros. Emily still hasn't seen Mexico, so I'm taking her across the border."

"Sounds fun," Tim tried, but he already felt a pit in his stomach.

"What are you going to do? Eat with some friends? Should I send you some money so you can all go out?"

Eric was having a party, but Tim hadn't committed yet, saying he needed to check the family plans. "What are you guys doing for Christmas?"

"Your father wants to see snow. Isn't that mean? He's taking me to—"

Tim barely heard the rest of the conversation. Once again, he would be on his own for the holidays. What angered him most was that he kept getting his hopes up, still caring if he saw his parents. Events played out like this every year, and foolishly, he kept putting himself through it. Ella kept chirping happy thoughts into the phone, Tim making just enough noises to prove he was still there. Then Travis brushed past him on the way to class. Maybe there was hope after all! As quick as he could, Tim got off the phone and ran to catch up with him.

"Hey!"

Travis looked at him like he was crazy. "Long time no see," he said sarcastically. "What's it been? Half an hour?"

Tim grinned. "I know. You should stop by my place sometime."

"We live together."

"Do we?" Tim played dumb. "Funny, I never noticed." This earned him a smile, so he pressed on. "My parents are bailing on me for Thanksgiving. Isn't that lame?"

"Mine are being cheap," Travis replied. "They said they could either fly me home this week or for Christmas, but not both, so I'll have to drive up there to see them."

"What is that, a fifteen-hour drive?"

"More like eighteen."

"All that for some turkey." They stopped at a crosswalk, the morning traffic too heavy to cross without the pedestrian light turning green. Tim wished it never would. "You could hang here with me. A friend of mine is having a party. It'll be more fun than a long boring drive."

"Nah, I'm flying up there," Travis said. "Thanksgiving is the only time the whole family gets together. My sister lives in Minnesota and doesn't come down for Christmas anymore, and my brother is heading to boot camp in December. I'm thinking I might spend the winter break slowly driving up there, maybe seeing the sights along the way."

"Or you could stay with me." Tim said it with enough meaning that Travis's expression became guarded. They hadn't slept together for weeks now—drunk or sober—and Tim felt like he was trying to catch one big Kentucky catfish with a shining, spinning lure made of sex. "I'll get a place for us, somewhere away from here. Somewhere secluded. Just you and me."

The light turned green. Travis started crossing the street. Over the idling engines, Tim just barely heard him say, "I'll think about it."

Tim let him go. To catch a fish, sometimes you had to let up on the line before yanking it in.

Eric's kitchen had come to life, pots bubbling and steaming, ovens baking and grills snapping. There wasn't a burner or surface not in use. Eric moved from spot to spot with baster in hand, even when he wasn't working on the four turkeys, but before long he'd be back at the ovens, squirting juice on the birds' roasted skins.

"It's good that you came early to help," Eric said over the din.

Tim glanced at the small army of caterers and cooks Eric had hired for the party. So far Tim hadn't been much use at all. "You owe me," Tim said, hoping for a laugh, but Eric had singed a finger and was sucking on it sullenly. "I have big news."

Eric pulled the finger from his mouth. "Do tell!"

"He said yes." The way Tim grinned, anyone would have thought he had successfully proposed, but Eric understood.

"Travis is letting you take him on a trip?" Eric passed the

baster to one of the cooks and joined Tim at the kitchen's edge, dragging along a stool to sit on. "I know you said not to, but I called my friend about that cabin in Colorado Springs. It's still available."

Tim had checked out the website the first time Eric mentioned it to him. The cabin was secluded and beautiful, perfect in all aspects except for one. "I'm hoping to find something cheaper."

Eric rolled his eyes. "I told you I'd pay for it. It can be my Christmas present to you."

"And I told you no. Get me a pair of socks or something. I'm not letting you spend that kind of money on me."

"The offer stands," Eric said with a shrug. Then he nudged him. "Well, it looks like you have something to be thankful for today."

"It's a Thanksgiving miracle!" Tim said with exaggerated glee.

"I mentioned the two snowmobiles that belong to the cabin, didn't I? Yes? Very well, I'll stop. Who has my turkey baster?"

Eric was on his feet and dancing around the kitchen again. An hour later, Tim finally found a way to make himself useful when the doorbell rang. Guests arrived in droves, many of them men around Eric's age, but a few younger couples came too and a group of rowdy lesbians who kept grabbing Tim's ass and calling him k.d. lang. The guests took care of themselves, for the most part. Waiters walked the room with champagne and *hors d'œuvres,* and soon Tim didn't have to rush to the door every couple of minutes.

He mingled while waiting for Eric to join the party, taking note of the guests' different reactions. Some of the older guys turned up their noses at him, perhaps preempting the attitude they expected. There were a lot of unfinished questions too, variations of "So you are Eric's… ?"

"Friend" was the only answer he gave, although clearly most of Eric's guests had already assumed otherwise.

Then there were the guys who hung on Tim's every word, laughing a little too loud at his jokes, eyes darting down his body when they thought he wouldn't notice. At least they were nice to him, even if it made him a little uncomfortable.

This made him realize just how rare someone like Eric was. He didn't seem to want anything from Tim except companionship.

So far, he hadn't made a move or flirted seriously. He could have been straight, considering how little he reacted to Tim's appearance.

Unlike the guy eyeing him from across the room right now. Tim was used to guys sneaking peeks, but this man was shameless, leering at him even when Tim looked his way.

The man was Eric's age, but hadn't taken care of himself. He was heavy, bearing in weight a lifetime of indulgence. His thick fingers were adorned by jewel-encrusted rings, his suit finely tailored, and his dark hair slicked back against natural curls, a few of which had broken free. If Eric had an opposite, this man was it. Tim couldn't stop looking his way, mostly because he felt his constant gaze. This soon lured the man over.

"Marcello," he said, extending a warm and slightly sweaty palm.

"Tim."

"Tim!" Marcello repeated. "How nice to meet you. Eric said he had a new friend, but he failed to mention how young and attractive you are."

"Maybe he was trying to protect me," Tim said.

Marcello barked laughter at this, delighted at the subtle slight. "He may have been indeed. Well, it's too late now. The secret is out. Are you still in college, Tim?"

Almost reluctantly, Tim answered the basic questions about himself while Marcello shamelessly sized him up like a prize bull. Tim wasn't sure what to make of him. The name sounded foreign, but Marcello's husky voice held no trace of accent.

"I deal in multimedia," Marcello explained, swiping two glasses of champagne from a tray passing by. He handed one to Tim. "Art, really, stationary images or moving pictures. The Internet has revolutionized the way we experience art, don't you think?"

"I'm not really sure." The room applauded as Eric finally made an appearance.

Marcello kept his attention on Tim. "I mean that we don't have to leave our homes to visit an exhibit or museum. We can enjoy all kinds of imagery from the privacy of our own homes, which of course has made people more honest about what they want to see. That's the blessing of anonymity."

"Funny," Tim said. "I've found that the more anonymous a

person is, the more free they feel to lie. Ever read a personal ad?"

Marcello barked laughter again. "Too true. I suppose anonymity makes people honest about what they want, but not what they are. I'm sure you've never felt the need to lie about your appearance, have you?"

"Oh, hello, Marcello!" Eric stepped between them. "So nice to see you. I'm afraid I need Tim's help in the kitchen for a moment."

Marcello bowed as if to royalty. "I've always said, Eric, that everyone enjoys your parties except for you. Try not to work so hard."

"Tell me that again once you taste the turkey!"

They chuckled together politely before Eric led Tim down a hallway. "Sorry for interrupting," he said, "but I didn't want you being taken advantage of. Did he make you an offer already?"

"An offer?" Tim shook his head. "No."

"Oh, he will."

"That guy deals in porn, doesn't he?"

Eric stopped walking and turned to face him. "Marcello has his fingers in a lot of pies. If it has to do with exploiting beautiful men, Marcello makes money from it."

"Don't worry, I'm not doing porn."

"Good, but Marcello doesn't deal only in pornography. He owns a modeling agency, for instance, and you can make good money at a photo shoot. That's what I wanted to speak to you about. If he offers you a job, say no. At first. Marcello goes to ridiculous lengths to get what he can't have. He won't give up, so name an astronomical price. Money begins to lose meaning when you have as much as he does. Play your cards right, and you'll easily be able to afford that cabin for Travis."

"Think so?"

"Yes. Or you can accept a gift from me and not deal with Marcello at all."

Tim shook his head. "I can deal with Marcello. Why are you friends with a guy like that, anyway?"

"Oh, he's not so bad. He does a lot for the community, even when distracted by the latest pretty thing. The charity balls he hosts every year raise so much money that entire organizations depend on them. *But,* Marcello can be pushy. Don't let him be in charge of you."

"I won't."

They returned to the party together, both ignoring a few knowing glances directed at them.

"Quite a turnout this year," Eric said.

Tim nodded. "I'm surprised so many people came. Thanksgiving is usually a family thing."

"Yes, but gay people choose their families, especially when they get older. I'm sure everyone here has parents or siblings they could be with, but there comes a time when all relatives seem to talk about is their children or grandchildren, problems at school, or parent-teacher conferences. The list goes on." Eric sighed. "Sometimes you just want to be around others who are on the same page as you are, no matter how little you might have in common."

On second thought, Tim was glad Travis wasn't here, since this is exactly what he feared most. Somehow Tim would have to give him the traditional family he wanted. "Gay people can adopt."

"Yes, we can," Eric said, "and we have our own special way of doing that."

Eric put an arm around Tim's shoulder. The gesture was proud, affectionate, not creepy or lecherous. Forget kids! As Eric guided them both into the party, Tim wondered if anyone had adopted someone as their father before.

Five thousand dollars. Five thousand dollars. Five freaking thousand dollars!

This mantra ran on a loop through Tim's mind. When modeling for Marcello, he had expected to fend off unwanted advances and have his integrity repeatedly tested. None of that had happened. What he hadn't expected, however, was hard work.

Currently he was posing in front of a lake, wearing nothing but a swim suit while two photographers stalked around him, grumbling.

"Your stance isn't natural at all," one of them complained.

"Maybe because it's the middle of fucking winter!" Two weeks into December, in fact. Shouldn't he be decked out in burly sweaters, posing in front of a Christmas tree? Tim glanced over at Marcello, who was bundled up and toasty in a knee-length fur coat. Where were those PETA activists when you needed them? "Can I at least sit in the car and warm up for a minute?"

Marcello grunted. "The cold is good; makes your skin tighter."

Tim glanced down self-consciously. What was wrong with his skin normally?

"However," Marcello continued, "I think I'll sit in the car until we're finished here."

When Tim glared at him as he wobbled away, one of the photographers gasped happily and began turbo-snapping pictures.

"What are these even for?" Tim said. "Who wants to buy a swimsuit in the middle of winter?"

"Winter is over, darling," said one of the lighting technicians. "At least as far as the industry is concerned. You have to stay ahead of the game!"

"Less talking, more sulking," one of the photographers ordered.

That part Tim could handle. This had been the weekend from hell. He had felt so proud at Eric's Thanksgiving party when haggling with Marcello. Tim had started at ten thousand. Marcello had barely blinked, but still he talked Tim down to five, with the promise of only having to work two days. And Tim had jumped at the offer, thinking he had the upper hand. Now he wasn't so sure.

Yesterday morning was spent being passed around from beautician to beautician. First they cut Tim's hair. Gone were the lanky locks that he had preferred since high school. He loved having his hair long, especially since his father always complained about it. His mother would come to his defense, saying, "In Mexico, men can have beautiful hair too." Sorry, Mom, because now his hair was buzzed short on the sides and gelled into messy spikes on top. They had wanted to give him highlights, but Tim had drawn the line there.

Then came makeup, not just for his face but for nearly his entire body as well. The first photo shoot yesterday involved swimsuits, but at least they had been in a warm studio. Then Tim was put into outfit after outfit, Marcello consulting the list as they went along, naming fashion brands too exotic to be cheap.

In the afternoon, another model was brought in, a guy with

long blond bangs and arms so toned that Tim felt like hitting the ground for some push ups. Both he and Tim were outfitted in the same kind of pseudo-letter jackets that high school kids wore in the fifties. Then they had to get tangled up in just about every position imaginable, the clothing coming off piece by piece. Sometimes they were posed like buddies with their arms around each other. For other photos they might as well have been dry humping.

"Stick your tongue in his ear," the photographer said at one point.

"Which one of us?" Tim had asked.

"Don't worry, dude," his modeling partner replied, bringing his tongue close to Tim's ear. "I'm straight."

"Aren't we all?" Tim muttered as his ear canal was filled with saliva and a barrage of flashes blinded him.

The endless outfits, poses, makeup, and homoerotic modeling partners went on and on, well into the evening. Then Tim went home to sleep. Unfortunately for him, the next day brought crisp clear winter weather, which the photographers loved. This meant he was paraded from location to outdoor location, all of them freezing.

"I think that's it for the light," one of the photographers said, checking a meter. "We'll have to make do with what we got."

"Gee, thanks," Tim grumped, grabbing a bathrobe from a nearby folding chair and stomping toward the limousine. After climbing into the backseat opposite Marcello, he slammed the door extra hard to make his unhappiness clear. "You're really getting your money's worth, aren't you?"

"I always do." Marcello chuckled. "You know, there are less time-consuming ways to make money. They pay better too."

Tim was too smart to ask. Porn was out of the question, and Eric had warned him about Marcello's escort service that catered to an elite clientele. Instead, he pulled the robe tighter around himself and watched the crew outside gathering their equipment. The sun was going down, which hopefully meant that they were done for the day.

"Just one more shoot," Marcello said. "This one on the rooftop with Austin's lights glittering in the background."

Tim sighed. "And me in a swimsuit?"

"In a gentleman's suit, actually. A tuxedo."

That was a welcome change. "Do I have time to grab dinner first?"

Marcello checked his watch. "Plenty, but don't overeat or your stomach will show."

He was one to talk! "Don't worry. After a day like today, I'll probably just drink my dinner."

"Or you can dine with me."

Tim shook his head, attention still on the crew outside. "If we're heading back to your house, I thought I'd visit Eric."

Eric's home wasn't far from Marcello's place, and right now his grounded presence would be a welcome relief. Tim could rely on Eric not to treat him like a piece of meat. Those photographers were brutal!

"I've been meaning to ask," Marcello said. "How is Eric holding up?"

Tim tore his eyes away from the window. "Holding up?"

"Well, you know." Marcello watched him, playing subconsciously with the rings on his fingers. "Or don't you?"

"What?" Tim snapped.

"Never mind," Marcello said, as if the topic suddenly bored him. "Get out there and tell those damn photographers they're riding with the crew if they don't hurry up. I'm starving!"

Tim watched him a moment longer, but Marcello acted as if the conversation had never occurred. If this was some new game, Tim wasn't playing it. Instead he went and told the photographers that Marcello *wanted* them to ride back with the crew. They were furious, but weren't about to complain to their employer. Tim grinned all the way back to the limo.

Once back at Marcello's home—just as grand and ostentatious as its owner—Tim hopped into his car, enjoying the solitude as he drove to Eric's. Try as he might, he couldn't purge Marcello's words from his mind. *How is Eric holding up?* Since Eric and Gabriel split up, maybe? Wasn't that ancient history? There had to be something else, unless Marcello was screwing with him. Even for Marcello, that seemed too childish, like a kid declaring with glee that he had a secret.

When Tim got to Eric's house, an old Honda Civic was pulling out of the driveway. Tim slowed in the street, blinker showing he intended to pull in after it. The car backed out and crept forward in his direction, a chubby-cheeked woman checking him out with interest.

She slowed when their windows were lined up, rolling hers down. Tim did the same, recognizing her from last month. This was the woman Eric described as being too chatty. Maybe she intended to have a long conversation with Tim right here in the middle of the road.

"Are you family?" she asked.

Wasn't that slang for being gay? Or did she want to know if he was related to Eric? Tim barely remembered Eric describing this woman as neither friend nor family, so he winged it. "Yeah, I'm family."

"Well, bless you! I know this isn't easy."

What the hell was going on? Like a secret phrase passed from spy to spy, he tried Marcello's mysterious words. "How's he holding up?"

The woman was exasperated. "I don't have to tell you that Eric is a stubborn old goat! That'll keep him strong for a while, but he certainly won't listen to me. Have you tried talking to him about chemo?"

"Chemo?" Tim repeated with dry lips.

"He can at least give it a try instead of throwing in the towel. I've seen it help people in his situation before."

Tim nodded dumbly. "Cancer," he managed to say.

"I know, dear. It's horrible, isn't it? Well, you stay strong and see if you can't convince him, okay? Do you have my number? You can always call if you have questions or if you need someone to talk to."

She reached across the space between their vehicles to hand him a business card. Tim took it and thanked her. Then he pulled into the driveway and stared at it. *Lisa Ownby: Austin Heights Hospice Care.* This couldn't be right. Eric wasn't sick. He was in great shape and full of life. Besides, he would have told Tim about something like this. Maybe they had only known each other for a month or two, but they were close. Weren't they?

But Eric did have that cough he was always quick to dismiss. Tim knew all about keeping secrets, and the more he thought about it, the more the pieces fell into place. Marcello hadn't been baiting Tim. He really had slipped up! And that hurt worse, because Marcello knew and Tim didn't. Why would Eric trust a sleazebag like that instead of him? The thought angered him enough that he started the car so he could pull out and leave.

But he couldn't. He was pissed and would tell Eric so.

Tim killed the engine and stormed to the front door, ringing the bell mercilessly. Then it opened and he saw Eric—appearing smaller and more fragile than usual against the light. Tim grabbed him into a hug.

"What in the world?" Eric said, voice strained. "Are you okay? Did things go badly with Marcello?"

"No," Tim said, letting go. "I'm just hungry, is all."

Eric's gaze flickered over him with concern before he smiled. "You know I'm always good for a sandwich. Come in!"

Once in the kitchen, Tim watched Eric carefully, as if signs of his illness would be apparent now that he knew. But Eric seemed fine. Maybe that's why he chose to hide it—because he could. Tim knew that game all too well. But it still hurt him that Marcello had Eric's confidence and he didn't.

"Do you trust me?" Tim asked.

Eric paused in the midst of buttering a slice of bread. "Of course!"

"I mean, I feel close to you. Like I can be open with you. I want you to feel the same way with me."

Eric nodded, continuing his work in silence. Butter, lettuce, ham, cheese, mayo. Tim's stomach growled in anticipation. He practically snatched the plate away from Eric when it was ready.

"He works his models hard, doesn't he?" Eric looked him over. "I hope you weren't put in any situations that made you uncomfortable."

Tim shook his head while chewing.

"That's good," Eric said. "Marcello, for the bad impression he can make, is an absolute professional. He was one of Gabriel's friends when we first met, and to be honest, I couldn't stand him. I used to call him the Fat Man. You know, from the old *Maltese Falcon* movie?"

Tim shrugged.

"Anyway, first impressions aren't everything. Marcello might not embrace traditional ideas of romance and relationships, but he cares about people in his own way." Eric leaned back against the counter and crossed his arms over his chest. "I've known him for longer than you've been alive. Sometimes that much history alone can make you comfortable around a person."

Comfortable enough to confide in him that you have a

deadly disease. Tim broke eye contact and kept chewing. Truth be told, there were still plenty of things Eric didn't know about him, little things that he preferred to keep to himself, like his painting. To anyone else, an interest like that wouldn't be worth keeping secret, but Tim needed to because his art made him feel vulnerable. He could only imagine how cancer could make someone feel the same, but for very different reasons.

So Tim would pretend, if that's what Eric wanted. But there were other things he needed to know, subjects he avoided to be polite. Marcello knowing Eric so well made Tim feel like he needed to catch up somehow.

"All that business with the fraternity—" Tim began, but he didn't need to finish because Eric nodded.

"You want to know what really happened. Tell me, is that old gazebo still behind the fraternity house?"

Tim shook his head.

"I'm not surprised. It was practically falling down when I was your age. Anyway, there was someone in my life, another brother. We weren't roommates like you and Travis are. That would have saved us a lot of trouble. Michael and I discovered each other anyway, and occasionally we managed to find private moments alone. Back then I was still willing to compromise. Those closest to me knew I was gay, as did my family, but it seemed prudent to keep a low profile.

"Michael and I were together for more than a year this way, and I have to admit our relationship being a secret made it all the more thrilling. Perhaps that's why we became more and more daring. One evening, during a party at the fraternity house, we snuck out to the gazebo. The weather had been terrible, so everyone was staying in. Unfortunately, we got carried away and let down our guard. A young lady came outside and caught us in a compromising situation. Do you need me to—"

"No," Tim said, his throat tight. "I can imagine."

"Okay. Well, we heard the young lady gasp and scrambled to pull up our pants as she headed back to the house. We didn't know how much she had seen, or if she recognized us. I wanted to leave, but Michael thought our absence would be twice as damning. Instead we returned through the front entrance and tried to mingle. When the young lady saw Michael, she looked right past him, not recognizing him. But when she saw me..."

"What happened?"

Eric exhaled. "It got ugly. There was no discretion. The brothers didn't wait until later to discuss this with me. The party came to a grinding halt and suddenly I was on trial. I didn't dare look at Michael. Doing so would have incriminated him. But I kept waiting for him to come to my defense. All the hateful things that were said that night, being pushed around, called names, even being thrown out on the street—none of that hurt as much as Michael turning his back on me. Afterwards he wouldn't speak to me, privately or publically. Not a single word."

"I'm sorry." Tim hopped to his feet and went to Eric, his chest aching. The story was all too familiar. Hadn't he hurt Ben in the very same way? "I'm sorry," he repeated, speaking now to the past. Eric was in his arms, patting his back and reassuring him that it was okay, but it wasn't. Giving into fear and turning away from love was never okay.

Chapter Sixteen

Snow brings silence. Tim had never become used to the mild Texas winters. Except for the occasional frost or freak scattering of snow, they were just a shadow of the Kansas winters he had grown up with. Every year he missed the calm that snow brought. Most people would stay inside to keep warm and cozy rather than venture out, but the frozen season held a tranquility that Tim never felt when living in Texas.

Holidays on campus came close. Even before the official first day of winter break, many of the students had already made the pilgrimage home. Some lagged behind, trying to keep the parties pumping, but most thought of family, reliving memories of a more innocent time when Christmas was still magical.

For Tim, that magic was back in full force. By the morning of Christmas Eve, the frat house was virtually empty. Even Quentin had left his collegiate kingdom for the comforts of home. Tim woke early and grabbed a quick shower, making sure to be noisy enough while dressing to rouse Travis. Then Tim pushed him toward the bathroom and went downstairs to check the car and their supplies. Of course he had already checked the night before, and triple-checked after packing the first time, but he wanted everything to be perfect.

When he went back upstairs, Travis was clean and dressed, sitting groggily on the edge of his bed. Tim dragged him downstairs and into the car. Then they were on the road, Travis falling back asleep as soon as they hit the highway. That was fine. They had a fifteen-hour drive ahead of them if they were to make Colorado Springs today, and he would need Travis to take the wheel later.

And drive they did. With Travis out of commission, Tim made it nearly to noon without taking a break, chugging energy drinks to keep him going. Of course his bladder nearly exploded, but he held it in until stopping at a Burger King. Finally ready to face the rest of the day, Travis ordered three Whoppers for himself, devouring them each in just a few bites.

"Hungry?" Tim chided.

"Always." Travis downed the last of his cola. Then he said with a more exaggerated accent than usual, "On the farm, we're used to big breakfasts!"

Tim laughed. "Did you really grow up on a farm?"

"No, but you'd be surprised how many people assume I did, just because of the way I talk."

Guilty as charged. Tim loved the country boy fantasy.

"My mom really does make the best breakfasts," Travis continued. "She knows how to keep a boy fed."

"I'll try and make sure you don't starve this trip," Tim said. They would have to eat out a lot because Tim couldn't cook. Eric had helped out, though. A cooler full of food was in the trunk, including a foil-covered lasagna that Tim was supposed to pop in the oven. He was fairly certain he could manage that much.

"Of course, because of my size," Travis said, "people also think I'm a dumb jock."

"You mean you're not?"

Travis punched his arm playfully. "No, I'm not. That's why I wanted to come here. Austin has one of the best schools of pharmacy, and I want to be the very best."

"At counting out pills?"

"Laugh if you want," Travis said. "There's job security and money all right there in one package. What are you going to do?"

"I don't know," Tim said. "Borrow money from you, I guess."

"Seriously."

"Architecture. At least I used to think so. Job security is something I didn't consider. There's not an architectural firm on every corner like there are pharmacies." All he'd been thinking of was combining his love of art with a practical trade, but so far his classes had left him cold.

"Still, good money." Travis nodded his approval.

"I didn't know you were so materialistic."

"It's more about being able to provide for my family, give them a good life."

Travis talked like he already had a wife and kids waiting behind a white picket fence. In a way, it was sweet that he was so family-oriented. But it was also depressing, since Tim couldn't make that dream come true for him. Not the wife part, at least, but he hoped he could show Travis a new version of that dream. He had four days in Colorado Springs to do so.

As much as Tim didn't want family overshadowing this trip, it was the one topic of conversation guaranteed to keep Travis talking. Otherwise he would lapse into long silences, no doubt pondering what they would be doing at the cabin. But this was good. Away from family, the pressures of school, and all the perceived risks, Travis should be focusing on the positive. This would be aided by a couple drinks, a few laughs, and of course tons of sex.

Already Tim had caught Travis checking him out, occasionally shifting in his seat and pulling at his jeans. After not having sex for the better part of a month, they were both ready to go, but Tim would draw it out a little longer, make sure the mood was right for Travis to see it as more than just release.

In the afternoon, Tim traded places with Travis and let himself doze until evening. For the rest of the trip they swapped driving duties every time they stopped. As the roads climbed into the mountains, the ground covered in honest-to-goodness snow, their progress slowed even further. The trip seemed like it would never end. It was nearly four in the morning before it did.

When they turned down the drive to the cabin, their long hours in the car were instantly justified. The two-story cabin was surrounded by a rustic stone wall, snow heavy on the roof and the branches of pines that towered over it. The front porch light was the lone beacon of civilization for miles around.

"You weren't kidding when you said it was secluded," Travis said, yawning himself awake.

"The very edge of Colorado Springs is another five miles away, and Eric says that's just a gas station and convenience store." He reached over to touch the back of Travis's neck, causing him to flinch, so Tim stated the obvious. "It's just me and you out here."

Travis took a deep breath and nodded. "Okay."

"Let's check it out."

Tim found the key in a hollowed-out rock to one side of the cabin, just as the owner had promised. He fetched it while Travis started unloading the car, and was glad he went after the key alone because two tarp-covered forms were also there. Travis still didn't know about the snowmobiles. That would be tomorrow's surprise. For tonight, the cabin was the main attraction.

They toured it together. While appearing simple and homey from the outside, the cabin was state of the art on the inside. Three bedrooms each sported a fireplace. The kitchen was fully equipped, a sauna was tucked away downstairs, a Jacuzzi awaited them in the bathroom and—as if that weren't enough—a hot tub was built into the back patio. Each of these amenities was bursting with potential romance.

But for now, they dragged their weary bodies to the bedroom, undressed in front of each other while laughing nervously like inexperienced honeymooners, and got under the sheets. Their skin touched, the warmth reassuring. Tim kissed Travis, not tasting alcohol for once, and despite being horny as hell, he was also tired. He rolled over on his side, wrapping Travis's arm around him. Their bodies pressed together, he could feel that Travis was hard. Maybe sleep could be delayed just a *little* longer. But even though he thought about it, Tim didn't find the power to move. Travis didn't budge either, and soon their breathing slowed, each breath growing longer as they drifted toward sleep.

Like a swarm of angry bees shot out of a cannon, a buzz blasted past Tim's left ear before Travis cut in front of him, kicking up a wave of snow for Tim to crash through. He slid to a stop and wiped the snow from his goggles before giving chase. After ramping off a snowdrift, launching five feet into the air, and hitting the ground again with a thud, he lunged forward with another twist of the handlebar.

Snowmobiles were freaking insane. The two they had been enjoying all day were fiberglass shells attached to skis, an engine powering the central tread at the rear. This meant they were relatively light and could practically take flight. Or cruise up the steep mountainsides like spiders scaling a wall. There didn't seem to be any limit to places snowmobiles could reach. Or the amount of trouble they could get into with them. Tim and Travis had spent much of the day howling with laughter, usually after falling off their snowmobiles, or more accurately, losing their grip on the handlebars and watching it rocket ahead without them.

Tim's body ached all over and his face felt frozen, so he signaled that they should head back to the cabin. Like a good Boy Scout, Tim was well prepared for their return. Before leaving that morning, he made sure the hot tub was heating up. Sure enough, when they reached the cabin and stripped out of their snow gear, they found a steaming cauldron of pleasure awaiting them on the back patio.

"That's going to feel so good!" Travis crooned. "Hey, what are you doing?"

"What does it look like?" Tim had pulled his jeans and underwear down at the same time. His shirt was already off, his socks the last to go. "I didn't pack a swimsuit," he said as he climbed into the tub with a moan of pleasure. "Besides, you don't have anything I haven't seen already."

Travis turned around to pull down his boxers, but he had to face Tim to get in the hot tub. When he did, Tim noticed with some satisfaction that Travis was already halfway hard. Tim would be on his best behavior, though. He envisioned a very specific way he wanted the night to play out. They still hadn't had sex since arriving here, and it was important that a few things happen first.

Travis gasped and hissed as he inched into the hot water. Eventually he adjusted, sighing and relaxing. For a while they were content to lean back, listening to the bubbles or staring off into the winter wonderland around them.

"This is amazing," Travis said. "Thanks for doing this."

"Thanks for coming up here with me." Tim moved closer to him. "Merry Christmas."

"Man, I almost forgot! It doesn't feel like the holidays without family around."

Tim snorted. "Thanks a lot!"

"It's not a bad thing. Just different."

That was the point Tim was trying to make by them being here. He moved in for a kiss, Travis pulling back a little before giving him an innocent peck. Then he really moved away. "It's been a perfect day. All that's missing is a beer."

Or his courage, Tim thought, but he was determined to show Travis he didn't need alcohol as an excuse. "Remember how nice it was last time?"

Travis was quiet a moment. "Yeah."

This time when Tim went to kiss him, Travis didn't pull away. In fact, he kissed Tim back and pushed against him, his hands delving beneath the water to grab his cock. Tim moaned. Or was it a groan, because he couldn't let it happen like this.

"Not so fast, man." Tim slid along the hot tub's bench to get away.

"Sorry," Travis said. "I'm just so hot right now."

Travis pushed out of the water, arms rippling with muscle, to sit on the tub's edge. His legs were spread, steam coiling off his body. Forget the plan! Tim couldn't hold back anymore. He moved through the water to reach him, Travis's dick at eye level before Tim took him in his mouth. When Travis shirked his inhibitions, he dropped them completely. He grabbed Tim's head, thrusting against it and growling out one syllable words of pleasure. *Yeah. Fuck. God. Ungh.*

Travis seemed determined to pass Go as quickly as he could, so Tim pulled away and stood, feet spread on the hot tub bench. With Travis still seated on the edge, their roles were reversed. Tim wasn't any more gentle than Travis had been. They had a lot of frustrations to work out. When he got close, he glanced down to see Travis pumping his fist, muscles tensing. They were both teetering on the brink, so Tim focused on keeping his balance as he let out a guttural growl of pleasure. Travis lasted a few seconds after he did, Tim watching him in satisfaction, but suddenly he was slipping backward. Tim's fall was broken by the water, his head barely missing the far edge of the tub. Had Travis pushed him? He righted himself and looked at Travis in confusion just in time to see him spit into the snow.

"You all right?" Tim asked.

Travis glared at him.

"Sorry." Tim chuckled. "I should have warned you before I came."

Travis nodded, then cast his eyes downward. "Cold," he said, slipping back into the tub.

Tim waded over to him, wanting to be close. He sat on the bench and slid over, pressing his leg against Travis's and putting an arm around him, but Travis shrugged him off and moved further down the bench. He still couldn't look at Tim.

Cold indeed.

Tim *knew* he should have waited. He had wanted it to be romantic, to have some sense of emotion when they slept together. Instead it had been feral, only physical. But he wasn't giving up. They still had three more nights to get it right. Tim sank into the tub, water all the way up to his neck, getting himself warm again before he got out.

"You hungry?" he asked.

He didn't have to wait for an answer. They hadn't eaten since that morning when Tim drove into town for some doughnuts. Time to heat up Eric's lasagna. Good food, wine, a little candlelight, and music. This was the ritual needed to summon up Cupid. The night could still be saved.

Tim lit the candles and stood back, examining the table and wishing he knew some fancy way of folding napkins. Still, for his first attempt at laying out a table, it wasn't bad. He went to the door, flipping the lights off and examining his work again from afar. The setting looked pretty damn romantic to him. He could smell the lasagna from the other room, the juices sizzling on the baking sheet when they splashed over the edge. Elsewhere the television blared, brief moments of silence every other second as Travis flipped through the channels.

Tim's chest went tight. All of this felt familiar. He didn't have to dig far into his past to figure out why. A night when his parents were out of town and a thunderstorm had killed the power. Ben had lit candles so they could keep eating dinner. He had joked it was romantic, and though Tim wasn't ready to admit it then, it had been. A simple meal together in their private little world. What had it been, frozen pizza? Or something Ben had cooked? He hated that he couldn't remember anymore. Some memories should never fade, should be forever retained in perfect recall, but he supposed all of it slipped away eventually. All but the essence.

"How much longer?" Travis called from the other room. "It smells done."

That it did, so Tim hurried to the kitchen. Good ol' Eric! The lasagna, when pulled from the oven, looked heavenly. Wrestling with a knife and spatula, Tim got two thick pieces on to plates without making too much of a mess. He hurried with them to the table, noticing that he hadn't poured the wine yet. Oh well. He could do it like waiters at the restaurants Eric took him to, uncorking the bottle in front of Travis and pouring a tiny bit for him to taste. Of course if Travis rejected it they were screwed, since Tim had only brought one bottle. He didn't want them getting too drunk. Just a little to help loosen up.

Dinner was ready. A small boom box in the corner played classical music. Tim wasn't crazy about that, but all the other stations were marathoning Christmas music, so classical would have to do. Food served, candles lit, wine ready to flow. All he needed was his date.

"It's ready!" Tim hollered. "Get your ass in here!"

He chuckled nervously to himself, feeling the tension that came with giving someone a present and being desperate for them to like it. Tim held his breath when Travis came into the room, watching his face closely. He looked sort of amused. That was good, right?

Travis laughed. "What the hell is this?"

"Dinner for two, *monsieur!*" The amusement fled from Travis's face. Was Tim's French accent that bad? "Take a seat."

"No." Travis looked angry.

"What's up?" Tim said. "It's just dinner."

"A *candlelight* dinner, like we're a couple or something?"

Tim clenched his jaw. "Fine, we can blow out the candles if it makes you feel better."

"And the stupid music," Travis huffed. "Turn the freaking lights on! We're not on a date."

Tim left the lights off. The food was getting cold, and Travis wouldn't even sit down. "What's your deal?"

"You! You're trying to make this all so… We're not a couple!"

"No, we're just in a cabin alone together on Christmas Day after screwing in the hot tub. Completely platonic. Nothing gay about it, right, buddy?"

Even in the candlelight, he could see Travis's face turn beet red. "You know what I mean! We're not a guy and a girl. You can't pretend it's the same. This is stupid!"

Travis tried leaving the room, but Tim moved to block his way. "Why can't we, huh? What's stopping us from doing whatever we want? It's just you and me here, Travis. We can be anything we want for each other."

"No, we can't!" Travis jabbed a finger in Tim's face. "You can't give me kids! I can't have a family with you! All you're good for is a blowjob, which I can get from any cheap hooker."

Tim shoved him. It was that or take a swing. Travis looked like he was about to charge, but instead he swung around and swiped at the table, sending a wine glass, cutlery, and a plate of lasagna smashing to the floor. "I don't want any of this!" he shouted. "This isn't going to be my life!"

"Right," Tim shouted back. "You're going to find a woman

and get her knocked up, and everything will be picture-fucking perfect—aside from you getting drunk so you can sneak off to a cruise park to suck dick. I hope your future family likes living in the goddamn closet with you!"

"At least I won't be alone!" Travis looked ready to kill. "I want out of here! Now! Drive me back to Austin."

"It's the middle of the night!"

"Then I'm calling a cab."

"To drive you to Texas?"

Travis crossed the room, his face inches away from Tim's, heat coming off him in angry waves. "I'd rather walk back than stay another minute here with you."

"Fine." Tim stomped into the other room for his coat, digging in one of the pockets until he found his keys. When he turned around, Travis was right behind him. Tim tossed the key ring at him. "Take my car. Drive yourself back to Austin."

"I will!" Travis shoved his feet into his shoes and grabbed his coat.

Then the situation got awkward, because Travis walked around the cabin, collecting his things. Why couldn't he just go? But Tim didn't really want him to, not like this. His temper cooled enough that by the time Travis headed for the door, he was sure they could get past this. Tim would ask him to stay, and they would talk everything through.

"Hey," Tim said softly, touching his shoulder. "Wait a minute."

Travis spun around, knocking away his hand. "Don't touch me again. Ever! Don't even fucking look at me!"

Then Travis was out the door, slamming it behind him.

"Don't fuck up my car!" Tim shouted after him. The car engine revved into life, headlights cutting through the front windows before the sound faded into the distance. Then Tim yelled, primal and harsh, because he felt like he was going to explode if he didn't.

For a while he just stood in the living room, waiting for the engine sound to return. When it didn't, he went back to the dining room, turned off the music, and sat at the end of the trashed table. Then he opened the bottle of wine, drinking from it directly and still listening for any sign of Travis returning. Surely he would come back. The dam had burst and Travis would break down and cry, finally admitting who he was. But when the bottle was empty and the candles had burned down, Tim knew hope was gone.

He shoved away from the table and went to the front room, taking his cell phone from his jacket and dialing Eric. He would understand. The phone rang and rang before a recording of Eric's voice explained the obvious: He wasn't there to pick up the phone. Tim left him a message, trying to tell him what had happened, how everything had fallen apart, and that Travis had gone. Then his time was up and the voicemail cut him off with a beep.

Tim tossed aside the phone and glanced around the cabin. He didn't want to be here anymore. The TV was still blabbering from the other room, left on the last channel Travis had landed on. He needed to get away, maybe head into town for something more to drink. Tim was turning to retrieve his phone when he noticed a glint of moonlight on a slick surface outside. The snowmobiles were parked out front. Colorado Springs was what, ten miles away? Twenty? Snowmobiles were just as fast as cars. Tim would be in town in no time, and more important, away from here.

He put on his coat and snow boots, made sure he had his wallet, and stumbled outside, slipping once. The ground was icy tonight, but that's what snowmobiles were made for. Tim revved the engine, hating the machine for being a part of his failed fantasy. Racing up and down the mountains with Travis seemed a million years ago already, a distant dream too bright and optimistic to have been true.

The snowmobile kicked forward. Tim headed toward the highway. He wouldn't follow the roads, of course, or he'd probably get run over by some hick drunk on eggnog. Instead he would cut across to the nearest valley and travel parallel to the highway until he reached town. When he reached open space, Tim twisted the accelerator, the snowmobile's engine snarling through the night's silence. The speed felt like an escape, like he was getting away from his stupid mistakes, the pain, all Travis's cruel words that kept bouncing around in Tim's mind.

Once he reached the line of trees, he slowed, but only to adjust to the new environment. The snow on the ground glowed white in the night, the trees dark pillars, like that painting Eric was so fond of. Tim steered toward the white, zooming around dark obstacles. Maybe he deserved this. After all, isn't this what he had done to Ben? Left him standing in the middle of the night just because he couldn't accept who he was?

Karma was a bitch.

Tim twisted the accelerator, momentarily confused by the way the ground seemed to become a wall. A snowdrift! He hit the brakes much too late. The snowmobile slid up the drift like it was a ramp and went airborne. From this new height, Tim could see he had crested a hill. Even if he hadn't hit the drift, he would have caught air. But he might have had a better chance of regaining control. The snowmobile twisted in empty space, and Tim could no longer see what was in front of him.

He was debating whether he should let go of the handlebars and take his chances with dropping to the ground when the world smashed into him. The snowmobile took most of the impact—a crunching noise followed by a terrible whirring from the engine—but the vehicle was rolling against whatever it had hit. Tim instinctively pressed himself flat against the vehicle as it rolled over him, but still the impact hurt. Something sliced into his right arm, leaving him with white-hot pain that ripped a scream out of him. Then the mess of vehicle and rider briefly spun again in free air before hitting the ground with a crunch.

The wind was knocked out of Tim as he skidded across the ground, tumbling sidewise like a rag doll until he landed on his back. Eyes wide in panic, he pulled and pulled and pulled until air finally sucked back into his lungs. His entire focus became making sure he could breathe, but his nose never cleared. Hand shaking, he reached up to touch it, his glove coming back covered in blood and dirt. That matched the taste in his mouth. Swallowing and then gagging, he tried taking stock of himself.

His body hurt all over, especially his right arm, up by the shoulder, but at least he was in one piece. As for the snowmobile… Tim lifted his head to check and found it had rolled further away. No smoke. No fire. At least it wasn't going to explode. He hoped.

Cautiously, Tim sat up, testing each limb to see if anything was broken. Everything seemed to be working. With a stiff neck, he turned his head to examine his arm. He saw blood on the outside of his jacket and something red and wet sticking out from the flesh. Head swooning, he was sure it was a broken bone, but when his vision cleared he saw a little offshoot.

Like a twig? He touched it and the pain increased, but some bloody bark shed from it. Sure enough, a twig was stuck in him. He looked at the skid mark the snowmobile left when it hit the ground. Not far away was a tree, the snow below it covered in wood splinters and shavings. Tim's arm must have been punctured by a branch when hitting the tree. Gruesome, but better than a broken bone sticking out.

Tim touched the twig experimentally a few times. He didn't think it was in too deep, so after a few steady breaths, he yanked it out. Then he screamed, because motherfucker—it hurt like hell! He let the pain motivate him, forcing himself to his feet and walking in a circle. He was okay. Sore, but okay.

Tim hobbled over to the snowmobile, which hadn't fared so well. A large piece of the fiberglass shell had broken off, as had one of the handlebars. Worse than that, the tread that gave the vehicle traction had torn loose. As much as he loved cars, Tim was no mechanic. The snowmobile was useless to him.

He patted his jacket pockets, searching for his phone before he groaned, remembering he had never picked it up off the floor. So much for help. Tim would have to walk, and he needed to start soon if he was going to stay warm. He hesitated, trying to decide how far he had traveled. His journey out here was a blur. He could be just a few miles from Colorado Springs for all he knew, but in the end, he decided he should retrace the path the snowmobile had made. If he tried going forward while disorientated, he might end up lost or dead. Limping over the hill, he found the drift that had launched him into space and began making his way back to the cabin.

Chapter Seventeen

Cold. No matter how fast he walked—even when sprinting up a hill so fast it left him dizzy—Tim was cold. With no sense of time, he didn't know how long he'd been walking, but now he was sure he'd been close to town when he wrecked the snowmobile. Judging from the way the snowmobile tracks weaved back and forth, he was drunker than he thought, probably since breakfast had been his last meal.

Something else was wrong. Tim's right arm was soaked, the inside of his sleeve drenched, but not in sweat. He was sure he was bleeding from his wound, but didn't dare strip off his jacket to check lest more of winter's death touch his skin. Snow brings silence, and as Tim slipped and fell more and more often, he was sure that silence was coming for him.

Reaching the valley nearest the cabin, Tim picked up the pace, his breath shallow, hardly showing in the air as heat anymore. When he crested another hill and saw the cabin, he made a joyous croaking noise, feeling like his mother had finally noticed him crying with a scuffed knee and picked him up. Tim fought off a wave of exhaustion, his thoughts barely making sense anymore. All he knew was that he needed to get inside the place of light and warmth.

Tim hit the door in a panic to get it open, terrified that he would be locked out. The door opened and he stumbled inside, struggling with choices. Fireplace. Hot tub. Sauna. Shower. That last one sounded the best. Tim stripped as he walked toward the bathroom, every part of him numb except his arm, which screamed with pain. He glanced at it once his jacket was off and saw a mess of dried and fresh blood, but he refused to look further. Not until he was warm and the blood was washed away.

The shower water felt hot to his frozen skin, even when he first turned it on, but as soon as he saw steam he stepped beneath the flow. He ached as sensation returned, blood flowing again and his arm stinging because of the open wound. He tried to keep it sheltered from the water's direct impact while he cleaned it. The wound was worse than he had imagined. The stick hadn't just punctured him; it had left a five inch tear in his skin. Even as water washed away the blood, more was still flowing.

Tim felt dizzy, on the threshold of passing out. He pressed against the shower wall until he was steady again. Then he shut off the water, grabbed a towel, and barely patted himself dry before wrapping it tightly around his upper arm to slow the bleeding.

Please let there be a first aid kit! Tim had seen a freaking apple corer in the kitchen. If they had that, then surely they also kept bandages or something here. He checked the medicine cabinet, which was empty, then under the sink, where a white plastic box with a red cross on it became the world's most valuable treasure. He grabbed it and shifted through the contents, finding antiseptic. How infectious could a tree be? Instead he went for the gauze, covering the wound with every bit before wrapping it around with cloth bandage. He made sure this was tight to stop the blood flow before he taped it.

Tim stared at the bandages, waiting for red to seep through. When it didn't, he looked in the mirror and nearly flinched at his reflection. His nose was puffy and swollen, blood and dirt still crusting the edges. Hell, he felt like each nostril was stuffed full of that combination, but he was too tired to wash anymore. Heading for the nearest bedroom, Tim slipped beneath the down comforter. Toasty. Warm. Safe.

When he woke, the day was bright and the birds were chirping their pretty little heads off. Tim was shivering, but the comforter was still wrapped around him. Despite the chill, he was sweating, his head burning hot. His throat felt like he had swallowed hot powdered glass, so he forced himself from bed to get a drink. Shoulder and arm throbbing, he glanced blearily at the bandages which were dark now. He had probably slept on it and made it bleed again, but he was sure the dressings were tight enough to stop the blood flow.

Tim cupped his hands under the bathroom faucet and managed four handfuls before he decided he wasn't done sleeping. Just a little more rest, and he would get up and pull himself together. He probably needed to eat, but the thought of food turned his stomach. Crawling back into bed, he covered his head with the extra pillow to shut out the light. When he opened his eyes again, the pillow was gone and the room was dark. The birds had fallen silent.

Night already? But Tim had bigger concerns. His entire

body felt like it was on fire. He threw off the blanket and started shivering, his arm throbbing like it had a heart of its own.

"I'm so fucked up," he said to the room, but he couldn't hear anything except the television downstairs, still on after, what? A day? His mind reeled in confusion. Was Travis sitting down there watching TV? Tim nearly called out when events caught up to him. He lay in bed, his breath labored as he tried to make sense of his situation. The cabin had seemed a sanctuary when they first arrived, warm and full of potential. Now the room around him had grown dark and alien.

He would die here if he didn't get help. Tim felt sure of it. If he could get downstairs to his phone, he could call someone, but first he needed to build up his strength. Tim braced himself to get out of bed but instead dozed off again. When he jerked awake, outside was still just as dark, but he heard tires on the gravel drive.

Travis had come back! Sorry for their fight, sorry for the things he had said, Travis had turned around and come back. Tim would forgive him, give him another chance, do anything he could to make it right, and this sickness would flee his body to be replaced by love.

"Tim?"

The voice wasn't right. When it called out again, he realized he hadn't answered and shouted a reply, his throat aching. Footsteps on the stairs, a light in the hallway. A silhouette filled the door before the lamp above him switched on. Then he saw the face he wanted to see most, the one who could make everything right again.

Eric.

"Are you okay?" Eric pressed a hand to his forehead. "You're burning up!"

"I've felt better."

"Can you sit up?"

Tim nodded and grunted with effort, the blanket slipping off his chest and exposing his arm. Eric's face registered shock, and when Tim followed his gaze, he saw the black cherry color beneath the bandages and the crust of blood surrounding them.

"What happened to you?"

Tim smacked his lips, mouth like sandpaper. "I had an accident with the snowmobile. I think I'm sick."

Eric's laugh was manic. "We need to get you to a hospital! Can you make it to the car?"

Tim thought so. Now that Eric was here, his head felt clearer and he realized how fucked up he was. Taking a walk through the cold, even getting cut, that didn't make a person sick. Not like this.

"Tim?"

"Huh? Yeah. I can make it. But stay by me."

Tim managed to stand. Eric left the room when he saw Tim was nude and returned with a bathrobe and slippers. As soon as Tim was covered, Eric put an arm around him and walked him down the stairs. Tim was doing okay. He could stand on his own. He just felt like complete shit.

"I'll bring the car around to the door," Eric said, seating Tim on the shoe bench in the entryway.

Tim leaned back and closed his eyes, flinching in surprise when Eric touched him to help him up and outside. The cold was a nightmare, even though Tim was fevered, but soon he was in the warmth of a car that smelled like a rental. Music was on low, Christmas carols coming from the glow of the radio.

Eric opened the driver's side door and hopped in, putting the car in gear and taking them away from there. "You're going to be okay," he said.

Tim closed his eyes again, comforted by a feeling of home he had long since thought lost.

Warmth. Not the overbearing heat of a fever or the chilling bite of cold. Just warmth in perfect balance, inside and out. Tim's head hummed with a familiar sensation, the blissful kiss of opiates. He hadn't felt this high since Ben jacked up his ankle.

Tim opened his eyes, expecting to see his foot in a cast and Ben sitting next to the hospital bed, jangling the keys of his 3000GT. He was nearly right. The person seated there was about the same size but a good deal older, calmly reading a newspaper folded in half.

Tim's memory was muddled. He remembered Eric taking him to the hospital and not having to wait in the emergency room for once. A nurse, or maybe it was a doctor, gave Tim something that chased away the pain. And consciousness. Then there were brief flashes of waking up to see Eric's concerned face, much like now, his brow crinkled up even as he read.

"Hey," Tim said.

Eric moved the newspaper to his lap, looking somewhat relieved. "Hey! How are you?"

"Good." Tim raised his head to look himself over. He was wearing a horrible hospital robe. He started to lift the sleeve so he could check out his arm when he noticed the tube stuck into his hand. "Oh, man! These things creep me out!"

"That's how they fed you breakfast," Eric teased. "Lunch too."

Tim's head swam. "Have I been out that long? What day is it?"

"The twenty-eighth." Eric checked his watch. "Almost four in the afternoon."

"Well, that's three days of my life gone."

"I'm glad it wasn't more." Eric moved the chair closer to the bed, turning it so he was facing Tim. "What happened to you? I got your call about Travis and kept calling you back. When you still weren't answering the next day, I caught the next flight."

"Sorry," Tim said. "Once Travis left I made some stupid decisions. I feel bad making you come all this way."

Eric shook his head as if it didn't matter. "On the phone you said you had a fight with Travis and he left. Sounds serious."

"Permanent," Tim corrected. "Travis chose fear. I don't think there's any hope at this point. I really don't."

"I'm sorry." Eric leaned back, glancing out the window where two birds swooped through the air, chasing each other. "Do you love him?"

Tim swallowed. "No. I don't think so. But I could have, you know? He's the first person since Ben who could have meant something. I thought I understood where he was coming from, but I guess not."

Eric, to his credit, didn't lecture Tim about other fish in the sea. Instead he nodded at Tim's upper arm. "What happened there? The doctor pulled out a lot of splinters."

Tim remembered the injury and checked it out. The area was clean now, purple from bruising, and stitched up with black thread. He was going to have one hell of a scar. He pulled the robe sleeve over the injury and found Eric still waiting for an answer. "I sort of downed a bottle of wine and thought I'd take one of the snowmobiles through the woods to town. It's still out there somewhere. Trashed."

Eric closed his eyes and shook his head.

"I'll pay for the damages," Tim said quickly.

"I don't care about the snowmobile," Eric said with a glare. "You could have killed yourself!"

"I wasn't trying to," Tim said. "I mean, I'm not suicidal or anything."

"No, you're just young. And stupid." Eric exhaled his worry and took Tim's hand. "Don't worry. Love, or even just infatuation, has a diminishing effect on intelligence. It's lucky you still remember how to speak."

Tim made some ape noises to show how far gone he was. Eric laughed.

"Next time I plan a romantic get-away," Tim said, "I'm taking you with me instead. Forget the stupid frat boys." He didn't care how Eric took this. He wasn't even sure what he meant. Tim just knew there was one person in his life most worthy of spending time with, which he intended to do.

"I'm flattered," Eric said, comically fanning himself with his newspaper as if he were overheating. "If you insist on courting me, you can start by inviting me to dinner. I understand this establishment has won Michelin Stars for its phenomenal Jell-O *a la carte!*"

Tim grinned at him. "It's a deal."

The doctor insisted on keeping Tim another day, rambling on about aspiration pneumonia and intravenous antibiotics to silence any protests. Apparently Tim had sucked some nasty stuff into his lungs during the wreck—probably the dirt and blood that also clogged his nose—and was lucky not to have infected lungs drowning in pus, or something like that. Rather than suffer more nauseating details, Tim agreed to treatment.

Soon Tim was bored out of his mind, especially after Eric left to stay at the cabin for the night. Television, Tim's only distraction, was turning his mind to soup when Eric returned with a Mylar balloon tied to a teddy bear.

"This is embarrassing," Tim said, scowling at the bear but secretly loving it. He just couldn't imagine bringing it back to the frat house.

"Well, maybe you'll like this better." Eric handed him a book on Japanese sports cars. "I also bought myself something to read."

"You don't have to stick around here all day," Tim said, not meaning it.

"What else am I going to do?" Eric settled down into the chair by his bed. "I already straightened up the cabin. Shame about the lasagna."

"Travis," Tim said, happy to shift the blame. "Sorry it went to waste."

"Not a problem. I spoke to Robert, the owner of the cabin, and told him about the snowmobile. Do you think you can give him a rough idea where you left it?"

"Sort of." Tim's face flushed. "I'll pay for everything. I still have some of Marcello's money left."

"It'll be fine," Eric said.

"How much does a snowmobile cost?"

"Oh, around eight thousand I think."

Tim let his head thump back on the pillow. "Think I can still model with a big ugly scar running down my arm?"

Eric chuckled. "I hope not. Once was enough."

"True."

They chatted for a while, Tim happy for a sympathetic ear. Then they settled down like an old married couple and read together. Tim flipped through his book, but his eyes kept returning to the cover of Eric's. The painting on the front was of a woman sitting on a bed and looking out a window. The subject matter wasn't the most interesting, but the way daylight flooded into the room made it exceptional.

"What is that?" Tim asked, setting down his book.

"Edward Hopper," Eric replied. "You probably know the—"

"Café painting, yeah. I never really liked that one, but the painting on the front… Can I see it?"

Eric handed him the book, waiting patiently while Tim browsed. Inside were more paintings like the one on the cover—simple, clean, and almost always featuring light bathing a wall or pressing against the night's darkness. Tim lost himself in the book, embarrassed when he finally came back to find Eric still watching him.

"He's good, isn't he?"

Tim laughed. "He's brilliant!"

"I'd love to own one of his paintings," Eric said wistfully.

"Why don't you?"

"Because they cost quite a bit more than your average snowmobile." Eric winked. "You really like art, don't you? Have you ever tried?"

"Painting?" Tim licked his lips. Why not? Without Eric, he might have croaked in that cabin all miserable and alone. "Yeah. I paint."

"Really?" Eric sat up straight. "Are you any good?"

Tim just laughed.

"Regardless, I'd like to see," Eric said. "If you don't mind."

Tim did mind. Sharing his paintings was a huge deal to him, but he thought he could trust Eric. "They're all at my parents' house. I haven't painted in ages. A frat house isn't the most inspirational environment. And I'm sort of private about the whole thing."

"Oh."

Eric sounded disappointed, so Tim was quick to add, "Next time I visit my folks, I'll grab a few of the less embarrassing ones to show you."

"That would be nice."

The nurse barged in to the room with Tim's lunch, and Eric headed to the cafeteria to fend for himself. In the afternoon, the doctor came in and finally cleared Tim for takeoff. Eric dialed a number on his cell phone and conjured up some plane tickets to get them home that evening. Tim felt even more in his debt, not that Eric seemed to expect the slightest hint of gratitude for what he was doing. But Tim would find a way to pay him back. If not financially, then somehow.

Chapter Eighteen

A new year always brought change, and Tim suspected most of that would happen at the frat house. Maybe that's why he avoided returning to campus. He had only shown up once at night, shortly after he and Eric had returned, to pick up his car. It was there, no worse for wear. In fact, there was no sign Travis had driven it at all, which Tim found disappointing. A letter of some sort would have been nice, or maybe a lonely rose on the passenger seat or dried tears on the steering wheel. But there was nothing. Tim drove the car back to Eric's house, where he stayed in one of the guest rooms.

Life was good for that solitary week. Eric cooked for him or took him out for dinner. In between meals they hung out around the house and talked or went for little walks in the neighborhood. Then New Year's Eve came, with it one of Eric's famous parties, and the calm serenity was chased away by drunken revelry.

This fantasy life of luxury and wealth couldn't go on forever. On the first of the year, Tim made an appearance at the frat house. No one questioned where he had been, since most of the brothers were still gone for the holidays. When Tim entered his room, he wasn't surprised to see changes. His side was much the same, but the family photo was gone from Travis's nightstand, replaced by a basketball trophy. A number of cardboard boxes were in various states of being unpacked.

A tall redheaded guy named Rick came in shortly afterwards. Tim had seen him around the house before, but didn't know much about him. They made small talk before Tim wandered downstairs to hang out in the common room. A lot of the guys were smoking pot to cure their hangovers. Tim ignored them, sitting on the couch and staring blankly at the television until Quentin plopped down next to him.

"Hey, Little. Have a good holiday?"

Tim nodded. "Not bad. You?"

"My sister's a bitch and my mom can't cook. Same as every year."

Tim laughed, but mostly because he was expected to.

"Did you see Rick is your new roommate?"

"Yeah," Tim turned his attention back to the television.

Quentin dug in his pocket for his chewing tobacco. "Travis asked to be reassigned the second he saw me. Looked sort of pissed."

Tim shrugged. "I guess I snore."

"Is that it? He wouldn't say."

"I don't know. He's so damn quiet. It'll be nice to have someone I can actually talk to."

"Yeah," Quentin said after watching him a moment longer. "Travis is kind of reserved. I'm surprised he made it through hazing. Hey, did you get any last night?"

"Just your mom," Tim said, laughing when Quentin slugged him. And just like that, the topic had blown over. A little casual banter was all it took.

Life returned to normal after that. Occasionally Tim saw Travis around the house, but they managed never to be in the same room. It was back to going to classes, getting ripped at parties, and hanging out with Eric on quiet nights when he wouldn't be missed. Tim passed the rest of the winter this way, comfortable in the routine.

Until the day he saw her.

Tim had come from his boring Mechanics of Materials class, eager to get out into the spring weather, when he noticed his shoe was untied. Someone walked by him, singing to herself while he stooped and tied the lace, her tune vaguely familiar. When he stood, he saw a tall black woman further down the hall but didn't think much about it until she looked back. Then he froze.

Allison Cross.

She was older, naturally, and even more beautiful. She could almost be a different woman, but the way her eyes widened slightly before she turned away from him gave her away.

"Hey!" Tim chased after her, nearly running to catch up. "Allison, wait!"

Allison stopped, looked up at the heavens, and sighed. Then she turned around to face him, cradling a couple books against her chest.

"Hey!" he said, smiling at her. The gesture wasn't returned. "Long time no see."

Allison nodded slowly. "There's a reason for that, isn't there?"

"Yeah," Tim said, growing serious. "How is he?"

"Ben?" Allison looked smug. "He's great!"

"That's good," Tim said. "I mean, that's what I hoped. Man, I can't believe you go to school here. Does Ben—"

"Chicago," Allison said, anticipating the question. "Other side of the country. Very, very, far away from here."

"Yeah, okay," Tim said, trying to laugh it off. "Don't worry. It's not like I'm going to track him down and ruin his life again. He's better off without me."

This earned him a little sympathy. "There's a music college up there," Allison said in more civil tones. "He's still singing away with that beautiful voice of his."

Just the thought of Ben's voice made Tim's heart ache. "What about you? I remember you belting out a tune or two." *That's* what she had been singing under her breath. The song she and Ben had performed together at the talent show, the one with the lyrics designed to cut him up inside.

"I still sing," Allison said, "but I don't plan on making a career out of it. Well, it was nice seeing you."

"Wait!" Tim hated how desperate he sounded. "Did Ben ever… I mean, he found someone, right?"

Allison chewed her bottom lip. Normally her answers came fast and snappy. "He moved on," she said. "Eventually."

But did Ben have someone new? If he did, then surely Allison would have said something. "As long as he's okay. Too bad you guys don't live closer together. It's hard to picture you being apart."

Allison smiled, and this time it wasn't smug or sarcastic. "I still manage to see him occasionally. On the holidays and such."

"That's good. Well, tell him I said 'hi' next time you talk." Tim hesitated. "Do you think that's a good idea?"

"Probably not."

They laughed together, exchanged a few more pleasantries, and went their separate ways. When Tim left the building and walked outside, the birds were singing and a breeze rustled his hair. He felt lighter than he had in a long time. Benjamin Bentley, up in Chicago and taking the city by storm! It had been so long since Tim had heard anything new about Ben. The last few times he had seen him—well, none of them had been exactly positive. But now he had something new to picture, a happier ending for the greatest love of his life. Tim hopped in his car and headed over to Eric's, eager to tell him all about it.

*****

"Allison Cross!" Tim said for about the ninetieth time.

"A very exciting development," Eric said. He'd already heard the whole story, Tim retelling some parts of it twice. Eric had listened patiently, eyes closed as he soaked up the sun next to the private pool behind the house. The weather wasn't warm enough for swimming, but being outside felt good.

Tim resisted saying Allison's name aloud again. He'd already made her sound like a celebrity. "It's just that she's connected to Ben," he explained. "Sometimes that whole year I had with him feels unreal, like a story I convinced myself was true."

Eric smiled. "But it *was* real, and there's no reason you can't have that again."

Tim shifted on the patio chair. "With Ben?"

"Why not? Have you thought about contacting him? You know where he is now."

"Allison said he had moved on."

"So have you. I'm pretty sure you don't cry yourself to sleep every night over Ben, and I doubt he has a dart board with your photo on it."

Tim frowned. "Yeah, but *I* left *him*. Maybe he's not angry anymore, but I doubt he's forgiven me. I mean, if Travis showed up here out of the blue, I wouldn't give him a second chance."

Eric opened his eyes and considered him. "Don't compare yourself to Travis. You might not have been perfect, but you gave Ben a year of your life, and it was more than just physical. That's completely different than drunken sex and a cold shoulder the next morning."

"I guess so." Tim thought about it. "What if Gabriel came back into your life and said he regretted leaving you?"

Eric's cheeks flushed, but he smiled. "Don't think I haven't fantasized about that. I'm sure Ben has too."

"Yeah?"

"I can almost guarantee it."

This made Tim entertain several fantasies of his own. He had never dreamed he'd have another chance with Ben. Lightning didn't strike twice, did it?

"A lot has changed," Eric prompted.

Tim snorted. "Hardly. I'm still in the closet. It's just that I've gotten really comfortable with the idea of being there. Besides, Chicago isn't exactly close."

"A thousand miles is nothing in the name of—" Eric's voice caught as he started coughing, a fit that lasted almost five minutes. This had been happening more and more recently. Tim was getting worried, but Eric still hadn't confided in him. "Damn smoker's cough," he said once he could breathe again.

"What brand?" Tim asked.

"Sorry?"

"The brand you smoked. Which was your favorite?"

"Oh." Eric looked surprised. "Uh, Camels."

"Yeah, but what kind?"

Eric grasped for an answer before he looked at Tim anew. "Why does it matter?"

Tim just stared in response.

Eric sighed. "You know, don't you?"

Tim swallowed and nodded.

"For how long?"

"Since before Christmas. I kept waiting for you to tell me."

"Marcello?"

"Not really. I bumped into your hospice nurse on the street."

"And you didn't run her over?" Eric took a sip of his iced tea, leaning back in the patio chair. "I hope I didn't hurt your feelings by not telling you. For what it's worth, I don't like anyone to know."

"Why?"

"Because people look at you differently. You become frail in their eyes, and anything you do imperfectly they interpret as a sign that death is creeping closer. Instead of talking about themselves, people are always asking how you're doing, but they do so with such finality, just waiting for you to confirm that you're one foot in the grave."

Tim shook his head. "I haven't treated you differently."

Eric was quiet for a moment. "No. You haven't."

"Then don't hide it from me, okay?"

Eric nodded before laughing. "Looks like I'm just an old closet case myself."

"Two peas in a pod," Tim said, nudging him. Then he grew serious. "So what are we dealing with exactly? Lung cancer?"

Eric nodded.

"My aunt's ex-husband had that, and he pulled through after chemo. Last I heard he was doing fine."

Eric remained quiet.

"It's worth a shot, right?"

"Chemo is an option," Eric said grudgingly.

"Whatever keeps you here," Tim said. "Don't you dare give up on me because I'd be bored to tears without you. I told you that my new roommate collects basketball cards. Not baseball, *basketball.* Who's ever heard of such a thing? Any time I'm in the room he reads the backs of them to me."

Eric managed a smile.

"You're my favorite person," Tim said. "Stick around, okay?"

Eric nodded, but Tim knew it wasn't as simple as making a promise. One thing he had learned from being in the closet is that coming out happened slowly. Now that Eric had confided in him, maybe he could convince him to do more for his health, but he would have to play this carefully.

Tim waited in the hallway, shoulders and one foot pressed against the wall. The temptation to talk to Allison again had been constant since their chance encounter, but Tim avoided giving in. For one whole week, at least. Today he had excused himself early from his Mechanics of Materials class just to be sure he wouldn't miss her. When Allison did show up in the hall, she stopped in her tracks, wearing a deadpan expression.

"Buy you a coffee?" Tim said, pushing off the wall and walking toward her.

"I'm more of a cappuccino girl." Allison resumed walking.

Tim fell in step at her side. "Okay. I'll buy you one of those."

"No thanks."

"Can I walk you to your next class?"

Allison kept her head high. "I'm heading home."

"Then I'll walk you home."

Allison cracked a smile. "You can walk me to my car. Final offer."

"Sounds good." Tim had gone over the questions in his mind all week, trying to decide which was the most crucial. The little details had him most curious. How did Ben look these days? Was he still a terrible driver? Did he still rub his nose when concentrating really hard? "Does he ever mention me?"

Allison sighed. "For a while you were all he talked about. Of course that was a long time ago. How long has it been?"

"Ninety-seven was when it all fell apart. Man, that makes it three years this summer."

Even Allison looked surprised. "Time just flows on by, doesn't it?"

"Yeah. Too fast for my liking, sometimes." Such as now. They had reached the exit door and stepped outside to the parking lot. He prayed that Allison had parked far away. "So you said Ben comes down to visit sometimes?"

"No."

"No?"

"I mean no, I won't tell you when so you can see him." Allison glanced over at him. "He loved you, Tim. I mean, really *really* loved you. It took a long time for him to get over you completely, but he has. Seeing you again will just reopen old wounds, and I won't help you hurt him like that."

"I don't want to hurt him!"

Allison shrugged. "Regardless, that's what would happen." She stopped at a car that was a lot nicer than the junk heap she used to drive in high school.

"You don't like me much, do you?"

Allison considered him. "You know what sucks? I used to. It took me a while at first. I was sure you were just like the other guys Ben messed around with. They would have their fun and ditch him as soon as he got too close or they got girlfriends. But after everything you went through together, I finally accepted it was going to be different."

"It was," Tim said.

She nodded. "That's right, because you weren't a horny straight boy who felt like experimenting. You're gay, which meant you could give Ben what he needed. Then you got scared or lord knows what and threw it all away. But before that, I liked you just fine."

"I fucked up," Tim admitted.

"Yeah, and I honestly don't hold it against you anymore. Ben's an amazing guy, and I bet losing someone like that hurt pretty damn bad. You both paid for what happened, which is a shame, because love shouldn't have a price." Allison opened the car door. "The older I get, the more I realize it always does."

Tim stepped back, watching her through the window. Allison offered a sympathetic smile before starting the engine and driving away.

Chapter Nineteen

Some ghosts haunt you for life. The best you can do is make room on the couch and get used to living with them.

That's what Eric had said before Tim made the drive back to The Woodlands. Here it was, Spring Break, when most of his fraternity brothers were flocking to the beaches for booze and babes. And Tim? He was on a familiar street in a sleepy suburban neighborhood, standing across from a house that once felt like home. Not the whole house. Just one room on the second floor. Tim wanted nothing more than to knock on the door, pat Wilford on the head when Ben answered, and trot up the stairs to their special place.

In his mind, Ben was still seventeen years old, skinny legs exposed from the knee down, because of course it was summer. Whenever Tim pictured Ben, it was always summer. He wondered, if by some twist of fate he knocked on the door and Ben answered, if he would even be recognizable. Maybe Ben had changed since high school, finally hitting a growth spurt and taking on the features of a man. Would he still be impressed by something as trivial as Tim's muscles or marvel that he could paint?

Remembering why he had returned to The Woodlands, Tim sighed and walked down the street to his car. Then he drove a few blocks to his parents' house. He had memories here too, so many secret nights in his bedroom, but Tim had already muddied them in his senior year, tearing them apart and fighting them to exhaustion. The memories at Ben's house—they were untouched, still pure in his mind.

"*¡Gordito!*"

Tim's hand slipped off the knob as his mother opened the door. Smiling, she pulled him into a hug. "Mom! I didn't know you would be here."

"Of course," she said as she ushered him in. "You called to say you were coming."

Just to let them know. He didn't expect them to wait for him. "Is Dad here?"

"No, he had to work, but I took the day off. Let me look at you!"

Tim basked in her attention. She took him to the kitchen, where she began heating up some leftover rice pilaf as a snack, promising to take him out to eat for a real meal.

"Then I thought we could go shopping," she said. "You could use some new clothes. Look how big you are!"

She made this statement like he was still growing inches taller every day. Tim smiled anyway. He wasn't expecting a welcome like this. Not by far.

"You eat. I'll finish getting ready."

His mother already looked fabulous, but Tim liked that she was getting dressed up for him. If only every day could be like this. He finished the leftovers, then put the plate in the sink and went upstairs to his old room. Little had changed, aside from the clutter. He hadn't packed much when he left for Austin. Before leaving for college, Tim moved everything from his studio to here, knowing his father would want the space back. His paintings—and he had produced a lot of them that final year—were everywhere, all positioned so the fronts couldn't be seen.

He flipped through them, scoffing at those he found embarrassing and setting aside the few he liked enough to show Eric. That familiar itch came back to him when he touched canvas, smelled the long-dried paint. How had he survived the last year and a half without this? Then again, painting at the frat house seemed impossible, even if he had the nerve to ask for studio space, so Tim dismissed the thought and took the paintings he still liked down to the car.

When he came back in, his mother was ready. The funny thing about parents was how easily they fell back into old roles. Tim might as well have been twelve again. His mother drove, then decided where they ate and where they shopped. She even tried to pick out his clothes for him. Luckily her taste wasn't too different from his own, so Tim didn't have to assert himself much. In the afternoon they walked the mall, both reluctant to call it quits, even though they had bought everything they wanted.

"Do you need cologne?" his mother asked.

"I have four bottles back in Austin."

"Maybe you aren't using enough," his mother said. "Women like a man who smells good."

He thought about telling her, right then and there. What did he have to lose? She would cry, but eventually she would get over it, he hoped. If not—well, he would miss days like these, but they were far and few between.

"When am I going to get a grandbaby?" Ella asked.

Tim laughed, mostly because his parents had never been ready for kids. But then he supposed grandkids might suit them better. Pick up the kids when they needed a fix and send them home when they were tired of them. His stomach sank. Of course she would be sad about that possibility flying out the window. Adoption was still an option, but he wouldn't do that without a partner. For that matter, why should he come out when he didn't have anyone? What was there to gain?

"We should probably head home," Tim said. "I want to drive back to Austin before it gets late."

"You aren't staying?"

He shook his head. There would be no point once his father got home and his mother's attention returned to him. Lucky bastard! Tim would love to have a person like that in his life, someone he could rely on. Someone who made him feel loved.

Then Tim realized that such a person already existed.

"It's not about having something to gain," Eric said. He was sitting at the dining room table, piles of mail and bills spread out on the wooden surface. The house had an office, but Eric always seemed more comfortable in an environment suited to food. "Coming out isn't about convenience, either. You do it so that others can love you."

"Funny," Tim said, "I *don't* do it so others will keep loving me." He was beginning to regret telling Eric about his day out with his mother. Tim sat across from Eric, tipping back in a wooden dining room chair while watching him work. Eric wore half-moon glasses that made him look both silly and cute.

"They don't love you," Eric said, half-distracted by writing a check.

"Wow. Thanks."

When Eric realized what he'd said, he looked surprised and shoved away the checkbook. "What I mean is that they can't love you. Not completely, because they don't really know who you are. The good news is that they love the version of you they know, and the real Tim isn't so different from him. He just prefers guys, that's all."

Tim wasn't convinced. "If it's not that big a part of me, I'd rather keep it from them."

"Because if you don't, they might not accept you."

"Right."

Eric shook his head. "That's one of the biggest misconceptions gay people go through. While in the closet, we want everyone to accept us, when in truth, people are only accepting a lie. Do you like women?"

"I'm a four on that Kinsey scale or whatever it was, remember?"

Eric peered over his glasses, looking very much like a stern teacher. "You know what I mean. Are you going to marry a girl, settle down, and spawn children like your friend Travis plans to?"

"No. Not a chance."

"But that's what they expect. What they've accepted isn't you. Since you haven't really been accepted by them, you shouldn't worry about being unaccepted. Does that make sense?"

"In a convoluted way, I guess so." Tim mulled it over. "Of course, right now I sort of have a neutral status, which is better than being unaccepted."

Eric moaned dramatically. "Now I see what poor Ben had to put up with."

Tim grinned. "There were benefits too."

"I can only imagine."

"Hey," Tim let all four chair legs hit the floor, "do you want to see my paintings?"

"You brought some with you?" Eric perked up. "Of course!"

Tim went out to his car and returned with the six paintings that had made the cut. He showed them to Eric, one by one, making excuses for little things he wished were different. Eric was encouraging, saying two nice things for every self-criticism. When show and tell was over, Eric appeared thoughtful.

"What strikes me most," Eric said, "is how each painting is in a different style. I wouldn't have thought they were from the same artist if I didn't know better."

"Yeah, well, most of them were painted at totally different times of my life. I experimented a lot, I guess because I was always looking for my own style. I just never found it."

Eric tapped a pen on his lower lip while he thought. "It's not too late."

"To start painting again? I don't know." But Tim did. Even tearing apart his favorite work with criticism made him want to try again.

"I'll hire you to paint me," Eric said with a bashful smile. "You can't be filthy rich without an arrogant portrait hanging on the wall. Marcello has three."

"I'm not surprised." Tim looked at Eric anew, hunched over the long dining room table, overwhelmed by a mess of envelopes, stamps, and checks—looking small in the face of it all. The secret burden of being rich. It would make a great painting. "I'd have to get back into shape, practice before I even try."

"Do that," Eric said. "I've always wanted to play patron to a real artist."

Tim sat across the table from him with the one other thing he brought with him from home—his old sketch book. It was only half full, since he didn't really enjoy sketching, but it made a good starting point. He scratched out some rough ideas, enjoying working quietly alongside Eric. That is, until he heard a gasp.

"What is it?"

Eric was holding up a magazine, the free kind made from the same cheap stock as newspapers. Mouth open in surprise, Eric turned it around so Tim could see the cover. He noticed first the title, set in rainbow letters: *Gay Austin!* Then Tim noticed the image below. There, for all the world to see, was a photo of himself, naked except for a pair of designer briefs. What he *was* wearing, was an annoyed expression caused by the hot surfer dude sticking a tongue in his ear.

Tim gripped the wheel with one hand, scrolling through the contacts on his phone with the other. Where was the bastard? Aha! Highlighting Marcello's name, Tim pushed the button to call him and scowled against the morning light. His head hurt from the six-pack he had downed last night after Eric's discovery. Tim had been a whiny nuisance and Eric had been a saint, listening to a list of worries so old that even Tim had grown tired of them.

"Good morning, Mr. Wyman!" Marcello sang in his ear.

"Fuck you!" Tim responded.

"I'd be honored to let you, if I weren't such a domineering

top." Marcello chuckled at his own joke, before asking, "What's wrong?"

"The cover of *Gay Austin!*"

"Ah, I just saw that myself. I wish the print quality of those magazines was better. They don't do the photo justice."

"You didn't know about it ahead of time?" Tim asked, his anger taking a smoke break.

"I only deal in sales for the big clients. The little ones buy from our catalog."

"Well, someone could have warned me about that before my face was plastered on the cover of a gay magazine!"

Marcello scoffed. "I thought you would be thrilled."

"I'm in the closet, you asshole!"

"Oh!" The line crackled quietly before Marcello spoke again. "What's the point?"

"Of what?"

"Of being in the closet."

Tim snarled, hung up the phone, and tossed it to the passenger seat. What a dick! *Gay Austin!* was the sort of magazine given away for free in bookstores, along with other independent publications and real estate guides. Surely it was only a matter of time before someone recognized him.

He pulled up to the frat house, expecting his brothers to spill out the front door, howling with laughter. But when he got inside, everything was normal. The few guys who were awake were just as hung-over as he was, so no one paid him much attention.

Two days later, and still nothing had happened. Maybe he had overreacted. Tim hung around the frat house more than usual, waiting for the bomb to drop, but eventually let down his guard. He shouldn't have. Returning to his room one night, he found a copy of the magazine on his bed.

"What's this?" he said to Rick, but his roommate just stared at Tim with wide eyes, like he was going to be assaulted by a syringe full of gay at any second. "Did you put this here?"

When Rick didn't answer, Tim tossed the magazine at him and went downstairs to the common room. The atmosphere got a whole lot thicker when he entered. Three brothers were lined up on the couch, each holding an open copy in front of their faces, snorting and snickering behind them. Tim noticed a couple more copies scattered around the room.

"Tim."

He spun around. Quentin stood in the doorway. He was smiling, but his lips were tight.

"What's up?" Tim said like nothing was wrong.

Quentin shook his head. No dice. He wasn't getting off easy this time. "You want to explain yourself?"

"I needed some money and did some modeling." Tim shrugged. "So what?"

"*So what?*" Quentin walked over and grabbed a copy from one of the guys on the couch. He looked at the front again, as if he couldn't believe it. "It looks to me like you're doing more than just modeling."

"The other guy was straight," Tim said. "It was just a job."

"Oh, okay," Quentin said sarcastically. "The *other* guy was straight. That's good to know, Tim, because we're real concerned about him."

Quentin crossed his arms over his chest. A couple more brothers had entered the room, attracted by the raised voices. They weren't looking too friendly.

"Is there something you want tell us?" Quentin pressed.

Travis walked in the room. The second he saw Tim, he turned and walked back out. Fuck him. Fuck everyone! Tim wasn't going to stand there and beg for them to believe him. They never would anyway, not completely. "I've got nothing to be ashamed of," he said.

The room grumbled like thunder before a storm, the tension desperate to break.

"Fag."

And there it was, the first flash of lightning, the first drop of rain. Tim wondered if this was the room Eric had stood in years ago, facing accusations that shouldn't have mattered. Instead of feeling fear, Tim felt oddly proud to be following in his footsteps. Eric was a good man, better than anyone here, and Tim wasn't about to act like a coward when Eric had once bravely endured such hate.

"Am I a fag?" Tim glared in the direction the slur had come from. "Because last time I checked, I was your brother."

"You can't be both." Quentin said.

That made it final. The others would follow his lead, no matter how they felt.

"Thanks, Big. Way to take care of your Little." Tim made his way to the common room door, turning around to face them one last time. "I'm not the only one, you know. Not by a long shot." Tim made eye contact with a lot of them—not the ones he knew about or suspected, but those who were probably straight. With any luck they'd start a witch hunt and end up burning themselves.

Tim went upstairs to his room—Rick fleeing for safety—and grabbed his suitcase from the closet. He didn't have much to pack except for his clothes. He spent more time at Eric's these days than he did here. Hopefully Eric wouldn't mind him staying over a few nights until he found a place of his own. On the way out of the room, Tim spotted the magazine on the floor and picked it up.

"Call me whatever you want," he said to himself. "I look damn good."

He rolled up the magazine and stuck it in his back pocket. Then he left the frat house with his head held high. He heard laughs and jeers, but somehow they weren't as upsetting as he'd always imagined. By the time he got in his car, he felt prouder than he had in years.

When he rang Eric's doorbell, suitcase in hand, Tim put on his best puppy-dog eyes. "Will paint for food," he said when Eric opened the door. "And a roof over my head."

Eric smiled and opened his arms wide, welcoming Tim home.

Chapter Twenty

People change. Catching them in the act, that's the trick. No one has seen a wrinkle etching itself into skin, or witnessed the moment a hair turns gray. Stomachs become flabby and muscles begin to jiggle, the transformation not hidden and yet undetectable. None of this happens overnight, but age often comes as a surprise. Usually an old photo is to blame, indisputable evidence that skin had once been tighter or eyes brighter. Other times aging is revealed in a chance reflection, a moment of confusion over this older person who looks strikingly familiar.

For Tim, the process of aging was presented to him like a play, one he repeatedly dozed off through. He would wake from the distraction of everyday life and see Eric with fresh eyes, realizing how much he had aged in the last year. Or even the last six months. Eric insisted the chemo was to blame.

Winter had been hell for them both. Tim finally talked Eric into trying chemotherapy, even sitting with him while the drugs were pumped into his veins. Then came weeks of illness, with Tim taking care of Eric as best he could during his recovery. At the end of the month, when Eric was back to being his old self, he returned to the hospital for another round of chemo, and the cycle would repeat.

Convincing Eric to return for each subsequent treatment hadn't been easy, but they made it through together. Having recovered from the final round of treatment, Eric seemed like his old self again. Except in appearance. Chemotherapy hadn't stolen his hair, but his face was more gaunt and his frame thinner, as if a black hole was eating him up from the inside.

"Stop doing that," Eric said, lowering the book he was reading.

"What?" Tim said innocently from the opposite end of the couch where he was curled up.

"Looking at me that way. You promised you never would."

Tim shrugged dismissively. "I'm a painter studying his subject. That's all."

"Well, study me when I don't look like hell." Eric set aside the book and massaged his temples. "Do you have classes tomorrow?"

"Just one. Nothing I can't skip. Why?"

"I know it's short notice, but I need you to drive me to MD Anderson."

Located in Houston, MD Anderson is one of the most comprehensive cancer centers in the United States. Tim had already ferried Eric there multiple times, especially lately, since the strong painkillers he was on made Eric the equivalent of a drunk driver.

"Can we take your car?" Tim asked.

"Of course."

"Then it's a deal." Tim reached out a socked foot and affectionately nudged Eric's leg. "What's the reason? Time to see how the chemo did?"

Eric nodded. "That, and a few other things. Bring a book. It's going to be a long day."

Tim knew that from experience. The next day he brought not only a book, but the laptop Eric had given him for Christmas. Eric dozed for most of the three-hour ride to Houston, which was just as well, since riding in cars made him nauseous lately. Plus, this meant Tim could drive the Jaguar XJR like the racecar it was meant to be.

Tim settled down in the waiting room as soon as Eric was called away by a nurse. As open as Eric now was about his cancer, he still didn't like Tim being there for the tests and consultations or even when the hospice nurse came around. That Tim was allowed to be in attendance for the chemotherapy was an honor, and one step closer in their strange relationship that Tim still struggled to define.

Today the appointment was taking longer than usual. Eric reappeared twice, sitting with Tim while waiting for the next doctor or test results. In between these periods, Tim tinkered with his laptop, playing card games and listening to tunes. The nurse on duty, a ramrod-thin woman with tired blond hair, gave him a sympathetic smile whenever she caught his eye. When he grew weary of music and took off his headphones, she stopped to talk to him.

"I've seen you here before," she said.

"Yeah, I might as well move in," Tim quipped.

The nurse smiled. "It's really nice of you to always be there for your father."

They got this a lot. Eric found it annoying, but Tim thought it was funny and rarely corrected anyone. "It's the least I can do."

"He's doing really great," she said. "For mesothelioma, it's amazing he's made it this long."

Tim's jaw nearly dropped. Were the nurses supposed to be so negative? "Of course he's made it this long. He'll make it all the way!"

"He will!" the nurse said quickly. "He'll be the exception to the rule, especially with a son like you. You're both incredibly brave."

She smiled again—a gesture Tim didn't return—before resuming her duties. For the rest of his wait, he remained haunted by the discussion. No wonder Eric was so private about his illness, when even the professionals were all doom and gloom about his chances. The feeling of unease remained with him even when Eric returned, finally finished for the day.

"What'd they say?" Tim asked as they walked down the hallway.

"Can't we discuss something else?" Eric snapped. "All I've talked about today is cancer."

"Sure. No problem." Once they were in the car, Tim buckled up but didn't start the engine. "Just give me a thumbs up or thumbs down. Otherwise I'll go crazy."

Eric sighed, but he raised a thumb in the air. "Now get going. I'm starving, and I know you must be too."

Thumbs up. Okay. Tim could deal with that. Maybe they weren't out of the woods yet—otherwise Eric would be happier—but they were headed in the right direction.

Car interior smelling like cooking grease from the golden arches, Tim swore under his breath. Eric had asked him to come straight home after class today, but Tim was running late. He'd only stopped to pick up french fries for Eric. Lately a lot of things tasted repulsive to him, but good ol' fries always made Eric happy. Lord knew he could use the calories, so Tim brought them whenever he could. Except today he had gotten stuck in the drive-through for an annoyingly long time.

He gunned it home—as he now thought of Eric's house. Tim really hadn't intended to stay there for so long, but Eric asked him to move in permanently, over and over again, until Tim happily relented. Today two cars were in the driveway. One belonged to Lisa, the hospice nurse. The other Tim had never seen before. Lisa usually didn't come by on Thursdays, so Tim ran inside the second his car was parked, fearing the worst.

He found Eric in the living room, the one based on René Magritte's horse painting. For Tim it had taken on special meaning. While it looked like a woman riding through the woods, much of the image was missing. People were no different—everyone had their hidden side, be it sexuality or illness.

Eric seemed to be in good spirits. Lisa was seated next to him, across from a man who reminded Tim of his father, probably because he looked fresh from a round of golf.

"There he is," Eric said. "What took you so long?"

"Fries," Tim said, holding up the bag.

"Oh, how nice! Just set them down for now and have a seat."

Tim sat, still tense and hoping for an explanation. "So—"

"Max Burnquist," the stranger said, sliding a business card across the coffee table. "I'm Eric's attorney."

"Okay," Tim said.

"There's simply some paperwork that needs to be filled out," Eric explained. "I need witnesses for this to be legal, which is why you are here. Please, Max, go ahead."

The attorney started a handheld tape recorder, set it on the table, and cleared his throat. Reading from a piece of paper, he said, "Eric Conroy, do you testify that you are of sound mind and memory and not under restraint?"

"I do." Eric sounded like he was taking his vows.

"And do you also testify that the content of this will, dated March 24th, 2001, is of your own creation or that the contents meet your approval and intentions?"

Tim's stomach twisted. A will?

"I do," Eric said.

The attorney moved some papers across the table to him. "Please sign here."

"Lisa Ownby, do you testify that the patient in your care is still of sound mind and memory—"

Tim barely listened to the rest, distracted by the implications. Did Eric think he was going to die? When the attorney got to Tim, he answered and signed as expected. Then he sat there numbly as more details were discussed, remaining in his seat when Eric rose and saw his guests to the front door.

"I hate this," he said when they were alone.

"I know." Eric sat, rustling in the greasy brown bag for some fries. "One of life's ugly necessities, especially when money is involved."

"But why now?"

Eric chewed and swallowed, sucking the salt from the tips of his fingers. "I have family, you know. I don't talk about them much, but I have a sister and a gaggle of nieces. My sister and I lost our parents, one to cancer and the other to drink, so we've seen the worst that can happen. We don't stay in touch much, but she has three daughters headed off to college. I've already made sure they have tuition and everything else they need. When I die, my sister will inherit most of what I have."

"Don't talk like that," Tim pleaded.

"A fair amount will go to charities I believe in," Eric continued unabashed. "As for this house, I would like you to have it."

"I don't want it!" Tim shouted. "I want you, so shut up about your stupid will!"

Eric didn't even blink. "Of course there are property taxes and general upkeep. You'll have enough money that, if you're careful, you'll be able to afford that and live comfortably off the interest."

"Shut up!" Tim was on his feet. "Are you giving up? Is that what this is about?"

"I'm dying!" Eric shouted back, his composure breaking.

The force of those words sent the blood draining from Tim's face. He'd never heard Eric raise his voice before. Never.

"You aren't. You can fight this!"

"Not forever," Eric said, his voice a croak. "I don't just have lung cancer, Tim. Do you know what mesothelioma is?"

Mesothelioma. That's what the nurse at MD Anderson called it. Not understanding, he shook his head.

"It's cancer caused from asbestos exposure—a particularly nasty kind that no one survives."

"What?" Tim's throat constricted so tight it ached. "Of course they do. Why else would you do chemo?"

"I've been fighting for time," Eric said.

Tim shook his head. "The nurse said you would make it through. She said you'd be the exception to the rule."

"I already am," Eric said. "They told me nine months, maybe a year, and I've lasted more than two."

"See? You've already proven them wrong."

Eric sat and studied him. Tim knew this was one of those moments. Eric would either point out the missing parts of the painting, or he would let Tim continue believing the illusion. When Eric did speak, Tim almost wished he hadn't.

"The chemo didn't help. The cancer barely responded, and I have been having... other problems. They did some tests and—" Eric shook his head, reluctant to say the words, tears spilling from his eyes. "They found a new tumor on my prostate, which they don't think is from the mesothelioma. I'm falling apart! I'm trying not to, but I'm just—"

A sob broke from Tim's throat as he rushed to Eric's side. Tim grabbed him, pulling him close and holding him while they both cried. Eric felt so small, so frail in Tim's arms. "Don't give up," Tim said, over and over again. "Please don't give up. For me. Do it for me."

"I didn't expect to meet you," Eric said, his head nestled against Tim's chest. "I would have given up a long time ago, but you keep asking me to stay. Had you not come into my life—"

Eric didn't finish the sentence. Tim didn't need him to. Maybe he was being selfish by insisting Eric stay, but surely living longer was a good thing. Eric was fighting just for him, a fact that filled Tim with love and sorrow—a pairing he was used to. Tim had walked with these emotions before, each taking one of his hands and leading him to dark forests he once found frightening, but now were disturbingly familiar.

Hope fills the heart of those facing death. They dream of a place where time never runs out, where the impossible can still happen, be it on this earth or elsewhere. Perhaps that was why Eric slept so much now, one foot already in a better place.

Summer had come, the windows of Eric's bedroom opened to let in fresh air so full of life that Tim sometimes believed it could cure him, that Eric could feed off the beautiful weather like a hummingbird did nectar. At least then he would be eating. A week ago, Eric had been too tired to get out of bed. Since then, Tim had been at his bedside, carrying him to the restroom when needed or making him roll over and change positions to avoid bedsores. When Eric wasn't sleeping they talked, although lately he had less and less to say.

Tim grew tired of sitting and staring and waiting, so he fetched the painting supplies he kept in one of the spare rooms and started working. No longer was he out of practice. Tim painted regularly, constantly encouraged by Eric, although he still hadn't found his own style. He didn't let that bother him. Instead he pushed on, letting come what may when inspiration struck.

Today the light flooding the room set him off. Edward Hopper would have loved it. Tim took this light, put it on his canvas, and twisted it around Eric like a blanket. Protecting him. Saving him.

"Tim." Eric's voice was dry, so Tim put down the brush to fetch the drinking glass from the nightstand. Eric sipped from the straw and nodded at the canvas. "What are you doing?"

"Painting you."

"Like this?" Eric smiled or grimaced. It was hard to tell. "You're cruel."

"I promised I would paint you," Tim said.

"That's right." Eric's eyes rolled around the room before coming back to him. "Make me a king, surrounded by beautiful young men."

"I'll make you an emperor with no clothes," Tim teased.

Eric chuckled before he winced. "Time for more of those poppies, Dorothy."

Taking the bottle of morphine from the nightstand, Tim drew more liquid into the medicine dropper than recommended, squeezing it into Eric's mouth. Even these extra doses didn't chase away the pain completely, but they helped. "Need to answer Mother Nature's call before that stuff kicks in?"

Eric shook his head.

"How about some soup? You need to eat something."

"Just keep working. I like the sound of the brush."

Tim toiled further, bending the light into a nest, bringing out the colors hidden deep in the spectrum. And as soon as Eric was asleep again, he let himself cry while he worked, because that's all he could do. Tim painted until his fingers went numb and his body ached from staying so long in the same position.

When he finished, he stepped back and stared until he was sure he had it right. Then he woke Eric, first saying his name, then shaking him gently until he stirred. "Look," he said, rushing back to the canvas and turning it around so Eric could see. His heart was thudding in his chest as he waited for a response. What was on canvas wasn't a lie—not Eric young and healthy. The painting was of him in his sickbed, but the light and the colors were like a filter that tore through the ravages of cancer, revealing the untouchable soul beneath.

"You made me beautiful," Eric said.

"You've always been beautiful."

Eric looked at him like he was being silly before closing his eyes. Tim stood there, arms limp at his sides, and watched him as the light outside dimmed, feeling disappointed that his magic spell hadn't worked. Eric was still sick. Eric was dying.

"I love you," Eric murmured, shifting beneath the sheets.

Tim went to him, sitting on the edge of the bed. "Eric?"

"Let me sleep, Gabriel," Eric murmured, his brow creasing as if concentrating, but his eyes remained closed. "I'm tired."

Tim opened his mouth, desperate to know if Eric had been addressing him a moment ago, or if he was thinking of Gabriel the whole time. Then Tim leaned back, biting his lower lip. Either way, he knew Eric loved him, and if he was dreaming of being with the greatest love of his life, maybe he was already experiencing a taste of Heaven.

"You know I love you, right?" Tim said. "I really mean it, Eric. I love you. I love you so much! I love you."

Tim clamped a hand over his mouth to stop himself. He wanted to say it a million times, because he realized that he'd never have another chance. This was it. No more relaxing nights on the couch together, the television off so they could talk the hours away. No more shared meals, Eric smiling over the table at the way Tim stuffed his face. All of this would be gone forever. No matter what he did, Eric was slipping away. Tim could scream all he wanted, punch the walls, cut his own skin, lie through his teeth or offer up his body and soul, but it wouldn't make a difference. Eric would die—and Tim was powerless to stop it.

He felt tears rolling over the fingers on his mouth, felt the breath from his nose coming in manic bursts. Tim moved his hand away and tried once more.

"I love you."

But Eric didn't respond, didn't wake up again, even the next morning. Tim called the nurse in a panic, which was silly, because he had known this was coming. He had read it over and over again in books and online, but part of him always felt that Eric would be one of the lucky ones. The exception to the rule.

"Oh, honey. That just means he's close," the nurse said on the phone. "If God is merciful, he'll take him soon."

If God was merciful, Eric wouldn't be dying, but Tim kept silent. He spent the next two days at Eric's side, giving him his medicine at the regular dosage times in case Eric was still inside there somewhere, feeling everything. And Tim took care of him in other ways he never thought he would have to, doing the unpleasant things that most people don't speak about, except maybe with others who have been through the same experience. He did everything he could for Eric, even talking to him so he wouldn't be lonely.

On the morning of the third day, Tim woke to find that God—merciful or not—had allowed Eric to slip quietly away in the night. Tim took his hand one last time, squeezing it desperately, but Eric wasn't there anymore. The soul he had managed to capture a glimpse of on canvas had gone home.

The funeral went by in flashes. Umbrellas. Rain. People dressed in black and gray. Faces Tim had seen only in photos, but now older. Eric's sister. The legendary Gabriel. Friends Tim had met in passing or not at all. So many people, their heads often turning in his direction, as if he had an explanation for this incomprehensible event.

Tim was lost, but Marcello was there, handling everything with the precise attention he gave his business ventures. "I buried too many friends in the eighties," he said to Tim. "Funerals have become disturbingly routine."

To Tim, the funeral felt like a circus. So many people were surprised that Eric was even sick, only in retrospect realizing why he hadn't thrown any parties this year or commenting how Eric seemed tired at the last one. Tim just kept saying that Eric didn't want them to know. Those final days were private, just between the two of them.

When everybody else finally went away, Tim found himself alone in a big house. He walked the hallways, exploring each room, opening drawers and cabinets and examining everything inside as if it had new meaning. And it did, because this was Eric. This was the story of his life—what he had chosen to surround himself with. He had left it to Tim so he wouldn't be alone.

But it wasn't the same.

Tim painted more than ever. He did little else, aside from eating and sleeping. What he needed to express was too big to fit on canvas, but he tried anyway. For a while he indulged in the morphine left on Eric's bedside table. The medicine helped fill the void, but its comfort never lasted. Once it was gone, Tim picked up the brush and kept working. The phone rang, and so did the doorbell, occasionally, but Tim ignored it all, shutting out the world. Eric hadn't left. His ghost was right here beside him. It was the rest of the world that had ceased to exist.

Until one morning, when Tim woke to find a very large man standing over his bed.

"I don't like the beard," Marcello said. "Maybe when you're older, but you're too young and handsome for it now."

"What are you doing here?" Tim said, pulling the covers up higher.

Marcello sat on the edge of the bed, Tim scooting over so one of his legs wouldn't be crushed. "I need a favor. There's a charity dinner tonight, and I'm short-staffed when it comes to waiters."

"Fuck you," Tim said. "I don't need your money."

Marcello looked over his shoulder at him, eyebrows raised. "I'm well aware of that. You would be doing me a favor, so I would owe you one in return. Having someone indebted to you is infinitely more valuable than money. You see, I can't hire just anyone for this job. Even gay charities revolve around men, and beauty is more effective than crowbars at getting wallets to open."

"Leave me alone."

"This isn't what Eric would want."

Tim didn't respond. Even hearing Eric's name hurt too much.

"Seven o'clock, my house." Marcello stood again. "If you aren't there, I'll bring the entire party here. Don't think I won't!"

Tim didn't doubt it. Once Marcello was gone, he got out of bed and stomped and raged around the house. Then he took a long look in the mirror and saw a stranger. The beard was alien, his hair unruly, his complexion pale and bloodless. Marcello was right. This isn't what Eric would want.

When he reported to Marcello's house that night, the man

of the hour wasn't in sight. Instead, an Asian guy in charge of organizing the event had him dress in an outfit suited for a Chippendale's dancer and informed him how the evening would work. Luckily it didn't sound hard. Tim would only be handing out drinks, not serving food.

A speech in the main room was followed by applause. Tim sulked in the corner of the kitchen until the time came to bring out the champagne. Once in the midst of the party, he found he couldn't maintain his foul mood, not while surrounded by so much life. Nearly six weeks alone in the house made the prospect of conversation enticing, and most of the men here were more interested in talking to him than getting a drink.

Marcello came over half an hour in, guiding him away from the crowd and to the side of the room. "Well, what do you think?"

Tim sighed. "You were right. I needed to get out of the house."

"And shave." Marcello smiled. "You look much better now. But I mean, what do you think of that?"

He pointed to one end of the room where a banner read *The 1st Annual Eric Conroy Foundation Fundraiser.*

Tim felt a lump in his throat. "What's the foundation for?"

"To support the arts," Marcello said with pride. "Mostly by funding underprivileged artists through scholarships. Eric always loved his art."

And Tim loved the idea. "I'll give everything Eric left to me."

"No," Marcello said with a chuckle. "The men here have plenty to spare. Eric wanted you to have what he gave you, not give it away. What he wanted most of all was for you to be happy. You've grieved, and you can keep grieving, but you also have to resume living. For Eric. For yourself. Understand?"

Tim nodded.

"Good. Now get back to work and make sure these men are all drunk and horny before I ask them for their hard-earned cash."

Tim laughed as Marcello floated back into the crowd, graceful as a Zeppelin. All around voices were babbling, laughter filling the air. Life went on. Painful and treacherous as it may be, life went on.

Part Three:
Austin, 2002

Chapter Twenty-one

Ben.

Tim had dreamt of running into him countless times. Usually these fantasies were triggered by a visit home, especially around the holidays. Tim would go shopping, hit the mall, Walmart, or even the grocery store, and part of him would always be looking, just in case Ben was home visiting and needed to buy markers or whatever in the middle of the night.

One time Tim saw him, or so he thought, in the greeting card aisle. The person's build was the same, the hair color right. Any other discrepancy in resemblance could be explained away by age. Tim browsed the cards, eyes never on the folded cardboard in his hand, until the other person had finally looked at him. And didn't react. Not his Benjamin, then.

Outside these odd moments, Tim went on with his life, struggling through his last year of college and trying not to think about what the past had been or what the future held. So when he entered the coffee shop, annoyed by the loud espresso machines and bean grinders, his thoughts weren't on the past at all. Instead he was looking forward to getting an Italian soda so he could return to the sunny weather outside. The clueless person in front of him was sounding out the words on the menu, so Tim glanced around in exasperation.

A pair of eyes darted away as he did so. Big expressive eyes that stood out against dark skin. Well, well! Allison Cross. Tim hadn't seen her since the end of sophomore year. As always she looked good, if a little nervous, her attention locked stubbornly on the person she sat across from.

Blond hair, medium length, half covering the ears. His build was right too, but Tim didn't need more evidence. If asked to paint those ears from memory, he couldn't have. There was nothing significant about them, but seeing them now, even half obscured, got his neurons firing. Tim was already moving around the tables, feeling detached from the world, like in a dream. He could see the person's profile now—the nose that curved upward ever so slightly at the tip, the brow cocked in an all-too-familiar "what the hell?" expression. Tim opened his mouth to speak the impossible.

"Benjamin?"

As soon as their eyes met, Tim felt light, as if the molecules in his body were separating and would soon dissipate, floating away in a happy cloud. Maybe this heady sensation caused him to reach out and place a hand on Ben's shoulder. Even through the light blue T-shirt, Tim felt sparks—real, honest to goodness tingles.

Tim caught his breath. "It's really you, isn't it?"

Ben looked just as taken aback, mouth hanging open as he stared. Those lips, the pointy incisors, every detail was still so familiar. "Yeah," came the answer.

They were together again. Finally. Already it felt so good. Except the feeling wasn't mutual. Ben's watery brown eyes turned hard as he jerked away his shoulder, breaking physical contact.

Damn.

"Man," Tim breathed, grasping for a lifeline. "So are you just visiting or what?"

Ben's jaw clenched. Tim could see a hint of afternoon stubble. That was new. He stared as Ben's mouth formed words that puzzled him. "I'm enrolled here."

"Since when? I thought you were in Chicago?" Tim looked at Allison for an explanation, but she focused on Ben, trying to explain everything in a meaningful expression.

"I'm guessing we go to the same school?" Ben asked her.

Allison pressed her lips together and nodded. "Yeah."

"Jesus!" Tim took a seat. All these years and they had been so close without even knowing it.

"I have to go." Ben stood, his chair scraping across the floor. He practically tripped over it on his way out the door.

Tim stared helplessly before turning a glare on Allison. "You should have told me!"

"Why?" Allison crossed her arms over her chest. "What would be the point? You might have pushed him away, but he made the decision to move on and never once said he regretted it."

"Fine." Tim watched through the window as Ben rushed off. "I know I fucked up, but things are different now."

"Are they?"

He didn't have time to answer her, not unless he wanted to risk another five-year separation. Maybe Tim should have searched for Ben in that time, and maybe Allison was right and there wasn't a point. But now that Tim had seen Ben again, he wasn't going to let him get away without at least telling him one thing.

Tim was on his feet and out the door, leg muscles pushing hard against the concrete when he saw Ben was already halfway down the block. Not this time! Tim was running to him, not away. The world seemed to move in slow motion, as if no possible speed was fast enough to close the distance. Tim called his name, and eventually Ben halted, but he hung his head like it was the dumbest thing he'd ever done. The world sped up again, Ben just inches away from him now. Tim wanted to reach out and touch him but didn't dare.

"Hey," he tried.

Ben studied the ground. "What do you want?"

"I don't know," Tim admitted. "I just want to talk to you, I guess."

After a barely perceptible shake of his head, Ben said, "I can't."

Can't? Or won't?

"I know you're mad at me." Tim lowered his head, trying to catch his eye, but Ben still wouldn't look at him. This was bad! If he didn't back off now, he would scare Ben away. But Tim couldn't leave without a way of finding him again. Reaching into his pocket, he pulled out his cell phone. "Take this."

Ben was so despondent Tim had to place the phone in his hand.

"I'll call tonight, okay? We're both in shock right now and need time to think, but I still want to talk to you. Cool?"

Ben nodded. Thank God, Allah, Santa Claus, or whoever was out there, because Ben nodded.

"All right. I'm going now." Tim started to back away, but it was possible Ben would change his mind and throw away the phone. Then Tim would never see him again, so he decided to tell him the one thing he needed to say the most. "You were right, Benjamin."

Ben raised his head, the line of his mouth relaxing. "About what?"

"About a lot of things." They looked at each other for one eternal moment. "See you around!" Tim smiled at him, because if this was the end, Ben might as well know how he made him feel. Then he did one of the hardest things ever. He turned and walked away.

When Tim was sitting in his car again, he allowed himself a nervous laugh. Another chance. Was it possible? What in the world would he say when he called Ben tonight? What he needed was advice. Tim started the car, thinking of Eric before a dart of sorrow hit his heart. Fuck it. He wouldn't let that stop him. Putting the car in drive, he headed across town to Austin Memorial Park where Eric was buried.

The grave was at the edge of the property, the last at the end of a row, shaded by trees. Tim came here sporadically, only sometimes feeling the need for extra closeness. As he parked his car, he was glad to see the wildflowers covering Eric's grave were still thriving. The headstone could barely be seen beneath a floral wreath, which was just as well. Marcello had chosen the headstone, and although it was elegant, there wasn't a grave in the world that Tim would describe as beautiful.

"I found him," Tim said once he was sitting at the edge of the flowers. "I found Ben. Or he found me. Neither, I guess." He laughed, picturing Eric's patient expression. "I need to know what to do. I mean, I know what I want, but Ben didn't seem happy to see me."

He waited for comforting words he knew wouldn't come, his thoughts wandering to the life he once shared with Eric. One fall day came to mind, when the weather was mild enough that he and Eric opened all the windows in the house. Then Gabriel had called, which was a rare occurrence. Eric went out on the back patio, staring into space or pacing occasionally as he spoke to him on the phone. Tim had sat nearby in the recreation room, pretending to read a magazine while listening as Eric laughed and chatted, mentioning names and places Tim wasn't familiar with. The call had lasted nearly an hour, Eric smiling when he came back inside.

"I love that man," he had said cheerfully.

"I don't see how you can," was Tim's reply. "I mean, he left you for another person."

"Ancient history. And besides, you never stop loving someone, no matter what happens. Do you still love Ben?"

"You know the answer to that."

"And have you loved anyone since?"

That had given Tim pause. His relationship with Eric felt like love. But they were never intimate. Not physically.

Eric continued anyway. "Take it from an old man with a lot of experience. When you do fall in love again, you'll still love Ben just as much. You might not think of him every day or yearn for him, but those feelings will still be there to catch you off guard. They never go away."

Tim had been skeptical. "Tons of couples break up or get divorced."

"Even love can't stop people from becoming incompatible."

Tim breathed in the scent of wildflowers, addressing the present once more. "I hope you were right. Ben and I are compatible now. I think. If he still loves me—" The thought was too huge to finish.

Tim allowed himself more time lost in memory, mulling it all over with Eric's ghost. Then he stood, determined to make Benjamin Bentley love him again.

Had life existed before the Internet, a time when endless information wasn't just a click of the mouse away? How else had people stalked their former flames, mapping a route to their houses in the middle of the night to peep in their windows? Tim hadn't gone *quite* that far yet. He was leaning against his car and staring at dark windows, but from a respectable distance. Maybe Ben wasn't at home.

Tim sighed, wishing he had more liquid courage coursing through his veins. Since his snowmobile accident, he was careful about drinking and driving, so he'd only indulged in one beer before coming here. While at the bar, he went over every possible outcome this night could have. Some were good. Most were bad.

Tired of wondering, Tim used the new phone he bought to call the one left with Ben. He watched the windows as it rang, waiting for one to light up. None of them did, even when the line clicked and Ben's groggy voice answered.

"Hello?"

"Hey! Were you sleeping?"

Ben suddenly sounded much more alert. "No! I mean, yeah."

"It's only 11 p.m.," Tim chided. "What sort of college boy are you?"

There was a heavy pause on the line. "Where were you?"

"Oh. I had a study group," he lied, "and we went out for—"

"No. I mean, *where were you?*"

"What? You mean the last five years?" And there he goes, ladies and gentlemen! Benjamin Bentley, right out of the gate! "All right, uh, high school. Fuck. Senior year I went to Conroe High School instead."

"Just to get away from me?"

"To get away from myself." Tim paced in front of the duplex. All remained dark. Was this the wrong address? "Man, you aren't going to make this easy, are you?"

"No."

"Maybe doing this over the phone was a bad idea." There! A light on the side of the house. Checking the street to make sure no one was watching, Tim walked toward it. "Can't we meet up? Talk face to face?"

"No, I don't think so."

He reached the window and peeped in. Jackpot! Not only was Ben in bed, phone pressed between shoulder and ear as he flipped through some photos, but he was stark naked. Well, nearly. He had underwear on, but Tim could see enough to get his libido raging. Many a moon had passed since Tim had gotten laid, and the rush of hormones sent his courage meter hurtling up to the max.

"Why? Are you indecent?" The window was open, only a screen separating them. "Lying in your bed with nothing but your boxers on?"

Ben tensed and turned around.

"You're still so damn scrawny!" Tim closed his phone. "But it suits you."

Ben's expression was pure disbelief. "What the hell are you doing here?"

Tim pressed his face against the screen. "Let me in before somebody calls the cops."

"I should call them myself! How did you find me?"

"Looked up Allison in the phone book." Another lie, but it sounded slightly less stalkerish. "C'mon, let me in."

Ben flashed a hint of a smile before getting out of bed. Tim hurried around to the front door, like a dog desperate to get out of the rain. Except it was hot, humid, and sweaty out, which made him even hornier. When Ben opened the door, he was wearing a T-shirt. Unfortunately. Tim stepped close to him, but Ben placed a hand on his chest to hold him at bay and shook his head.

"You know what? This isn't a good idea. Wait outside. I'll get dressed and we can go for a walk."

Tim shrugged and stepped back. The door closed. He took a deep breath, trying to summon his brain's higher functions again. Ben wouldn't let him off the hook unless he explained… well, everything. He strolled back to his car, wishing it was the old 3000GT, if only for the nostalgia factor. Still, a brand new Mazda Miata was easy on the eyes, and who didn't love riding in a convertible? Tim leaned against the car, imaging Ben's impressed response. Except when Ben came outside, he walked right past Tim and down the street.

"Same old Benjamin," Tim said, hurrying to catch up. "Always knowing what you want and getting it."

"Yeah, well, not everything's the same." Ben glanced over at him. "So how did Conroe High treat you?"

"Same shit, different school. Well, not completely the same. There was no you."

The obvious flirtation was ignored. "What about girls?"

Tim fought down a grin. Ben was in for a big surprise if he thought girls were still in the picture. "Tried to avoid them. Just had a prom date senior year."

"Krista Norman again?" Ben's voice dripped with venom when he said her name. Eric would probably claim it proved underlying passion. Jealousy equals passion equals love—or something like that.

"No. Not Krista. I stopped seeing her shortly after we beat the crap out of Bryce." That broke the ice. They both smiled at the memory, the space between them feeling a little warmer. "That was another reason to switch schools. I'm sure Bryce was aching for a rematch. They give you any more trouble?"

"Not really."

Well done, Stacy Shelly.

A small park at the end of the block became their destination, a view of the river past some overgrown brush. Ben sat on a flat rock, its edges buried in the dirt. Tim joined him. Their legs brushed against each other, Ben shifting uncomfortably and pulling his legs up close. Not a good sign. This wasn't going well. Maybe Ben had someone.

"So what about you? Drag any lucky guys to the prom?"

The question was ignored. "So straight from high school to Austin?"

"Yeah, pretty much. My dad graduated from here and insisted I do the same. I didn't know what I wanted to do, so I agreed. It's worked out pretty well so far." Time to pull the ace from his sleeve. "People are so liberal in Austin that it's easy to be gay here."

Ben's reaction was priceless. Flabbergasted was probably the right word. Best of all, Ben was so surprised, he let down his guard completely. "You came out?"

"Yeah. Got kicked out of a fraternity because of it too."

"Seriously?"

"Yeah. It was stupid, since I'd slept with half of them before coming out. Well, not *half,* but you know." Great. Now he was making himself sound like a slut. Tim rewound the conversation to coming out. "A lot of the frat boys were the same way I used to be. Some just liked to mess around, which was all right, but other guys were so closeted they couldn't even admit it to themselves. I got a good taste of what I put you through."

Ben lapsed into thought. Everything had changed. Surely he could see that now; would realize the implications. They could be together. Nothing was in their way anymore.

When Ben remained silent, Tim bumped shoulders with him gently. "So tell me about your life. Was Chicago just a lie to keep me away from you?"

"No. I was there for almost two years."

"Did you like it?"

Ben's face lit up "I loved it. Everything but the weather. The museums were amazing, the shopping—just the city itself. There was always something going on. Culture thrives there. It didn't feel like a dead city, like Houston."

"Austin must seem boring in comparison."

Ben shrugged. "Not really. It's taken me a little while, but it's starting to feel like home."

"You know," Tim leaned toward him, "they say home is where the heart is."

"They also say you can never go home again,"

"*Touché!*" Tim did his best not to frown. He needed to know. "So what about guys? I guess you've probably dated a lot?"

Ben seemed to hesitate before he leaned away to get at his back pocket. He pulled out a photo, handing it to Tim. "His name is Jace. We've been together for over two years. Someday he's going to take me to Paris."

Tim took the photo reluctantly, not wanting to see. There was Ben, wearing a grin free of inhibition, his face pressed against that of another guy with killer cheekbones and a cool expression. To Tim he almost looked smug, as if he knew Tim would see this moment captured in time and realize how damn happy he could have been. That should be him there, pressing his cheek to Ben's and stretching out his arm to snap the photo.

"I guess I deserve this." Tim's throat burned with the effort of holding back tears.

Ben stared, as if seeing something he never expected. When he spoke again, his voice was soft, like it used to be. "I'm sorry."

"Don't be." Tim pulled himself together. "I missed my chance, right? A guy like you doesn't stay single."

"You either."

Tim shook his head. "Nope. Not since you."

"But you said— The frat boys?"

"That was just sex. All the guys I've been with were nothing more than a one-night stand or fuck buddies. None of them meant anything." Not even Travis. Next to Ben, he had been nothing. Only Eric mattered, but who knew if he even counted. Since him, Tim hadn't connected emotionally with anyone else.

"You can't tell me none of those guys fell for you," Ben said. "If not a frat boy, then someone."

Fair enough. Tim had hit the bars a few times since Eric died, and he did find guys interested in more than a single night, but Tim hadn't felt that spark. "There were a few, yeah, but they weren't…" He let a glance at Ben finish the thought. Time to slink home and lick his wounds. He stood and stretched. "I tracked you down tonight in the hopes of seducing you, but instead the evening was completely embarrassing."

"No, it wasn't."

"You aren't the one who almost cried. I think I'm going to cash in my chips and call it a night. Hey, you still have my phone?"

"Yeah." Ben stood to dig it out.

"Good. Here, trade me. You can have this one," Tim handed him the new phone. "It's all paid up."

Ben looked uncomfortable. "I can't."

"You can. Besides, I like the idea of being able to get a hold of you whenever I want."

"Oh. Well, thanks."

They began a slow walk back to the car, both introspective. Tim wished it would have gone differently, that they could have met again while single, but he understood. If things had been good between him and Travis, had they fallen in love, been together all this time, and Ben had shown up in his life again—Honestly? Tim would have dropped Travis in a second. He couldn't picture loving anyone more than Ben.

Eric was right. Those feelings didn't go away, even when someone else was in the picture. Ben hadn't spent their years apart sad and lonely, which was good, but it was time for him to come home. Tim would have to be smart about this, not mopey or jealous.

"I'm happy for you, Benjamin," he said. "I'm glad that someone recognized how special you are and held on tight."

"Thanks." Ben stopped next to Tim's car. "I'm sure there's someone out there for you too."

"Oh, there is."

Tim wanted to kiss him right then and there, but he was going to do this right. He winked instead, hopped into his car, and drove into the night. Tomorrow he would return and keep coming back every day if that's what it took. He glanced in the rearview mirror at the rapidly shrinking figure and smiled.

See you soon, Benjamin!

Chapter Twenty-two

Tim called first thing the next morning. Ben was already up, and from the noise in the background, he seemed to be driving.

"Hello?"

"I dreamt about you last night," Tim said.

"I don't want to know," Ben replied.

"You really don't. Horribly obscene things happened."

"I bet they did."

"Worst of all, we were both wearing clown makeup."

"Ugh."

"I know."

"I have to go," Ben said, but he sounded amused.

The conversation was short, but it was a good start to Tim's day. He called later in the afternoon between classes. The phone rang longer this time, and when Ben answered he sounded angry.

"How the hell do you turn the ringer off on this thing?" he grumped. "I got kicked out of class!"

"You took me to class with you? That's so sweet! Tell me where you are, and I'll come carry your books for you."

Ben laughed. "I'm going back to class. Don't call me again."

"Then let me take you out tonight."

"No, Tim."

"Go-karts. Me and you. We need to finally settle our differences."

"I have to wash my hair."

The line went dead, but Tim wasn't discouraged. That evening he went home, got gussied up, and was halfway to Ben's duplex when he called again. "I'm picking you up in ten minutes. That's enough time to brush your teeth, check the mirror, and get your butt to the curb."

After a long pause Ben said, "Hurry up."

He wasn't waiting at the curb, but he did answer the door a few seconds after Tim rang the bell. Tim offered his arm, which was ignored, but soon enough Ben was in his car. If he could find a way to permanently lock the doors, he would have driven straight to Mexico and never looked back. Instead he made good on his promise and took him to a family fun center that had a lot more than just go-karts.

They were walking through the arcade, game cabinets buzzing and bleeping, when Tim put an arm around Ben's shoulders. "High school, take two," he said.

Ben smirked. "You couldn't pay me to go back there again."

"You sure? Five hundred bucks? A thousand?" The reaction to this was strangely awkward, so Tim tried again. "It wasn't all bad. Junior year was pretty nice."

Ben didn't exactly sigh and lean into him, but he didn't pull away, either. When they were out on the track, racing each other, Tim became frustrated. Usually he loved engaging in a miniature race, but not when it meant being separate. Then again, when he purposely lost near the end, Ben wore the same goofy smile as in the photo. Take that, new guy! I can make him happy too!

"Another round?" Ben asked when they were getting out of the karts.

"I can't stand the humiliation of another loss. Besides, I owe you your prize."

"Prize?"

"Yeah, the loser always buys the winner a beer."

Ben shook his head. "You don't have to do that."

"I can afford it, trust me."

Now Ben looked downright uncomfortable, but Tim couldn't figure out why. "Still don't drink?"

"I do. Not often, but occasionally."

"Then let's go."

Tim supposed it would be like this for a while. Ben would have fun with him and get caught up in the past before remembering his current boyfriend. But eventually he would make a choice, and Tim was feeling more and more confident about what that choice would be. A couple of beers and some horrible chicken wings later, Tim was driving Ben home when the storm that had been hovering over the city finally broke, rain pouring down.

"Good." Ben sighed in relief. "We need that!"

"We do?"

"I mean plants and things," Ben explained, but Tim had already hit a button on the car's console. "Hey, what are you doing?"

With a whirr of motors, the convertible top opened, letting the weather in. Ben shouted in shock, and Tim howled with laughter. Soon Ben joined him as they cruised through torrents of rain. They reached Ben's home a few blocks later, but it was enough to thoroughly soak them both, Tim's shirt and shorts plastered to his body.

"Mind if I come in for a towel?" he asked once the convertible top was up again.

"Allison is home."

"So? Just think of what we used to do when your parents were home."

"Ha." Ben gestured toward the duplex with his head. "Come on. But in and out, okay?"

"Of course."

Allison was on the couch watching TV when they entered. She didn't look happy, shutting off the television and rising to have a hushed conversation with Ben. Tim idly examined the surroundings, feeling like a home wrecker. When the whispers became more like hisses, Ben broke away briefly.

"Wait in my room," he said, pushing Tim in the right direction.

Perfect.

He didn't find anything recognizable about Ben's bedroom, the furniture and decorations completely different from those of their teenage years. With one exception. The painting Tim had given Ben for his birthday—two hearts overlapping—hung on a wall opposite the bed. Tim stared at it, part of him criticizing his work from so long ago, but the rest of him feeling elated.

He spun around when Ben came in, wanting to scoop him up into his arms. Instead he took inspiration from the towel Ben had fetched for him and started stripping off his wet shirt. Slowly.

For one fleeting moment, familiar lust made those brown eyes appear anything but innocent. Then Ben tossed him the towel and looked away. "I need you to go."

Need. Not want. Tim dropped his shirt on the floor and towel-dried his hair. "Mind if I keep this? The car seats are pretty wet."

"Sure." Ben remained in the doorway, eyes on the carpet.

Just come closer, Tim thought. We both want this. "I had fun today," he said. "Just like old times. Better maybe, since I'm hiding in your bedroom from Allison instead of the whole world."

"It was a nice day," Ben admitted.

"How about dinner tomorrow? You deserve a better meal than those chicken wings."

Ben raised his head. "You broke my heart. You know that? I picked myself up and brushed myself off, but it never stopped hurting."

Tim swallowed. "If it's any consolation, I broke my own heart in the process."

"Did you?"

Tim put his hand over his chest. "I swear. I won't pretend to know what you went through, but I sent myself straight to Hell. I deserved everything I got, but you didn't."

Ben looked away, chewing his bottom lip. Tim struggled to find another way of expressing how much regret he felt, but there were no adequate words. He was sure he had lost when Ben said, "Maybe a quick lunch."

"Deal!" Tim walked toward him, towel draped over one shoulder, and Ben stood aside for him to leave. That was okay. Tim showed himself out, nodding cordially to Allison on the way. Not bad for the first date. Not bad at all.

Tim had an enemy in Allison. A shame, since he really did like her, but her intent became obvious the next day. He met Ben for lunch on campus, which was nice, but not conducive to romance. When they made plans for that night, Tim knew they were on the fast track. He could feel the tension between them growing. A little more time spent together and the outcome was inevitable.

Then Ben called in the late afternoon to cancel, saying Allison needed a night out with him. Tim didn't hold it against her. She was only trying to protect Ben from getting hurt again. She'd come around when she saw how happy Tim would make him. Instead of getting angry, he made further plans.

Saturday morning, Tim collected Ben and whisked him away to a nearby amusement park for another blast from their past. It wasn't the same park they'd visited as teenagers, but it wasn't so different either. They fell right back into their old routines, except this time Tim was desperate to touch Ben in public, to hold his hand or just put an arm around him. He didn't, not wanting to move too fast, but Tim did mentally kick his teenage self around for all the missed opportunities.

The day was ideal, the sun steadily sinking, when Ben's new guy found a way to ruin their fun, even from out of town.

"Samson!"

"Who?"

"Jace's cat. I totally forgot to feed him today."

Tim had forgotten the new guy's name until Ben said it again. Jace hadn't come up in conversation at all, and Tim had been happy to pretend he didn't exist. Ben—well, who knew what he was thinking? But now they had to head back to Austin just to feed the damn cat.

"I hope Samson's okay," Ben fretted once they were back on the highway. "Usually I stay over there when Jace is out of town."

"So why haven't you been?"

This earned a thoughtful pause, but one that ultimately backfired on Tim. "I'll crash there tonight. Gotta make sure the apartment looks nice before Jace comes home."

"When's that?"

"Tomorrow night."

"So I have you to myself until then." Tim glanced over at him. "We can do dinner tonight. We'll feed the cat and then head out. My treat."

"You don't need to pay for everything," Ben said. "I have money too, you know."

"I can afford it."

"How?"

That single word was loaded. Heavily. Come to think of it, Ben acted weird every time the topic of money came up. Tim's stomach sank. He knew what people said about him at school. The rumors had started after he moved in with Eric. The following fall, the fraternity had sent their usual fund-raisers to the alumni, including Eric. Tim had answered the door, recognized one of the brothers, and told them they could go fuck themselves. The rumors had spread after that, lies that would explain Ben's curious reactions.

"I inherited some money," Tim said. "A lot, actually."

"From who?"

"No one you would know," Tim snapped. He regretted it and took a few steady breaths. "His name was Eric. He was a friend of mine. He died last year."

"I'm sorry." Ben paused. "Still, it's a bit unusual. Inheriting money from a friend, I mean."

"Is it?"

"Yeah. Unless he was your sugar daddy or something."

Tim felt his temper rising. "I guess Allison has filled you in on the rumors, then?" Why did people have to be so stupid? Maybe the situation was unusual, but that didn't give them the right to cast judgment. Especially on Eric. He was amazing and wouldn't have needed to buy anyone. Ever. "I guess there's no point in telling you what you already know. Eric was rich, old, and gay. What else could it have been, right?"

Ben looked guilty. "I don't know."

"Well, it's bullshit! People think the whole world revolves around sex and money, but they're wrong. Eric was a good person and one of the best friends I ever had. All he ever wanted was friendship."

"I didn't mean to pry."

"Yeah, you did, but it's okay." Tim exhaled. "I just get tired of what people say. They don't know me. They take a couple of facts and warp them into something they can feel superior about."

"Yeah, that does suck." The hum of tires on the freeway accompanied an awkward pause. "So what's the truth, then?"

Complicated, to say the least. Tim explained the parts of it he could, how Eric was like the father he'd always wished for. How they could spend hours just being in each other's company and talking. And how, at the end, Tim found himself playing a role he never expected to. That part was much too complicated to express, so he kept it simple. No details, no breakdown of those final days. Tim had been his nurse. Simple as that.

"So sex was never involved?"

"No! Christ! Can't gay people just be friends?"

"Sorry. It's just the money thing—"

The money. Sometimes Tim felt like burning it all just to shut people up. "Yeah, well, what else was Eric supposed to do with it? He didn't have any kids. Just a sister. She got most of it. I got a small part, which was still a tremendous amount. And the house. She didn't want it, anyway."

His little outburst made the rest of the drive awkward. It only got worse for Tim when he followed Ben into Jace's apartment. He wished it was a horrible dump, cluttered by empty beer cans and smelling like a dirty litter box. Instead it was respectable and comfortable. Samson was cute, a gray furball who Tim felt gave him knowing looks. As soon as the cat was fed, Tim was eager to get Ben away from there, luring him back to the car with promises of dinner. But he needed to step up his game if Jace was due back tomorrow, and that meant finding somewhere private.

"Why don't we avoid the crowds? We'll go back to my place and I'll cook for you."

Ben's spidey sense must have tingled. "Eh, I don't know."

"It'll be cool." Tim switched lanes without waiting for permission. "You'll like it there." As he took the next exit, he wondered if that would be true. He couldn't imagine anyone but him and Eric in that house; the idea of Ben being part of the scenery seemed somehow surreal. But he had to try.

Ben sat on one of the bar stools, glancing around at the large kitchen, unaware that Tim watched him from the doorway. In front of Ben, the countertop held little except decorative bottles of oil. And a container of dry cereal, which had a surprising number of memories surrounding it. Eric loved a bowl of cereal in the morning. Tim always found this amusing. Eric had been such a food connoisseur, but in the mornings he went for artificially colored and heavily sugared cereals, usually with marshmallows. He would always sit where Ben sat now, Tim on the next stool over, as they munched away together.

"It's a huge house," Tim said, startling Ben as he walked into the room. "Too big for me. I plan on selling it and finding a place in Allandale, so don't go getting used to it."

Ben rolled his eyes. "Allandale is a nice neighborhood, but I don't know if you're enough of a hippie to fit in there."

True enough. Besides, Tim doubted he could really part with this place. He walked around the kitchen island and leaned against one of the counters.

Ben considered him. "So Eric lived here alone?"

"Yeah, when I first met him. It wasn't long before he asked me to move in. Don't give me that look! I can see what you're thinking."

"What would you think if anyone told you the same story? You have to admit it sounds fishy."

"Yeah, I guess so. You believe me, right?"

Ben shrugged. "Why not? The world's a crazy place."

"I would have, though."

"What?"

"Slept with Eric." Tim kept his head held high, not ashamed of this confession. "If it would have made him happy, I would have, but he never even hinted at it."

"Did you want to?"

"I don't know." Tim turned around and opened one of the cabinets, grateful for the excuse not to face Ben while he talked. "Sometimes you can't tell your friends from your lovers, you know what I mean? The line gets kind of blurry. That's how it was with me and Eric. Maybe if he wasn't on so many meds he would have wanted something physical. Maybe not."

"What was wrong with him?"

"Cancer. Multiple kinds, multiple places."

"Geez."

"Yeah." Tim grabbed a handful of ingredients and turned to set them on the island. "Eric toughed it out until the end. He never complained, never felt sorry for himself. He had so much spirit. That's why I can't sell the place yet. I feel like he's still here." Tim stared at the tiled surface of the island, thinking how he'd give anything for one more shared breakfast there. When he noticed Ben watching him, he tried to sound chipper. "Anyway, what did you have in mind for dinner?"

"You don't know how to cook, do you?"

Tim glanced down at the ingredients for the first time. Pineapples and pasta? Brown sugar and rice? Tim laughed. "No, I don't, but I had to get you here somehow. We could do delivery. Or we could get nostalgic and you could cook for me. I'll even lay myself out on the couch and pretend my ankle is jacked up."

"Tim—" Ben's warning tones matched his expression.

"Too far? Sorry. I just wanted you to see my home, since it's so connected to my past." And because he hoped Ben would be part of its future. "You being here really livens the place up. I wouldn't mind you visiting more often. Bring Jace along. I'd love to meet him."

Ben scrutinized him. Okay, so maybe Tim was laying on the nice guy act a little thick.

"All right," Ben said. "I'll cook, but you have to help. I don't care how rich you are, everyone should know how to make at least one meal. What have you got here?"

"Just a bunch of canned stuff." Most of it had been in the

cabinets when Eric was alive. "Uh, you better check the expiration dates. I eat a lot of take-out."

Ben was at his side, rustling through the counters. "Canned tomatoes—these are still good. Where are the spices?"

Tim followed Ben around, discovering cupboards he'd forgotten about, which was refreshing. Eric used to cook with these things, and now Ben would too. Tim liked that.

"Seriously? No onions?"

"I think there are green ones in the herb garden out back." Automatic sprinklers watered those. "Lots of things grow wild out there, if you know what you're looking for."

They raided the garden, tearing leaves off different plants to taste them and laughing about getting poisoned, but they found some familiar flavors and the onions. Ben fired up the oven, put a pan on the flames, and threw in some olive oil. He made Tim wash and slice the onions while he put water to boil on another burner.

"Toss the onions in and stir them around," Ben commanded like a drill sergeant. "Now the can of tomatoes and the spices."

"Yes, sir!"

Then Ben started stirring the concoction with a wooden spoon. "I learned to cook when taking care of you," he said.

"Seriously?"

Ben nodded, smiling at the memory. "You didn't notice? For two whole weeks everything you ate was either burnt or undercooked. I didn't know what I was doing. I'm surprised you survived."

"I remember it all tasting good."

"Must have been the painkillers." Ben glanced over at him, his eyes shiny. "I loved taking care of you."

"Well, you know where I live, and I'm still needy as hell."

"It's different now," Ben said.

"Exactly." Tim came up close behind him. "So is there a trick to stirring? Let me try."

He moved his arms around Ben, who let go of the wooden spoon before Tim could place his hand over his.

"Seriously?" Ben said. "That tired old move? Stir away."

Tim took the spoon and jabbed at the sauce. "I don't know how."

"Oh, come on!"

Tim moved forward, their bodies in full contact now. "Guide my hand."

"So lame!" Ben shook his head, but then he put his hand over Tim's.

And it felt so damned wonderful. Ben made a little effort to stir, but Tim let go of the spoon, splaying his fingers and inviting Ben to interweave his own. Ben moved his hand away and rolled to the side to free himself from his embrace. He didn't look angry though. Instead his skin was flushed.

"Keep stirring," he said.

"I'm not really hungry," Tim tried.

"But I am, and you promised me dinner."

"I suppose I did." Tim stirred, but kept his eyes on Ben. "You should come by more often, maybe in the morning. I miss those burnt waffles you used to make."

"They were pancakes," Ben protested, "and I thought you didn't remember my food being bad!"

Tim nodded at the pot. "It's starting to come back to me."

Ben laughed and shook his head, pushing Tim aside so he could resume cooking, tasting and adjusting the sauce, and testing the noodles. When he was satisfied he drained the water. "Grab some plates."

"Nah, just throw the pasta in the sauce and we'll eat it here. That's what I do sometimes with mac and cheese. Eat it straight out of the pot right here at the stove."

Ben stared at him. "That's the saddest thing I've ever heard."

"You feel sorry for me?"

"Yes."

"Good. Misery loves company. Grab a couple forks from that drawer and join me."

As it turned out, the food wasn't much better than the instant food Tim occasionally wolfed down, but the process had been fun. They attacked the pot, occasionally sword fighting with their forks, and snacking away until most of it was gone.

"I wish it could be like this every day," Tim said.

Ben toyed with a few leftover noodles in the pot. "This used to be my dream."

"And I ruined it. Do you ever regret it?"

"What?"

"The time we had together."

Ben snorted. "Are you kidding? Never. Not once."

Tim straightened up. "Really? I figured you hated me for what I did."

"I never hated you. I just hurt. When we were together—" Ben exhaled. "Don't let it go to your head, but even when it was bad, it was good."

Tim leaned forward, ready for a kiss, but Ben returned his attention to the stray noodles in the pot. So much for Lady and the Tramp. Maybe dessert would work better than pasta. Tim went to the freezer. "I know I have some ice cream in here somewhere."

"I really need to get back to Jace's."

"Aw, you can't leave. You haven't even done the dishes yet!" Tim winced from Ben's glare. "Only kidding. Geez! There is a pool here, you know. We could go for a swim, have a couple of beers. You can even crash here."

Ben scoffed. "I don't think so!"

"Your virtue will remain unchallenged, Princess, you have my word." Not true. "There are two guest rooms. Take your pick. I'll even sleep in the car." Also not true!

But Ben was adamant. Short of pouncing on him and taking him on the kitchen floor, Tim's only option was to give in and drive Ben back to Jace's. He pulled up to the apartment, wondering if he should walk Ben to the door, but of course being close to the lair of the enemy probably wouldn't help his chances.

"Thanks for the last couple of days," Tim said. "I know I went a little overboard, but it's been a long time since I've had someone like you around."

Ben shifted in his seat. "I liked it too, but I'm also looking forward to Jace coming home tomorrow."

"Hint taken." Unwillingly. What if Jace being back in town put an end to their little reunion? "I'm serious about meeting him. The man behind the legend and all that."

"Yeah?"

"Yeah."

"Okay."

Where a goodbye kiss should have been was a nervous chuckle. Then Ben was out of the car, released back into the world. If you love somebody, set them free…

Chapter Twenty-three

Waiting should always be avoided. Good or bad, confronting the future is better than torturous anticipation or crippling dread. Tim called Ben early the next morning with the intent of talking him into cutting class. There was no answer. He tried again closer to lunch. Still no answer. With Jace due back in the evening, Tim was forced to wait and wonder.

He didn't remember how long Jace and Ben had been together. Perhaps he had tuned out that information. Regardless if their relationship had lasted years, months, or even just a few weeks, they would most likely celebrate their reunion in the bedroom.

The thought alone made Tim seethe with jealousy. He tried not to think about it, giving his full attention first to his classes and now to painting. Tim worked in silence, just him and a canvas, occasionally glancing toward the fading light on the other side of the garage window. He had moved all of his equipment into the garage some time ago. Marcello had a habit of letting himself into the house, occasionally commenting on Tim's work. His words were encouraging, but still invasive.

Later, when Tim brought home a one-night stand who turned out to be an art student, the guy had stood there and critiqued one of Tim's paintings. Like it was any of his business! Of course Tim didn't admit the work was his own, but that had been the final straw. The paintings were as private as his emotions—not to be shared with just anyone.

So Tim had cleared out the garage and made it his studio. Usually he found painting therapeutic, but today it only seemed to increase his frustration. Nothing came out like he wanted it to, the canvas growing darker as he added more and more layers of failure. He was trying not to think of Ben, desperately avoiding thoughts of where he was or what he was doing. Or what was being done to him.

Still the images came unbidden. A hello kiss for Jace when he came in the door. That shy feeling that comes from being apart, especially when the other person means so much to you. Jace picking Ben up. Carrying him down the hall. Laying him on the bed.

Tim tossed aside the paintbrush. Part of him felt like driving over there, kicking in the door, and begging Ben to run away with him. Despite how pathetic this would make him seem, the idea was tempting.

Instead he picked up the brush, closed his eyes, and thought of Ben. Not what he was doing at this moment, but who he was, how complete he made Tim feel. When they were in high school, Ben had given Tim the affection he was desperate for while showing him how to be free. Now Ben represented hope, the promise of an end to his solitude. Someone he could share his life with.

Taking a deep breath, Tim opened his eyes and continued painting.

Tim understood why Ben didn't answer his phone that first day. That he didn't answer the second day was an ill omen. Tim tried anyway, hoping to get through. On the third day he abandoned all subtlety and called every hour. He cursed himself for not setting up the voicemail before giving Ben the phone. At least then Ben might give into temptation and listen to what he had to say.

Tim didn't have a plan. He had nothing.

He was deep into one of his evening painting sessions when he heard a car pull in the driveway. He shot out the side door in seconds, hoping to see Ben smiling at him through the windshield. Instead he found a huge man getting out of an even bigger Rolls-Royce Phantom.

"Hello, my handsome prince," Marcello said theatrically.

"Hey," Tim replied, forcing his eyes away from the car. Whenever Marcello came around, he made some excuse to enter the house. Tim understood why. Others visited graves, but he and Marcello were lucky to have this piece of Eric left behind.

"It's hotter than Satan's butt crack out here." Marcello dabbed at his forehead with a handkerchief. "Please tell me you have the air conditioner cranked up to the max."

"Of course." Tim led him inside to the living room before fetching drinks from the kitchen. He always kept a bottle of champagne in the refrigerator for Marcello. Tim popped the cork, grabbing a glass to go with it and a bottle of beer for himself. When he reentered the living room, Marcello was glancing around as if at an exhibition.

"The parties that used to take place here," he said as Tim poured his champagne. "You know, I don't think a single party at my house has ended without someone getting into an argument, but here people behaved respectably. Ah, thank you!"

Tim raised his bottle in a quick toast, took a swig, and sat in the chair opposite Marcello. "It was Eric. People never argued here because they didn't want to upset him."

"Quite so." Marcello nodded. "Do you ever think about continuing the tradition?"

Tim shook his head. "It wouldn't be the same."

"I suppose not. Well, speaking of parties, guess who's turning fifty?"

"Your nephew?" Tim teased. "I know it can't be you, because I was at your fiftieth last year."

"And that wasn't my first." Marcello took a dainty sip of his champagne, the light catching the glass and the rings on his fingers. "I'm having a real bash this year, no expense spared."

"If you want me to jump out of the cake, you can forget it."

"I'd rather you jump out of those clothes." Marcello chuckled at the idea, then tutted when Tim didn't look amused. "You seem tense tonight."

Tim sighed. "Sorry. Don't take this as a hint, but I'm sexually frustrated."

"Easily cured," Marcello said. "I can't imagine you having trouble attracting bees to the flower. Or if you're tired of the scene, I'd be happy to send over one of my boys."

Tim shook his head. "There's only one guy who can scratch my itch."

"And? Has he never laid eyes on you?"

Tim smiled at the compliment. "It's Ben's boyfriend that's the problem."

Marcello waved a hand dismissively. "That's only a problem if you get caught."

"It's more than just sex," Tim said. He took another swig. "Have you ever been in love?"

"I've always been in love with the idea of being in love, if that counts."

"Seriously." Over the years, Tim had seen a number of guys on Marcello's arm, most of them young and gorgeous. And they didn't seem to be there under duress. At first Tim thought it was the money, and maybe it was for a few of them, but others seemed to genuinely find *something* about Marcello appealing. "You never seem to have trouble getting what you want."

"Success in love comes much as it does in business. Aggression and persistence will get you most of the way, with a little sweet talk to seal the deal." Marcello appraised him. "In your case, a pair of Speedos should do the trick. My birthday party is at Splashtown this weekend. I won't be swimming, but I always enjoy the view. I have the whole park reserved for me and my friends."

"Isn't that down in San Antonio?"

Marcello nodded. "I have two party buses reserved to shuttle us all there. Why don't you come and bring this Ben person with you?"

Tim leaned back. "I doubt his boyfriend will allow that."

"Bring him as well."

Tim snorted.

"I'm serious." Marcello leaned forward. "Do you really think he can compete with you?"

That was a tricky question. Tim avoided conversations about Jace, so he didn't know much about him. From the photo he had seen, he was an okay-looking guy. Handsome in an offbeat way. But Tim had taken good care of his body, and it wouldn't hurt to remind Ben of his assets.

"When Ben sees you and this other person together," Marcello said, "one of you is going to pale in comparison. I wouldn't bet a penny on this boyfriend of his. If it doesn't work out, I'm inviting the handsomest boys in Austin. I'm sure you'll find someone to soothe your broken heart."

"That won't be necessary."

When it came to advice, Marcello made a poor replacement for Eric, but he might be on to something this time. He knew how to get what he wanted, and Tim sure as hell wanted Ben.

The next day he called only once, unperturbed when he still didn't get an answer. Tim went through the motions of the day, waiting until evening when he was sure Ben would be out of class. Then he drove over to the duplex and rang the bell. Allison opened the door, eyebrows raised as if his every thought was transparent.

"He's not here," she said.

"Does he have a class this late?"

"He's usually home by now. Just not this home."

"Jace?"

She nodded. "Sorry."

Well, that was something. At least she didn't look smug as she shut the door. Of course she probably didn't realize that Tim knew where Jace lived. Or that Tim was crazy enough to head straight into enemy territory. Why shouldn't he? Jace was invited to the party too. Besides, it was time he learned firsthand what he was up against.

His self-assurance remained intact even as he knocked on the apartment door. He imagined Ben opening it, shocked and maybe a little thrilled by Tim's audacity. He felt less certain when Jace answered.

There is a big difference between seeing someone in a photo and meeting them in real life. Jace was taller than he was—which Tim didn't like—and dressed in a nice button-up shirt and casual slacks that made Tim feel scuzzy in his T-shirt and shorts. His blond-brown hair was styled intentionally messy, matching his controlled-but-casual appearance. Jace looked Tim over with a flicker of recognition, but with no hint of interest.

"Hey," Tim said, flashing a smile. Even that failed to provoke a reaction, causing him to wonder if he wasn't looking his best today. "Jace, right? I'm Tim."

He extended a hand, which Jace accepted. Because Jace was tall, he looked thin, but his hands were warm and strong. Tim hated to think of all the places they had been.

"Tim, of course," Jace replied. "Ben said he had run into you recently."

In other words, *I know all about you.* "Yeah, it was just like old times. Hey, I was hoping to talk to you both about an idea I had."

"Ben isn't home," Jace said.

"But he usually is by now, right? I don't mind waiting."

Jace took stock of him. Tim was sure Jace was about to tell him to go fuck himself and to not come around anymore. That's what Tim would have said were the situation reversed, but instead Jace shrugged easily and gestured for him to enter.

The apartment felt more alive with Jace there. Even Samson seemed peppier. He still did the creeping, cautious sniff thing that cats did, as if seeing a person wasn't proof enough that they weren't really a giant pudding monster. Then Samson happily followed Jace to the living room and hopped up on his owner's lap as soon as Jace was seated in the recliner.

Tim spread out on the couch, trying to make himself as large as possible. Hey, it worked in the animal kingdom. "So, Ben tells me you're a stewardess or something."

Jace smiled as if this didn't bother him. "Yes. That's exactly what I am, although I prefer to think of myself as an astronaut of the stratosphere."

Huh.

"That's funny," Tim said without humor. "Seems like all they talk about on the news lately is airline employees having to take cuts. Must be hard making a living in your line of work."

"I don't live in a mansion," Jace replied, "but I managed to take Ben to London recently. That was nice. Still, I'll be glad when Ben has graduated and is earning money. What are you studying?"

Tim mumbled something about architecture while trying to come to grips with the situation. Here he was, a high school sweetheart back from the past and gorgeous enough that most gay guys would love to get into his pants—and yet Jace calmly sat there watching him with the same casual curiosity as his cat. Was Jace always like this? If so, Tim could understand the appeal of being with someone so confident.

"I don't know much about architecture," Jace said, "although I did see one of Hundertwasser's buildings once, and that was a real eye opener."

"He was amazing," Tim admitted. "Shows you what's possible if people think outside the box. Buildings can be art."

"True. I suppose it's like poetry. I've never really enjoyed it either, but someone like Dr. Seuss makes it so wacky and fun that it's impossible not to like."

Tim nodded. "Although it's odd how if you make a painting that's strange and different, most people dismiss it. Everyone scoffs at modern art or art installations, when really that's also being playful within a medium. These days you have to grab people's attention any way you can."

Hold on now! Tim felt like leaping to his feet and pointing an accusatory finger. Jace was disarmingly charming when he should be biting his nails and fearing for his relationship. Even now, he was checking his watch as if he had other concerns.

"If he's this late, I should probably start dinner."

"No problem," Tim said, whipping out his phone. "I'll order us some pizzas. Ben still likes cheese and tomatoes, right? What about you?"

Ha ha! Take that! Your boyfriend is being fed by another man!

But this small victory went unnoticed by Jace, who pet and talked to his cat while Tim was ordering on the phone. When waiting for their food to arrive, Tim gave up taking cheap shots at Jace and kept conversation civilized. After all, the plan was to invite him to a party, and being the only one behaving maliciously made him feel like a royal asshole.

Not that he was done completely. The second the doorbell rang, Tim leapt up to answer it, like he owned the place. When he opened the door, he found something much more appetizing than dinner. Ben stood there slack-jawed, arms full of books and take-out.

Tim grinned at him. "For a pizza boy, you're pretty hot."

Chapter Twenty-four

Water slides, a wave pool, and all the overpriced snow cones you could eat. As far as Tim knew, there were only two Splashtowns: one in San Antonio and another near Houston. Back in high school, Ben often hinted that they go, but of course Tim had been too twisted up with fear then. That they were finally going now tied in nicely with his high school nostalgia tour, even if the "astronaut of the stratosphere" was tagging along. Tim was just happy Jace had agreed to this nutty plan. Maybe Marcello knew what he was talking about.

Only Allison's presence threw him off. Why did Ben insist on bringing his fiercest chaperone? As Tim drove them to San Antonio, Ben spent half the trip down in the backseat with Allison, laughing it up or singing—especially when Tim tried making conversation with Ben. Hearing that voice again—even slightly changed due to age—was worth the beating Tim's confidence was taking.

A guard at the gate checked Tim's name against a list before they were allowed into the park. Party headquarters was at a restaurant near the entrance. Despite Marcello's promise of Austin's hottest guys, all the other party-goers were much older and fully clothed. Maybe the eye candy was out enjoying the actual park, like Tim was eager to do, but he wanted to at least put in an appearance. Marcello greeted him dressed in a ridiculous Hawaiian-patterned shirt, complete with hula dancers and pineapples.

"Happy 49th," Tim teased, giving him a hug. "I didn't get you anything because you're already too damn rich."

Marcello batted his eyelashes. "The only thing I've ever wanted is your happiness. Speaking of which, who do we have here?"

Tim made the introductions. When he got to Jace, Marcello snuck Tim a look of approval. Wrong guy, dumb ass! Even Marcello thought Jace was hot, and he'd been around the block—maybe even the globe—a few times. After a little more birthday banter, they were free to hit the locker room. Allison went her way, while he, Jace, and Ben got changed on the boys' side.

When they met again back outside, the sun warming their skin, he caught Ben looking him over. Tim stretched and casually flexed. Of course he wanted to win Ben over with more than just his body, but he'd take what he could get.

They started with the nearest water slides, and for a while Tim forgot about his intended conquest and just had fun. The park was nearly empty except for nomadic groups of gay guys. The lifeguards on duty appeared either amused or uncomfortable, many seeming happy to see a girl in their group. Allison soon abandoned them for the attention of one of those lifeguards. One down, one to go.

The wave pool came next. They lost themselves in the oddly enjoyable experience of getting knocked around by water. More than once Tim let himself "accidentally" collide with his former flame. Ben even forgot himself enough to smile, his eyes half-lidded before he seemed to wake from his dream and look around for Jace.

As fun as flirting was, Tim figured he wasn't likely to get anywhere while Jace was around. They tried tubing next, Tim preferring to swim along the slow-moving river. After a break for lunch, they hit the artificial lagoon. Ben caught Tim staring and splashed him, so Tim splashed back before Jace playfully came to his rescue. Soon they were in the middle of a huge—but friendly—water fight. As much as Tim wanted to, he couldn't dislike Jace. Regardless, he was still glad when Ben's boyfriend waded back to shore to dry out in the sun.

Tim headed toward a wall of rocks, showing Jace that Ben was left alone. Once he climbed onto a stony outcrop, Tim watched them both—Jace to see if he was checking on them and Ben, who was floating on his back. Tim couldn't stop staring. Ben's body had matured, but he would probably never be very big. He didn't really have any muscle, but Tim didn't care. He liked Ben's size, how it made him feel stronger in comparison. He wanted to wrap his arms around that narrow torso, squeezing until Ben laughed and told him to stop, just like they used to.

And then he wanted to do a whole lot more.

Three waterfalls coursed over the wall of rocks, behind one a grotto. Glancing toward the shore, he saw Jace lounging there. Chances were, his eyes were closed behind the shades he was wearing, so Tim moved toward the cave.

"Check it out!" he called, hopefully just loud enough for Ben to hear. "There's a cave behind this one."

Ben waded over to see. Tim stood beneath the waterfall,

the pressure of the flow relaxing his muscles, the cool water helping keep down one muscle in particular. As soon as Ben was near, he held out an arm, breaking the water flow and creating a door for Ben to duck through. The cramped interior was lit solely by filtered light from the entrance. The small pool inside was probably designed for kids, only deep enough to reach Ben's waist. Tim waded in, the water lapping at his crotch as if encouraging him.

Ben still played the angel, looking at the water, the walls, anywhere but directly at Tim. "You know this is where everyone comes to pee," he said.

Tim grinned. "Or to do other things."

Ben didn't react. "They should put a hot tub in here. That would be way cooler."

Come on, Benjamin! Stop playing. "I liked hearing you sing today." Tim moved a little closer to him. "In the car. It was nice."

"Thanks."

"Sometimes at night, on the very edge of sleep, I swear I could hear you singing." Tim laughed at himself. "That sounds cheesy, but it's true. Never in a million years did I think you'd be in my life again, that I really would be able to hear the sound of your voice."

Ben's attention was on the ceiling now, as if praying to God to help him avoid temptation. "Do you still paint?"

No more changing topics. No more talk. Tim remained silent, thinking about how long it had been since they had kissed, how Ben's hand over his on a wooden spoon could feel more intimate than sex. Finally Ben looked at Tim with eyes both vulnerable and wanting. He started to say something, but Tim shook his head and moved in close. Wasn't it about time they picked up where they'd left off?

Tim touched a lock of Ben's hair, heavy with chlorinated water. He brushed it behind Ben's ear and let his hand keep moving to the back of his head, pulling Ben in for a kiss.

Their lips met, but it wasn't electric. Ben's lips were mush beneath his, not responding, and Tim knew he had lost. He had tried everything he could, but Jace was the better— Fire! Ben's lips came to life with hunger, his body pressing against his, and then Tim knew why Lucifer was so desperate to conquer Heaven and make it his own. He hadn't been wrong, his memories polished by nostalgia. In fact, they had grown dusty and tarnished, because Tim had forgotten how wonderful kissing Ben could be.

Tim grabbed Ben tight, hands clenching at his back while Ben seemed so desperate to touch every part of him that he couldn't settle at one place. He felt Ben's hardness rub against his own and wished he could shout down the walls of the cave, sealing them safely away from the outside world forever and ever.

The constant roar of the waterfall was broken before Jace spoke. "About done?"

Ben shoved Tim away hard enough that he fell backward, splashing into the water. At the cave entrance, Jace's towering form blocked out the light, and Tim wondered if he would have to fight. Except Jace's face wasn't angry but drawn and hurt. He didn't even look at Tim. Only at Ben who spluttered an apology.

Tim got to his feet, Jace's gaze flicking in his direction.

"Maybe you should wait for us outside, Tim."

He didn't like the sound of that. Maybe Jace hid his anger well, only revealing his demon when others weren't looking. Tim left through the waterfall, staying close to the entrance and straining to listen. If Jace flipped out, Tim would step in to save Ben, and it would be check and mate.

Ben was apologizing again, the regret in his voice like a knife in Tim's chest. How could Ben regret what had felt so perfect? Tim soon forgot his pain when he heard Jace's response.

"It's all right."

Ben's reply mirrored Tim's thoughts. "What?"

"I said it's all right." Jace was closer to the entrance and easier to hear. "I knew something like this would happen eventually, if it hadn't already."

"I didn't do anything with him before!" Ben replied. "Just now, I promise." There was a pause, Tim straining to hear more when Ben spoke again. "Aren't you angry?"

"Not really. Old feelings don't just disappear overnight. It's normal that you and Tim still find each other attractive."

Great. Now Jace was channeling Eric, sending a surge of guilt zipping down to Tim's stomach.

"That's it?" Ben didn't sound happy. "I wish you *were* pissed. At least then I could tell that you care."

"I care." Jace's voice was louder now. "I just thought I'd give you the benefit of the doubt."

"What's there to doubt? You saw everything. I did something stupid, and you should hate me for it."

No, it wasn't stupid. They did what they both desperately wanted. Tim leaned closer to hear Jace's response, his ear grazing the waterfall.

"I'd never hate you."

Nice move, but Tim wasn't about to let things turn sweet again. He pushed through the entrance, grinning shamelessly at Jace as he waded into the pool. "Hey, it's my fault. I grabbed him and started kissing him. Ben wasn't even kissing back. Really. Please don't blame him."

Jace nodded as if considering his words. Then he pulled his fist back and swung so fast that Tim didn't even have time to flinch. Boom! Those big gentle hands of his fucking hurt! Tim fell backwards into the water, laid out so flat that this time his head went under. He felt hands grab him and pull him up again, but he didn't need to wipe the water from his eyes to know they belonged to Jace. Tim's head was still reeling from the punch, but as soon as it cleared, he would tear Jace to pieces. The asshole even helped Tim lean against a wall so he could recover, making him all the more livid.

Jace released him and turned toward Ben. "How's that for angry? Come on, we're going home."

Tim looked at Ben, waiting for him to say no, to declare his love for him. But instead he followed Jace out of the cave, only sparing him the smallest of glances. Tim let him go. There would be another time when Jace wasn't around, when they couldn't be interrupted, and then Ben would be free to give into the feelings they both shared. Tim wasn't giving up. Not now. Not ever.

Rubbing his jaw, Tim made his way to the front of the park, hoping to catch Ben and Jace in another argument on the way, but they seemed to have disappeared. He didn't know how. Were they going to walk back to Austin? It was that or wait for Marcello's party buses to shuttle most people home.

The restaurant hosting Marcello's party was packed now, people trading fun in the sun for cool drinks in the shade. Tim wished he hadn't driven down so he could have a stiff drink. After changing back into his clothes, Tim grabbed a beer anyway, leaving it closed but pressing the cold bottle to his jaw. No sign of Ben and Jace here either, but Marcello spotted him and made his way over.

"From the red mark on your cheek," Marcello said, "I take it your friend said no."

"He said yes." Tim grimaced. "His boyfriend said no."

Marcello chuckled, clapping his hands together. "Well, be sure to make your next move before the dust settles."

"Huh?"

"Little infidelities can either tear a couple apart or push them together again. It just depends on how forgiving the other person is."

Great. Jace was ridiculously noble and would probably try harder in their relationship. "Round two will have to wait because I think they took off. I'm about to do the same."

"Not before I blow out the candles on my cake."

"Yeah, all right." Tim tried to put the whole incident behind him and act cheerful. After all, it was Marcello's birthday. But after a slice of cake he said a quick goodbye and left the restaurant. On his way, he bumped into Allison.

"Tim! Where are the boys? I've been looking everywhere."

Man. Couldn't they have taken Allison with them? "I'm pretty sure they left."

"Without me?"

He shrugged.

Allison gave him a knowing look. "What did you do?"

Tim rolled his eyes and headed for the parking lot, Allison on his heels.

"You can't just abandon me here!"

"There are shuttle buses leaving later."

"There's a bus leaving now, and I'm the only passenger!"

Tim glanced back at her. They were two peas in a pod, Ben and Allison. "Come on then."

He was sure he would get the third degree, but as they hit the highway, Allison had other things on her mind.

"Twenty-three, a licensed lifeguard, and drop dead gorgeous," she raved. "And he still lives with his mother?"

"I don't think being a lifeguard pays very much," Tim replied.

"That doesn't matter, not to me. He *likes* living with his mother and was talking about me meeting her. I suggested dinner. He suggested lunch with his mom. I'm sorry, but if you already have a lady in your life, I'm not interested. Especially if you're related to her."

Tim laughed. "If he was that hot, you could have slept with him before bailing."

"Only guys think that way." Allison paused. "Okay, so maybe women think like that too, but we don't act on it as much. Speaking of which."

"What?"

"You know what. You did something to chase Ben and Jace away."

Tim shrugged. "It takes two to tango."

Allison sighed, shaking her head. "Ben, Ben, Ben. Why does he never listen to me?"

"Nothing personal, but I'm glad he doesn't."

"I bet!" Allison gave him a playful slap on the arm.

Tim glanced over at her. "You aren't pissed at me?"

"I don't know all the details yet. Give me time."

Why the hell not? Tim told her everything that had happened. She'd hear it all from Ben anyway.

"It's just nostalgia," Allison said when he was finished.

"No, it's not."

"It is. You're both in love with the person you remember from high school. Have you changed?"

"Yeah, of course, but—"

"So has Ben."

"That doesn't mean it won't work. We're more compatible now *because* we've changed."

Allison wasn't convinced. "That's what you think. You won't know until you try. Everything is different now. When you first met Ben, he was desperate for any kind of relationship. He would have fallen for any guy willing to have him. After high school, he never had trouble finding a boyfriend, and since Jace, he's been totally happy."

"And yet he kissed me back."

"Nostalgia," Allison repeated. "Maybe it could work, but to find out, you would have to wreck a two-year relationship."

"Ben and I were together a year," he retorted, but that sounded lame even to his own ears. How much of that time did Ben spend trying to get Tim to ditch Krista and admit his feelings? With Jace, it was probably fireworks and valentines from the very beginning. Maybe Allison was right. He didn't stand a chance.

But once he had dropped her off, Tim's mind wandered back to that kiss in the grotto, how more than their bodies had caught fire. They belonged together, and Tim wasn't about to make the same mistake again. This time he wouldn't let Ben go.

"We need to talk."

Tim tried to analyze Ben's voice. Over the phone he couldn't rely on facial expression. Did he sound wistful? Reluctant?

"About what?" Tim replied.

Ben hesitated. "Everything."

That was vague. "Okay. Like this, or—?"

"Can I come over?"

"Yeah! Of course. How about right now?"

"All right." Ben didn't sound particularly happy or excited. "I'll see you soon."

Tim paced the house for the next hour, walking to the front windows and checking the driveway. This was bad. Had Ben said "I *need* to see you!" he wouldn't be worried right now. Instead they were going to talk, but what couldn't be said over the phone? Of course this could be a good thing. In person, they could pick up where they had left off.

When Ben's car pulled in the driveway, Tim was already out the door and standing in the yard before the engine went silent. Ben seemed preoccupied, barely looking in his direction. Then the car door opened and something small and fat hopped out and ran to him, its whole body quivering with excitement.

Tim stared in surprise. "You got a dog?"

"No," Ben corrected, "*you* got a dog."

Tim squatted, the puppy doing little leaps to lick at his face. The little booger was ugly in the most adorable way possible. Tim stroked its head and jiggled its furry sides, laughing at the loose skin that looked like a kid dressed up in grownup clothing. "This is a bulldog, right?"

"Yeah." Ben kneeled on the grass, the puppy running back and forth between them. "I was on my way over here and stopped for some beer—uh, which I totally forgot about—and there was this lady looking for a good home for these puppies. I figure not many people have a home better than you."

Tim sniffed, but not because he was moved. "What smells like pee?"

"That would be me." Ben winced. "She got excited and peed all over my shirt."

"It's a girl? Hm. She needs a good Spanish name. *Pepita* maybe."

Ben flashed him a smile, always loving it when Tim broke out the foreign lingo. "What's that mean?"

"Pumpkin seed. Sounds cute, doesn't it?"

Ben shook his head. "Too random!"

Tim grabbed the puppy, trying to get her to hold still for a few seconds so he could take a look. The little fat body and squashed face reminded him of another animal. "Then she'll be my little Chinchilla! Isn't that right, my stubby little puppy? Are you my Chinchilla?"

The dog barked, causing them to laugh. Tim met Ben's eye, catching the tender admiration there, but he was still worried. This hadn't been the plan. Ben meant to pick up beer for their big talk, which was probably intended to soften the blow. But maybe Chinchilla had earned him another shot.

"I don't have anything a dog needs. Let's go shopping!"

"What, now?"

"Yeah, why not?"

After running into the house to fetch Ben a clean shirt, they piled into Tim's car like a perfect little family and headed to a huge pet store. Normally Tim tried to be cautious with the money Eric had left him, but not today. He splurged on everything a dog could need from the very best puppy food to just about every toy the store offered. He even ordered a dog house to be delivered—not that Chinchilla would need to sleep there unless she wanted to.

Then they brought her home, letting her tear into her new toys and chasing after her as she plowed through the house. Finally, when it seemed she would never stop peeing, barking, and chewing, Chinchilla rolled over on the floor and conked out. Tim looked at Ben with exaggerated relief, catching something in his expression that made him nervous. They stood as quietly as possible, letting the puppy snooze on the carpet as they snuck over to the couch.

"This was a nice surprise," Tim said casually. "I thought

you were coming over to tell me that Jace wants my head on a platter."

"No." Ben's face became guarded. "Jace was very understanding about everything, but there is something we need to talk about."

"Oh yeah?"

"I can't handle this." Now the mask slipped, Ben looking strained. "My feelings for you, I mean. They never went away—"

"That's a good thing," Tim interrupted.

"No, it's not. I love Jace. I've been with him a long time, and I plan on staying with him."

Tim grabbed his arm. "I can give you everything he can. More, even."

Ben shook his head, jaw clenching. "I'm with Jace. And that's how it's going to stay."

Tim let go. The words stung. Maybe he had moved too quickly, but it wasn't too late. They could start over, build up slowly. "Okay. Fine. That doesn't mean we can't be friends."

"Yeah, it does, Tim, because that's not how I see you."

"That's not how I see you either, so why fight it?"

"Because I love Jace, and I've already hurt him more than I ever should have."

"And you don't love me?" Tim pleaded. "I know you do, because I feel the same way."

Ben stared at him wide-eyed and confused. Then he leapt to his feet, Chinchilla's head whipping up in response. "I have to go. I don't think we should see each other. For a while, at least."

Ben headed for the door, breaking into a run when he reached the hallway.

"Benjamin, wait!"

Tim chased after him, Chinchilla following like it was a game. Ben was getting in his car when Tim made it outside, but Chinchilla didn't see him, stocky legs pumping as she kept running for the sheer joy of it. She was heading for the street, and Tim had a nightmare vision of Ben—blinded by tears as he sped away—running over her. Tim sprinted and leapt, nearly tackling Chinchilla to stop her. She squirmed safely in his arms as he raised his head to see Ben leaving him all over again.

Chapter Twenty-five

Tim didn't realize he had a routine until it was broken. No longer could he shuffle to the fridge in the morning, bleary-eyed and miserable until he chugged that first can of Coke. Now he barely managed to get his bathrobe on before a little monster had bitten the hem, tugging and growling playfully. Sometimes Tim managed to grab a drink on the way to the backyard so Chinchilla could pee—on the rare occasion she went outside to do so instead of piddling on the carpet. Then Chinchilla had to be fed, after which she wanted to play.

The dog came first, and only after her needs were satisfied did Tim make time for himself. This helped the weeks pass less painfully than they would have otherwise. But as he got used to his new life as a doggy dad, Tim found himself stewing more on what had happened.

Anger and jealously toward Jace troubled him for a couple of weeks, along with a healthy portion of blame toward his teenage self who had given it all away. Then he became more reasonable, telling himself it was time to cut his losses and move on.

There *was* one prospect. Aaron was in Tim's contemporary art course. They had noticed each other early in the semester, mostly because Tim caught Aaron staring so often. Aaron was gay. He was too primped to be anything else. Tim had known frat boys obsessed with their appearance, but they normally drew the line at powder and base.

Aaron's style had a strange appeal, an alluring touch of femininity with all the benefits of being a boy. So Tim had playfully winked at him one day. Ever since, Aaron made excuses to talk to Tim after class, practically panting each sentence in his enthusiasm. Today was no exception. As they walked through the halls, Aaron filled the silence between them with an air of desperation, as if searching for the magic phrase that would make Tim want to be with him.

"It's like, I wish there was another year of college," he was saying. "I could use the time to figure out what the hell I want to do, you know?"

Tim nodded. He certainly did.

"When you're a kid you think, 'oh, I'll be a doctor,' and it's as simple as that. What am I going to do with a degree in fashion design? I like dressing up, but I could give a shit what anyone else wants to wear. You know what I'm thinking of doing after I graduate? Going to a beauty academy."

Tim glanced over at him. "You need a degree to get into one of those places?"

"More like five thousand bucks." Aaron laughed madly. "My parents are going to kill me, but I don't care. They made me come here. I told them after high school that I just want to cut hair and give makeovers! Me, making the world more beautiful, one middle-aged woman at a time."

Shamelessly proud of who he was, Aaron had the blond hair and the slender frame. He wasn't so different from Ben, really. Maybe he would be close enough. Tim stopped, Aaron walking a few more steps before he noticed.

"What's up?"

"Come here," Tim said, voice husky.

Aaron fidgeted and flushed before he complied. When he was close enough, Tim put a hand on his neck, leaned forward, and kissed him. Aaron tasted like the gum he'd been smacking, his breath minty fresh. He was a good kisser, letting Tim lead but not remaining passive. And Tim felt nothing. Not even a stirring in his pants.

"What was that for?" Aaron grinned when Tim pulled away.

"Just because. I'll see you around."

Once outside, Tim walked around the building to get away from the parking lot where their cars were. When he felt enough distance, he leaned against the brick wall of the building and resisted the urge to bang the back of his head against it. So stupid! Of course no one could compare to Ben, but it had seemed worth a shot anyway. Life would be so much easier if he could move on.

Tim knew now that he couldn't.

Nights were sleepless, even though he jogged more than usual, or played countless games with Chinchilla. Even with his body exhausted, Tim's mind was fevered, refusing to rest as he considered scheme after scheme of getting Ben back. One thing was for sure: as long as Jace was in the picture, he didn't stand a chance. So his focus shifted to separating them somehow. The plan he came up with wasn't brilliant, but it was his only shot.

The following week, after his contemporary art course, he invited Aaron out for coffee. What he proposed would probably get him slapped in the face, considering how perked up Aaron was. They sat across from each other at a table with a chessboard surface. This was the same coffee shop where Tim had found Ben again, providing him with all the motivation he needed.

He told Aaron a condensed version of his history with Ben, and slowly Aaron's shoulders began to droop. Only when Tim got to the end did Aaron straighten up hopefully.

"So it sounds like it's over between you two," he said.

Tim nodded. "Yeah. But I can't move on. I keep trying…" He looked at Aaron meaningfully. "This guy Ben's with—he's no good." A lie. Jace was *too* good, but the truth wouldn't help his cause. "Maybe if they weren't together anymore I could get over it."

"There's not much you can do about that," Aaron said dismissively.

"I think there is."

"Oh?"

Tim leaned back. "What if someone wrote Jace a love letter? The guy travels all the time, which would give him plenty of opportunity to mess around on Ben."

"So… what? You send a love letter to Jace and hope Ben finds it?" Aaron scoffed. "Jace will just throw it away."

Time to move in for the kill. "Right, but if Ben sees this guy leaving the letter for Jace, maybe tacking it to his door…"

"A-ha. Let me guess. You want me to be that guy."

Tim gave a slow smile. "I can't exactly do it myself."

Aaron pursed his lips. "I'm not stupid, you know. You just want them to break up so you can get to Ben."

Fuck. Time for a new strategy. "I can make it worth your while."

"Really? How?"

There was something disturbing in the way Aaron looked at him, like he thought Tim would gladly whip it out in return for this favor. "I mean money," he said. "Beauty school tuition."

Aaron rolled his eyes. "Yeah, right."

"We can go to the bank right now. All you have to do is write the letter and make sure Ben sees you delivering it. I know what time he gets out of class. He always heads over to Jace's afterwards."

"You're crazy."

Tim shrugged. "Might as well take advantage of me. Five grand for what, ten minutes work?"

Aaron's eyes narrowed but his lips twitched at the corners. Tim had him hooked.

There is always some madness in love. But there is also always some reason in madness. Friedrich Nietzsche was certainly right about that, but Tim wondered if the German philosopher had ever hidden at home while paying someone else to do his dirty work. Tim wasn't alone, either. Next to him perspiring over textbooks was his alibi. Jessica was a fellow student, and to Tim's credit, when she had advertised needing a study buddy, he hadn't yet hatched his evil scheme. But he knew Ben was smart. Tim would be under instant suspicion, and so he took advantage of the opportunity.

Tim invited Jessica over for the afternoon, trying his best to focus on the study material. Mostly he let her talk, only occasionally asking a question to fake interest, when really all he could think of was his stupid plan.

He had felt convinced of the idea until this morning. So much could go wrong. What if Jace found Aaron tacking it to the door? Or what if Ben had plans with Allison and didn't even go to Jace's apartment? As the afternoon wore on, Tim was convinced it had been a failure.

Then he heard a pounding on the door.

"Be right back," Tim said, running to answer it and finding Ben, his face crimson with anger.

"Who's here?" he snarled.

Uh oh. "Just someone from school."

Ben glared in disbelief before pushing past him. Oh man, was he pissed! Tim followed him to the living room, waiting just outside the door and imagining Ben discovering Jessica surrounded by books and notes.

"Is that your car outside?"

"Huh?" Jessica sounded completely lost, which was perfect. "Yeah. Do I need to move it?"

"No. Sorry." Ben's voice sounded more embarrassed than angry now, so Tim made an appearance.

"Actually," he said to Jessica, "we're going to have to do this tomorrow. Something's come up. Sorry, but it's important."

Jessica panicked. "There's only two days left!"

"I know. We'll really nail it tomorrow, promise."

Jessica gathered her things and left, the look of terror never leaving her face. Oh, those pesky finals! Tim would be worried about them if he didn't have Eric's money, but these days his focus was on Ben.

Chinchilla danced at Ben's feet as he sank into the couch. She yapped for his attention, peeing in excitement, but Ben was too deflated to respond. Tim grabbed the paper towels he always had nearby and cleaned up, glancing up at Ben. God, it was good to see him again! Even if he did look miserable.

"You didn't leave a note on Jace's door, did you?" Ben asked. "Or have someone else do it?"

"No." Tim sat up, as if concerned. "Why? What happened?"

And it all played out, just like in his fantasies. Well, almost. Ben didn't throw himself into Tim's arms, but as he talked, his anger was directed only at Jace. Tim grabbed a couple of beers to help the process along as Ben became more and more agitated. And then it all went terribly wrong.

"You know, if he was going to cheat on me," Ben said, "I wish he just would have asked. I would have let him, if he wanted to. I don't care. I mean, it would have hurt, but it's better than him lying to me. That's the worst part, because it makes me wonder what else he's lied about. Not about cheating, but—" Ben's voice cracked. "What if he lied about loving me? Why else would he sleep around?"

There were tears. Only a couple, but like the ghost of Christmas past, they brought Tim right back to the night when he watched Ben crying in his backyard. That moment had been the lowest in Tim's life, and now he had done it all over again. Ben was hurt, and it was all his fault.

"I'm going to throw some pizzas in the oven," he mumbled, getting to his feet and feeling unsteady as he left the room. He couldn't stand to see Ben like this, didn't want to face it.

Once in the kitchen, he tried to compose himself. The damage was done. Ben would be hurt either way, whether he believed the lie or knew the truth. His anger might focus back on Tim, but the hurt would remain. Swallowing the bitter taste of guilt, Tim decided to press forward.

He brought another couple of beers with him to the living room, needing a drink as much as Ben did. Even the alcohol didn't allow Tim to enjoy his victory. Night came and Ben was too drunk to drive home, so Tim invited him to stay over. When Ben stumbled into his arms, making a clumsy pass at him, Tim felt repulsed by what he had done and guided Ben to one of the guest rooms. Then he went to his own room, helping Chinchilla into bed before crawling in himself. Lying on his back, he stared at the ceiling, prepared for another sleepless night.

I can make him happy.

These simple words carried Tim through the next three days. Ben was busy with finals, and Tim had little time himself, but he would have given up graduating if Ben wanted to be with him. He called Ben whenever he could and talked him into a quick lunch once. The subject of Jace never came up, Tim too scared to broach it. He prayed that all of this hadn't been for naught, but ultimately decided to stop agonizing over hurting Ben and to focus on his conviction.

He could make Ben happy. Much more than Jace ever had. If he had made Ben happy in their teens, when Tim's efforts had been half-assed and incompetent, then surely now would be so much better.

Saturday was hellishly hot, and while Ben had told him on the phone that he'd be busy working on his thesis, Tim called anyway and invited him over for a swim. The second Ben said yes, Tim sprang into action, fishing leaves out of the pool, whipping up a pitcher of Kool-Aid, and checking his appearance in the mirror. He already wore suggestively tight swim trunks—not that Ben didn't know what he was packing—and he fussed over his hair, trying to decide if he should gel it into messy spikes or leave it natural since they would be swimming. He still hadn't decided when he heard Ben open the front door.

"Chinchilla, come!" Tim ran for the back patio, picking up the serving tray with the Kool-Aid and balancing it like a waiter. He had hoped Chinchilla would stand obediently at his side, but instead she attacked the stack of towels and was dragging one away.

Then Ben came through the sliding glass door, wearing a navy blue pair of swim trunks, a light blue tank top, and flip flops. He was dressed like a beach bum but still had finals gloom hanging over him. They would soon fix that.

"*Monsieur.*" Tim gave a cordial nod and brought the tray around, setting it down and pouring Ben a glass.

"Thanks," Ben gasped after a big swallow, "but the pool is the only thing that'll cool me down."

"After you," Tim said. He watched Ben strip off his shirt, wanting to do it for him, to run his hands along the sides of his torso, brush his fingers along his ribs and tickle the blondish-brown wisps of armpit hair. Ben locked eyes with him as he stepped out of his flip-flops. The last time they had been this undressed together, they had kissed in the grotto at Splashtown. Now it felt as if they were starting from where they'd left off. Or so Tim hoped.

Ben went to the pool and sat on the edge, testing the water with his feet before plopping in. Tim cannonballed after him. Ben bobbed beneath the water and came up again, his hair slicked back. "This is really nice."

Tim waded closer to him. "It's not bad. Too small to do any laps, making it a glorified bathtub."

"Pools are meant for relaxing, not working out."

"Working out *is* relaxing."

Ben smirked. "Whatever, muscle boy."

"I don't remember you ever complaining." Tim dove, showing off with an underwater handstand before surfacing again. "Finals out of the way?"

"Yeah." Ben nodded.

"And Jace?" he said casually. "You two patch things up yet?"

Ben turned away from him, his expression hidden. "Kind of the opposite. We're taking a break."

Tim mentally exchanged a high-five with God. "Wow. Benjamin Bentley is back on the market."

"Not exactly."

"No?"

"I don't know."

Okay, that was vague, but a break was a break. Tim didn't want him thinking about Jace, so he playfully splashed Chinchilla, who grumbled and barked from the pool's edge. Ben laughed and joined in, missing on purpose. Then Tim challenged him to a race, a quick swim to the end of the pool and back.

"Ready?" he said, poised to win. "One, two, three!" Tim took off, reaching the end of the pool and turning to head back when he noticed Ben was still there.

"Beat you," Ben said.

"You never left!"

"How do you know? Are there any security cameras around here? Check them and you'll see my lightning-fast swimming skills."

Tim shook his head and swam back to him. "Why don't you show me while I sit this one out."

Ben looked offended. "Are you kidding? Moving like that is exhausting! I need a break." He swam over to the ladder and climbed out, the weight of the water pressing the swim trunks close to his body and revealing every detail. Then Tim followed, flopping facedown on the deck chair next to Ben's.

"Put some oil on my back?" he invited.

Ben snorted. "Could you think of a more clichéd line?"

"Tried and true," Tim argued. "It's withstood the test of time for a reason."

"Fair enough."

Tim waited until he felt Ben sitting on the edge of his deck chair, blood already pounding at their closeness. Then he rolled over. "Think my front needs some, actually."

Ben looked at him, his eyes almost pleading, but Tim wasn't sure whether it was for him to stop or keep going—until Ben turned the bottle upside down, drizzling oil on to his chest. Then Ben placed his hand there, fingers warm despite the dip in the pool. Tim wanted to cry. The emotion turned to lust when Ben moved his hand across his skin, slowly making his way south.

Tim couldn't take it anymore. He took Ben's arms and pulled him down forcefully. Their lips met, but this time Ben didn't hesitate, and there would be no interruptions. Their lips mashed together with desperation, as if they were both starving for each other. Then the rest of their bodies caught up as they scrabbled at each other's swimsuits.

As soon as they were nude, Ben climbed onto Tim, the deck chair creaking as they pressed against each other. If the kiss at Splashtown had been fire, this was an inferno. Tim couldn't remember ever burning like this, his need shutting out thought as he gave way to raw sensation. He took the oil, using it to lube them both as Ben ground against him, but he needed everything, needed to be as close to him as humanly possible. He shifted Ben upward, grabbing his wrists and pinning them behind his back so Ben's full weight was on him. Ben writhed and Tim shifted until they were lined up. Then Tim gently pressed inside.

Ecstasy! He wanted the moment to last the rest of their lives. Let them grow old and turn to dust in this very deck chair, because what they had now was perfection. They were one, inseparable, the five years between them melting away like a bad dream. When they exploded together, their panting bodies sticky with sweat, Tim was sure it had been just that—a horrible nightmare, but now they had woken up together.

Tim released Ben for only a second so he could wrap his arms around him. "Welcome back."

Ben sighed against his chest, but when he raised his head, he was grinning. "You have no idea how many times I fantasized about this."

"What, sex by the pool?"

"You know what I mean." Ben let his head rest on him again. "Us somehow finding each other and giving in one more time."

"I want way more than once," Tim said, squeezing him.

"Ow!" Ben wheezed.

"Sorry."

When he could breathe again, Ben laughed. Then he rolled to his side, propping himself up. "I never stopped thinking about you. I wanted to. Sometimes I would make it days or even weeks, but inevitably, you'd pop up in my mind."

"Same here," Tim said. "There's probably a reason for that. A sound, scientific explanation."

Ben rolled his eyes and gave him a playful nudge. "We're having a moment here."

"Sorry." Tim put on a sober expression. "You want to move in with me? Get married in the morning? I'll even build you a white picket fence."

Ben sighed. "Of course in my fantasies, I forgot how full of shit you are."

"Try me," Tim dared. "Whatever you want. Name it."

When Ben looked at him, Tim was sure he finally understood how serious he felt. Then Ben gave a gentle smile. "How about dinner with your parents?"

Tim laughed. "All right, but you have to show up like it's an accident. I'll call you the next time my mom is making *chile rellenos.*" Ben chuckled, but Tim wasn't done. "I'm serious. About what I said, I mean. Whatever you want."

Ben exhaled as if facing a serious decision. "Let's let it develop naturally. By that I mean slowly. Things are still a little weird for me right now, you know?"

Jace. But Tim was no longer worried about him, so he nodded. "It might not be my mom's cooking, but I can take you to dinner. I read about this place where you bring your dog and they also cook for her."

"Seriously?"

"I shit you not."

Ben glanced over at Chinchilla. "But she's not potty-trained."

"Maybe they ask you about that like a smoking preference. 'Would you like pissing, or non-pissing, sir?'"

Ben laughed at his dumb joke, just like he always had… and with a little luck, always would.

Chapter Twenty-six

Tim drummed along with the song on the radio, the steering wheel doubling as a percussion instrument as he shot sidelong glances at the phone in the passenger seat. To call or not to call? Ben had stayed late on Saturday but hadn't slept over. The next day Ben was home working on his thesis and wasn't available. Tim had given him his space, but was beginning to regret it. On Monday, once he was done with his only class, he was tempted to drive straight to Ben's house and would have if Chinchilla didn't need to go out. Twenty-four hours without an "accident" was a big deal, and Tim hoped to keep the record going.

When he got to his house, Ben's car was in the driveway, sending his pulse racing. Oddly enough, Ben appeared from around the side of the garage. Was he snooping? Tim would be worried if the garage wasn't locked, so he pushed the thought from his mind and grinned his approval at the surprise visit.

"Wow," Tim said as he got out of the car. "Think hard enough about something and it'll come true."

"What do you mean?"

One suggestive look, and Ben was enlightened.

"I'm done with school today," Tim said. "You?"

"Home free."

"Good. Come inside."

Ben was uncharacteristically silent as Tim turned the key in the lock. But it wouldn't turn because it was already unlocked.

"I let myself in around the back," Ben said sheepishly.

"Want a key to my house?" Tim said as he ushered him in. "I'll put it on a necklace for you and everything."

"And then I'll sneak upstairs to your room at night?"

"Yeah."

The words sounded humorous, but they carried weight. Tim took Ben's hand, leading him through the house and up the stairs to his bedroom. Standing next to the bed, he brought Ben close, pressing their hips together and swaying slowly, as if it were the last dance of the night. Ben's eyes glittered, considering Tim anew. That was good. He wanted Ben to see that everything had changed, but so often he lacked the words to express how. What could he say that would communicate what Eric was to him? What words were sufficient to explain the years of regret that plagued him since the summer of ninety-seven?

So instead, Tim slowly undressed Ben, and unlike Saturday's blur of heat and passion, today he took his time, kissing Ben everywhere, running his hands along his skin, rediscovering every part of him. When they lay together on the bed, the sex was secondary, a byproduct of their closeness. Even after they came, their touches didn't cease.

Ben lay in the crook of Tim's arm, tracing the contours of his muscles. "What are we?" he asked.

"After that? Exhausted."

"Seriously."

Okay, time to get real. "Well, I'd like to think that you're my boyfriend."

There was a heavy silence. The Ben of old had been so happy when Tim finally confirmed their relationship, but now he was pensive. For the first time, he truly believed Ben had changed just as much as he had.

When Ben finally spoke, Tim was surprised at the topic. "Are you staying in Austin after you graduate?"

"I guess so. I don't really want to go back to Houston. Do you?"

"No. Do you ever visit?"

Tim readjusted his position, trying to remember the last time he'd gone to see his parents. He kept his answer simple. "For the holidays, yeah."

"Your parents will be surprised to see me in your life again."

Surely the dinner thing the other day had been a joke. And why the hell would Ben think that Tim would *want* to bring him back there?

Ben tensed. "They don't know you're gay, do they?"

Okay, so some things hadn't changed. "Why bother telling them? They're hardly part of my life."

Ben propped up on an elbow. "You said you came out!"

"I did! To friends and lots of other people. I don't tell my family anything about me."

"But what if they found out?" Ben said. "Last time that almost happened you ditched me rather than be discovered."

"I'll tell them if you want," Tim snapped. "Am I supposed to call them right now, or can we relax?"

Ben swung his legs over the edge of the bed. He sat there a

moment before standing and putting on his clothes. Tim was sure he was about to leave, but Ben glanced back and said, "I'll make us something to eat."

"Want me to help?"

"No. I can handle it."

Tim let him go downstairs, staying in bed and thinking it all over. They needed more than this, more than sex to renew their closeness. Maybe he really should take Ben to his parents, correct the mistakes of the past. He could even find Krista Norman and patiently explain to her that he had loved Ben all along. Is that what Ben needed?

Tim got out of bed, put on his boxers, and headed downstairs. The kitchen wasn't full of sizzling meat or rattling pot lids. Nothing had been disturbed. Ben stood leaning against the counter, doing nothing.

"What's going on?"

Ben straightened up, heading for the refrigerator. "I was just about to start. Hey, you went shopping!"

"Seriously," Tim said, walking to him. "Just tell me."

Ben turned around and sighed. "Look, I know you're secretive. I remember that about you, and I know you need time to open up."

Tim raised his hands in defense. "I'm not hiding anything."

Ben glanced toward the window, and Tim was sure. Ben had been snooping in the garage. "You mean my paintings?"

"Why are they all stuffed in the garage like that?"

"It's my studio."

"And it's full of finished paintings. You practically live in a castle. Hang a few up!"

Tim stared at him. "Seriously? You're mad that I'm not full of myself and don't surround myself with my own art?"

Ben's shoulders slumped. "No. I'm not. I'm just scared that history will repeat itself." He looked up at Tim. "I'm falling in love with you again. Or I never stopped being in love. I don't know. It's so confusing, and everything feels so intense, even more so than when we were younger. Do you know what I mean?"

"Yeah," Tim said, voice hoarse. He knew.

"Just think how much more it'll hurt when it doesn't work out."

"You say that like it's a certainty."

Ben shook his head. "I don't mean to. Look, just promise me that I can trust you. That whatever secrets you have can't hurt us."

"I don't have any secrets," Tim lied. How could he ever confess what he and Aaron had done? But Ben needed more, like he always did. "Earlier, in bed, you asked about the scar on my arm."

Ben nodded "You said it was a mistake, whatever that means."

"Yeah. A mistake. His name was Travis."

Tim took a deep breath and told Ben his story.

His contemporary art final completed, Tim walked out the classroom door, wishing he could magically end up on stage to accept his diploma. His college education was at an end, assuming he passed. He was certain he'd squeaked by, at the very least. Despite still not knowing what to do with his future, he felt a sense of pride for buckling down and getting through it all, especially in the last year when Eric's money made dropping out a strong temptation.

"How'd you do?" Aaron said outside in the hall.

Tim had been hoping to avoid him. He had plans to meet Ben for lunch, but he could spare a few minutes. "On the final? No problem. You?"

"I'm sure I passed, not that it matters."

"Taking my money to the nearest beauty school?"

Aaron laughed. "Something like that. How's it going with Ben?"

"Good." Tim nodded slowly. "I think we're getting there."

Aaron's expression was a little snide, but he said, "He's lucky. It's sort of romantic what lengths you went to. I mean, it's twisted, but also kind of sweet."

"Thanks. Listen, I'm sorry if I sent any mixed signals. It's been a very weird year."

Aaron rolled his eyes but didn't look angry. "No big deal. I figure I'll find the right guy while cutting hair. If I get a job at a ritzy salon, I'll have my pick of rich old—"

Aaron never finished his sentence because someone grabbed him and spun him around. When Tim saw who, his stomach sank.

"You go to school here?" Ben said incredulously.

"What the hell?" Aaron snapped before he caught up with the plot. "Oh god! Leave me alone!"

Aaron tried pulling away, but Ben kept his grip on his shoulder, grabbing the other. Tim hadn't seen him like this since their brawl with Bryce and his cousin.

"I thought you were from out of town." Ben snarled. "You're a student here, aren't you?"

"Ask Tim!" Aaron whined. "Leave me out of your little love triangle."

Aaron was released, backing away before he turned and fled from the building. The fight had gone out of Ben, but his breathing still came fast as he stared into space, the puzzle pieces coming together. Then he glanced over at Tim, abhorrence in his eyes before he turned away.

"Benjamin, wait!" Tim started after him, ducking in front of him. "Let me explain."

"You lied! And I was stupid enough to believe you. And now Jace—" Ben's voice strangled to a halt, Jace's name little more than a whisper. He looked at Tim, shaking his head as if the truth was too horrible to believe.

Tim was losing him. Again.

"I would do anything to be with you." Tim put all of himself into his words, desperate to convince Ben that this time he was telling the truth. "Yeah, I lied, but I don't regret it. If that's what it took to get you back, then it was worth it."

He tried embracing Ben, hoping he would cry this one last time, get it all out so they could move on. Instead Ben exploded, arms lashing out and knocking Tim away. Unrestrained, he rushed toward the daylight at the end of the hallway.

"I fucked up, okay?" Tim called after him.

Ben kept moving.

"I didn't know how bad leaving Jace would hurt you."

Ben reached the doors and shoved them open, Tim hot on his heels and struggling to find words powerful enough to make him stop.

"You kissed me! It's not like everything was perfect between you two. You wanted to be with me as much as I wanted to be with you."

Ben was beside his car now, shaking his head and fumbling with the keys.

"You wanted to believe the lie."

The keys clattered to the ground. Tim felt one feeble thread of hope reach out to him.

"You wanted an excuse to come running to me. You wanted your relationship with Jace to fall apart just as much as I did."

Ben turned and leaned against his car like he was about to faint. Tim took hold of his arms, happy for the excuse to touch him, to breach the distance that threatened to consume them.

Ben was incredulous. "What is it with us? Our lives are always so fucked up when we're together. Is that what makes us attracted to each other?" He shook his head again. "It's like those studies where a woman meets a man on a swinging bridge over a crevice and finds him extremely attractive, but when she sees him in a safe environment she barely gives him a second glance. We like each other now, but what happens when the danger dies down, when our love is no longer forbidden or a secret? What's left between us then?"

"A lot," Tim said. "I promise."

The way Ben looked at him, he might as well have been speaking gibberish. "How can I even trust you anymore? You lie about coming out, you hide your paintings. Is there anything real about you? Do I even know you?"

"Don't say that," Tim pleaded. "You know me. You might be the only one, but you know me."

"Well, maybe I don't want to anymore."

Tim let his hands fall. The second he was free, Ben picked up his keys and got into the car. Tim watched him, hoping he would stop, roll down the window, and say he didn't mean it, that passion had shaped these false words. But Ben didn't even glance at him—not once—before he drove away.

The phone rang and rang on the other side, a sad whale song against his ear. Usually there was no answer, but when Allison answered, she would tell Tim that Ben wasn't home. He kept calling anyway, desperate to apologize, to explain himself, even though he knew it wouldn't help. Tiring of never getting anywhere, Tim showed up in person.

Allison answered the door.

"He's not here."

Tim sighed and spun around to check the driveway. Ben's car wasn't there, but maybe he had parked around the block.

"Want to come in?" Allison offered.

"No. I believe you."

"I wanted to talk to you anyway," she said.

Tim hesitated. She didn't seem angry with him. "Did Ben tell you what happened?"

She nodded. "It was lower than low, but I have to give you props. I never thought you'd do something that crazy to win Ben back."

"Seriously? You're just now figuring out how much he means to me?"

Allison shrugged. "You aren't the most forthcoming guy with your emotions. Before, I thought you only wanted Ben in your life when it was convenient for you."

"Believe me," Tim said, "our relationship has never been convenient."

Allison's smile was sympathetic, but her expression became somber. "They're getting back together."

"What?"

"Jace and Ben. Right now Ben is avoiding both of you, but he regrets what happened with Jace and wishes they could start over."

Tim shook his head. "Jace won't take him back when he finds out about me."

"He will," Allison said. "I told him everything. Jace still wants him back."

Seriously? Could anyone really be that nice?

Allison read his expression. "The man is a saint. I know you and Ben have your history, but so do they. And Jace has never hurt Ben. Ever. Maybe he will someday, but not intentionally. He's too good a man."

"So they keep telling me," Tim muttered.

"Graduation is tomorrow."

"I know." Tim had thought about it obsessively because Ben was sure to be there. He didn't want to patch up things in public, but it might be his only hope.

"Jace will be going," Allison said. "It's a surprise. Ben doesn't know. It's their best chance of getting back together, and I need you to do the right thing. If you love Ben, if you want him to be happy, you'll back off and let them be."

"I don't want to," Tim said, but without defiance. Instead he felt like a child struggling against the inevitable. "I want to be the one to make him happy."

"Well, here's your chance," Allison said. "A lot of guys tried to fill your shoes, but they were either trash or weren't good enough for Ben. Then Jace came along, and all Ben's dreams came true. Give them their space. Let Ben be with the person who makes him happiest."

"Is he really that good?" Tim asked.

"Jace?" Allison nodded. "He's pretty damn incredible."

Tim couldn't say yes—at least not verbally. He didn't trust his voice to be strong enough. But he nodded, and Allison hugged him.

"Thank you," she said with a squeeze. "And I'm sorry."

"Yeah, me too." Tim took a few steps back. "Listen, if it doesn't work out between them, let me know, all right? Just on the off chance that Jace is a serial killer or something."

"It *is* always the nice ones."

They shared an awkward laugh before Tim said goodbye, the words meant more for Ben than for anyone else.

Goodbye, Benjamin.

Chapter Twenty-seven

"Lovely, *Gordito!* The whole ceremony was just lovely. We're so proud of you!"

Tim's mother raised a wine glass, prompting Tim and his father to do the same. The restaurant was full of other fresh graduates and their parents, celebrating after the big event. Tim clinked glasses and smiled, even though he wasn't in the most festive mood. Not since Ben's name was called at the ceremony. Tim had half-stood, catching his last glimpse of Ben before he resumed the idyllic life that Tim had interrupted.

"Now what?" his father said with a knowing smirk. "That's what you're wondering. I remember the feeling, worrying about job prospects or if you graduated with the right degree."

"Yeah, exactly." Somehow Tim managed to hide his sarcasm.

"You'll find your way, son. You could always work for my company. We could use a new sales rep in Austin."

Ella beamed at the idea. "That would keep you on your feet until you find the right architectural firm."

Tim nearly laughed. Architecture wasn't his future. It was merely a convenient answer when people asked what he planned to do. "Actually, I'll probably take a break for a while. Maybe travel or focus on my painting."

"You can't make a living on your art," his father said.

That was for sure, but they didn't know about the money. Eric had left him enough that Tim could live off the interest without touching the actual inheritance, if he was careful. But his parents were clueless, thinking he still lived at the frat house. They didn't know a thing about his real life. Or Eric.

He thought of Ben, of how much secrecy had already cost him. That was Jace's true advantage. As cool and confident as Jace might be, Ben never would have left Tim if he hadn't clung so desperately to his secrets. But he had, which allowed Jace to slip in and take his place, unhindered by any neurotic hang-ups. Now it felt no matter how hard he ran that he would never catch up to Jace. Or Ben.

Maybe it was time that changed.

"I have my own place now," Tim said as dinner wore down. "Come see it."

"We have a three-hour drive," his father replied.

"Just stop by," Tim pressed. "Mom wants to see it, don't you?"

"We have time, Thomas."

"Very well."

Tim led the way, alone in his car as they headed up to West Lake Hills. He could only imagine what his parents were thinking as they drove through a neighborhood of homes worth astronomically more than their own. They must have thought he was joking when he pulled into the driveway.

"What is this?" Thomas said, shutting the car door. "Is this a frat house?"

"It's my house," Tim said, walking to the front door so his parents had to follow. An awkward silence accompanied them until Tim opened the door, Chinchilla scampering around in greeting. Then Tim started speaking. "There was this guy. Eric. He was also a brother in Alpha Theta Sigma, although a little before your time, Dad. Eric Conroy. Did you know him?"

His father shook his head, and Tim led his parents to the living room. Once seated, he told them the truth. All the important parts, at least. He didn't tell them about Travis, but he did say Eric had once picked him up when he was down, and possibly saved his life. He told them everything wonderful about Eric, even if it didn't help ease their confusion, and then he told them how he had died.

His father was incredulous. "And he left all this to you?"

"Yes."

"I don't see why he would," his mother said.

"Because we cared about each other."

Thomas cleared his throat. "If you have all this money, then why have we been paying your tuition?"

"I'll pay you back, I don't care. Just listen to me. Eric was a good person, and we weren't more than friends, but we loved each other. The thing you need to know about Eric, even though it shouldn't matter, is that he was gay."

"Oh, Tim," his mother said as if Tim had been conned or coerced.

"I wasn't with him like that."

"Of course you weren't!" his father nearly shouted. "But he was obviously deluded enough to think he could buy you."

Tim clamped down on his anger. "Do you remember Ben? From back in high school. He had dinner with us that one night."

His mother nodded, and when she spoke, her voice was quiet. "They called his name at the graduation ceremony." She still remembered him, and that confirmed that she had always wondered.

"As you know, he's gay too, and he and Eric are about the best people I've ever met in my life. And I know you're not going to want to hear this, Mom, but the Bible is wrong. Or maybe people have changed it or twisted the words, because there's nothing wrong or sinful about being gay."

His mother's eyes were brimming with tears, his father's scowl creating dark crevices between his eyebrows. They knew. Tim had said too much for them not to know, so he might as well get it over with. "I loved Eric, and I love Ben. I've already lost them both, but if I'm lucky, I'll find someone else. But it's not going to be a woman."

"That's enough!" Thomas stood, grabbing his wife's arm and pulling her to her feet. Then he let go of her and swung a finger in Tim's direction. "You better get your head straight, young man! We didn't raise you so you could play these sick games."

"You barely raised me at all!" Tim shouted. "Don't act like I've disappointed you when you've never given a shit about me. You're worried about what your friends or coworkers will think? Fine! Tell them I'm married to some bimbo with big tits. I don't care."

"You watch your mouth!" His father came at him and slapped at him like he was a child. Tim raised his arms in defense, the idea that his father wanted to hit him far worse than the actual blows.

"Thomas! Stop it!"

The assault ceased. Ella hung on to her husband, who was huffing like a bull.

"I'm sorry, Mom. About what I said. But not what I am." Her eyes pleaded with him to take it all back, but he couldn't. "I've always wanted to be a bigger part of your life, but now I guess the roles are reversed. It's up to you. If you want to be a part of my life, you'll have to accept who I am. You always said God has a plan for me. Well, this is it."

"We're leaving." His father pulled free from his wife and stormed out of the room.

Tim's mother lingered for a moment, a trail of tears glistening on her cheeks. Why was he so good at hurting people?

She hugged him, but he knew better than to get his hopes up. "I'll pray for you," she said, a hand on each side of his face. "You pray too. I don't want you to go to Hell."

Sure, why not? Even though he hadn't prayed for a very long time, Tim would, but not for forgiveness. Instead he would pray for God to make his parents finally come to their senses. When they were gone, Tim put Chinchilla on her leash and went for a walk, shedding the anger and disappointment. Long ago he had feared what he would lose by coming out, but his parents had given him so little that there was virtually nothing they could take away.

The men in his life had done the opposite. Eric had given him guidance and a home, not just a house. Ben had given him love—and although he might never know it, tonight Ben had given him a reason to be brave. And he had made sure Tim wouldn't be lonely again.

"If people want unconditional love, all they need is a dog."

Chinchilla stopped sniffing the ground long enough to look at him, but when she saw he wasn't talking about a treat, she went back to her hunt for the perfect place to potty. Feeling oddly content, Tim continued his long stroll through the night.

Part Four:
Austin, 2004

Chapter Twenty-eight

Time flies when you're having fun... unless that's all you're having. Then time starts to drag. Tim had spent the last year doing exactly what he wanted. First he took a month to fix up the house, doing little repair jobs he had been putting off or rearranging rooms to give the place a fresh feel. He had a fleeting affair with photography, but the medium felt too easy, so he returned to his most loyal of lovers and painted the nights away. Then he discovered a dog park, which he often took Chinchilla to. Every time he went, women there eagerly flirted with him, as if all that guy-seeking magazine advice had finally paid off. Tim enjoyed it regardless, a small collection of phone numbers piling up in a kitchen drawer.

Tiring of Austin, he put Chinchilla in the car and drove down to Mexico City to see his grandmother. He spent the better part of a month there, living with her and brushing up on his Spanish. Of course she had heard the news. When he tried broaching the subject, she stuck out her chin stubbornly and said, "God judges. I don't."

The subject of sexuality was closed to her, but his grandma still treated him like a prince, heaping love and affection on him. He was tempted to sell the house and move close to her permanently, but the American in him soon became homesick for familiar sights and the easy comfort of English, so he headed back. He made a few more excursions like this, but without a friendly face awaiting him at each destination, the trips seemed empty and aimless, a feeling that followed him home from his last journey.

Tim could do whatever he wanted, but what he really wanted was something to do. A real purpose, not just goals he created and accomplished for himself. Maybe a career would help, even if he didn't need the money.

These thoughts were on his mind one night as he headed to Oilcan Harry's. Drinking beer at a gay bar usually meant not getting much thinking done. Before long, someone would come along to chat him up. Tim enjoyed these conversations, and the attention of course, although it was rare these days that anything more happened.

On his way into the bar, he noticed a figure hunched against the wall outside, hoodie up and pulled tight around a lean frame. Occasionally some hustler would be hanging around outside, looking for money, but tonight it was raining. Why didn't the guy just go inside? Unless he was underage. Scoping him out as casually as possible, Tim was taken aback when the hooded head raised. The face was beautiful, framed by blonde hair that came to a point at each side of the chin. Eyes as blue as any sky in Heaven locked on to his, pleading for help even though the delicate lips didn't open to ask.

Tim gave a friendly nod, those angel eyes widening in hope, but Tim looked away and pushed into the bar. An explosion of dance music and cigarette smoke greeted him. He only made it a few steps before he stopped, pinching the bridge of his nose. What could he do? He wasn't interested in escorts. Occasionally Tim attended Marcello's parties, which were full of handsome faces, but he never felt comfortable getting close to those guys. Any of them might be models, a profession he respected, but there was an equal chance of them belonging to Marcello's elite escort service. The hotter the guys were, the more Tim became suspicious and kept his distance.

The guy outside was handsome enough to be a hustler, but he couldn't have been working the streets for long. Even indestructible youth showed signs of wear from such a life. But what else could he be doing out there so late at night? A young guy, looking for his first experience? But those eyes had been desperate, not horny. Growling at the universe in general, Tim turned around and headed back out the door.

"What are you doing here?" he demanded.

The guy's head whipped up, expression guarded. "You bounce here or something?"

"No, I'm not the bouncer." Tim cocked his head. "I just don't get why you're out here in the rain when you could be inside."

The blue eyes blinked. "I'm not old enough."

"Never stopped me." But Tim had looked older—had surely been older—when he had first come here. "Don't you have somewhere better to be?"

The hooded head shook. "I don't have anywhere at all." The guy's stomach grumbled loudly. If this was a scam, it was a damn good one.

"Come on," Tim said. "I'll buy you dinner."

"I don't need charity." But the lack of conviction in his voice said he did.

"Fine, then I'll take you on a date. Happy?"

The difference was small, but it was enough to get the kid following him to the car. "What's your name?"

"Ryan. You?"

"Tim. And don't worry, I'm not some pervert."

"Then you'd be the first," Ryan mumbled.

"I mean it," Tim said, looking at him across the top of the car. "I'm not picking you up. I don't go for hustlers."

Ryan eyed him, assessing the truth of this and then nodded. "I guess guys like you don't need to pay."

Don't be so sure, angel eyes! Tim had met plenty of Marcello's clientele, and some were very handsome. That usually meant they had weird kinks only escorts were willing to indulge. Or that they required discretion.

Tim drove them to Denny's, figuring the diner chain was good enough to give Ryan a full stomach while avoiding a romantic atmosphere.

"I love their veggie-burgers," Ryan said, flipping through the menu. "Have you tried those?"

"Nope. I prefer the real thing."

"How do you know if you haven't tried?" Ryan raised a thin eyebrow. Were they plucked, or naturally so fine? With his hoodie pulled back and some color returned to his cheeks, Ryan's beauty positively stunned.

"How old are you, exactly?"

Ryan toyed with the straw of his drink. "Nineteen. You?"

Not jailbait then. "Twenty-four."

"So you already graduated?"

"College? Yeah."

"Lucky! I still have three more years. Well, supposedly." Ryan's lips grew tight, but he perked up when the waitress came by. "Two veggie burger platters, please!"

Tim chuckled. "Is one of those for me?"

"Mm-hm." Ryan nodded, his expression mischievous. Tim could imagine him being quite the handful, in more than one way.

"So tell me why you were outside that bar, wet and hungry like an abandoned puppy."

"Oh, I like that!" Ryan grinned, but then his eyes dropped to the table. "It's just been a rough month."

"How so?"

"Well, freshman year was definitely awesome. Instead of getting called a fag every day, I was meeting all these other gay guys. Finally, you know? If only high school could have been like that. Anyway, I guess the freedom went to my head, because when I went home for the summer, I didn't stop being me."

"You came out?"

"Yup! First to my mom, who totally flipped." Ryan made a face. "She gave me the whole 'it's just a phase' spiel, which sucked. Then she told my dad, and the shit really hit the fan. He blamed me, my mother, and eventually college. I stuck to my guns, but now I wish I hadn't."

Tim sighed. "My coming out story wasn't quite that bad, but my parents didn't take it well, either. I don't regret doing it, though. Living a lie felt worse. Believe me, you end up paying the price eventually."

"Maybe. It's too late now anyway." Ryan rolled his eyes. "I kept fighting with my parents, and things got bad enough that they kicked me out. Well, maybe I threatened to leave. Either way, I'm not going back there. I was staying with some friends, but then I got in a fight with them over something stupid." Ryan gestured down his torso. "And thus the pathetic creature you see now."

"I'm sorry."

"Yeah, me too. I'm not a hustler though. I mean… you saved me just in time."

"Yeah?"

"Yeah." Ryan looked him over. "So what do you do?"

"You mean my job?" Always an awkward question. "I have a degree in architecture, but I'm on sabbatical."

"What's that mean?"

"It means I'm not working or doing much of anything right now."

"Lucky," Ryan said wistfully.

"I suppose. It gets boring."

"I wouldn't get bored." Ryan's eyes twinkled as he dreamed. "I would sleep in every morning, and when I woke up I'd stay in bed until noon watching television. Then I would get up, take a shower and make myself pretty so I could order pizza."

"Why bother if you aren't going out?" Tim asked.

"*Never* let the public see anything but your very best," Ryan said with celebrity wisdom. "Even if it's just a delivery boy. Then I would take my spoils to the couch and eat slowly while watching daytime soaps or talk shows."

"That's a lot of TV," Tim pointed out.

"Which is why in the evening I would grow restless and go out dancing. It's the only way to burn off the carbs. Then I would end the perfect day by getting drunk or whatever." Ryan cutely crinkled his nose. "In my fantasies I'm old enough to buy beer, so there."

Tim shook his head. "Sorry, but that sounds boring."

"Hm," Ryan mused. "What if you added another person to the equation? The morning in bed wouldn't be spent watching TV, and those daytime soaps are a lot more fun if you trash-talk them with someone. No need to go on the prowl in the evening, either, not if you have drinks and music at home."

"It just so happens I do," Tim said, willingly taking the bait.

Ryan demonstrated his bedroom eyes. "Then let's go."

Tim mentally took a few steps back. "I promised you a meal. First we eat. If you really need a place to stay, you can crash with me this weekend and fulfill that dream of yours. But you'll have your own room. No—" Tim hesitated as the waitress approached with their food, finishing with a whisper. "No funny business."

"Funny business?" Ryan snorted, then shrugged. "Suit yourself."

When Tim brought him home later, he was true to his word. After letting Chinchilla out in the backyard, they made their way upstairs. Tim didn't offer Ryan a drink, mostly because he didn't want one himself, or the weakness it would bring.

"This is your room," he said, holding open the door.

"Thanks." Ryan poked his head in without much interest. "Listen, do you think I could take a shower?"

Alone?

"Sure. Make yourself at home. It's been a long day, so I'm going to crash."

Tim showed Ryan the guest bathroom and made sure he had everything he needed before whistling for Chinchilla and heading to his room. Once undressed and in bed, he lay there with his eyes open, feeling ill at ease about having a stranger in his home. Then again, what's the worst Ryan could do? Steal some things and take off? Tim could afford it.

He rolled over, watching Chinchilla sleeping in her new bed, the side of her body rising and falling. The motion was soothing, as was the gentle sound of her snores. More than once that sound had helped lull him to sleep. He was drifting off when his bedroom door clicked open. The hall light burst around a silhouette—lanky hair, a slender frame, and the scent of body wash.

Ryan walked to the edge of the bed, but Tim didn't make a move until the towel dropped to the floor. Then Tim threw open the covers in invitation. Ryan barely had one knee on the bed before Tim had sat up to meet his kiss. Ryan didn't miss a beat, his lips not leaving Tim's as he climbed into bed and straddled him. Then he pushed Tim back against the bed with surprising force, his tongue tracing a path down Tim's neck, across his right nipple, diagonally across his abs to his hip before returning to the center again.

Tim's back arched as Ryan's mouth was filled. The kid knew his stuff! Adjusting to the pleasure, he settled, sighing and moaning. He was lost in a cloud of bliss when Ryan stopped and flopped over to the middle of the bed. Tim raised his head and opened his eyes to find him on his stomach, a wild grin on his face. His ass being in the air probably had something to do with that.

"Come fuck me," he said.

So much for taking things slow. Casual encounters for Tim rarely involved more than trading blow jobs. What Ryan wanted was special to him, with a few rare exceptions. But damn if he wasn't pretty! Tim grabbed a condom and lube from the nightstand, hoping that such things didn't have expiration dates because it had been a long time. Then he positioned himself over Ryan, kissing his neck and smelling his freshly-washed hair while letting his cock rub against Ryan's inner thigh.

"Come on," Ryan said impatiently. "Show me who's boss!"

Tim didn't like to disappoint. He bit and nipped playfully at Ryan's butt cheeks while getting the condom on, grinning at the *yipes* this caused. He meant to start slow, a little finger play and a reach around, but Ryan expressed impatience again.

"Stop messing around and give me what I deserve! Fucking use me!"

Unsure how much of this was just dirty talk, Tim slowly slid inside, but soon Ryan was bucking against him and begging for more. Spurred on by more trash talk, Tim let go of his inhibitions and really started pounding him. Only then did Ryan stop talking and start moaning. The bed shook as their flesh continued to slap together, Tim grunting in ecstasy, but he missed those pretty lips.

"Sit up," he commanded.

Once Ryan was only on his knees, Tim wrapped one arm around his chest and the other around his neck, holding Ryan's back flush against his chest as they twisted their necks to kiss. Tim held him there as he kept thrusting, Ryan's breath huffing against his lips, sometimes in his mouth. Then Ryan squirmed free, falling forward on to his hands.

"Slap my ass!"

Tim was already doing so with his hips, but he started slapping the side of Ryan's rump, responding to chants of "harder, harder, harder" until Ryan's words became groans. Tim felt more like an animal than a human being, skin drenched in sweat and nearly howling when they finally came together. As he recovered from this bestial low, he felt a pang of guilt, worrying that he had hurt Ryan, had damaged his delicate beauty. But when they rolled over on their sides, Ryan squirmed up against him and sighed contentedly.

"You all right?"

"Yeah," Ryan said, then after a couple beats, "but next time you don't have to be so gentle."

Tim laughed in relief, wrapping an arm around him and dozing off into an endorphin-induced sleep.

The weekend of Ryan's dreams stretched into ten days. Tim, who had found the idea so boring, couldn't get enough. During the day they would sleep in, waking up for progressively rougher sex. Once purged of these demons, Ryan was sugar-sweet the rest of the day. Forget the lost puppy from the first night. Ryan was more like a kitten in the way he would cuddle up to Tim when they watched TV, head on his lap so Tim could stroke his hair.

For food they called on any delivery service they could find, sometimes making brief excursions together for take-out. Or to stock up on beer or whatever liquor Ryan was in the mood for that evening. He kept researching cocktails on the Internet, begging Tim to get the different ingredients so they could try them. So far they'd had appletinis, bloodhounds, cosmopolitans, daiquiris, and *el presidentes.* The rest of the alphabet was sure to follow.

Tim was used to having the occasional beer, not drinking every night, but he was having fun. Ryan always got silly when he had a buzz, putting on music and dancing or making them do dumb things like shutting off all the lights both inside and out and going for a swim under the stars. Ryan was always at his side, even in the shower. All he wanted was to be with Tim, and Tim found all he wanted was to be with Ryan.

"We need to get you something to wear," Tim said while folding laundry. "I'm tired of you looking all baggy in my clothes."

"Should I take them off?" Ryan teased. "Or you could take me shopping."

That sounded good. Fun as staying in had been, Tim needed to get out of the house for more than a quick errand. "All right. We'll go shopping, but I'm not buying you an entire wardrobe. If you're going to keep hanging around, you'll have to fetch some clothes from home."

For their shopping trip, Tim took Ryan to Soco, a neighborhood on South Congress Avenue full of weird and funky shops. Ryan ran from store to store like he was on a shopping spree, and Tim had so much fun that he indulged him, spending more money on clothes and music then he had intended.

After a quick meal of tacos from the food trucks at the farmers' market, they drove by Ryan's parents' home. On the way, Ryan kept insisting the clothes they had bought were enough, fighting against seeing his family. Tim promised to take him out for dinner if he went through with it. The house they pulled up to was big—the neighborhood not quite as exclusive as Tim's, but Ryan clearly came from money.

Tim waited in the car, not wanting to meet Ryan's family. Their age difference wasn't too drastic, but that, combined with Ryan's parents not accepting his sexuality, made Tim keep his distance. Besides, meeting the parents was a big step, and Tim had no idea if this was an extended fling or something more.

As he waited, staring at the house, Tim could imagine walking through the door and discovering his mother's often-cleaned but rarely used living room. Or maybe he would hear his father in the den, shouting at a football game on TV. Regardless of what he would actually find behind the front door, Tim felt certain he and Ryan came from similar worlds.

After twenty minutes, Ryan came out of the house lugging a stuffed duffle bag and wearing a scowl. Tim hopped out and popped the trunk.

"How'd it go?"

"Let's get the fuck out of here!" Ryan went to the passenger side and got in, slamming the door after him.

Tim looked at the house, expecting to see his own parents at the window, judgment on their faces, but no one was there. He drove in silence, letting Ryan decide when he was ready to talk. Sometimes Tim had needed physical distance from his parents before he felt free enough to express himself.

"They're cutting me off," Ryan said.

"What do you mean?"

"School. They won't pay my tuition. My dad acts like going to college made me gay or something. He says the environment there 'supports my bad decisions.' So now I'm on my own, unless I want to move back in and go to the stupid Nazarene college he went to."

"I'm sorry, man."

"It's fine." Ryan's laugh was bitter. "I told them I was moving in with my boyfriend. You should have seen the looks on their faces!" Their expressions probably matched Tim's, but he hid it before Ryan turned to face him. "Is that all right?"

"The boyfriend thing or moving in?"

"Whatever," Ryan scoffed, his scowl deepening before he turned to the window. "Never mind. I'll find somewhere else to crash."

Not the best time to kid around, apparently. "It's cool," Tim said, not knowing if it was. "Both things, I mean."

Ryan didn't react at first, still watching the scenery whiz by outside. Then he exhaled, shoulders relaxing, and reached for Tim's hand.

Chapter Twenty-nine

Ryan crept into the bathroom, draped in a pink robe and matching slippers, taking comically large steps like Elmer Fudd sneaking up behind Bugs Bunny.

"Burglar!" he hissed.

Tim peered at him in the steamed-up mirror, shaving razor poised. "Huh?"

"There's someone downstairs!" Ryan stage-whispered. "You're being robbed!"

In the middle of the morning? This had to be a joke. "Think he'll take the couch? We could use a new one."

"I'm serious!" Ryan's eyebrows came together, stage one of the "soon to throw a fit" warning system.

"All right," Tim said, dropping the razor in the sink and grabbing a towel to wrap around himself. "I'll check it out. Is he a big guy?"

"Huge!" Ryan held his arms out like a hula-hoop, and Tim nearly laughed.

"And what exactly is he doing down there?"

"Poking through the refrigerator." Even Ryan looked uncertain at this behavior.

Tim hid his smile, splashing the remaining foam from his face before heading for the hallway. "Come on. If I'm going to risk my life defending my home—and my vegetables—I want a witness."

"Wait!" Ryan darted into the bedroom, returning with a cell phone that he held before him like a crucifix. "I'll take photos. We can use them in court."

"Good idea." Tim marched downstairs like he had something to prove. When he entered the kitchen, Marcello was already perched on a bar stool, glass of champagne in hand.

"Well!" he breathed, eyeing Tim in his towel. Then he noticed Ryan. "Well, well!"

Tim charged him, which took Marcello by surprise, but as soon as he was close enough he gave him a hug that nearly knocked him off the stool. Tim grinned. "Why are you always creeping around my house?"

"Isn't it obvious?" Marcello nodded at Ryan, who had stopped taking photos and was now looking puzzled.

Tim gave basic introductions, not bothering to explain who was who. The reasons Ryan was there were fairly obvious, and Marcello—there was no explaining him.

"I came to drag you out of the house again," Marcello said, "but I see you have a very good reason for staying in."

"What's up? Another Eric Conroy fundraiser?"

"Not until autumn," Marcello replied. "No, this one is a good ol' fashioned shindig."

Ryan perked up and came closer. "A party?"

"*The* party," Marcello corrected. "My fiftieth birthday, in fact!"

"Those are always fun," Tim said coyly.

Marcello was shameless. "Indeed they are. This year I'll be hosting from home, and there will be more beautiful boys and bubbling booze than ever."

Tim nodded knowingly. "I'm sure there will be, but we sort of have our own thing going here."

"Ah, the honeymoon phase! But there's no excuse for you not to pop in, not when you live so close."

"It sounds cool," Ryan said.

Tim glanced over at him. He appeared genuinely interested. Was he getting bored of his dream life already? "All right," Tim said. "You heard the little lady. We'll be there."

The party took place the following evening. Ryan suggested they buy fresh outfits to wear, which Tim agreed to. Ryan ended up with five new outfits, but Tim had no one to blame but himself. When those sky blue eyes were turned on him, his willpower simply vanished. And he had to admit that Ryan looked good wearing a form-fitting dress shirt and ultra-tight jeans. Tim kept sneaking peeks at him on the drive to Marcello's, planning to make it an early evening so he still had plenty of energy in bed.

The party was in full swing when they arrived. Marcello's palatial home had its own ballroom, which is where the festivities were centered, but guests were free to roam all but a series of rooms that Marcello referred to as his inner sanctum. As soon as the birthday boy spotted them, he disengaged himself from a conversation to join them.

Marcello always made time for Tim, as if he were an important old friend. In a way, they had transferred the love they felt for Eric to each other, even though they were both poor replacements.

"Happy fiftieth, old man," Tim said, giving him a hug. "This year I actually got you a present."

"Oh, thank you!" Marcello accepted the small package before turning to Ryan. "And I owe you a debt of gratitude for dragging Tim here. You know, sometimes I think he's older than I am."

"Keep celebrating your fiftieth every year and I will be," Tim retorted.

"Pay him no mind," Marcello said.

But Ryan wasn't paying attention to either of them. Instead he was looking across the room to a group of younger guys, most of them nearly his age or pretty enough to pass as such. "Is everyone here gay?" he asked, eyes not leaving them.

Marcello's head bobbed along with his chins. "Nearly."

Eyes alight, Ryan's head whipped around to Tim. "Mind if I mingle?"

Tim shrugged. "Have fun."

Marcello chuckled as soon as Ryan was out of earshot. "Feels like releasing him back into the wild, I imagine."

"Exactly. I found him with a broken wing, took him in, and made him all better. Now he's ready to fly again."

"So the honeymoon is over?"

Tim blinked. "I hope not. I've gotten used to him being around."

"Never fear. I don't think he's ready to build his own nest just yet. Let him have his fun now, and he'll be back in your bed tonight." Marcello tore the paper from his present. "One of your paintings? No, too small for that. Ah!"

Tim waited while Marcello examined the small frame. He had found a box of Eric's old photos in a closet, among them one of Eric and Marcello clinking wine glasses with exaggerated grins. Both were much younger in the photo, Marcello a few pounds lighter.

Marcello opened his mouth, no doubt to say something witty, but then shook his head, eyes misty.

"You all right?" Tim asked, patting him on the back.

"Fine, yes," Marcello said. "It's just... Sometimes you think you have it all, but then you remember how youth and friendships slip away."

"I didn't mean to make you sad."

"No! It's a happy reminder, in a melancholy sort of way."

Marcello considered him. "Love suits you, you know."

Tim glanced to where Ryan had already made new friends. "Do you think it's love?"

"You tell me."

Tim thought about it a moment. "I need a drink."

The party was pleasant. Tim had attended enough of these occasions that he had plenty of conversation partners when Marcello wasn't available. He tried hanging out with Ryan and his new crew, but they were all so young and wired that Tim really did feel fifty. Ryan had forged a fast friendship with a guy named Stephen, who—aside from having short hair and a slightly broader build—could have been Ryan's twin.

Tim wandered around the party, constantly deflecting questions about his post-college life. Eventually he grew tired of making excuses for himself and dragged Ryan out of the party and back to the car.

"So how long have you known him?" Ryan asked on the ride home.

"Marcello? Years now. Ever since my sophomore year in college."

"Oh, so you have a sugar daddy too?"

Tim nearly hit the brakes. "No, and what do you mean *too?* Marcello isn't my sugar daddy, and I'm definitely not yours! Got it?"

"Don't freak out. It was just a joke."

"It didn't sound like one."

Ryan made a face, like Tim was being over-sensitive. "So where do you get your money, then? You never work."

"I told you about Eric already."

"Oh, that's right. *He* was your—"

Now Tim really did hit the brakes, shocking Ryan into silence. "What the hell is wrong with you?"

"What's wrong with you?" Ryan shot back. "Jesus Christ, lighten up already."

Tim reined in his anger. "Eric was special to me. I don't like jokes about him."

"You didn't let me finish," Ryan said. "You don't know what I was going to say."

"Fine. Finish the sentence."

"*He* was your sugar daddy."

Ryan cackled in amusement while Tim stared at him in grim silence. Then he took his foot off the brake and drove the rest of the way home, refusing to look at Ryan until they were inside. When he did, he thought Ryan's pupils looked funny. Was that a trace of white powder on his nostril?

"Everyone fucks to get something," Ryan said, following Tim into the kitchen. "Sometimes it's love and sometimes it's money."

"You don't know what you're talking about."

"Don't I?"

"What the hell is that supposed to mean?" Tim shouted. "If all you're here for is money, you can leave right now!"

Ryan strutted close to him. "Some people fuck just to get fucked."

When Ryan kissed him, Tim tried to remain cold, but he couldn't. He kissed back, enjoying himself when suddenly he felt pain. His bottom lip had been bitten hard enough to draw blood. Ryan pulled back, eyes brimming with satisfaction. Was this part of the game now? Tim was so disgusted that he felt like smacking him, but Ryan had taught him a better way to deal with pent-up aggression. In case he'd forgotten, Ryan was already undoing Tim's pants before working on his own. Needing to be purged of his anger and wanting those angel eyes to come back, Tim spun Ryan around, bent him over the kitchen counter, and took out his frustration. Ryan grinned the entire time.

The honeymoon was over. Marcello's words were prophetic. Tim didn't know what he had done, if anything, to cause the change, but Ryan's dark side had slipped out of the bedroom and into the light of day. Usually this materialized as sadistic humor, Ryan taking unprompted cheap shots.

Ryan spent much of his time with his new friends. Even when he was home, his ear was glued to the phone while he chatted with Stephen or one of his circle. Ryan also possessed an eerie sense of knowing when he had pushed Tim to the very edge. More than once Tim had been ready to kick him out. Then, out of the blue, his sugar-sweet boy would return.

With the fall semester drawing near, Tim kept encouraging Ryan to re-enroll. Of course money was an issue, so he pulled a few strings with Marcello, as Eric had probably once done for him. He got Ryan model work that would earn him enough in just a few weekends to pay for his sophomore year. Ryan seemed thrilled at first, especially since he would be working with some of his new friends, but he came home after only a few hours on the first day.

"That wasn't fun at all," Ryan complained.

"It's work. It's not supposed to be fun." Tim remembered the experience all too well. "When do you have to go back?"

"I don't. I quit."

This led to another argument, but by the end of it, Tim agreed to pay Ryan's tuition as long as he promised to attend classes. Even when the school year started, Ryan still went out and partied most nights. Every time he came home, he lashed out like Tim had done something wrong.

"Some like their freedom," Marcello advised when Tim stopped by. "Others hold it against you. It sounds to me like you either need to live his lifestyle or cut him loose. I speak from experience when I say you should cut your losses now."

But Tim didn't agree. He had just turned twenty-five, not fifty, so the next time Ryan planned to go out, Tim invited himself along. And Marcello was right. Suddenly those angel eyes were shining again. They hit the clubs together and danced, Stephen's crew unsure at first, but when they offered Tim a pill to "enhance his fun," he took one look at Ryan and his encouraging nod and swallowed the pill down with a swig of beer.

When they got home that night, Tim's head spinning in a million different directions, there were no cruel barbs, no taunts. There was only Ryan, pulling him into the bedroom with a smile so they could play his favorite game.

Hell came every morning. No, not morning. Time had gone topsy-turvy nearly a year ago. Dawn was for going to sleep, the afternoon for waking up. Regardless of the hour, every time Tim woke, he felt like hell. Usually hangovers were to blame. Those could be chased away by a nice greasy meal. Other times Tim was strung out, which was particularly bad, because the only cure was to tough it out or try to figure out what they had been taking so he could get more.

In those hours when he was sober, he was always tired. Ryan seemed immune to all of this, always ready for the next adventure. The nights when Tim couldn't find the energy, Ryan left him at home, heading out with Stephen to find the next big party. When they couldn't find it, they would make one, returning to Tim's house with a convoy of vapid youth in tow.

And although all of this was taking its toll on Tim, he could deal with it. Partying and college went hand in hand, so Ryan's desire to indulge in the experience was understandable. Except Ryan was no longer going to class. Tim kept pushing him to return and get caught up, but sleeping the day away made this impossible. Once Tim had stayed home, abstaining from partying for an entire week and remaining clean to set a good example, but this had accomplished nothing. Ryan still went out and Tim had barely seen him.

The partying was nothing compared to the petty theft. All Ryan had to do was ask, and yet Tim's credit cards went missing once, Ryan turning up with shopping bags, saying Stephen had bought him an early birthday present. A call to the credit card company revealed the truth. Tim felt more confused than angry. So often it seemed Ryan was punishing him without explaining why. Those moments when Ryan rewarded him with sweetness were becoming rarer and rarer. Tim was already thinking of calling it quits when Marcello came to visit.

"You look tired," Marcello said, settling on to the couch. For once he declined his traditional glass of champagne.

"Thank you." Tim stood over him, arms crossed over his chest. "Is that what you came to tell me?"

"Sit down." Marcello looked away until Tim was seated across from him. "I recently had a disturbing conversation with one of my escorts, Stephen. I believe you know him?"

"Ryan said he was a model."

Marcello harrumphed. "Stephen *did* model for me once, but they weren't the sort of photographs advertisers are interested in. No, Stephen has worked for my escort service for a few years now. In fact, he recently recommended Ryan do the same."

Tim gritted his teeth. "Not a chance!"

"Of course not. I don't mean to pry, but do you and Ryan have an open relationship?"

Tim didn't like where this was going. "No. We're monogamous."

"I see." Marcello was pensive. "I think it's best we verify something. Stephen recommended Ryan as an escort because of how he behaves in bed. We have clients who ask for—"

"What did he say?" Tim interrupted.

"That Ryan likes it rough. *Very* rough. He claimed to be speaking from personal experience."

Tim leapt to his feet with a growl. "You need to leave!"

"Please don't be angry with me," Marcello said, placing a hand on his chest.

"I'm not! I'm going upstairs to deal with the little shit. Thank you for telling me. You can leave now."

"Let him go," Marcello said as he got to his feet. "No amount of yelling is going to change who he is. Cheaters cheat, liars lie. But there's something else."

Tim, already on his way out the room, spun around. "What?"

"The reason I was talking to Stephen in the first place is because of a complaint from a client. He said Stephen offered unprotected sex for extra money."

"So?"

"So, have you been safe with Ryan?"

"Yes." Mostly. Of course a few of those nights were blurry, but after being with someone for a year, he shouldn't have to worry about being safe. Or so he thought.

"There's no harm in getting tested, Tim."

"Fine."

"I'm sorry."

Tim sighed. "I know you are. Thanks, Marcello. Now get out while I'm still angry enough to do what I have to do."

Tim kept his cool as he walked Marcello to the door, but by the time he headed up the stairs, he was shaking with fury. After all he had done for Ryan, everything he had put up with, the bastard had the nerve to screw around on him.

Tim barged into the bedroom, Ryan muttering a complaint and pulling a pillow over his head. That was fine. Tim went to the walk-in closet, grabbed luggage from the back, and began filling it with Ryan's clothes. When he returned to the bedroom, he tossed the luggage on the bed and went to the drawers.

Now Ryan woke up. "What are you doing?"

"Throwing your ass out!"

"What? Why?"

"Because of Stephen!"

The daintiest of pauses preceded Ryan's response. Tim never

would have caught it had Marcello not tipped him off. "What about Stephen?"

Tim spun around. Ryan's hair was sticking up, and even after all the partying they had done over the last year, he still looked good. Tim glared at him, his accusations silent until Ryan rolled his eyes.

"It was an accident. We were high and drunk, and it just sort of happened."

"He looks just like you," Tim spat. "You might as well have fucked a hole in a mirror."

"Yeah, I'll give that a try next time," Ryan shot back.

"Were you safe?"

Ryan climbed out of bed. "Just shut up and let me get a coffee, okay?"

"Were. You. Safe?"

"I don't know!"

Tim shook his head in disgust and turned to grab more socks and underwear from the drawer. "Better figure out where you're sleeping tonight because you aren't staying here."

"I don't have anywhere to go!"

"You should have thought of that before you let Stephen fuck you. I can't believe you weren't safe! Do you know what he does for a living?"

Tim felt a hand on his shoulder and went tense. When he turned around, Ryan's face was soft instead of defensive. His angel eyes could be deceptive, but Tim was sure he saw regret in them.

"I messed up," Ryan said. "This is why I like you to go out with me because I know you'll stop me from being stupid."

Tim huffed. "But you go out anyway, even if I'm not there."

"I'm still young, okay? I can't be all grown up like you."

But Tim had been anything but grown up. He hadn't done a damn thing since finishing college. "Things have to change," he said. "I can't do this anymore. It's not working."

"It can still work," Ryan said. "Don't turn your back on me like my parents did. You know that will kill me!"

Fuck him for playing that card. Tim knew Ryan didn't deserve his sympathy, and yet it was the most effective thing he could have said. Tim moved around him, dropping the socks and underwear into the suitcase.

"One more chance," Ryan pleaded.

Tim shook his head, but then sighed in resignation. "Prove that you're willing to change. Stop hanging out with Stephen and go back to school. We'll take a break, okay? If you love me, get your shit together and then come back. Otherwise I don't want to ever see you again." Tim slammed the suitcase shut. "Are you going to take a shower before you go?"

"Maybe a bath," Ryan said. "Are there any razors in there?"

Tim's blood went cold. "Don't talk like that."

"Why not? What have I got to live for?"

"It's just a fucking break, Ryan! Stop bitching and prove that you care, okay?"

Ryan didn't answer. He didn't speak in the car either, except to tell Tim where to bring him. Their destination was an old apartment building on the other side of town. He prayed it didn't belong to Stephen, but didn't ask.

Tim said goodbye, his words gentle, but Ryan slammed the car door anyway. Instead of letting it get to him, Tim drove downtown to a clinic that provided anonymous testing, rolled up his sleeve, and watched his blood spill into a vial.

Chapter Thirty

The house was eerily silent that night, the bed feeling too large and empty, but somehow Tim found sleep. In his dreams he lurked in the wings of a theater, eyes transfixed on a figure center stage—Ben, older than Tim had ever seen him but still every bit as handsome. Tim yearned to hear him sing. The dream shifted, and Tim found himself seated at a piano. His fingers moved in a way they never could in the waking world, summoning music for Ben to sing to. Once that voice had sent him away but now it was calling him home again. His penance was done, the wait was over.

Come home.

Tim awoke, body tense with adrenaline as if waking from a nightmare, but he didn't feel afraid. Instead he felt a longing that made his heart ache. Chinchilla grumbled in puzzlement when he got out of bed, following him into the bathroom where he grabbed his robe. It hung next to Ryan's, which gave him pause, but that song still filled his head, so he went to the office and turned on the computer.

Google don't fail me now!

Tim had looked Ben up before, hoping to glean some insight into his life, but never found much. He had no reason to believe this time would be any different. But it was. Clicking a link to a potential lead, he poured over the website's text like it might vanish at any moment.

Con Man's Heart – A musical drama of heartbreak and deceit. Austin's Twilight Theater proudly presents an original Brian Milton production, set in colonial times and told in the traditional style of—

Tim scanned through the play's description, trying to find what the search result had to do with Ben. And there it was, that wonderfully familiar name, and in full!

Staring the musical talents of Linda Anderson as the Duchess of Derby and Benjamin Bentley as silver-tongued Bo Williams.

Theater? Scratch that. Dinner theater! Tim grinned at the screen as he learned everything he could about the theater and the play. The website even had cast photos, little headshots that were frustratingly small. He could see Ben's familiar features, but the resolution was too low to tell how much he had changed. Of course Tim could always go and see for himself. The play was running for the next three weeks. He practically did cartwheels out of the office to get his credit card.

When he was about to click "submit" to complete his order, he hesitated. Was this the right thing to do? What if Ben noticed him, and the play came grinding to a halt? Tim chuckled at the idea and clicked the mouse with glee.

Ben's face and that wonderful singing voice… If neither could be his, Tim could at least bask in their presence again.

The theater interior was tastefully decorated and well maintained, having been rescued by the local historical society some years back. This meant the stage area was grand, framed by tall pillars that ran all the way to the second story balconies. Tim felt a strong sense of relief at this, not wanting Ben to be working on a trashy stage with an audience more interested in the cheap buffet. In fact, no buffet was offered. Instead the theater functioned as a restaurant, waiters taking orders from each table, but Tim stayed in the lobby, nursing a beer at the bar until he heard the play begin. Only then did he make his way to his seat in the dark, taking a fresh beer with him.

Tim's frustration grew as the play went on with no sign of Ben. So far the story was about a duchess who had fled England for America, and who despite being beautiful and rich, was inexplicably single. Tim supposed he could relate. When Ben strolled on stage, he sat upright in his seat. The historical clothing and fake beard made Ben almost unrecognizable at first, but his voice was the same. Part of Tim felt like hiding. The other part wanted to leap on stage and make himself known.

He barely paid attention to the plot, instead staring at Ben no matter which characters were speaking, but he picked up on the basics. Ben, aka Bo Williams, was a con man after the duchess's money. Naturally, Bo ends up falling in love with her, but just before the wedding, a person from Bo's past exposes his history. This sets off a series of misunderstandings that end in heartbreak, just as the website promised.

Tim didn't care much for theater, and if he was being honest, Ben wasn't an exceptional actor. But the play featured musical numbers, and when Ben sang, Tim became enraptured. Sparing a glance for the audience, he could tell everybody else was equally impressed. At the story's end, the duchess tosses Bo out of her life, much to Tim's dismay. Not because he really cared about the characters, but because it meant Ben left the stage.

When the play was over, all the lights came on at once, and the cast walked out on stage in one big line, bowing and grinning at the applause. Tim felt exposed, but Ben was on the opposite side of the stage and didn't notice him. Still, the distance between them was relatively small. They were ridiculously close, and Ben would never know.

Tim hastily made his way out of the theater after that, feeling heady at having seen Ben again, even if Bo and his fake beard were in the way. He'd like to see Ben as he really was. Maybe Tim could write the theater and ask for an autographed headshot or something nutty like that.

Stopping outside his car, Tim turned on his cell phone. Three new messages, which was unusual. *Any* message was unexpected. Barely remembering how to access his voicemail, Tim listened, feeling a chill despite the summer evening when he heard the key words. St. David's Hospital. Ryan. Emergency room.

Tim was in his car and gunning it across town in seconds, ignoring the speed limit and quite a few red lights. If a cop wanted to pull him over, he would have to chase him all the way to the hospital. By some miracle he made it there unhindered and ran across the parking lot, panting by the time he reached the nurses' station. God damn, he was out of shape!

"Ryan Hamilton," he said.

The nurse calmly typed the name in the computer, one of her coworkers speaking up. "He's the overdose."

Fuck!

"Oh, right." The nurse looked him over. "Are you family?"

"I'm all he's got," Tim said. "Is he okay? Can I see him?"

"Just a moment." The nurse who knew about Ryan disappeared down a hallway. When she returned, she brought a doctor with her. Tim knew she was a doctor because she had that frazzled "way too much too do" air about her.

"Dr. Phillips," she said, not offering a hand. "We think Ryan overdosed. Do you know if he's a regular drug user?"

"Yeah, he is." Tim's throat felt tight. "Is he okay?"

"He was barely coherent when his friends brought him in. Since they've gone he's lost consciousness. Do you know what he took?"

"Could have been anything," Tim said. "Probably a mix."

"Okay. Well, if you'll wait here, we'll start the gastric lavage and see how he does."

"What?"

"We need to pump his stomach. Please have a seat."

"I want to be there with him."

Dr. Phillips sighed testily. "It's better if you wait. It isn't a pleasant process."

"I'm his boyfriend. I have a right to be there." Tim doubted that was true, but Dr. Phillips gave in.

He followed her to a small room. Ryan lay motionless on his back, the color drained from his face, reminding Tim of Eric's death. For a moment he was sure Ryan *was* dead, that his conversation with Dr. Phillips had cost them precious time, but the doctor didn't seem overly concerned when she checked on Ryan. Soon a nurse entered, rolling equipment behind her.

"You can sit next to the bed if you want," Dr. Phillips said.

"Can I hold his hand?"

"Of course."

The doctor took a clear tube from the tangle of machinery and inserted it into Ryan's nose, slowly feeding more and more in through the nostril. That was all Tim could take. Gripping Ryan's clammy hand, he looked away, sometimes even closing his eyes to pray. Where were those friends of his now? How long had Ryan been messed up before they decided to bring him in? If Ryan died, Tim would never forgive himself. He should have been there with him, keeping him safe, even if Ryan was a selfish brat.

Once the process had begun, the doctor left them in the nurse's care. After what felt like an eternity, the tubes were pulled out of Ryan's nose and the nurse took away the horrible machine. The room smelled like bile. Tim found traces around Ryan's nostril and wiped it clean with a tissue. Then he kissed Ryan's forehead, whispering to him that everything was going to be okay, that all was forgiven.

Hours passed before Ryan awoke, but when he did, Tim was still at his side, holding his hand.

"I don't feel good," Ryan rasped. "Where am I?"

"The emergency room."

Ryan's eyes found him and his face grew pained. "What are you doing here?"

"You gave the nurses my number."

Ryan tried to pull his hand away but Tim wouldn't let go.

"You don't have to stay here," Ryan said. "I know you don't want to. I don't blame you for hating me."

"I don't hate you, but you can't keep doing this. You overdosed. Do you realize that? You almost died."

"I don't care." Ryan's face crumpled. "I'm such a fuck-up. I ruined everything!"

"You didn't ruin anything." Tim stood. "I'm going to get the doctor and tell her you're awake. We're going to get you better, and then you're coming home with me. Okay?"

Ryan wiped away the tears and nodded, Tim stooping to hug him. They could make this right. If Ryan was willing to try, they could fix this.

Three days of sweet Ryan holding his hand, cuddling against him on the couch, listening to his stories and laughing at his jokes. For seventy-two hours, everything was back to normal. At the end of the third day, they tried having sex, Tim telling Ryan he needed to be tested in between kisses. But then Ryan's dark side revealed itself, and Tim couldn't continue. Hitting, biting, spanking, choking—Tim was literally sick of it. The idea of returning to that made him nauseous, and he couldn't stop thinking about where Stephen had been and what they had done together.

"I'm tired," Tim said, shifting away from Ryan and pulling up the covers.

"I'm not! What the hell?" Ryan tugged at him and fumed, eventually stomping out of the room. Tim let him go.

The next morning he found Ryan passed out on the couch, an empty bottle of champagne on the coffee table. Tim had thrown out all the alcohol before bringing Ryan home from the hospital, but hadn't thought of the bottle he kept chilled for Marcello. When Ryan woke up that afternoon, he was all piss and vinegar, every word venomous and calculated to infuriate Tim. Maybe he was expected to get angry and take it out on Ryan sexually, but Tim couldn't play that game anymore. Instead he went upstairs to his office, whiling away the hours on the Internet. Naturally he kept returning to the website for the Twilight Theater. Ben was performing again tonight.

Would Ryan be up for a show? He knew all about Ben, of course, but unless Ryan carefully read the playbill, he would never suspect a thing. It could be good, the two of them getting out. Maybe they could talk over the whole sex thing afterwards.

When Tim went back downstairs, he noticed a pungent smell in the air, like burning plastic. And Ryan wasn't alone. Stephen wasn't with him, thank god, but another of his friends was. He and Ryan were giggling incessantly, even when Tim walked in the room.

"What?" Ryan challenged.

"What are you doing?" This caused a fit of laughter. "Seriously, what are you smoking?"

"Pot," Ryan said.

Tim had smoked enough to know what marijuana smelled like. He marched over to the coffee table where a glass pipe leaned on its side.

"Are you fucking kidding me? What is this, crack?"

Tim grabbed the pipe and headed for the kitchen. Ryan chased him, pulling on his arm. "Give it back! It's not yours!"

Tim threw the pipe in the trashcan with enough force that it shattered against the champagne bottle. When Ryan saw this, he started screaming shrilly, like a child throwing a tantrum. Tim wanted to backhand him, but instead he grabbed him by the arms and started shaking him.

"What the hell is wrong with you? Are you trying to kill yourself? Huh? Fucking answer me!"

Tim let go of him in disgust. Ryan slumped to the floor in a sobbing heap. This was too much! He had to get out of here. Now.

"I'm leaving," Tim said. "When I get back, your friend better be gone and you better be sober."

Ryan glared at him. "Where are you going?"

"Out. Alone."

Tim whistled for Chinchilla—not wanting to leave her alone with someone on crack—and loaded her into the car. Then he went back in for a blanket and one of her favorite bones. She would need to crash in the backseat for an hour, if tickets were still available at the Twilight Theater box office. Tim had his own dragon to chase, and right now he needed a fix.

*****

Busted. So very busted. Tim was at his third showing of *Con Man's Heart.* During the previous show, the night he had fought with Ryan, he was sure Ben had noticed him. He certainly kept looking in his direction, but by the time the lights went up, Tim was already gone, not wanting to leave Chinchilla alone so long.

During tonight's show, Ben was staring in his direction so intently that one of the other actors had to prompt him. Tim couldn't help grinning. Nothing like a ghost from the past to make you miss a line. The smile was his first in days. Nothing Tim said or did made a difference anymore. Ryan kept partying, seemingly set on self-destruction. All Tim could do was steer clear.

After losing himself in the show as much as possible, Tim left the theater when Ben's last scene was over. He checked his phone once he was on the street, always expecting the worst. This time it came in the form of text messages.

i know were u r

From Ryan, of course. But he couldn't really know, could he?

con mans hart? how appropriate

Tim glanced around, expecting to see Ryan's accusing glare. The play was over now, people leaving the theater, but he didn't see Ryan. When were these messages sent? He checked the last one and sighed.

hows benjamin?

Tim dialed Ryan's phone, disconnecting when he got his voicemail and trying a few more times before giving up. This relationship was a nightmare, a mess he couldn't crawl free from without Ryan doing something stupid. Ben was Ryan's opposite. Giving instead of selfish, reliable and steadfast instead of unpredictable and insane.

Tim could use his help now, ask Ben what he would do if he were foolish enough to get in such a situation. He realized after a second that he could. Ben was just yards away, probably in a dressing room ungluing his beard this very moment. Tim could pop in, say hello, and ask for some quick advice. Chances were, Ben wouldn't even speak to him. But Tim wanted to try.

He turned around and made his way to the back of the theater, where he imagined a metal door guarded by bouncers, a flock of fans desperate for a glimpse of the star. The door was there, but Tim was alone. Feeling like an idiot, he pounded on the door a few times until a man with thinning hair and trimmed beard—this one real—opened it.

"Yes? Can I help you?"

"I'm here to see Ben. I'm an old friend of his."

"Oh." The man looked taken aback. "Well, he's already in reception talking to someone. If you go around front again—" He checked his watch. "Actually, the doors might be locked by now. Um. Follow me."

The man led Tim through the theater, a strange world full of hallways, scenery pieces, and props, but he barely paid any attention. This was a terrible idea. He knew he looked horrible. Not only was he out of shape, but he hadn't bothered to shave this morning, and lord knew he hadn't slept much recently. He could at least chew some gum to hide the smell of beer on his breath. But it was too late. The man opened a door to the familiar reception room and bar.

"Another one for you."

There he was! Not Bo Williams and his fake beard but Benjamin Bentley. And he looked fantastic. Age had done him more favors than harm. His once-blond hair was cut short, darker now and closer to matching his brown eyes. The summer sun made his skin appear radiant and healthy, and he didn't seem to have an ounce of fat on his thin frame.

Tim could see by Ben's expression that he was having entirely different thoughts about him. Was that pity?

Then Tim heard a familiar scoff. Ryan was standing farther away, wearing a smug expression.

"What are you doing here?" Tim said, jaw clenching.

"Me?" Ryan shouted. "I should be the one asking that, if it wasn't so obvious. I checked your computer. I know you've been coming here!"

"So what? It's a theater!"

"With *him* in it? Like that's an accident?" Ryan marched forward; Tim met him halfway. "You're pathetic, you know that? You have the nerve to kick me out for sleeping around on you—"

Too much! Tim couldn't take it anymore. Here he was in front of Ben again after all this time, looking and feeling like hell, and Ryan was spouting everything ugly about his life. Red blinded his vision. He just wanted Ryan to shut up, to stop spewing venom and go away.

"Let go of him!" The voice sounded like Ben's, but it was far away. "I said let go!"

A hand grabbed his shoulder, and Tim swung around defensively. Then the world came back into focus and Ben was staring at him in fear.

Oh god.

"That's right, show him how you treat me!" Ryan shouted. When Tim turned around, Ryan was lifting up his T-shirt sleeves to reveal the bruises he got last week when Tim had shaken him in anger. Now, just above them, were fresh red handprints. "Did he do this to you too?" Ryan said. "Is that why you left him?"

Tim turned to explain, but Ben no longer appeared afraid. He looked angry. Tim couldn't hold his gaze.

"I'm going to kill myself," Ryan shouted. Tim heard the front door open. "I'm going to kill myself and leave a note blaming it on you!"

The door slammed after him. The silence that followed was thick. This was humiliating.

"I guess I should go after him," Tim said lamely.

"I guess you should."

He reached the door, his hand on the push bar. He couldn't leave it like this. Ben had seen him do plenty of terrible things, but this was too low. Tim turned his head. "La Maisonette, tomorrow. Seven o'clock?" When Ben didn't answer, he added, "Please?"

Ben sighed. "All right."

Tim left the theater, head hung low. He found Ryan half a block down, waiting at a bus stop, arms wrapped around himself.

"Come on," Tim said, not bothering to stop. "I'll drive you home."

Half a minute later Ryan rushed to catch up to him. "I hate you," he said.

"Yeah. I kind of figured that."

Ryan sniffed. "You still love him, don't you? Admit it."

"I have a bad habit of loving people I shouldn't, but don't worry. He shares your opinion of me."

They didn't talk during the drive home or the rest of the night. When Ryan announced he was having a party the next day, Tim merely shrugged. At least it would keep Ryan occupied while he went to dinner with the love of his life and tried to explain the colossal mess he'd gotten himself into.

Chapter Thirty-one

A fresh haircut could work wonders. Today, Tim needed something more miraculous than that. He stared forlornly at his reflection in the car's flip-down visor. The stylist had done the best she could, but even cleanly shaven he still looked like life had taken a dump on him. Too many parties, sleepless nights, and arguments. Too much Ryan.

Flipping up the visor with a resigned sigh, Tim went into La Maisonette early and had the waiter bring him a bottle of wine. He intended it to be ready and waiting when Ben arrived, but his nerves got the better of him and he poured himself a glass. Or two.

When Ben showed up, led to the table by the waiter, he looked wary, as if Tim had some ulterior motive. Tim felt much too insecure to even contemplate seduction. He gave his best smile anyway—just enough to convince Ben to sit.

"I'm sorry about yesterday," he said, lifting the bottle. "Drink?"

Ben nodded, watching Tim pour a glass and set it before him, but he didn't touch it. "Is your boyfriend okay?"

"Ryan? Yeah, he says stuff like that all the time."

Ben's posture was rigid. "And do you react like that all the time?"

"No! I never hit him. Nothing like that." Tim moved his hand across the table out of habit, wanting to touch Ben. Instead he lamely fondled the salt shaker before retreating. "We had a fight last week, an argument, and I grabbed him just like last night. I guess I don't know my own strength." Ben didn't look convinced. "Ryan really knows how to push my buttons. Usually I keep my cool, but lately— I'm afraid of what might happen if things don't change."

Ben considered his words before his body language relaxed slightly. "All right. Tell me everything."

Tim poured out his heart, grateful for a sympathetic ear. Marcello wasn't a bad listener either, but he regarded Ryan as a defective product that needed to be exchanged for something better. Marcello transitioned through love affairs with ease. For Tim, every relationship had gravitas, and when things went wrong, he felt like Atlas struggling under the weight of the world.

"Ryan is your opposite," Tim said. "You always brought out

the best in me, changed me for the better. With Ryan, I just don't know. I used to see myself in him. His parents are just as cold as mine. I saw the pain hidden behind that pretty face of his, but he has a mean streak. Ryan turns his hurt back on the world, and I don't know what I can do to make him better. I think he's who I would have become had I never met you."

"You would have been fine," Ben said.

"No, I wouldn't have. Hell, look at the mess I've made of my life." Tim shook his head. "You never would have let me get away with any of this."

"I still won't." Ben smiled for the first time since arriving. "You inviting me here tonight gives me free reign to meddle."

Tim shrugged. "Meddle away. As long as you can fix things."

"You could leave him," Ben said.

"I could," Tim said, "but the sex is great, and you know how needy I get. If only I had someone to take his place."

Ben rolled his eyes. "Jace knows I'm here."

"That's fine." Tim took another sip of wine. "Did I cause an argument?"

"Nope."

"Despite what happened last time, he still let you meet me here tonight?"

Ben nodded.

"He's not human."

"Probably not," Ben said as if exasperated, but he was smiling. "He trusts me, and I'm not about to make him regret that. Not this time."

"Good," Tim said. Amazing how one little word could still be a lie.

The waiter came to take their orders, but neither of them had even glanced at the menus yet. Tim ordered the suggested appetizer, but by the time it came, they both were eager to leave. This wasn't the right environment. Had they ever eaten dinner out together? Doing so now seemed unnatural, so they settled the bill and left.

"You should probably get home," Tim said. "Jace might make Gandhi look intolerant, but I bet he's still worried."

"You can't drive. Not after all that wine."

"It was just a few glasses."

"It was enough." Ben started toward the parking lot. "Come on. I'll give you a ride."

Familiar discomfort settled over Tim once they were in Ben's car. He imagined Jace sitting in this very seat, wondered how much of the interior smell came from him. Was that a hint of his cologne? Tim still didn't like the idea of someone else being with Ben, but he no longer felt he had a claim on him. Especially now. Ben probably thought he was pathetic, the furthest thing from being worthy of love.

"This isn't how I meant for it to be. How I wanted us to meet again, I mean." Tim glanced over at Ben, rows of shadow and light from the streetlights passing over his face. "I had this dream about you being on stage. Isn't that crazy? I had no idea you did theater, but I dreamt it anyway."

Ben's eyes darted to meet his. "And that's how you found me?"

"Well, that and some Google-powered stalking."

"I may have indulged in that myself," Ben said.

"You tried looking me up?"

"Yeah. I was curious. I didn't find anything, though."

Because Tim didn't do anything. He hadn't left his mark on the world, hadn't made a difference in any way. The thought was almost as depressing as the cars that filled his driveway and lined the street. Ryan's party. Tim had nearly forgotten. "Walk me to the door?" he said jokingly, relieved when Ben pulled over and killed the engine. Ben felt like a lifeline to sanity, and Tim wasn't ready to let go just yet.

They could hear loud music blaring even before they got out of the car. Once they did, shouting voices were added to the din. And a howl that made Tim's gut twist with guilt.

"I told him not to leave her out back. She hates being alone at night."

"Chinchilla?"

"Yeah." Tim nodded toward the house. "Come on. She'll be glad to see you."

Having property enough to not need a privacy fence was nice, but Tim was considering having one built. That way Chinchilla could be unchaperoned when outside. Currently he had to keep her on a leash tied to a tree. When Chinchilla saw them, she bounded around in circles, stubby tail wagging when Ben knelt down to pet her.

Tim squatted, unclipping the line and trying to get it untangled. "This happens almost nightly," he muttered. If he wasn't having a party, Ryan would get sick of the dog being in the way and put her outside, knowing Tim would bring her back in every time. Ryan probably did it just to piss him off.

"I don't mean to state the obvious," Ben said, "but why don't you just break up with him? I know, I know, you said the sex is really great, but things are only going to get worse."

"You're right, but I don't know how. You heard him last night. He always threatens to kill himself. The night he overdosed was because I suggested taking a break."

Chinchilla was on her back now, Ben rubbing her belly absentmindedly. He suggested a scheme to get rid of Ryan, one about shipping him off to some tropical gay resort to find someone new. The idea was completely unrealistic and just crazy enough to make Tim smile. Ben still held that power, even now. Tim was miserable and felt embarrassed at the state of his affairs, but Ben could make him smile.

Their joking around was interrupted by the sound of smashing glass. What the hell was Ryan doing, trashing the place? Disturbingly, this was within the realm of possibility.

Ben sighed and stood up. "All right. Time for me to make everything better. Come on."

As they entered through the back door, Tim saw the chaos around him through Ben's eyes and realized just how screwed up his life had become. The house was full of guys, many of them probably still in high school, all of them intoxicated. Ryan's circle of friends had spread beyond Marcello's escorts and models. Many of the faces were familiar, but only from previous parties like this one that seemed to get worse every time. A group of teenagers stood next to a broken window, a potted plant on the other side.

Tim picked up Chinchilla, worried about her stepping on shards, and shut her in the laundry room. At least there she would be safe. Often Tim would take Chinchilla and retreat upstairs to his bedroom until it all blew over, but tonight he had a feeling things were going to become much worse before they ended.

The heart of the party thudded and beat in the living room. Ben marched in like he owned the place, walking over to the stereo and yanking the cord from the wall. At the sudden silence, every head in the room turned toward them, Ryan's included, and Tim felt scared. Not for himself, but for Ben. As emotionally strong as Ben was, Ryan was bat-shit crazy and already moving toward them.

"What the hell is he doing here?" Ryan spat, clearly high on something.

"I'm here with my boyfriend," Ben said.

Boyfriend? Tim was even more surprised when Ben took his hand. Okay, so maybe Ben was a little crazy too.

Ryan pulled his lips back in a snarl, then launched himself in Ben's direction, pushing party-goers out of the way.

No. Absolutely not! Tim changed his stance, ready to deck Ryan before he could lay a finger on Ben.

Tim tensed as he felt a hand on his check, one that turned his head. He barely had time to process this before Ben's lips smashed into his and everything was forgotten. The party, Ryan, the years of mistakes and regrets—all gone. There was only Ben, and he was everything love should be.

When their lips parted again, the room silent, Tim understood. Ben knew that Tim would never leave Ryan. He would have done so already if he could. But they could drive Ryan away if they convinced him they were an item. Tim didn't need to pretend. Not about this. He looked over at Ryan, leaving his emotions exposed. When Ryan saw the truth, a sob escaped from his throat.

"I'm moving in," Ben said, twisting the knife. "Tim asked me to. You are leaving and never coming back. All of you."

When no one reacted, Ben mentioned cops and drug dogs. That did the trick. The street value of the illegal substances these kids were carrying in their pockets and bloodstreams was probably worth a fortune, and none of them wanted to lose what they had. The house cleared out quickly. That left Tim and Ben alone with Ryan, whose sorrow was shifting back to anger.

"I'll kill myself," he said. "I swear to God I will!"

"No, Ryan, you won't." Tim slowly walked toward him. "I know you won't, because you're too much of a coward. You've been running away since the day I met you, away from your family's disapproval, away from the one person who loves you, but most of all you've been trying to escape from yourself. I was once that cowardly, and you still are."

"I overdosed!" Ryan whined.

"And I was there holding your hand in the hospital as they

pumped your stomach. When I told you that you almost died, you cried. I thought there was still hope for you then, but I've seen you almost overdose every night since. I don't know how to fix you, Ryan. I wish I did, but it's not going to be my money that helps destroy you. Not anymore."

"You need me! Ben won't stick around. He'll leave you and you'll be alone. Then what will you do?"

"I guess we'll find out," Tim put a gentle hand on Ryan's shoulder, guiding him out of the room. "Come on. We'll pack your things."

"I'm not packing anything!"

"Then you'll watch me do it." He tightened the arm he had around Ryan, trying to make it feel supportive when really he just wanted to get him away from Ben. Thankfully, Ben didn't follow them out of the room.

"You can't make me leave," Ryan said on the way up the stairs. He kept stopping like they would stand there and discuss it. Tim tried to keep him walking. Eventually he gave up and went into the bedroom by himself, gathering up Ryan's things while listening for signs of trouble from downstairs. But soon Ryan came into the room, his face contorted with anger. "How long have you been seeing him?"

"Ben?" Tim smirked. "Since I was seventeen."

"You know what I mean!"

Tim grabbed a bunch of shirts from the closet and stuffed them in the suitcase, hangers and all. "We never stopped seeing each other. Not really."

"So you've always been cheating on me?"

"Yeah." Lying to him—hurting him intentionally—wasn't a good feeling. But it had to be done.

Ryan sat on the edge of the bed, head down, and Tim started getting angry himself. What right did he have to act so hurt when he's the one who cheated? Tim packed the rest of Ryan's things with little care, then called a taxi while watching Ryan cry.

"Where are you going to go?" Tim asked him.

"I don't know."

"Go home. Your parents will take you in."

"I hate them!"

"You hate everything." Tim headed for the door. "Come on."

"No."

"I'll call the cops if I have to. Now come on."

Ryan stood and took hold of his arm. "Please," he said. "Please don't make me go. I'm sorry."

Tim ignored him, walking to the front door and practically dragging Ryan along. Even when they passed Ben on the way, Ryan kept begging, and Tim felt oddly embarrassed for him. When the taxi arrived, he gave the driver a hundred bucks and told him to take Ryan wherever he wanted. As the taxi drove away, Tim stood in the street watching it go, the brake lights blazing red before the car turned at a corner and disappeared from sight.

"You okay?"

Tim turned around to find Ben there. "Yeah." Then he gave in to instinct and wrapped Ben in his arms. Everything about him brought comfort. The feel of his body, the familiar scent of his skin, the warmth of his neck. "You always know how to make things right. I'm a mess without you."

"I'm awesome, I know." Ben gently pulled away. "I'm also in trouble. Jace is going to give me hell when he finds out I kissed you, no matter what the reason. You *are* going to make all my suffering worth it by never seeing Ryan again, right?"

Tim stepped close. "Since you're going to be in trouble anyway—"

Ben playfully pushed him away and they laughed.

"Oh, man." Tim looked toward the house. "Chinchilla is still locked up."

"She's fine," Ben said. "While you were upstairs I let her out and gave her some honey ham I found in the fridge."

"That's good." Tim stared at him and couldn't help wishing things were different. He supposed he always would.

"I should probably go," Ben said.

"Don't. I mean, not forever. We could hang out sometime. After all these years, we should be able to be friends, right?"

Ben studied him. "Do you mean that?"

Of course not. "Yeah. It'll be a test of just how nice Jace really is." He chuckled nervously. "Maybe I can have you guys over sometime. Uh, but not like Splashtown. No ulterior motive. I just want you in my life."

That was true. After all this time, Ben should be more than just a painful memory. Being friends was better than nothing.

"No promises," Ben said, "but I'll talk to Jace." He hesitated as if he had something more to say, but then he shook his head and headed for his car.

"Thanks, Benjamin!" Tim called after him, and despite it all, he couldn't help grinning. Then he went inside, ready at last to clean up his mess. And maybe look up a good maid service to help get him started.

Chapter Thirty-two

Tim threw a party that weekend. Not a Ryan-style puking-on-the-carpet, overdosing-in-the-bathroom party, but a much more respectable Sunday barbeque in the backyard. Of course he waited until Ben and Jace agreed to come before making arrangements, inviting Marcello and some of his more pleasant friends. As a show of goodwill, he even invited Allison and her husband.

And now they were all here, gathered together in a comfortable scene worthy of Norman Rockwell—if he had ever painted gay guys and interracial couples grilling steaks beside a private pool. Marcello's date was a younger Asian guy who seemed bookish, and Brian, Allison's husband, was just as plain as she was pretty. Brian, it turned out, was the owner of Twilight Theater and the very same person who had let Tim in the other night. Then there were a handful of older gay guys and a pair of lesbians who were eyeing the pool like they wanted to strip down and dive in.

Tim manned the grill, letting his guests enjoy themselves while he made every effort not to stare at Ben and Jace. They sat across from each other, deep in conversation at one of the picnic benches Tim had bought for the occasion. What did couples talk about after so many years together? One thing was certain: They looked happy.

When Ben came up to him alone, grabbing two paper plates, Tim played it cool and said, "What can I get you and your dashing boyfriend?"

"I don't know where to begin," Ben said, eyeing the food. "Did you make all this yourself?"

"Of course," Tim said. "How hard is it to marinate meat?"

Ben nodded at one of the tables. "Even the dates stuffed with cream cheese and wrapped in bacon?"

"Is that what those are?"

Ben chuckled. "You either talked some lovesick guy into making all this or you hired a caterer."

"Caterers," Tim admitted. "I may have to fire them. These hot dogs look a little gray."

"They're bratwursts, and they're supposed to look that way."

"Oh!" Tim replied innocently.

Ben took two, and after loading his plate with other goodies, headed back to the bench where Jace waited. Tim shouted that lunch was ready, and soon his guests were plundering the spread. He watched them with satisfaction, serving brats and feeling a little embarrassed when Allison and her husband approached. Hopefully the guy hadn't overheard his argument with Ryan in the theater.

"Thanks for having us," Brian said.

"My pleasure," Tim replied. "Have a wiener. You too, Allison." He eyed the gold band on her finger as she took the plate. "How's married life treating you?"

"Good!" Allison beamed. If Jace and Ben were going for world's happiest couple, they had some competition.

"How did you two meet, anyway?"

Allison glanced over at Brian, who gestured that she should tell the story. "I was volunteering at a hospital. Brian was in one of the programs I was leading, and we just sort of hit it off."

Tim cocked an eyebrow. "Putting the moves on a patient? Isn't that immoral?"

"Absolutely," Allison said shamelessly. "Besides, that was just my apprenticeship. I'm a counselor now."

"Which means no more flirting with patients," Brian chimed in.

Tim laughed. "Wow, a counselor. Go Allison! Maybe you should leave me your card. With all my problems, I'll keep you in business for years."

"Actually," Brian said, scratching at the reddish-brown hair of his beard, "I wanted to invite you to something similar. I'm a recovering alcoholic. Haven't touched a drop in two years. Ben was telling us how he's worried about your drinking. I'd be glad to have you at one of our AA meetings if you're interested."

Tim shifted uncomfortably. "I know this is going to sound like I do, but I don't have a problem. I just need to slow down."

"Well, if you find it harder to slow down then you thought, my phone number and email address are right here."

Tim accepted Brian's business card, feeling somewhat embarrassed. He wasn't an alcoholic, was he? He thought longingly of the cold beer bottles buried in ice in the cooler, and realized he'd be going without today—and for a while after. He was sure he didn't have a problem and wanted to keep it that way.

After more chitchat, Tim excused himself and kept grilling, snacking between serving hungry guests. Ben was worried about him, huh? That was something, at least. After everyone had eaten their fill, even Marcello, Tim did something he'd been nervous about all day and went over to Jace.

"Can I talk to you for a minute?"

Jace looked between him and Ben and nodded. "Sure."

Tim led him away from the party to the side of the house, willing his pulse to slow. This could get ugly. Hopefully the legends about Jace's niceness were true.

"What's up?" Jace asked. His expression wasn't entirely friendly, but he wasn't sneering, either.

"I just wanted to apologize," Tim said, extending a hand. "I figure it's long overdue."

Jace eyed his hand but didn't accept it. "What exactly are you apologizing for? And before you answer, do us both a favor and think about it carefully. If there's one thing I won't put up with from you, it's more bullshit and lies."

Ouch! Was it too late to scamper back to the party with his tail between his legs? But Jace was studying him, waiting for his response. The truth? Tim didn't regret trying to get Ben back or kissing him when he had the chance. He wasn't sorry for trying to steal Ben away from Jace. When he considered the absolute truth, the answer was obvious.

"I'm sorry for hurting Ben."

Jace grabbed his hand and shook it. "Apology accepted."

Tim laughed in relief. "Jesus, dude! Everyone says you're a saint, but you're kind of scary, you know that?"

Jace winked. "Remember that right hook?"

"My jaw still twinges when the weather gets cold."

Their laughter brought relief as they slowly relaxed. "Thanks for letting me be around Ben." Tim said. "You didn't have to do that."

Jace shrugged. "It's not my choice to make. He's his own person."

"Well I appreciate you being cool about it anyway. It's nice having him in my life again. I really hope he and I can be friends."

"And if not?"

"Then I'll bow out," Tim said. "There's no way I can take him from you without breaking his heart in the process."

Jace nodded in appreciation. "Ben told me about Ryan. Sounds like a rough time, but don't give up. I had to go through a lot of Mr. Wrongs before I finally met Ben."

"Yeah, but imagine if you had met him first."

"And then messed it all up," Jace said without any malice. "I've thought about that, which is why I try not to blame you. There was someone else in my life, once. Someone I loved almost as much as I love Ben. There's no chance of getting him back, but had Ben not come along and I had one more shot, I would have taken it."

"Yeah?"

"Definitely. If our roles were reversed, I also would have done something to win back that love. Although I'd like to think I would have done it with charm instead of trickery."

"Hey, I'd be more than willing to try it your way if you want to give me some pointers."

Jace smiled. "Not a chance."

After a little more banter they returned to the party. Jace really was nice, except when life demanded otherwise. Tim wasn't into self-depreciation, but maybe, just maybe, Jace was the better man. The thought wasn't too depressing, because it meant Ben was going to have the best life possible.

Tim was sitting cross-legged at the edge of the pool, breaking apart a bratwurst and feeding the pieces to Chinchilla, when Ben came over and sat next to him. "What did you guys talk about? Jace won't tell me."

"You, of course," Tim said. "Your morning breath, your terrible cooking—the usual."

"I see I'll have to keep you two separate," Ben said in mock exasperation.

"So catch me up on your story," Tim said. "Last time all I did was whine about my problems. How's life after college for Benjamin Bentley?"

"Good." Ben slipped off his sandals and dipped his feet in the pool. "I got a job as a speech therapist, which is nice. Makes me feel useful."

"So the dinner theater thing is just a hobby?"

Ben shook his head. "More like a second job. They're both

only part-time, but I like the variety. What about you?"

"You're looking at it. I'm a housewife without a husband."

Ben snorted. "Seriously. You once said something about celebrities working out of boredom, even after they get rich."

"Words of wisdom," Tim said with irony. "I *was* bored. Then I met Ryan and everything went crazy. Frankly, I'm looking forward to being bored again. Afterwards, I don't know. But I want to hear about your life. What else has happened?"

Ben took a deep breath. "I got married."

"Oh." Tim paused. "Does Jace know?"

Ben shoved him playfully. "That's who I married."

"Ah, I see!" Tim grinned even though his insides felt crushed. Better man or not, he couldn't help feeling jealous. "Is that legal in Texas?"

"Nothing fun is. According to the law, we're still second-class citizens, but they can't stop us from making the commitment. Marriage isn't a piece of paper, right?"

"True. Did I tell you I'm marrying Chinchilla?"

"Really?" Ben said with faux interest.

"Yeah. We haven't picked out rings, but I thought I'd give her a pair of my shoes to chew up. Then I would wear them around town as a sign of my commitment to her."

Ben looked impressed. "Sounds romantic."

"I thought so." Tim nudged shoulders with him. "Are we going to make this work?"

"You and me?" Ben nudged him back. "Yeah. We'll make it work. Somehow."

"Your eyes light up when you look at him."

Marcello was at Tim's right, startling him. For a big guy, he sure could move with stealth. Of course the orchestra music helped disguise his arrival, as did the sounds of the dancers in the ballroom. Another Eric Conroy Foundation fundraiser. Each served as a reminder of how long he had been gone, the years adding up quicker than Tim cared to contemplate. This year he invited Ben and Jace, and as they danced together in their rented tuxedos, Tim couldn't pull his eyes away. They were—

"Beautiful," Marcello said, having seen them as well. "No waging a war of the heart this time?"

"Me?" Tim grimaced. "I don't think I could wedge myself

between them even if I wanted to."

Marcello patted him on the back. "You could have anyone you want. Maybe Ryan wore you a bit thin, but the last few weeks have marked the return of that handsome face that sells so many photos. I'm still making money off that weekend of modeling you gave me."

Tim was flattered, but he wasn't quite there yet. He had started jogging again, but the pounds went on a lot easier than they came off. Staying away from beer helped, although tonight he allowed himself to sip from a glass of champagne to celebrate: His second round of HIV tests had come back negative. Any mistakes he'd made with Ryan wouldn't be permanent.

"No," Tim responded at last. "This time I'll let them be. I'd say they were made for each other, but it's more like Ben was made for me, and Jace was made for him. Does that make sense?"

"Few things in love do. Regardless, it's nice to see such a happy couple here tonight."

"Yeah. Don't let them give any money to the foundation," Tim said. "I mean, a token amount is okay, but I know they struggle."

Marcello nodded. "It's hardly needed. Some very generous donations have already been made this year. Enough that we'll be left with an excess, which is never ideal for a charity. No doubt there are artists who could use the money, but sorting through grant applications is time-consuming, as is conducting the interviews."

"Really? Sounds kind of fun, actually."

"I have enough on my plate," Marcello said dismissively.

Tim's plate was still empty, except for hanging out with Ben and Jace occasionally. He was beginning to wonder if he was living vicariously through them.

"Besides," Marcello continued, "you have no idea how desperate the applicants are to have anyone look at their art. I keep telling them to take a photo and put it online."

Tim shook his head. "It's never the same. Even the best photographer can't capture the full spirit of a painting. Have you thought of doing more than just giving grants? What if you rented a gallery space for new artists to exhibit at?"

"The idea is nice, but again, finding time is an issue."

"Not for—" Tim glanced at Marcello accusingly. "You're totally playing me, aren't you?"

The hint of a smile betrayed him. "Not at all," Marcello said. "But if you should happen to know someone who is willing to work long hours for free, then be sure to send him my way."

Tim stared at him. "I'll think about it."

"Good." Marcello offered his arm and nodded toward the dance floor. "Now how about we give Ben and Jace a run for their money?"

Hobbits fought a giant spider while elsewhere, elves and dwarves battled evil orcs. All of it was lost on Tim. He could only focus on the nearness of the body next to him, the warmth underneath the quilt that was just inches away. Forget magical golden rings. If there was one burden in the world impossible to bear, it was love.

Jace and Ben had invited him over for dinner. Of course Jace could cook. The meal was well prepared, the conversation pleasant and followed by the third and final *Lord of the Rings* movie on DVD. The extended edition of *Return of the King* was apparently twelve million hours long, or so it felt. And Tim was grateful, especially when Ben stretched out on the couch, resting his head on Jace's lap, and his feet— At first the bottom of those were flat against Tim's outer thigh. After focusing on this contact for the longest time, remaining completely motionless, Tim moved his hand beneath the quilt, taking hold of one of Ben's feet like they were holding hands.

Silly as it was, it meant everything to him that Ben didn't pull away. Instead he wriggled his toes in response, sighing contently. Is this what Ben wanted, both his ex-boyfriend and his husband at once? Tim had never entertained the idea, but right now he would agree to anything because things were getting bad. Terribly bad. He and Ben found a lot of excuses like this, little ways of touching each other—goodbye hugs that went on a little too long, or playful shoves where hands brushed down the other's body instead of pushing. They even snuck lunch together once without Jace.

No matter what they promised and how much they swore, they were slowly giving in to the gravitation between them. Tim had no doubt that Ben loved Jace, but Eric was right. Love wasn't exclusive, nor did it expire, and if one of them didn't act soon, there would be no turning back.

Except Tim didn't want it to end. This time together had been nice, even if Ben wasn't his. In a way, being friends meant getting to know him outside the pressure of a relationship. They had fun. Too much fun, maybe.

As for the movie, the damn ring finally ended up in the volcano, but even then Frodo was left haunted. There was no escaping this curse.

"I'll get the dishes done," Jace said as the credits rolled.

Ben sat up, pulling his foot away. "I'll help."

"Me three!" Tim offered.

"No, just relax," Ben said. "We'll have them done lickity split."

"I'm buying you guys a dishwasher for Christmas," Tim said. "It's like Amish-land here. Who does dishes by hand?"

"Us po' folks," Jace said, leading his husband away.

Once they were out of sight, Tim groaned and fell over on his side. He stretched out on the couch and pulled the quilt up to his neck. All he could think was how nice doing dishes with Ben would be, both of them wearing brightly colored rubber gloves. Jace and Ben weren't poor. They were richer than he would ever be.

Lickity split must have meant something different to them, because Tim was nearly nodding off by the time he heard footsteps padding across the carpet. He kept his eyes closed. Maybe Ben would wake him with a kiss. Whoever was in the room with him didn't seem to be doing anything. Were they just standing there watching him?

"Is he asleep?" Jace's voice said from farther away.

"Yeah." Ben's whisper came from just in front of the couch. "Let's let him crash here."

"Okay. Are you coming to bed?"

"I'll be there in a second. I just want to lock up."

There was an awkward pause, then Jace said, "Come kiss me goodnight."

Tim listened, the subtle sounds excruciating.

"Is something wrong?" Ben asked.

"It's just—" Jace sighed. "Your eyes light up when he's around. The same way they do when you look at me."

"I love you," Ben said, almost with desperation.

Jace's response was gentle. "I know. Come to bed soon. Okay?"

Tim listened as the living room lamps clicked off, one by

one. He felt the quilt pulled tight, Ben tucking it in around him. Tim wanted to open his eyes, to pull Ben down on the couch with him, but he didn't dare move. Then Ben caressed his hair, just a single gentle stroke as innocent as a mother's touch. But of course it wasn't.

Tim listened to Ben's sigh, his footsteps in the hallway as the wood beneath the carpet creaked, the bedroom door as it clicked shut. Then Tim got up and snuck out the front door.

Insects hummed, thriving in the humid night. Tim sat on the front steps, rolling a bottle of beer between his palms while Chinchilla slept on her side, enjoying the cool concrete. They could have been out back, next to the soothing waters of the pool, but Tim was waiting. Maybe it wouldn't happen tonight, but the storm was coming. The only question was whether or not it would rain.

Sure enough, Ben's car pulled up half an hour later.

"You're either here to do something that you really shouldn't," Tim said, "or you came to say goodbye."

"I'm sorry." Ben stood before him, not bothering to sit. This would be a short visit. "I wish we could just be friends."

"No, you don't." Tim managed a brave smile. "That's the problem, isn't it?"

"Yeah."

Tim took a deep breath. "You think we would have made it? Say we never had the cops chasing us that night, that we kept on going. Do you think we'd still be together?"

Ben thought about it, maybe considering the possibilities that could have been, but instead of answering he swallowed and said, "I have to go."

Desperation stole over Tim. He wouldn't be able to breathe if Ben walked away. "I don't know what I'll do without you, Benjamin. I don't have anything left."

"That's not true. You have plenty."

"Did I tell you that I came out to my parents?"

"No."

"Yeah. They weren't thrilled. If they were distant before—" Tim shook his head.

"They'll get over it. And if they don't, then they can fuck themselves."

Tim smiled at this resurgence of Ben's teenage attitude. That's probably what he would have said if Tim had come out way back then. His parents would have flipped out, and Tim would have come sulking to Ben, only for him to say those very words. *They can fuck themselves.* Then their relationship would have continued, no worse for the wear. If only Tim could have understood that back then.

"Don't go back to Ryan," Ben said. "You don't need him. Or me. Or anyone else, for that matter."

Tim shook his head. "I've always needed you."

"You might want us, but you don't need us. You said I bring out the best in you, but all those wonderful things were already there, even before I came along. Live for yourself, Tim. Decorate the house with your paintings. Don't hide them away. Don't hide yourself away, either. There's a whole world out there waiting to see you. The real you." Ben fumbled with his car keys, already turning to leave, but first his eyes poured over Tim with sorrow. "You're so beautiful, and I don't just mean your face or your body."

"Don't go," Tim pleaded.

Ben shook his head and walked away, slowly. Tim could leap to his feet, could spin him around and kiss him and tell him he had to stay. And maybe Ben would for the night, or maybe even a day or two. But eventually he would remember Jace, and his heart would break with what he had done. So Tim remained seated and watched Ben open his car door, pausing with his hand on the doorframe.

"Until next time?" Ben said.

Tim laughed, wiping away the tears in his eyes. "Until next time."

Part Five:
Austin, 2008

Chapter Thirty-three

So much of attraction depended on balance. Not too skinny, not too fat. Not too young, not too old. Everyone had a different definition of the porridge that was *juuust right.* Tim was currently trying to find the perfect balance of scent. Cologne should be strong enough to be noticed, but not strong enough to make the eyes water. How many sprays was that exactly? Two? Three?

The balancing game continued. Stylishly messy hair sounded easy, but was found only in a narrow range between careless and completely crazy. And of course the old battle between overdressed and too casual waged on. Tim had opted for a dress shirt to go with his jeans before deciding this was trying too hard. Anything could happen when his guest arrived. Of course if the news was bad, all of this was superficial.

Giving up on his appearance, Tim walked through the house, Chinchilla following dutifully behind as he inspected everything. Kitchen counters cleared? Check. Scented candles in the living room lit? Check. Big fat guy sipping champagne on the couch? Check.... God damn it! Not now!

"What are you doing here?" Tim demanded.

"I keep showing up," Marcello said, "and you keep asking why. Thus our dance goes on."

"Seriously," Tim said, wiping a ring of condensation off the coffee table. "This isn't the best time."

Marcello's crow's feet crinkled. "I haven't seen you this nervous in quite some time. He must be quite the looker. What's the lucky guy's name?"

"Allison," Tim huffed.

Marcello stuck out his bottom lip and shrugged. "Always try new things, I suppose."

"It's not a date. You remember Allison. You met her at that grill party a few years ago."

"Grill party?"

"Yeah. Afterwards you said you'd been to children's birthday parties with more debauchery."

"It's true!" Marcello chuckled. "I remember now. She's the pretty black woman who sang with Ben. Why is she coming over?"

"I wish I knew. She called me yesterday and said she wanted to talk in person."

"Probably needs money," Marcello said, pantomiming a yawn.

"I don't think so." Tim felt his pulse pick up. "I bet it has something to do with Ben. Anyway, I need you out of here. Go on! You can take the bottle with you."

"There's something I wanted to talk to you about," Marcello said. "I'll make it quick. You know we have the gallery opening in two weeks."

It had taken ages to find an available downtown spot with all the right elements. Location, parking, lighting, wall space—and most of all—price. Finally, Tim had found someone sympathetic to their cause. The Eric Conroy Foundation would have its gallery, but it wasn't opening as soon as Marcello thought.

"Four weeks," Tim corrected.

"Ah, but the space will be ready in two, and it would be a shame to let it go to waste just because that Belgium artist is on holiday."

Tim checked his watch pointedly.

Marcello continued unabashed. "You're supposed to point out that we have nothing to exhibit. Well, I was thinking that painting you did of Eric would be a perfect piece to hang in the gallery."

Tim stared at him. "It's in my bedroom."

"It doesn't have to be."

"No, I mean, how the hell did you see that painting? Do you snoop around my bedroom when I'm not home?"

"What else am I supposed to do with my free time?" Marcello said. "You have a gift, Tim. Eric raved about your talent, and the few paintings you've allowed me to see left me thoroughly impressed."

Tim's face flushed. "Thanks, but I'm still changing the locks on the doors."

"I'll find an open window," Marcello assured him. "Anyway, instead of boring empty walls, why not exhibit your best paintings? You've worked hard for the foundation. Treat yourself."

"It's a little self-indulgent," Tim said.

"You've worked hard," Marcello repeated. "And it would make Eric proud."

And Ben, if he ever found out. "I'll think about it. Now get out of here, you old windbag."

"Old?" Marcello said as if offended, but he smiled and took his leave.

Tim was watching Marcello drive away when Allison arrived. Her hair style might be different and her clothes more respectable, but the expressive eyes and wide smile made her instantly recognizable. She sized him up on her way up the walk, nodding in approval.

"You look good!"

"Thanks." Tim grinned. "You too."

"No, I mean really good! Last time you were so frumpy and scruffy."

"Thanks," Tim said a little more firmly. "I've been working out. Uh, come on in."

He led her to the living room, desperate to confront her in the hallway and demand to know if Ben was all right. Once seated, she mercifully turned down the offer of a drink, and Tim could hold back no longer.

"How is he?"

Allison did one of those slow, bobbing nods, like she wasn't quite sure of the right answer. "He's fine." Then she sighed. "Can't we do small talk first?"

"You're killing me," Tim said, taking a seat himself.

"Okay." Allison took a deep breath. "Jace passed away."

"What? How?"

"Aneurysm." Suddenly Allison looked much older. "We had a bad scare but they caught it in time. He made it through one surgery and things were looking hopeful—" She shook her head, unable to continue.

Tim's stomach sank. "I'm sorry. Ben must be in terrible shape."

"He's doing better," Allison said. "It's been a couple of years now."

"Since Jace died?"

Allison nodded.

Tim felt dizzy trying to consider all the implications. "Why didn't you tell me sooner?"

"I didn't want you to… Never mind, it's not important."

"What? Say it."

Allison looked at him squarely. "I didn't want you to think it was convenient."

"It's not convenient." Tim felt his temper rising. "When it happens to you, when someone you love is suddenly taken away, it's never convenient. When Eric died—" Tim shook his head. "Part of you dies along with them. That's what it feels like."

"Sorry," Allison said. "I didn't mean it like that."

Tim sighed. "It's okay. I'm not upset at you. I just hate thinking of what Ben must have gone through—is still going through."

"He's doing better." Allison bit her lower lip before continuing. "These days when you mention Jace, he smiles. I think he's over the grieving as much as anyone can be. But he's lonely. I know he is. All he does is work."

Tim could relate.

"He never goes out or talks about meeting anyone." Allison raised her eyes. "Except you. Sometimes he still talks about you."

"I'm here," Tim said without hesitation. "If he needs a shoulder to cry on, I'm always here."

"He's done enough crying for a lifetime," Allison said. "Do you still love him? I mean really *really* love him."

Tim didn't hesitate. "More than anyone in my entire life."

Allison nodded. "Then maybe you should get me that drink. We have a lot to discuss."

The Eric Conroy Gallery, located on Second Street, was the ideal space for exhibiting art. Long narrow rooms—barely more than hallways—lined three sides of a big space perfect for sculpture or installations. The previous tenant had used the biggest room to sell designer shoes and the narrow rooms for inventory. The layout would have been a nightmare for most other retail stores. Tim had discovered the location after the shoe store went bust, but the rent was too expensive, so he turned it down. After half a year on the market, the owner called, eager for Tim to take the property at a reduced price.

With weeks of renovation complete, the former shoe store had been transformed into the perfect blank canvas. Neutral white walls and track lighting guaranteed the art would pop. They even pulled up the cheap carpeting and brought the wooden floors underneath back to life. Tim had worked alongside the contractors, leaving nothing to chance.

So when Marcello suggested not letting that extra week or two go to waste, Tim would have agreed simply to show the public how beautiful the gallery turned out, even if his paintings weren't on display. But Allison thought it had romantic potential.

Romantic! What a cheesy, stupid word. Tim scarcely believed romance could be part of his life again. As opening day neared, he began to have serious doubts. Not about his own feelings. He wanted to see Ben again more than anything. But he was scared of what losing a spouse could do to a person. Maybe Ben would look right through him, thinking only of Jace.

Tim was willing to risk it one more time. Hell, he'd try a million more times, if that's what it took. He worked hard at making his first exhibition the right place for them to meet again. He was opening his life to the world, so he didn't choose just his best work. He chose paintings from every stage of his life, even childhood. This meant putting some very humble pieces on display. Somehow this felt more honest and less pompous.

Tim managed most aspects of the Eric Conroy Foundation now, but publicity for the gallery opening he left to Marcello and his expertise. Aside from begging him not to use shirtless cocktail waiters, Tim had complete faith in his abilities.

The big night came all too soon. The gallery preparations were enough to occupy his time, but Tim had also been busy finishing a new painting. He barely completed it in time to hand over to Allison. Now it was all up to her, because Tim found himself waiting in a near-empty gallery as the sun began to set. Opening night. What would people think? Would they sneer at his art, turn up their noses and walk away? Even worse, what if they laughed at his efforts? Or didn't show up?

The gallery's first visitors were an elderly couple. Tim kept his distance, watching them move from painting to painting before his curiosity got the better of him. Approaching them, he introduced himself and was rewarded with compliments. The old man's father had been a painter, and some of Tim's work brought back happy memories. While Tim was talking with them, more people came in. Before long, visitors were coming and going from the gallery in a steady stream. Some left unchanged by the experience, but others stuck around, honoring Tim with their time and questions.

"It's past eight," Marcello said, sidling up to him. "You were supposed to give a speech at seven."

Was it so late already? Tim glanced around the gallery. Still no sign of Ben and Allison. Maybe she had told Ben their plan and he had declined.

"Speech," Marcello prompted.

"Yeah, okay. I'm coming."

Tim made his way to the main room, checking each face in the crowd but not finding the one he wanted to see most. The larger space was much easier to navigate, since nothing was installed in the center of the room yet. Tim went to a microphone and small amplifier that waited for him next to the free drinks. That would keep the attention on him, even if people were just waiting for him to get out of the way.

Tim picked up the microphone, wondering how to capture everyone's attention and opted for a classic. "Is this thing on?" Horrible reverb shot from the speakers and crawled up dozens of spines. That did it! Every head turn toward him.

"Whoa! Too loud. Sorry." Tim adjusted the amp volume and grinned sheepishly at the crowd gathering in front of him. "Uh, I'm really glad you all decided to be here. I'm not really good at speeches, so bear with me."

A burble of laughter came from the crowd, thanks mostly to the free champagne.

"The art you see here is about twenty years in the making. I'm sure most of you have seen my crowning achievement, 'Frog Goes Sailing on Boat'?" Another round of laughter. Hey, this wasn't so hard! "That's from when I was eight and is the first painting I ever did."

Tim searched the crowd. If Ben was here, wouldn't he be right up front?

"I owe this art to a lot of people. The subjects in each piece, of course. My dog Chinchilla, or Eric, who was a father, a hero, and much more to me. Even strangers, like the old woman I saw lying in the grass at the park, staring up at the clouds and giggling like a little girl at what she saw there."

Tim licked his lips, eyes sweeping the crowd once more. No Ben. Well, if he was here, Tim could only hope he was listening.

"So many people have inspired me, but only one gave me the courage to show my paintings to other people. I hope he's here somewhere tonight, and as I finish this clumsy speech, I'd like you all to clap for him, not for me. Thank you, most of all, to Benjamin Bentley."

The resulting applause was impressive. Tim turned off the amp and gave an awkward little bow. The room began to clear, but some visitors remained behind to speak with him, asking him about certain paintings or even prices. The attention was wonderful. Why had he fought against this for so long? But as good as it felt, Tim kept searching the room, kept hoping. Then, in the center where a sculpture or some other work of art should be, was the ultimate masterpiece.

Ben looked small and uncertain, but still very much himself.

Tim ran to him and scooped him up in his arms, spinning him around. "I'm so glad you're here!" Tim set him down reluctantly. He could have run off into the night with him. Soon enough… "And even more glad that you're late! I just gave the most embarrassing speech!"

"I thought it was really good," Ben said with a hint of mischief.

Tim felt his face flush, but this was all positive. Ben wasn't broken or morose. A little more reserved, maybe, but still his Benjamin. And he was here! "I thought for a second that Allison had changed her mind," Tim said.

Ben appeared puzzled. "Where is she, anyway?"

"Running an errand for me." They eyed each other for a moment, soaking up the details. "Hey, have you seen much of the paintings?"

"A little," Ben said, "but a tour from the artist himself would be very informative."

"All right, grand tour, but only if you promise to buy something."

Ben exhaled. "Do the postcards count?"

"Those are free, and yes."

Tim led Ben from painting to painting, eager to show him the ones he hadn't seen, dragging him this way and that. Occasionally people would overhear their conversation and ask Tim questions or make their own comments. That was fun, but the night wasn't really about his art or this gallery. It was about Ben, so Tim spontaneously took his hand and led him toward the back exit.

"There's one more piece I'd like to show you," Tim said. "Something really special to me."

He led them out to the parking lot, expecting Ben to stop him and demand an explanation, but so far he was rolling with it. Hopefully Allison had kept her part of the bargain. He walked Ben to the passenger side of his car, letting go of his hand.

"Have any idea what sort of car this is?" Tim asked, opening the door for him.

"Nope."

"Care to know?"

"Not really."

Tim chuckled. "It's a Bentley. I figured it was the next best thing to the real deal."

Ben smiled, which alone was worth the expensive price tag.

Once Tim was in the car and driving, he glanced over to see Ben looking a lot less certain. He wanted to comfort him, to explain what was happening, but he also didn't want to ruin the surprise. Most of all he wanted to tell Ben he was sorry about Jace, to find some words to make the pain disappear from his heart, but Allison had said not to broach the subject. Tonight was about the future, or so they hoped.

"Won't you be missed at the gallery?" Ben asked.

"Me? No. We had one of those life-size cardboard cutouts printed of me that will go in the corner. No one will know the difference."

"What about me?" Ben said. "It's only a matter of time before someone calls the police."

Tim shrugged. "They'll have to pay the ransom if they want you back."

There was a heavy pause. "Where are we going?"

"Trust me. We're almost there."

Holy crap! How had any of this sounded like a good idea? Tim should have just called Ben and asked him out on a nice boring date. When he and Allison had planned this, it had all seemed so clever. Now...

Tim pulled into a neighborhood. Beside him, Ben grew tense. This was where Ben lived. Tim had driven past his house every night last week, looking at lit windows and marveling that the man he loved was just behind them.

"What are we doing here?" Ben asked when they pulled into his driveway.

"I wanted to show you a special painting of mine."

Ben relaxed visibly. "You mean the one you gave me for my birthday." He smirked. "You can't have it back."

But Tim knew that the painting was no longer there.

He followed Ben inside, feeling less and less certain. This was the house Ben and Jace had saved their money to buy, where they had shared their final years together. When Ben turned on the living room lights, Jace's old cat Samson woke up, watching Tim curiously from the couch. Ben was looking at the cat too, no doubt thinking of his husband.

"Jace—" Ben began.

"—was a good man," Tim finished for him. "The best, in fact. I would never dishonor his memory, and I will never, ever be able to replace him. No one could."

Samson hopped down and walked up to Tim, sniffing his leg and rubbing against him before doing the same to Ben. Then he returned to his place on the couch to continue his nap. Well, that was one vote in his favor. He turned to Ben, who was staring at a nearby wall. There, where the old painting had been before Allison took it, hung the one Tim had recently completed. The colors and spirit were the same as the painting from so long ago, but now the emotions flowed freely, no longer denied. Tim had poured all of those feelings on the canvas, choosing two hands instead of hearts, the fingers intertwined. One hand was clearly his own, the other what he remembered of Ben's. Glancing down, he saw that his memory hadn't failed him. Ben raised his hand as if seeing it for the first time, and Tim gently took hold of it, adjusting their fingers, weaving them together until they matched those of the painting.

"I love you, Benjamin Bentley. I should have told you that twelve years ago. I've always loved you."

Tim looked into Ben's eyes and saw uncertainty, maybe even fear. Once upon a time, it's what Ben must have seen when looking into his own. Tim didn't let it dissuade him. Ben had taught him how to bring a heart out of the dark. Tim could finally do the same for him.

"What now?" Ben asked.

"Now we start over."

Tim leaned forward for a kiss, only bridging half the distance. The rest was up to Ben—had to be his choice. Ben closed his eyes and leaned forward, their lips touching, and they were teenagers again. Time had granted them mercy, turned back the clock, and given them a second chance.

"Wait," Ben said, pulling away. His cheeks were flushed. "This is going so fast."

Tim chuckled. "Twelve years later and you think a kiss is too fast?" Tim leaned forward again, and this time the kiss lasted longer. But then Ben fell into him, clutching arms around his torso and hiding his face against Tim's neck. He could feel tears against his skin.

"I know," Tim whispered, wrapping arms around him. "I mean, I don't know, but I can imagine."

This had to be weird. Ben had kissed Jace for years, had kissed him last, and maybe what he was doing now felt like betrayal. Or maybe it just felt strange, because it really was a lot to process, even for Tim.

"We'll take it slow," Tim said. "There's no need to rush into anything. I just want to spend time with you. Okay?"

Ben's head nodded against his neck, and when he pulled away, his smile was brave.

"I love it," Ben said, glancing at the painting. He took hold of Tim's hand with firm determination. "I love seeing you again."

"Yeah, it feels good. Crazy and unreal, but good."

Ben sniffed, sighed, and composed himself. When he spoke again, he sounded like his old self. "Where's the old painting? If you sold it at the gallery, I demand half the proceeds."

"You'll have to ask Allison," Tim said. "Maybe she's planning to give it to Brian as a present."

"She better not!"

Tim squeezed his hand. "She's probably back at the gallery by now. We could return there if you want. I should probably be there since it's my show."

"It's your first exhibition, right?"

"Yeah, but I don't mean that as much as the gallery opening. I'm heading the Eric Conroy Foundation now."

Tim told him all about his work as they headed back to the gallery, glad he had something to report that he could feel proud of. No more spoiled rich boy wallowing in his own misery. Everything was different, and maybe this time it would be enough.

The nightlife had poured into Austin's streets, the vibe at the gallery more like a party now. Taking care of the visitors and maintaining order occupied most of Tim's attention, but every time he searched the crowds he found Ben not far away. Their eyes would lock and they would smile. Definitely a promising start, but so much still needed to happen.

At the end of the evening, Tim offered to drive Ben home. Allison complained teasingly, insisting that Ben was her date before winking and leaving them alone. The ride back to Ben's house was quiet. Tim wasn't sure of Ben's thoughts, but he dreamt of spending the night together, even if they only stayed up talking. Regardless, he would keep his promise to move slowly.

"Can I have you tomorrow?" Tim asked as he pulled up to the curb.

Ben raised an eyebrow. "Interesting choice of words."

"I mean, do you have any plans?"

Ben shook his head. "There's a new play starting soon, but rehearsals aren't until next week. What did you have in mind?"

"I thought we'd go for a drive. Maybe head over to The Woodlands and chase after some old memories."

"Okay."

Tim shifted in his seat. "I don't suppose a good night ki—"

Ben's lips were on his before he could finish the sentence, and of everything that had happened that night, the kiss was the most meaningful. A debut art exhibition and a successful gallery opening simply couldn't compare.

Chapter Thirty-four

The Woodlands had been many things to Tim over the years. At first the city had been a chance at a new beginning, a fresh start after the events in Kansas that now seemed small and distant. Like a sapling, Tim had sprung up out of the dirt only to find his pot was too small and cramped, that he wasn't getting enough sun or water. Of course the metaphor fell apart right there, since the city wasn't to blame for his stunted growth. Tim took full responsibility for that now, but in his mind, The Woodlands remained a place of failed potential.

Not anymore. In the passenger seat next to him was Ben, and like a magic totem, Tim was rushing him back to the past to banish those clouds and bring back the sun. Together they could rewrite history, he felt. Of course it would help if Ben stopped looking at him like he was a total stranger.

"So you'll be running the gallery?" he was asking.

"Yeah." Tim checked his blind spot and cruised over to the fast lane. "I about flipped when I started working for the foundation. After all those years of having nothing to do, it felt good to have a purpose. Most applicants come around in the spring or summer. Besides that there's only a fundraiser in the fall, so I still have a lot of free time."

"How terrible," Ben interjected.

Tim grinned. "I know, right? My life's so hard. Anyway, I figure the gallery will keep my hands full the rest of the year by giving me a chance to help out other artists." He glanced over, hoping to see Ben impressed, but instead that puzzled expression had resurfaced. "Am I not making sense?"

"You are," Ben said, turning his attention to the road. "That's how speech therapy makes me feel."

"You're still doing that?"

"Yup. Sometimes I wish it was full-time, since it's a lot more fulfilling than theater work. Being on stage is more self-indulgent than anything. An excuse to sing for an audience."

"I wouldn't mind hearing you sing again," Tim said.

"The show coming up is just straight-up acting," Ben said, not taking the hint. "I don't like doing those as much, but Brian always gets Allison to talk me into them. I need the extra money anyway."

Tim resisted the urge to offer him everything he had. He would give it, if Ben asked, but he also worried about making everything feel weird. Instead he nodded at the highway sign. "Ten more miles and we're there!"

They exchanged looks that both said the same thing: Is this really a good idea? Then they laughed and scrutinized their surroundings, pointing out familiar landmarks as they entered the city limits.

"Where to first?" Tim asked. "Want to see your parents?"

Ben shook his head. "Not this time. I can only imagine all the questions they'll have."

Tim had a few himself. They hadn't shared any kisses today or any other sign that they were more than old friends. Their reunion might have been fueled by dwindling flames of nostalgia and nothing else. For Ben at least. What Tim felt was so much more.

"I know where we'll go," he said, turning down the street.

"No!" Ben laughed. "You've got to be kidding."

"Nope!" Tim pulled into the high school parking lot. "Memory lane!"

"More like death row," Ben said. "We're not going in there, are we?"

"Why not? If anyone stops us, we'll just say we're picking up our kid."

"We're not that old! Besides, what's the point? It's not like you and I have many memories here. Not together, at least."

"True." Tim considered the school. "Maybe I want to walk down the hallway with you, hand in hand, like I should have done a long time ago."

Ben's eyes softened. "You don't have to do this."

"I want to."

Their hands didn't touch until they pushed open one of the doors and stepped into an empty hallway. Ben was right. The place didn't hold a lot of memories for them. Tim had only attended this school his junior year, but the universal smell made it feel like every school he'd been in. Dingy lockers, cheap carpet, textbooks, and a touch of desperation. That was the smell of institutionalized education.

Tim reached over, the side of his hand bumping Ben's, whose fingers responded by tangling up with his own. "So, can I walk you to class?" Tim said.

Ben laughed nervously. "We can leave now."

"Come on, just down to the end of the hall and back. We'll be gone before anyone notices."

That seemed to be the case until they had started heading back. Then the bell rang. As much as Tim said he wanted to do this, when countless teenagers swarmed into the hall around him, he couldn't help but feel uncomfortable. Not really because of the gay thing—even though they heard plenty of laughs already—but because the students made him feel old while reminding him of how awkward those school days had been.

He scanned the crowd as they walked, looking for the new Stacy Shelly or Bryce Hunter. And of course they received plenty of stares. Girls giggled and guys glared, but a few students they passed looked at them with a mad sort of hope in their eyes. Tim grinned at one of them, nudging Ben after they walked past him. Ben nodded, having seen him too.

"Oh man!" Tim said, laughing with nervous relief when they were outside again. "Could you imagine two guys walking down the hall holding hands when we were in school? I would have freaked."

"I would have loved it!" Ben said. "Besides, it's not so unusual anymore. One of my coworkers at the hospital, her son came out when he was fourteen and took his boyfriend to homecoming."

"Seriously?"

"The times, they are a changin'!"

"Would you have gone to prom with me?" Tim asked.

Ben snorted. "Are you kidding? I would have followed you to the moon."

Their next destination was even less a part of their history than the school was. Tim had wanted to revisit the past with Ben, but he hadn't realized until now how much of their relationship was restricted to their teenage bedrooms, hidden away from the world. Tim drove to their old neighborhood, parking near one of the bike trail entrances a few blocks over from either of their houses.

"Go for a walk with me?" he said.

Ben was quiet as they strolled into the trees, but he took Tim's hand, gripping it tighter when they reached a small man-made lake. Walking around it, they took another path that led to a small playground. The scene had changed, the jungle gym and swings replaced by new equipment, but neither had forgotten what had happened here. The night the police had nearly caught them, quite literally, with their pants down.

"Want to pick up where we left off?" Tim teased, but when he looked over, Ben wasn't smiling. So maybe this wasn't the best idea. They did have memories outside of their homes, but few of them were happy. Tim checked his watch. His parents would still be at work, probably. The den, or his old bedroom, those were happy places. "Come on. Let's get out of here."

During the walk, Ben's posture relaxed a little. "It's crazy. How many times do you think I snuck over to your house at night?"

"Hm." Tim pretended to do some mental calculations. "Once, maybe twice."

"More like one or two hundred times. I used to hide behind a tree whenever I saw a car coming, like the cops were doing a sweep for forbidden lovers. It was always so quiet, especially in the winter when all you would hear was the wind or a few lonely leaves skittering along. Just me and the stars above, on my way to Tim Wyman's house."

"And then you'd crawl into my bed with frozen hands," Tim said. "You remember my technique for getting them warmed up?"

Ben grinned sheepishly. "These days I can drive anywhere I want without anyone to stop me. I guess the lack of freedom back then made even the simplest thing seem special."

"It was more than just that," Tim said. "Sneak over to my house in Austin one night and I'll prove it." He stopped on the sidewalk as they reached a driveway and stared. "There it is. Home, sweet home. It looks the same."

"You sound surprised," Ben said.

"It's been a while."

How long exactly? More than a year, that was certain. Two, maybe? His mother called occasionally, and so did Tim, sometimes, but they didn't want him to share much about his life. Anytime he mentioned a guy, even just Marcello, she got quiet, no doubt wondering if that person meant something more to him.

At least the locks hadn't been changed. Tim entered the house with Ben in tow, and after a few murmured jokes, they toured the downstairs in silence. Like in a museum, they walked carefully, not touching any of the exhibits, stopping and staring in silence at some of the same places. The corner of the living room where the Christmas tree had been. The dining room table where they had their candlelight dinner, or the den, which had been their whole world together for the first few weeks. Then they crept up the stairs as if it were another of winter's midnights, but behind the bedroom door was now just an anonymous guestroom. Only the dresser against the wall was the same.

"Too bad," Ben said, sitting on the edge of the bed. "I was hoping you had obsessive parents that keep the room a time capsule after their kid leaves."

"It's not like I died," Tim said, even though sometimes it felt that way. He sat on the bed next to Ben. Their backs were to the window that looked out on the back lawn, for which he was grateful. "Ever wish you had a time machine?"

"For what?" Ben laughed, already guessing the answer. "What would you do, travel back here and lock teenage Tim in the closet?"

"Yup. Literally this time. Then I'd wait in bed like the wolf in Little Red Riding Hood."

"I think teenage Ben would notice you were older."

Tim leaned against him. "But would he complain? That's the question."

"I don't remember you being this weird," Ben said, changing subjects.

"Yeah, well, that's what living the life of a secluded millionaire will do to you."

Ben's response was cut short by the sound of the garage door rumbling. Tim tensed.

"Want to sneak out?" Ben offered.

"No. Come on. Let's go meet them."

His parents were already in the kitchen when they entered. His father yelped in shock, and his mother pressed a palm to her chest, but when they recognized him they relaxed. Somewhat.

"*¡Gordito!* What are you doing here? Your car isn't out front!"

"I just thought I would stop by." His parents' full attention was already focused on Ben. "Uh, this is Ben. Ben Bentley. Do you remember him? He had dinner with us when—"

Tim's father tossed his car keys on the kitchen table. "I'm going up to my office."

"Why?" Tim said, stepping in his way. "It's been ages since you saw me, and you're going to walk away just because I brought my boyfriend along? Seriously?"

His father scowled. "This is my house, young man, and I'll do as I please!"

Tim stepped aside, sparing a glance for Ben who had moved out of the way. He had his arms crossed defensively over his chest and appeared exceedingly uncomfortable. This made Tim all the more angry. His parents could at least act civil.

"Why do you even care?" Tim shouted after him. "You never wanted a kid, so why do you care that I turned out different than you expected? You couldn't give a shit about anything good I've ever done, but you've always been there to make me feel bad when I do wrong."

His father spun around, face red with barely contained rage. "Maybe if you weren't such a disappointment I would have cared more!"

"What did you want me to be?" Tim retorted. "Like you? Get a wife, run a boring business, and treat my kids to icy silence? If that's what I was supposed to be, then I'm glad I disappoint you so much." Tim glanced at his mother. "And thanks for the few times a year you remembered to pay attention to me. That was real generous of you."

Tim headed for the door, catching Ben's eye to make sure he'd follow. Time to get out of here. Tim couldn't imagine ever coming back. On his way out of the kitchen, he pushed past his father, wanting to shove him, knock him up against the wall—anything to make him hurt half as much as he did. But instead he kept moving, turning his back on him.

Ben followed him through the house, nearly running to keep up. Tim's hand was on the front door when a voice called after him.

"*¡Gordito!*"

And he hated himself for doing it, but he hesitated because he still loved his mother, even though he often wished he could forget her altogether. He turned around, noticing how miserable Ben looked. So he put an arm around him. His mother's eyes widened.

"What?" he spat. "What can you possibly say after all these years? Do you know how lonely I was growing up, how desperate for attention I was? And when I figure out the kind of person I need by my side to not feel that way, you turn your back on me completely. What kind of mother are you?"

"We weren't ready," his mother said quickly. "I'm sorry. We weren't ready for a child, and I tried, and I thought you had enough. Later I saw other parents with their children, and I realized how little we gave you. But you were already older then, too old to start coddling."

"It's never too late. I don't need you to coddle me, but you can treat me like I matter to you."

His mother took a step forward. "You *do* matter!"

"Then why aren't you a part of my life?" Her eyes flicked to Ben and back. "I thought if I brought him here, you would see... I don't know, that you would understand. It's just love. It's no different." Tim turned, opening the door for Ben so they could leave. "If you ever want to be a part of my life," he said over his shoulder, "you know where to find me."

He thought he heard his mother crying on his way out, but he could no longer let that dictate his actions. He had to live his own life, and her tears were her own doing. She could be laughing right now, cooking up a meal for them both and congratulating him on finding Ben again. She was responsible for her own pain. The choice was hers, not his.

"I'm sorry," Ben said as they walked back to the car.

"It's not your fault," Tim said.

"No, I mean for when we were younger. My parents aren't like yours. When I came out, they were worried about my safety. Maybe it took a little time for them to get used to the idea, but mostly they just had questions. I naively thought it would be the same for you, the same for everyone, so I kept pressuring you to come out."

Tim shook his head. "You didn't do anything wrong. Being in the closet didn't make me happy. You did. I made the wrong choice. Even when you weren't around, I was glad I came out. I spent so long wishing for their approval and living a lie that it was a relief not to have to try anymore. No more pretending."

Ben took his hand. "For what it's worth, I'm proud of you."

Tim sighed. "Maybe your parents can adopt me."

"Want me to ask?"

"Yeah. Or I could marry into the family."

"My sister Karen recently got divorced," Ben teased.

"That's not quite what I meant. Hey, did you notice when I called you my boyfriend in front of my parents?"

Ben hesitated. "Yeah."

"You didn't disagree. That makes it legal."

"Really? Is that a Kansas law?"

"Nope. Texas only. I looked it up."

"Okay."

Tim glanced over at him. "Okay?"

"Yeah. Okay. I'll even let you take me out to dinner."

"One more stop," Tim said. "Then I'll take you anywhere you want to go."

Once again they drove to a different neighborhood and parked near one of the bike path entrances. As they walked, Tim held Ben's hand with confidence. Maybe the previous surprises hadn't been a hit, but Tim was certain Ben would like this one. They walked down the path together, entering a stretch where the trees on one side fell away to make room for a drainage ditch. The grass was speckled with seasonal yellow. The ditch was just deep enough to cause an injury if someone fell in—a severely sprained ankle, for instance.

"Right here," Tim said.

Ben shook his head and pulled on his hand. "A little farther. Trust me, I remember this one. I had to come back for my Rollerblades."

Tim let Ben lead him farther down the path. "This far? Are you sure?"

"Yup. Right here. See that rock down there? It's probably still splattered with your DNA."

"Good," Tim said. "That way future generations can clone me."

Ben laughed, but his face grew somber as he stared down into the ditch. Was he remembering? If so, why did he look so damn unhappy? Tim had brought him here to show how far they had come, that they had started from something small and could do so again. Maybe Tim needed to take it a step further.

"I feel faint," he said, groaning dramatically before toppling over and rolling down ditch's slope. The keys in his pocket hurt like hell, but this time his fall was controlled. He managed to stop just before hitting the rock.

"Are you crazy?" Ben shouted after him.

"No, but I think I jacked up my ankle again."

"Whatever. Get back up here!"

"I can't!" Tim groaned. "You have to come rescue me." He stared at the sky until Ben's head appeared against the blue and white backdrop. He was smiling. That was something. Tim extended a hand. "Help me up."

The second Ben took his hand, Tim pulled him down on top of him. Ben's knee landed dangerously close to his crotch, and the wind was nearly knocked from him, but he didn't care. He wrapped his arms tight around Ben, who squirmed in protest before giving in.

"You'll have to let go of me eventually!" he said.

"Nope." Tim shook his head. "Never again."

"What if someone sees us down here?"

Tim gasped sarcastically. "Sounds like something I would have said."

Ben laughed and howled while trying to fight his way free, and eventually Tim loosened his grip. When Ben pushed himself up on his elbows, his eyes were wet from tears. And although the tears had come from laughter, Tim could still see something sad there.

"What's going on?" he said. "Whatever it is, tell me."

Ben sighed. "I get what you're doing today—taking me around to all these places. And standing up to your parents like that. That was both horrifying and wonderful at the same time."

"They had it coming," Tim said before searching Ben's eyes again. "So why do I feel like you're sad?"

"These places," Ben glanced around them. "I know exactly where you hurt your ankle because I came back here countless times. After we broke up, I'd walk by here or your house or even the playground by the lake. You asked if I ever wished I had a time machine, and the answer is yes. For months, maybe even years, I wished I could turn back time and stop that night from happening."

"Would you still?"

Ben rolled over on to his back. "No. Yes. I don't know. Part of me wishes we could have been together our entire lives. The other part knows that if we hadn't fallen apart, I never would have met Jace, and I wouldn't wish that away. Ever."

Tim sat up and turned to face him. "That's okay. I've thought the same thing before. I regretted leaving you for so long, but if I hadn't, I wouldn't have met Eric. I love him. Not in the same way you love Jace, but I'd hate to have never met him. Maybe I would have anyway, except we would have met him together."

Ben frowned. "I don't think that would have worked with Jace."

"I guess not."

"I want to be with you," Ben said. "You coming back into my life feels like a miracle. It's just that we both have so much baggage. All the bad things that happened here or in Austin, which is worse, because it's also full of happy memories with Jace. I wish we could start over somewhere without—"

"We'll move." Tim said. "New York, Canada, Europe. You name it. I'll sell the house and we'll start over again."

Ben shook his head. "It's not that easy. Austin feels like home now. I love my work, and Allison is there. And what about the gallery?"

"None of that matters."

But he knew it did. The gallery was part of Eric's legacy, and taking Ben away from everything else that made him happy wouldn't be good in the long run. Tim's pulse raced, feeling he was losing Ben again.

Then he took a deep breath and forced himself to relax. They had made it twelve years. Even if they weren't together for all that time, their feelings for each other had lasted that long. They just needed a neutral place to start over.

Tim reached out, taking Ben's hands and pulling him into a sitting position. "Let's get away from it all. Not permanently. Just for a little while. We'll take a trip but leave the baggage at home."

"Yeah?" Ben considered the idea. "I could push my appointments at the hospital back a week. Think that'll be enough?"

Tim laughed. "For you to fall madly in love with me again? How long did it take the first time?"

Ben's face flushed, but he nodded. "Okay. Let's do it. Where are we going to go?"

Chapter Thirty-five

"Mexico City?" said the woman behind the counter as she eyed their passports.

She had their reservation on the screen and probably wouldn't hear his response, but Tim went along with this strange airport ritual and answered in the affirmative. Then he glanced back at Ben, whose attention was elsewhere. Tracing his line of sight, Tim saw a group of flight attendants, chatting happily as they pulled their luggage behind them.

Of course.

That would explain the return of Ben's haunted look. The woman at the counter spoke again, Tim nodding through the rest of the process. Had another of his ideas failed already? If so, he only had himself to blame. Of course an airport would make Ben think of Jace—astronaut of the stratosphere. And now that Tim considered the situation, he remembered Jace had often whisked Ben away to exotic destinations.

The realization made him want to drive to Mexico City instead, especially when Ben remained silent all through the security screening. But once past this procedure, Tim began feeling optimistic. He loved the buzz of an airport, how everybody was jetting off to somewhere new or finally returning home again. Everyone was in transition, no one truly belonging there, which meant no one was an outsider. All were of equal status. At least until it came time to board.

"This is going to be fun," Tim said.

Ben managed a smile. "It's been a long time since I travelled. How long is the flight?"

"About two and a half hours."

"Should we stock up on drinks and snacks?"

"Why?" Tim asked. "They'll be serving us lunch, and we get all the drinks we want."

"Since when?"

"Since always. We're flying business class, baby!"

Ben perked up. "Really? I've only flown economy before."

This made all the difference. Faced with a new experience, Ben focused on where they were going instead of where he had been—and with whom. During the flight, they played with the seat controls like a couple of kids, taking shameless advantage of all the perks and privileges the overpriced seats brought them. The flight attendants—all of them female, thankfully—treated them like royalty. Time flew by like the clouds, and the plane soon began circling a sprawling metropolis as it began its descent.

Tim leaned over Ben's lap, both of them looking out the window. "Wait until you see the city at night. It's like the land is on fire."

Ben would see it every night. Tim hadn't just splurged on business class tickets. The hotel suite he had reserved was magnificent. From their room on the twenty-third floor, Ben would view the city like an emperor on high. Then Tim would drag him into the Jacuzzi built for two. Maybe he'd even have the tub filled with champagne instead of water. Tim would love to have a limo pick them up at the airport, but one small kink had formed in his romantic plans.

"I told you my *abuelita* is picking us up from the airport, right?"

"Your what?"

"My grandma, Nana."

"No." Ben shot him a nervous glance. "Does she know about me?"

Tim laughed. "Don't worry. She's not nearly as bad as my parents. I mean, I thought she would be worse. Not in a mean way," he added quickly. "I figured my sexuality would break her heart. Instead she mostly took it in stride."

"Mostly?"

"Well, we don't exactly talk about it much. And she's never seen me with another guy. That's going to be weird."

Ben stared until Tim nudged him, triggering a smile. "Well, I'm looking forward to meeting her. Remember how I did all that research on Mexico City to impress your mom?"

Tim groaned. "Yes, and please, just be yourself. No hammy book reports."

"Of course not." Ben paused. "Did you know that Mexico City has the largest public transportation network in the world?"

"Stop," Tim pleaded.

"And the most affordable, making it a form of transit that truly belongs to the people."

"Shoot me now," Tim begged. "Put me out of my misery!"

Ben kept teasing him with all the facts he could still remember, but as the plane touched down, Tim began to worry. What if his grandmother couldn't cope with seeing him and Ben together? Then again, they weren't going to make out in front of her or anything, even though Tim would jump at the opportunity. They still hadn't kissed since the night of the gallery opening. He respected that Ben wanted to take it slow, but waiting for him to make the first move was driving Tim crazy.

Stomachs burbling with nerves, they waited at the luggage carousel until their bags appeared. Tim took both of them, sending Ben a cocky wink that belied how uncertain he felt about the situation.

Nana, here is the love of my life. Love of my life, here is my grandma. Now duke it out!

Customs let them pass without much difficulty, the fogged glass doors opening automatically to generic airport corridors full of waiting people. He scanned the eager faces, aiming low since Nana was short. He spotted her hair first, which she wore high like a honey-colored helmet. Below this were huge amber sunglasses and a smile, her arms opening in invitation as she happily declared, "*¡Mi nieto!*"

Tim grinned, his worries temporarily forgotten as he set down the luggage and moved toward the woman who was stout, dark, and wrinkled—like a bag of brown sugar. As she took Tim in her arms, he remembered that she was just as sweet. She kissed both his cheeks. Holding his face in her hands, she examined him. "*¡Tan hermoso!*"

Feeling about eight years old, Tim gently moved her hands away and nodded to Ben. "*Nana, éste es mi novio, Ben.*" There. Just like in his fantasy, he said it. He used the word "boyfriend" instead of "love of my life," but it was out there now. Tim held his breath.

Nana looked at Ben and threw her arms open wide, giving him the same treatment she'd given Tim, except instead of calling Ben handsome, she said *bonito.* Beautiful. Tim agreed.

"It is very good to meet you, Ben," Nana said with practiced care. Her accent was so thick she made his name sound like "bean."

"It's wonderful to meet you," Ben replied.

"I drive you home," Nana said. "Then I make you for lunch."

Tim chuckled, imagining Ben tied up on the table with an apple in his mouth. "Your English is good," he said, picking the bags up again. "*¡Muy bueno!*"

"We have Englishman next door," Nana said, taking his arm on one side and Ben's on the other as she led them away. "I make him practice with me one time a week. We have tea together. Nice old man. One time he want to kiss me." She giggled like a little girl, looking back and forth between them as they headed to the parking lot. Nana chatted about her other neighbors, then family members Tim didn't know. She continued talking as they piled into her old Cadillac.

Traffic in Mexico City was notorious, rush hour turning the highways into parking lots. Nana was obviously mindful of this, checking the clock on her dashboard repeatedly as they drove in a race against time. She could barely see over the steering wheel, navigating the traffic with blind instinct as she continued to update him on family gossip, cars occasionally careening out of the way to avoid being hit.

Tim kept glancing at Ben in the backseat as she chattered. He was looking out the windows, no doubt wondering if coming here was such a great idea. Mexico City, like most places, wasn't best seen by car. Of course Tim could already spot architecture that made his mouth water, but the beautiful side of the city would reveal itself as soon as they reached his grandmother's neighborhood.

"How is my Ella?" Nana asked as they neared the south side of the city.

"Mom's fine."

Pencil-thin eyebrows just managed to rise above the sunglasses. "Fine? Nothing more?"

"As far as I know."

Nana slipped back into Spanish. «She never has much to say about you, either. I keep telling her that a mother is a part of her son's life, whether he likes it or not.»

«I'd love it,» Tim replied. «She's busy with Dad, as always.»

«Is that why?»

Of course not, but Tim wasn't about to explain the real reason to his grandmother. He felt lucky Nana didn't seem to be concerned about his sexuality, but he didn't want to hear her agreeing with his mother about who goes to Hell.

«I'll try harder,» Tim said. «I saw them just the other day, but I didn't stay long.»

Nana nodded as if satisfied and took the exit to Xochimilco, the neighborhood and popular tourist spot where she lived. On either side of the street were never-ending walls, obscuring most of the homes behind from view. The monotony of this wall was broken by windows and doors, gates and garages, flower boxes and ornaments.

Nana's house was pure comfort. As they pulled up, Tim took the key from her, hopped out, and opened the gate. Beyond was just enough room for her to park in front of the orange two-story building. After guiding the car in, Tim went to open Ben's door, smiling the whole time. Just being here felt good. He took Ben's hand and helped him out, amused by how hard Ben was trying to appear comfortable when he clearly wasn't. Then Tim went to the trunk for their luggage. They'd take a train to the hotel later instead of risking traffic again.

"Where is the fat one?" Nana cried as if they had forgotten something important.

"Chinchilla?" Tim asked, hefting a suitcase to the brick pavement.

Nana nodded, eyeing the suitcase as if she expected the dog to hop out at any moment.

"She's with a friend. She could have flown with us, but they would have put her in cargo." Normally Tim preferred to drive down, but Ben didn't have a lot of time off. So he had entrusted Marcello with Chinchilla's well-being. He just hoped Chinchilla didn't demand truffle purée and chilled champagne from now on.

"Ah!" Nana took Ben by the elbow. "Instead, you bring another beautiful creature. Come inside. I make enough food to kill an army."

Tim laughed as he followed them in. The best thing about any grandmother's house is the smell—like baby powder and fresh flowers, or maybe freshly washed sheets hanging in the sun, or sugar cookies cooling on a wire rack. If scientists could reproduce that scent and pump it into the open air, wars would cease, and whole armies would trade their guns for toys.

Nana's house was a series of small rooms, the walls decorated with the same frames and knick-knacks that had been there since his childhood. Only the photos changed as children in the family grew older. And of course the painting he had brought her last time. That was in a place of honor in the dining room. Aside from it, all the furniture and baubles were comfortingly familiar.

"I have work in the kitchen." Nana said in the small living room. "Then we eat."

"I can help," Ben offered.

"No, no. You a guest here. Relax. You can do the dishes later."

"She's kidding," Tim said as she left the room.

"I ain't scared of no dishes," Ben said in a gruff voice.

"You will be when you see the feast she's cooking up. Last time there wasn't a clean plate left in the house."

Ben pointed to a black and white photo of a little girl in a summer dress. "Is that you, *Gordita*?"

"It's *Gordito,* and no, that's my mom. Smart ass. Come on, I'll give you a tour."

They walked through the rooms on the first floor, avoiding the kitchen. Tim tried to express the memories he had made here, but most weren't great stories. They were just him playing with his grandmother or watching her cook his favorite dishes, even if the rest of the family was having something different.

Upstairs were a couple of rooms and a bathroom. In Nana's sewing room, Ben stood at the window, looking out at the neighborhood below. "It's so different here," he murmured.

"I know. Everything in the States is so polished and presentable. Mexico City, parts of it are completely relaxed, like when you put on a ratty old pair of sweatpants and stay inside."

Ben turned from the window. "I love those days!"

"Yeah, me too. But Mexico City also has its evenings out, places where it puts on its best to impress. Or sometimes it dons stuffy business clothing or the latest fashion trends. Best of all, these places are often jumbled together. Wait until you see the hotel room. Smack dab in the middle of the city, and yet it's so secluded and romantic that your poor little heart will explode."

Ben gave him a curious look, as if this wasn't the best news possible. "You should be a travel agent for Mexico," he said as he strolled the room, taking in the details. "I had no idea about this part of your life. I mean, you mentioned your parents bringing you on vacation, but this is a whole new side to you. For me at least."

"For me too, in a way. Since college, I've been coming down

here more often. Usually I drive. You should come with me next time. There are tons of little tumbleweed villages along the way, some of them just like in the movies. Flying is faster, but you miss out on so much. You're going to love it!"

Ben turned to him. "Already planning our next trip?"

Tim nodded. "Maybe."

Ben smiled coyly.

"Is that a yes?"

"Sure. Sign me up."

Tim grinned. "All right. If you're lucky, Chinchilla might even let you sit in the front seat. Hey! Come downstairs. I want to show you something."

Once back in the living room, Tim opened the wooden door to the backyard, which was just a strip of grass bordered by palms and a rickety old fence. Beyond this, water curved its way through the trees.

"There used to be a huge lake here," Tim said. "Now the lake is gone, but there's still a system of canals. And—well, check it out."

Right on cue, a long narrow boat glided by. The boat had an open deck with a canvas roof and was painted with enough colors to give Jackson Pollock a headache. Tourists sat at a bench on board, drinking beer and staring at them as if they were part of the tour. Tim's grandmother complained about the *gringos,* as if the loud tourists were there only to irritate her, but then she often sat out here and waved.

"Can we ride one of those?" Ben asked, sounding like a kid.

Tim grinned. "Hell yeah! But I wanted to show you this because it's typical of Mexico City. Sometimes it might look a little drab and worn compared to what we're used to, but then you walk around the corner or enter the right building and find something that blows you away. Something you'd never find back home."

"*¡Almuerzo!*" a voice shouted from inside.

Ben's puzzled expression made Tim want to melt. "That means lunch is ready," he explained.

"Oh, good. I'm hungry!"

"Trust me, that's the last time you'll say that at my grandma's house."

* * * * *

"You aren't staying here? Why you want hotel?"

Tim eyed Nana from across a table cluttered with half-empty platters and pans. Maybe her English hadn't been off when she said she would cook enough to kill an army. Tim doubted even a hundred men could eat everything on the table without exploding.

"We don't want to inconvenience you," Tim said.

"Inconvenience?"

"*Molestia.*"

"You think having my grandson here makes a problem?"

Of course not, but it did put a cramp in his romantic intentions. "I already have a room booked."

Nana waved a hand dismissively. "Your father always say the same thing. My own daughter never sleeps here."

Nana, master of the guilt trip.

"I'd love to stay here," Ben said, nodding at Tim encouragingly. "It'll be fun."

Tim looked at Ben, picturing the hotel Jacuzzi, the dimly lit room, soft music, and the twinkling city lights beyond. That's what they needed. Not the cozy comfort of a grandmother's home. He focused on Ben, trying to silently communicate all of this. Staying here isn't really what he wanted, was it? "Are you absolutely sure?"

"Yes!" Nana answered for him. "Oh, this is good. I better start dinner soon."

"We're going out," Tim said, forcing a smile. "I want Ben to see more than just your dining room."

"Yes, yes," Nana said. She waggled her eyebrows. "Go out and be romantic. You want my car?"

"No, thanks. I think we need to walk this one off. Ready?"

He and Ben lumbered to their feet like pregnant women. A little exercise and fresh air were the only cure. If they took a nap now they'd probably end up in a coma. Besides, Mexico City had plenty of potential. A stroll through the streets, a kiss or two by a roaring fountain, and he and Ben would finally have their fresh start.

Chapter Thirty-six

Back on the streets of Xochimilco, where the narrow alleys felt like hallways, Tim waited patiently for Ben to share his opinion of the woman he loved so much.

"She's cool," Ben said.

"Yeah." Tim nodded thoughtfully. "Cooler than I thought she would be. I figured she'd be uncomfortable. She was one of the main reasons I didn't want to come out."

"I worried about that too," Ben said. "Every kid is used to their parents being angry, and disappointing them is part of growing up, but grandmas are sacred. When they're unhappy, it feels horrible."

"Exactly. I thought she would be broken hearted. But she seems okay."

"Better than okay." Ben laughed. "She's awesome. I'm glad we're staying there."

Tim thought again of the luxurious hotel room, but didn't say anything. He'd cancel the reservation later, but for now, he was determined not to become discouraged. "What do you want to see first? The National Palace? Some ancient pyramids? The Metropolitan Cathedral?"

"What about that volcano you used to talk about. Popo-oh-no, or something."

Tim grinned. "*Popocatépetl.* That's more of a day trip."

"Oh. How about we ride those boats?"

"We can do that tonight. I don't want to sit down anymore, do you?"

"I guess not." Ben glanced around. "I don't know. It's all so new that anything will be interesting. You decide."

"Okay, then. It's straight into the heart of the city for us."

They took a train to the *Plaza de la Constitucion,* a huge empty plaza in the middle of Mexico City. The world's largest public square was impressive for its size alone, but something about all the concrete felt too militant. Tim considered the plaza an ideal starting place and nothing more. They wandered the city, soaking up the sights and sounds. Tim kept pulling Ben down small side streets to show him buildings that went from impressive to patchwork and weird.

"When I was a kid, this city felt like a wonderland to me," Tim said. "Have you noticed how nothing really fits a scheme?"

"Yeah." Ben glanced around. "No more cookie-cutter suburbs and strip malls."

"Exactly. It's like architects here just wake up every morning and say, 'Well, what the hell should we try today?'"

"Some of these buildings look a little homemade," Ben said carefully.

Tim laughed. "Some of them probably are, but that's what makes them unique. The possibilities are endless. Wait until you see the more modern buildings here."

"That's right. You studied architecture, didn't you?"

"Yeah, and man was that a buzz-kill. The practical aspects weren't nearly as cool as my dreams. Maybe if I had lived down here I would have stayed interested, but in the U.S., I felt like I was learning how to build a bigger and better Walmart."

"But think of all the people who need to buy cheap underwear and cheese in one convenient trip," Ben teased.

Tim shrugged. "They'll have to go commando and starve. I like painting better since I don't have to limit my imagination. Or worry about a roof falling in on people."

"Painting suits you better, anyway," Ben said, taking his hand.

"Yeah?"

"I think so. You look like a jock but have the soul of an artist. What more could a guy want?"

"A gorgeous singing voice?"

Ben grinned at this flattery.

"A brave heart?"

Now Ben's smile faltered. "I'm not so brave."

"That's not what I remember. The things you talked a teenage closet case into doing! Need I remind you?"

Ben turned a little red. "No need. I have a very good memory."

Tim looked him over. "You know, we could still check into that hotel room, just for a little while."

Ben looked uncomfortable, letting go of Tim's hand to scratch his nose and not offering it again. He headed toward one of the major streets. "Let's do some shopping. I think all this walking down back alleys is giving you the wrong idea about me."

Ben's tones were jovial, but he wasn't looking at Tim anymore. "Sounded like the right idea to me," Tim joked, stepping in at his side, but Ben didn't laugh.

Talk about mixed signals! What was going on? They were somewhere new, their pasts far behind them, and it sure as hell seemed like Ben was interested. But every time Tim tried to get intimate, it appeared to cause Ben pain. Was it Jace? Had his ghost followed them all the way down here?

"Ben?" Tim reached out and took his hand. "Hold up a minute."

Ben turned, his expression stopping Tim dead in his tracks. He could read Ben, knew his body language fluently, but Tim had never seen this before. The message Ben's face conveyed was crystal clear: *Not now. We're not going to talk about this now.*

Tim never expected that. Not from Ben, of all people. The bravest, boldest spirit he'd known in his life was avoiding a subject and asking Tim to do the same.

"Talk to me," Tim tried.

Ben's eyes softened. "Let's just do some shopping, okay?" He squeezed Tim's hand. "That's what I need."

"Okay," Tim said, feeling anything but certain.

They hit some stores but didn't buy anything since Ben only seemed interested in browsing. Ben didn't act moody during this. He still made casual conversation, Tim glad to join him, but the topics remained superficial. They even held hands, but this felt more like a consolation prize than anything. When their feet grew tired, they rested at a café and drank fruity *aguas frescas* as the sun went down. As much as Tim enjoyed watching people and taking in the sights and sounds, he found himself wanting to be alone with Ben. Maybe in privacy the truth would come out.

They caught a train back to Xochimilco, stopping in to check on Nana before heading for the canal boats. She loaded them up with leftovers, which Tim gratefully accepted. Bringing food and drinks on the *trajineras* boats was the norm for the natives, while tourists relied on enterprising individuals who would tie their smaller boats to the *trajineras* to hock their wares.

Most tourists left Xochimilco before nightfall, but some stuck around to party. Luckily, the atmosphere was fairly calm tonight. They approached one of the boat owners, whose dark eyes sparkled when Tim spoke the native tongue. Tim offered the man a much higher price than the norm. He wanted the boat for him and Ben alone. The owner accepted after haggling, Ben blissfully ignorant to the entire exchange.

"This is lovely," Ben said, taking a seat at the long bench that filled the deck.

A couple of sputtering gas lamps provided atmosphere as the boat coasted into the canal, the world around them dark. Only lights from the neighborhood could be seen in the night. As they drifted down the waterway, leaving the homes behind, the stars above were matched by lamps from other boats on the canal. Over the gentle sound of the punt pushing through water, they could hear voices laughing.

Tim didn't pay much attention to the surroundings. His eyes kept returning to Ben, face lit by flame, the shadows just enough to create the illusion that no time had gone by. Ben caught him looking and smiled before he stood and walked to the boat's bow.

Tim followed, coming up behind him and placing his hands on Ben's ribs. "Time for a Titanic moment? I'll lift you up and you sing. Ready, Celine Dion?"

Ben laughed, reaching down for Tim's hands and pulling his arms around him. "This was the right thing to do. This is what we needed."

"Is it?" Tim said, feeling more puzzled than ever.

Ben sighed. "I'm sorry about earlier." He turned around to face him, their hips close together, but Ben placed a hand on Tim's chest until he took a step back. "And I'm sorry if I keep leading you on."

"Please talk to me," Tim said. "If this is punishment for all those times I kept you guessing…"

"I don't play games," Ben said, shaking his head. "At least I don't mean to. Sometimes I feel like I can do this, that we can start over, but then I remember and—" Ben lowered his eyes. "I've been through a lot."

Tim's stomach sank. Of course. "Jace," he said.

Ben nodded. "There's so much you don't know."

"Then tell me!" Tim said in desperation. "Please!"

Ben took a deep breath and nodded. "I don't know how much Allison told you, but Jace suffered from aneurysms. He had a close call once, and that was terrifying enough. When it happened a second time—" Ben's lip trembled. "We were together. At home.

Jace wanted me to hold him, which was weird because he was usually the one to hold me. He knew he wouldn't make it, or he'd given up—I don't know, but we were in bed and I did what he said, even though it hurt like hell." Ben wiped at his eyes. "That's what he wanted, and I know it sounds stupid, but I thought if I held on to him tight enough, that it might make a difference—that I wouldn't lose him. I was still holding Jace when he died."

"That must have been hell for you," Tim said, clenching his jaw. "And here I am, stupid enough to think that I could just saunter back into your life and make everything perfect again. I'm sorry. Of course you can't love anyone else."

"No!" Ben took a step forward, shaking his head. "You don't understand! I *do* love you! I love you so much that I can barely keep it in! All I want to do is touch you, kiss you—anything to bring us as close together as humanly possible. But then I remember how painful it was to lose Jace." Ben grabbed Tim's hand, eyes wild. "I know you think I'm brave, but losing Jace almost broke me. I can't go through that again. The thought of watching you die one day, the idea alone is enough to break my heart."

Tim pulled Ben close, kissed his forehead before resting his cheek against his head. There was no solution to this problem, no way to guarantee Ben that he wouldn't get hurt again. Tim knew the pain that love brought. The two were inseparable, but both love and pain had taught him one thing. He kissed Ben's hair, let go of him, and took a step back.

"Jace was worth it."

Ben looked surprised. "What?"

"I'm not even going to ask because there's no question. Jace was worth going through all that pain, and you were worth the hell we went through as teenagers." Tim looked Ben straight in the eye. "I can't honestly say that I'm worth it, but I'll try my best, and I promise you that you won't have to see me die. No matter what happens in the future, I won't be the first one to go."

Ben blinked, and when his smile came, it brought along a sigh. "Of all the lies you've told me over the years, that one is the most beautiful."

Tim shook his head. "It's not a lie. No matter how hard I have to cling to life, no matter how many life support units and doctors it takes, I won't die first. My love for you is strong enough to keep me going. And when your time finally comes, I won't survive the loss and will be right behind you."

"You can't promise that," Ben said, but his eyes were shining.

"There's only one way to prove me wrong," Tim replied.

They passed a boat overloaded with drunk passengers, one of whom shouted "Whoooooooooo!" before they heard a loud splash. Okay, so maybe he could understand why Nana got sick of the boats, but soon the party had gone its way, leaving them in the evening's tranquility.

Tim put an arm around Ben's shoulder as they faced the water together. "So you love me, huh?"

"Love doesn't even begin to describe it." Ben exhaled. "And you're right. Jace was worth it. And so are you. Just keep that promise, okay?"

"You got it."

In the far distance they could hear a *mariachi* band. They had their own boats too, roving musicians who would play for money, and while Tim normally found that music annoying, the way the songs floated ethereal through the evening air made them sound beautiful.

Tim pressed his nose against Ben's neck, kissing him there. "Come back to the table. We have to eat some of this food or Nana will never forgive us."

They picked at the leftovers, offering the rest to the boat owner to take home. Hopefully the guy had a huge family. Then they sipped beers, looking out across the water as the boat slowly brought them home again. They were dropped off at Nana's house directly, where they squeezed through a gap in the old fence.

Tim held up two bottles he'd grabbed on the way off the boat. "Want another beer before we go in?"

Ben didn't answer, looking at him with an expression that probably matched Tim's own. He saw lust there, but it was more than that. Interest. Longing. Love. Tim set down the beers.

"We're starting over," he said. "This is the first day we met."

"Strange place to meet," Ben replied.

"Not right here," Tim said "I met you earlier in the day. You were wandering the streets and looking sad."

"Why was I sad?"

"That's the first thing I asked you."

"In Spanish?" There was a glimmer in Ben's eye.

Tim grinned in response. "You like that, don't you?"

"Well," Ben said coyly, "I figure I'm a lost tourist. You're the helpful native."

"Okay. I came up to you and said, '*¿Por qué estás tan triste, mi hermoso muchacho? Déjame que ahuyente esas nubes que ensombrecen tu rostro.*'"

Ben leaned against the wall of the house. "And I said, 'Huh?'"

Tim laughed. "So I tried again in English. 'Beautiful boy, why do you look so sad? Let me chase away those clouds from your face.'"

"How will you do that?" Ben asked.

"*Con un beso.*"

Before Ben could ask what this meant, Tim stepped forward to show him, placing one hand against the wall and gently pressing his lips against Ben's. Then he pulled back, basking in the resulting smile. "See?" he said. "There it is. The sunshine, even in the middle of the night."

Ben took a deep breath. "I was sad because I was lost. That's what I would tell you. But now that you've found me, maybe you can take me home with you."

"And that's how we ended up here." Tim gave a nervous chuckle. "Apparently we took a boat home. Let's go inside."

Ben nodded.

The house was silent, with only a single light on in the living room. Tim glanced at the note Nana had left. They were to sleep in the sewing room. Taking Ben's hand, he led them through the house and up the stairs, relieved when they arrived in the room without waking Nana. Holding his breath, he shut the door as quietly as possible and turned to Ben. Then they both smiled. Sneaking upstairs to a bedroom sure brought back memories.

The small bed in the corner was freshly made. Ben sat on the edge and took off his shoes. Tim kicked off his own impatiently, desperate to be near Ben, but he also knew what this moment meant. The last time Ben had shared a bed with someone had been his final moments with Jace.

Tim turned off the light and opened the window, letting in the sounds of the night—traffic, insects, voices, and the lapping of water on the shore—all reminders of the different world they were in. Hopefully this would keep painful memories away. Then he moved to the bed where Ben still sat.

Tim ran his fingers through Ben's hair and bent down for a

kiss. Ben took hold of him, leaning back and pulling him in. They shifted and scooted, lips never parting as they maneuvered the rest of the way into bed. Tim stripped off Ben's shirt, then his own, as Ben worked at their pants. Before he could get too far, Tim wrapped his arms around Ben and rolled over, kissing him deeply, wanting nothing ever again but this.

If Ben wanted to stop there, if he only wanted Tim to sleep next to him the rest of the night, he could have been satisfied with that. But even at the worst of times, they had always shared the same appetite. Ben moved his hands back down to their belts, and this time Tim let him do what he wanted, putting his hands behind his head as Ben finished undressing him and then stood to take off his own clothes. Tim glanced over, Ben standing at the side of the bed as he kicked off his jeans. In the dim light of the room, he was a dark silhouette, the edge of his body illuminated with light from the window, neck shiny with saliva where Tim had kissed him last.

"Come be with me," Tim said, reaching out a hand. He meant more than just this moment, this simple act. Ben responded, crawling into bed, and for a while all they did was hold each other. He waited for Ben to cry, feeling relieved when he didn't, but still he took it slow. Rolling over on his side, he let his fingers trace up and down Ben's skin, delighting in each shiver he caused. Then Ben began to reciprocate, rubbing his hands over Tim's body just like he used to, exploring him.

"Any new scars?" Ben asked.

"None you can see," Tim said, but his breath caught in his throat when Ben kissed his chest, his stomach, and then traced a path south with his tongue.

"Hold on!" Tim said, grabbing Ben's shoulder. "That's exactly what I want to do to you."

Ben resisted, wearing a mischievous grin. "We're starting over, and if you'll recall, *you* were first."

"That was then," Tim said, but an idea occurred to him. *"Sesenta y nueve."*

Ben paused as he tried to recall his high school Spanish. Then he snorted. "It sounds so much more romantic in your language."

"It's not romance I'm going for," Tim replied.

Ben's gaze could have made a volcano sweat. Crawling down to the end of the bed, he swung his legs over each side of

Tim's head. Tim was tempted to make a joke about the Sword of Damocles, but instead he moaned in pleasure—Ben having claimed his prize at the other end. The sensations made Tim writhe before he regained control. He put a hand on Ben's butt to bring his hips lower so he could return the favor.

They risked small moans and whimpers as their hips pumped, rolling to their sides, then over again with Tim on top. Though he felt he could ride these waves of ecstasy forever, he wanted to get back to those lips of Ben's that drove him wild. Tim crawled in a quick circle, lifting one of Ben's legs with his shoulder as he sought another kiss.

"Do you think we can—" Tim let the question hang.

"Have any lube?" Ben asked.

They glanced around the room in mad hope, finding only a sewing machine, doily-covered lampshades, and a statue of the Virgin Mary who appeared more smug than scandalized. Tim laughed. "Guess Nana is fresh out."

Ben's finger traced a path across Tim's pecs, running circles around one of his nipples. "Remember when we used to kind of fake it? Before I got up the nerve the first time."

Tim grinned at the memory, adjusting his hips. Both of Ben's hands lowered to hold their cocks tightly together. Tim began pumping, eyes locked on Ben as they rediscovered this old game. Then the sensations made them somber, Tim leaning forward and kissing Ben as he thrust harder and faster. He moved his kisses to Ben's chin, tracing the jaw line with his tongue before nibbling on his neck. Tim was leaking enough pre-come that Ben's hands were slick. He wondered if it would be enough to do more without needing lube when the thought sent him over the edge.

Ben's muscles tensed, his breath held, so Tim kept pumping until Ben bit his lower lip to keep from moaning. Then Ben's breath came out as a sigh and he relaxed. Tim gently lowered on to him, holding himself up just enough to keep from crushing Ben with his weight. Their heaving breaths soon turned to hisses of quiet laughter.

"*¿Ya no estás triste, mi mariposa hermosa?*" he asked. "No longer sad, my beautiful butterfly?"

"No." Ben shook his head with a dopey grin. "Not anymore."

* * * * *

«I've been going to a new church,» Nana said. She stretched her legs out straight, pushing back into her favorite recliner and wiggling her toes before she put her legs back down.

«That's nice,» Tim said, turning his attention back to the Spanish-English dictionary he was thumbing through. Being back in Mexico City always made him aware of the holes in his Spanish. The other day he was trying to ask a shopkeeper for aftershave and had to settle for saying "face water" instead.

«If you were staying longer, you could go to church with me,» Nana continued. «You would like it.»

He doubted that!

«Can't you stay longer?» Nana pressed.

«No. The flights are booked, and even if we changed them, Ben has to go back to work. So do I.»

«You must like him a lot to bring him here. I always pictured you bringing a beautiful American girl to meet me one day, but I like Ben.»

Tim listened to make sure the shower upstairs was still running before he remembered they were speaking in Spanish. Ben wouldn't know they were talking about him even if he was in the room. «I love him, Nana.»

«So will you build a home with him?»

Tim shook his head. «He already has a house, and so do I.»

«Those are places, not homes. A home is what you make together.» Nana picked some lint off the recliner's arm. «Two houses! How will that be a home?»

«No idea,» Tim admitted. «I think he's attached to his house, and I don't want to leave mine.»

Nana nodded as if this made sense. «Did you know I never wanted to live in this city? I grew up in a small village, and that's all I knew. That's all I wanted to know. Your grandfather was from Guadalajara, and he didn't want to leave there, either.»

«Then how did you meet?»

«He did business with my father, working for a bank that wanted to check on their investment. So when he came to see that everything in the company was going well, he would always be invited for dinner. That's how we met and kept meeting. When he said he wanted to marry me, I was happy, until I learned he wanted us to live in Guadalajara.»

«So what did you do?»

«I told him that if I had to leave my home, he also had to leave his. I told him to find a new job somewhere else. Then I would marry him and move there.»

Tim laughed. «And that's how you ended up here?»

«That's right.»

«Crazy old woman.»

Nana smiled proudly. «You think about it. Sometimes you can only make a home in a new place. Move here to Mexico City. Be close to your grandma.»

Now he saw what she was trying to say. Tim agreed with Ben. Too much connected them both to Austin now. They couldn't leave it behind. But there might be some wisdom in her words anyway. «We can't move here, but I'll try to visit more often. Okay?»

Nana nodded as if satisfied. «Next time you come with me to my new church. The priest, he's younger than me, but he says that love isn't a sin. You love a woman, you love a man, you love a tomato. God is happy, because he created love.»

Tim stared at her. «Do you agree?»

Nana shook her head. «No one should love a tomato. But the rest, yes.»

«Then maybe you can talk to Mom about that.»

Nana sat upright. «Is that why you don't spend time together?»

Tim shrugged, turning his attention back to the dictionary. He didn't want to send Nana after his parents like an attack dog, but hopefully she would broach the subject with them. Maybe it would help. And if not, Tim would no longer worry about the consequences. Nana was right. He needed to have his own home, his own family. The only question was how.

"Ready to fly home tomorrow?" Tim said, not hiding the concern in his voice.

Ben looked over at him. "Afraid I'll come to my senses the second we land in Austin?" He winked. "Stop worrying. Against all logic and reason, I've been hopelessly in love with you since I was sixteen. If I haven't snapped out of it by now, then there's no hope for me."

Tim grinned. "Glad to hear it."

"Besides," Ben said. "The past has to catch up with us eventually. When it does, we'll face it together."

The past was a funny thing. He and Ben stood on the apex of a pyramid, a green valley surrounding them—the Basin of Mexico. On the horizon, rolling hills and mountains turned blue as they faded into the distant sky. Here they were, on the Pyramid of the Sun, part of an ancient city built by a civilization that had risen and fallen centuries before even the Aztec Empire. The Teotihuacan people had never thought their time would come to an end, that centuries later, tourists would wander their city with cell phones and cameras extended to capture it all on video. Or that two gay guys would stand on the top of their tallest pyramid and contemplate their future together.

"I don't want to forget what we've been through," Ben said. "Not any of it. Even the painful memories belong to us." He shrugged. "That's who we are. Coming here was just to help us get on our feet."

"Really? I thought we were running away together." Tim meant it as a joke, but it didn't sound that way.

"Nah. There's nothing we need to run from. Not anymore, although the idea has a certain romantic appeal to it." Ben nudged him. "Besides, what about Chinchilla?"

"She can come with us."

"And Samson?

"Absolutely!"

"Allison too?"

"Sure, why not?" Tim grinned. "*And* her husband. Hell, we'll bring all of Austin with us."

Ben crinkled his nose. "That would sort of defeat the point."

"Maybe. I'm just having a hard time picturing what life will be like when we go back to Austin. I'm tired of living alone."

"Oh." Ben eyed the valley in silence for a moment. "Yeah. That is kind of weird. Jace and I scrounged every penny we could to buy that house. So many things happened there. Good or bad, every memory is special to me."

"I understand," Tim said gently. "In a way, I feel the same about where I live. It's never easy for me to talk about, but I was with Eric in his last moments."

"You were?"

He nodded. "We were at home together, instead of some horrible hospital—" Tim shook his head. "People talk about a haunted house like it's a bad thing, but it's not always. Not when it's someone you love."

Ben looked relieved. "I know exactly what you mean."

"I'm glad. So, the idea of me living with you seems somehow disrespectful to Jace's memory, but I also can't expect you to sell your house and move in with me."

"No," Ben sighed. "I don't like either of those options."

Tim swallowed. "If none of that were an issue, would you want to live with me?"

Ben pretended to mull it over. "Yeah, but not if I'm constantly serving you frozen pizzas and Cokes while you lounge around on the couch."

"Hey, it worked in high school!"

"Maybe on special occasions, then." Ben's eyes searched his. "We could just stay where we are. You'll come visit me sometimes, or I'll go to your place. It'll keep things fresh."

"I don't want fresh," Tim said. "I want to get old and smelly with you. Eventually you'll *want* me to keel over first, just because you're so sick of being around me."

Ben laughed. "Trust me, that will never happen."

"How about somewhere new?" Tim said. "Still in Austin, but a place that belongs just to us. We can take it slow, put our houses on the market, and see what happens. If they sell, we'll both be making a sacrifice, leaving something behind."

Ben chewed his lip. "That house *isn't* Jace. I can take the memories with me. Just like you can with Eric, right?"

"Right." Tim scooted nearer, wrapping an arm around Ben. "So you'll start a new life with me?"

Ben stole a kiss. "I already have."

Epilogue

Twelve seasons. Starting in summer—as they always seemed to—but now they were leaving another one behind and entering autumn. Three years of living together in this little house, surrounded by trees and land and hope. Ben had found the real estate listing. The photos didn't look like much since the house was hidden away deep on the lot. As it turned out, that's what made them fall in love with the place.

Ben and Tim still lived in Austin, but on the outskirts. They had land, enough that they rarely heard another car or saw any sign of civilization, apart from the occasional airplane overhead. When they were at home, the world existed only for them, just like it had once in a den at his parents' house or in Ben's teenage bedroom. Their little bubble world had come together again after all this time. Austin was still there when they needed it—the gallery, the theater, Allison, and Marcello. But when they were done, they returned home to solitude.

Of course they weren't completely alone. At the very beginning they had been four. When Chinchilla had first met Samson, the dumb dog had chased right after the cat. Samson stood his ground, waiting patiently until Chinchilla was close enough. Then he swiped—claws extended—hitting Chinchilla directly on the nose. Tim was painfully reminded of the time Jace had decked him. Regardless, that had ended the dispute of who was in charge. Samson reigned supreme for the next two years, eventually becoming fast friends with the dog.

When Samson died, he did so quietly. Curled up at Ben's feet one night, he simply slipped away. Ben had cried for days, Tim joining him a few times. In a way, Samson was the last piece of Jace lingering behind long enough to make sure Ben was okay. And now he was. Ben would never be alone again, never have to search for someone to love him because Tim did so with all of his being. But losing part of their family still hurt.

"He was always Jace's cat," Ben had said afterwards. "Now he will be again."

They buried Samson in one corner of the yard, planting flowers over his grave. A year later the flowers were still there, pink, white, and yellow. Tim was watering them now, Chinchilla standing solemnly at his side. When he was finished, she raced off across the yard, looking for a new game.

Tim returned to the back of the house to put away the watering can. He passed Ben, who was stretched out in a lawn chair with his eyes closed as he soaked up the sun, a forgotten book on his lap. Tim's heart pounded. Why was he so scared? After all this time, after years of being together, this should be the easiest thing in the world. He second-guessed himself as he slowly wound up the garden hose and then walked back to where Ben rested. A cloud blew over the sun, shadow chasing across his body.

"You awake?" Tim said so quietly that he thought Ben might not hear.

Ben turned his head, smiling at him with brown eyes like melted chocolate. They made Tim weak, even still. "Yeah. Nearly dozed off."

"Okay." Tim stood there awkwardly. Maybe this wasn't the right place. The right time. But of course it was. Where else could this happen but in their own little world. "Uh, could you sit up for a second?"

Ben looked puzzled, but he sat up, swinging his legs over the side of the deck chair. "Are you okay?"

Tim chuckled madly. "Ask me that again in a second." Then he reached into his pocket, took out the ring, and fell to one knee. The words he had planned were lost in his throat. He simply held up the ring and gave Ben a look of such hope that it was enough.

And then Ben cried, and Tim was sure he had made a terrible mistake, but as the sun came back out again, so did Ben's smile. Looking just as embarrassed as Tim felt, Ben nodded and held out his hand.

"Oh!"

Jace's ring was still on Ben's finger, but this didn't bother Tim. These days he felt a bond with the man who had been smart enough to love Ben from the very beginning. After all, Jace had been there for Ben at a time when Tim couldn't, and for that he was eternally grateful. Tim never expected Ben to take off that ring, so instead he reached for Ben's other hand.

"There's a reason God gave you two ring fingers," he said, sliding on the platinum band.

Ben stared at it in wonder for a moment before throwing his

arms around Tim's neck and kissing him. Ben's tears gracing his cheek, Tim hoisted him to his feet and held him near. As the wind blew through the trees, the first leaves breaking loose to fly free, they swayed together to a song only they could hear, their love perfect now, as it would always be until the end of their summer-filled days.

The story continues—

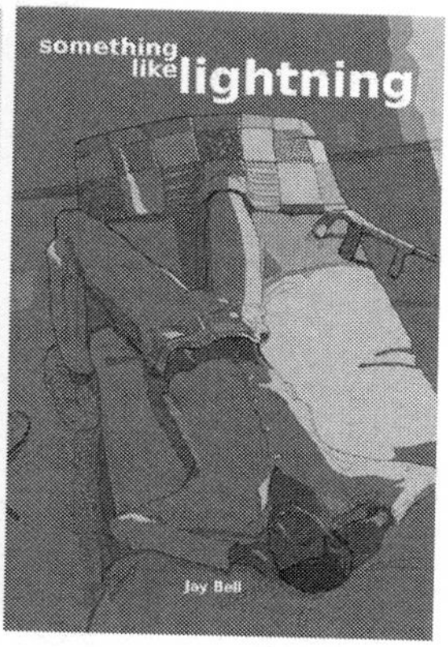

—in the *Something Like...* series, each book written from a different character's perspective, the plots intertwining at key points while also venturing off in new directions. The quest for love takes many different forms, changing like the seasons. Which is your favorite?

Current books in the series:

#1: *Something Like Summer*
#2: *Something Like Autumn*
#3: *Something Like Winter*
#4: *Something Like Spring*
#5: *Something Like Lightning*
#6: *Something Like Thunder*
#7: *Something Like Stories – Volume One*
#8: *Something Like Hail*
#9: *Something Like Rain*
#10: *Something Like Stories – Volume Two*
#11 *Something Like Forever*

Learn who each book is about and where to buy at:
www.somethinglikeseries.com

Also by Jay Bell:

Something Like Spring

Nothing in this world is permanent. Friends, lovers, even family, can all disappear in the blink of an eye. Without these anchors, it's all too easy to find oneself drifting.

Jason Grant doesn't have much, aside from a beat-up old guitar and knack for getting kicked out of foster homes. His latest placement is set to be just another in a long line of failures. Then he meets Caesar Hubbard, a handsome guy who lives down the hall. For the first time in his life, Jason wants to stay, which means learning to be part of a family, and not letting his feelings—or his actions—ruin his first real chance of falling in love.

Something Like Spring introduces a new character to the *Seasons* story, one with a troubled past and an equally turbulent future. Jason must traverse a winding road fraught with emotional conflicts and tough decisions… a road that might just lead to a certain couple in Austin.

For more information, please see:
www.jaybellbooks.com

Also by Jay Bell:

Something Like Lightning

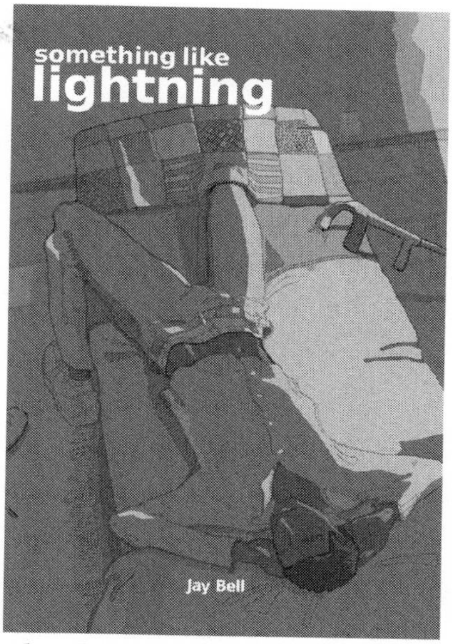

Kelly Phillips has been out of the closet since he was a young teenager, and thanks to the gay youth group he frequents, he has never been short on friends or lovers. But when you have almost everything, it's hard not to focus on what's just out of reach: A best friend, who would be Mr. Right if he wasn't already Mr. Straight. Or that handsome guy at school, who would be easier to wrangle if not for his angel wings. And then there's the one who might be a perfect fit, maybe even a soulmate… if only he wasn't convinced he didn't need anyone at all. Kelly has always been good at running. Now he must learn to chase, which will not only test his endurance, but the durability of his heart as well.

Something Like Lightning is a new beginning in the *Something Like…* saga, shifting the focus to a fresh set of characters while also revisiting a familiar face or two.

Also by Jay Bell
Kamikaze Boys

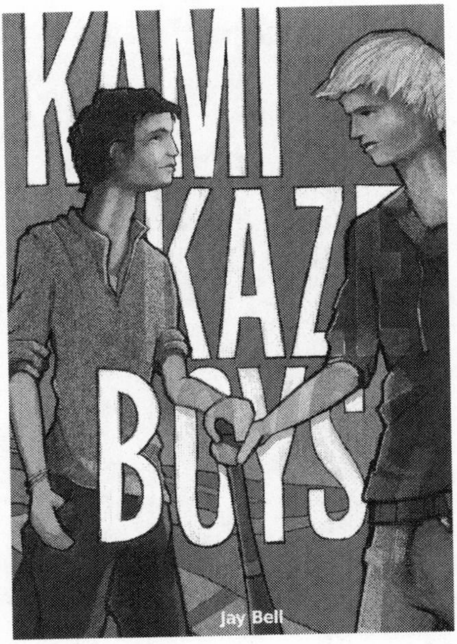

True love is worth fighting for.

My name is Connor Williams and people say I'm crazy. But that's not who I am. They also think I'm straight, and mean, and dangerous. But that's not who I am. The stories people tell, all those legends which made me an outsider—they don't mean a thing. Only my mother and my younger brother matter to me. Funny then that I find myself wanting to stand up for someone else. David Henry, that kind-of-cute guy who keeps to himself, he's about to get his ass beat by a bunch of dudes bigger than him. I could look away, let him be one more causality of this cruel world... But that's not who I am.

Kamikaze Boys, a Lambda Literary award winning novel, is a story of love triumphant as two young men walk a perilous path in the hopes of saving each other.

For more information, please see:
www.jaybellbooks.com

Something Like Summer has been reimagined as an ongoing web comic series! Join us on this colorful new adventure at www.gaywebcomics.com

Hear the story in their own words!

Many of the *Something Like…* books are available on audio too. Listen to Tim's tale while you jog with him, or ignore your fellow airline passengers while experiencing Jace's story again. Find out which books are available and listen to free chapters at the link below:

29882477R00224

Made in the USA
Columbia, SC
07 November 2018